I wobble, get my footing, walk unsteadily to the piece of paper that fell from the man's leather jacket. I pick it up.

It is lined and legal sized, creased and smudged with black grease. I unfold it and discover two names written in blue pen. One name is Sandy Vello. Doesn't sound familiar. The other name does.

"What is it?" The brunette puts a hand on my arm.

I point to my name on the piece of paper. She shakes her head, uncertain what I'm talking about.

"This is my name."

"What?"

"Nathaniel Idle."

"I'm Faith." She's still not getting it: My name was on a piece of paper that fell from the pocket of a man who nearly turned me into subway smoothie.

"That wasn't an accident."

THE CLOUD
MATT RICHTEL

By Matt Richtel

THE CLOUD
DEVIL'S PLAYTHING
HOOKED

MATT RICHTEL

THE
CLOUD

HARPER

An Imprint of HarperCollinsPublishers

This book is a work of fiction. References to real people, events, establishments, organizations, or locales are intended only to provide a sense of authenticity, and are used fictitiously. All other characters, and all incidents and dialogue, are drawn from the author's imagination and are not to be construed as real.

HARPER

An Imprint of HarperCollins*Publishers*
10 East 53rd Street
New York, New York 10022-5299

Copyright © 2013 by Matt Richtel
FLOODGATE. Copyright © 2012 by Matt Richtel
ISBN 978-0-06-199970-3

First Harper digest printing: February 2013
First Harper premium printing: February 2013

HarperCollins® and Harper® are registered trademarks of Harper-Collins Publishers.

Printed in the United States of America

Visit Harper paperbacks on the World Wide Web at
www.harpercollins.com

10 9 8 7 6 5 4 3 2 1

To the eMs: Meredith, Milo and Mirabel. Muses.

Acknowledgments

There is no "i" in Cloud. This was another team effort. Thanks to:

The Creative Fellows League: Josh Friedman, David Liss and Bob Tedeschi.

Carl Lennertz, great editor and friend. And the rest of the Harper team: Liate Stehlik, a publisher who gets people; publicity juggernauts Pamela Spengler-Jaffee, Andy Dodds, Jesse Edwards, Shawn Nicholls, and Jay Corson. Tessa Woodward, patient sherpa on the publishing journey.

Agent and sister-of-another-mother Laurie Liss.

To bookstores. Big and, especially, small.

Meredith, for patience, spark, encouragement and perspective. I love you. And for your fecundity. Books are nice. Milo and Mirabel are transcendent.

I can see clearly now the rain is gone
Gone are the dark clouds that had me blind

—Johnny Nash

As I write, highly civilized human beings are flying
overhead, trying to kill me.

—George Orwell

THE
CLOUD

Twelve Years Ago

Before it was chips in Silicon Valley, it was fruit. Orchards dominated the landscape here, a tapestry of cherries, apricots and plums, eventually giving way, acre by acre, to semiconductors and their spawn.

Manufacturing, labs, suburban offices, open-air Eichler homes and their knock-offs added enough concrete and density to cause a modest rise in the average temperature. It was sufficient to make the climate less than perfect for farming. But, no matter, the conditions remained plenty hospitable for the entrepreneurs, investors and engineers who combined forces to make magical electronics the region's chief export.

On this lazy March afternoon, a fruity fragrance carries on the light wind, a throwback to more pastoral times. Two girls frolic in the front yard of the Menlo Park house with the white picket fence. Without warning, the brown-haired one with the scrawny arms and purple blouse seems struck with an idea, and suddenly bolts.

She opens the white gate, seeing something, hearing something, something otherwise unseen, and runs into the street, like a fawn or an impulsive child half her age. She never sees the Volvo, nor its driver.

"An inexplicable catastrophe," the *Palo Alto Daily News* bemoans the next day. "It is the likes of which our cozy and insulated part of the world has been so often, thankfully, spared."

"What, we may ask ourselves over and over without ever getting a satisfactory answer, can possibly explain this tragedy?"

Roiling change, the complex swirl of progress, a future seductive and foreboding. What can possibly explain this tragedy?

THE CLOUD

Present Day

I stare into the dark tunnel and find myself imagining how it would look to Isaac.

To an eight-month-old, the shadowed subway opening wouldn't seem ominous. It would be a grand curiosity. Shards of reflected light frame its entrance like shiny pieces of broken glass. Would Isaac try to touch them? Would he finger a droplet of misty water rolling down the jagged wall and put it on his tongue?

The cavern wouldn't frighten my son. It would excite him with possibility and mystery.

A horn blares and I flinch. The night's last express approaches. I'm without company on the below-ground platform but I am joined by a wicked aroma. It's coming from a green, paint-chipped metal trash can that, from the scent, must contain a day's worth of half-eaten fruit and the carcass of an extremely dead sandwich. The trash can sits along the wall, beneath a dimly lit poster advertising a service that promises to turn your mobile phone into a day-trading terminal. More garbage. "Buy Low, Sell High, Commute Profitably."

Isaac would love little more than exploring the contours of the iPhone with his mouth.

I turn back to the track and squint across the platform. I'm looking for the woman with the tri-athlete's calves. I saw her upstairs at the turnstile, a brunette with darkly tinted skin wearing a skirt and a look of compassion. I watched her put some money in a cup at the feet of a figure sitting in the shadows upstairs, and she turned away with a kindly, worried look.

How come all the beautiful women who look like they were born to heal the damaged are going a different direction than me on the train?

Would she be a great mom?

Would she be impressed that tomorrow I become this year's recipient of a national magazine award for investigative reporting? Would she help me feel impressed?

A rumbling roars from the tunnel. It's not yet my train, the K, but the nearing Express, expressing.

Over the din, I hear rustling from behind me; something heavy hits the pavement. A boot step, then another. I turn to see a mountainous man in a leather jacket materialize from the darkness, stumbling toward me. He's the picture of a San Francisco drunk, downtrodden but wearing a fashionable coat with collar upturned, curly beard, and dark shades.

I'm tempted to ask him if he's okay as the train whooshes out of the tunnel into the station.

The drunkard lunges, or trips. He careens toward me, leading with his arms as if pushing through a revolving door.

The train's warning horn explodes.

Powerful palms crash against my chest, fingers claw my sweatshirt. I stumble backward toward the track. I flail to cling to his beefy forearms.

I feel the train pass behind me, airbrushing my scalp.

Isaac. My son. Will I see him again?

One last tactic.

I yank the drunk on top of me. Our momentum abruptly changes. We fall straight down to the pavement. My backpack slams into the ground. My spine unfolds.

Crack. I see an instant of light, then one of black, then a hazy return to the moment. I smell something like burning tires. Then cologne. I feel intense pressure on my chest.

The mountain man lies on top of me. I think: The base of my skull hit the edge of the concrete platform, but after the train passed. I'm alive.

I frantically push and kick the man from atop me. I claw the cement, then roll, panting in downward dog. I run a triage check. Limbs moving, no obvious fractures. I feel sticky warmth at the back of my skull, a cut but not deep, and shy of the heavy capillary bed on top of my head that would bleed profusely and require stitches. I attended med school a decade ago, before quitting to become a journalist, but I'm still fluent in the anatomy of survival.

I look up to see the drunk. He's ambling awkwardly. He holds his arms close to his chest. He disappears into a darkened stairwell. From his pocket, something falls, a piece of paper, onto the damp cement.

"Don't move. You might be hurt." The voice comes from my right.

It's the brunette, the one from the turnstile.

I blink hard. She's blurry.

"Breathe." She kneels and extends an arm and puts fingers on my shoulder.

Her touch brings attention to the acute pain near my deltoid. The strap of my ratty black backpack must've given me a nifty friction burn. But it also probably spared me a rougher fall. The pack, which follows me everywhere, contains an overflow of magazines and notes, the flora and fauna from which journalism sprouts and, tonight, a serendipitous pillow. Lucky I left my laptop home today, for its sake and mine.

I exhale.

I picture the man coming at me, falling but somehow purposeful, his face camouflaged.

"Say something," the brunette encourages. "Did you know that guy?"

"Scleroderma."

"What?"

I don't express my thought: the drunk's skin was pulled tight against his forehead and around his eyes. *Scleroderma* means "tight skin." Its presence can indicate a rare disease of the organs, very rare, so these days it is much more likely to indicate a visit to the dermatologist; this drunk recently had an injection of Botox that tightened his wrinkles. Rich drunk.

My scrutiny is a sign of my own condition: excessive medical analysis. Some people focus on faces, or names. I remember pathologies. My not-very-exciting sixth sense is seeing illnesses and physical conditions, a vestige of med school. Jaundice, clinical water retention, lazy eye, gout, misaligned spine, all the herpes variants, emphysema cough, flat-footedness. The obsessive medical labeler can identify the flat-footer even when the condition hustles by, wearing shoes. Even though I'd abdicated a career in medicine for one in medical journalism—after realizing I lacked the intensity and rigidity to be a good doctor—I can't shake associating humans with their conditions.

"It doesn't feel right." I look in the direction the man stumbled away.

"What? Your head?"

"That too."

I stand, feeling her fingers fall away. I wobble, get my footing, walk unsteadily to the piece of paper that fell from the man's leather jacket. I pick it up.

It is lined and legal sized, creased and smudged with black grease. I unfold it and discover two names written in blue pen. One name is Sandy Vello. Doesn't sound familiar. The other name does.

"What is it?" The brunette puts a hand on my arm.

I point to my name on the piece of paper. She shakes her head, uncertain what I'm talking about.

"This is my name?"

"What?"

"Nathaniel Idle."

"I'm Faith." She's still not getting it: My name was on a piece of paper that fell from the pocket of a man who nearly turned me into a subway smoothie.

"That wasn't an accident." I clutch the piece of paper in both hands.

"Do you think you need an ambulance? I suspect you're in shock."

I look at Faith. She's biting the edge of her bottom lip with perfect teeth, her head tilted, concerned, empathic. Early thirties, jet-black hair, arched eyebrows, soft features, irresistible grace of the genus Beautiful Person. My eyes lock on her for a millisecond more than is appropriate. I am struck by an urge to make her laugh. But it's overwhelmed by a more powerful compulsion.

I look at the stairs where the man disappeared. I sprint after him.

2

I bound up a steep set of metal stairs. They're slippery and dimly lit from a track on the low ceiling.

I'm halfway up when I'm hit by a wave of lightheadedness and nausea, and feel my toe slide, causing my leg to collapse underneath me. My knee smacks the edge of a stair. A burst of pain shoots forth from my right patella. I look down and curse my cheap canvas high-tops and their cheap rubberized soles that offer inexpensive-chic—and traction approximating paper plates.

I hear footsteps behind me. I glance back to see Faith.

"You're hurt. Wait."

I ignore her and stumble to the top of the stairs.

I'm looking down a long, empty tunnel, ending in the well-lit maw of the subway station. I start running again but with a decided hitch in my step.

At the station entrance, my eyes adjust to the wide-open space, with cathedral-like high ceilings, illuminated by bright light. Very bright. Another wave of nausea, one I can't suppress. I put my hands on my knees and heave spittle and hot breath.

I stand and focus again on the cavernous station. In front of me, a handful of ticket machines line a distant wall. To my left, stairs lead down the tracks for trains heading to the beach, the direction I wasn't traveling. To my right, turnstiles provide exit and entrance. Next to them, in a rectangular cage of thick glass that stretches nearly to the ceiling, sits a man in blue cap, gray hair overflowing, wooly sideburns, eyes turned down, lost in paperwork, or the paper. Oblivious.

There is no drunk or homeless man. There are no fellow travelers besides Faith, who I hear behind me.

I hobble to and through the turnstiles. Beyond them, a set of majestic stone stairs.

I walk ten yards to the top of the stairs. Outside, I inhale cool air, grateful for it, and peer into the darkness dotted by brake lights, headlights and a stoplight at the corner just to my right. It's just past 10 P.M., rainy, cold, windy. There's an empty bus parked for the night in front of the subway terminal, and a Volvo in the passenger pickup zone; its driver sits behind the wheel mesmerized by whatever is on his smart phone.

I return to the turnstiles and knock on the glass cage. The blue-capped man takes a deliberate few seconds to look up, communicating his superiority.

"Excuse me. I was attacked—on the inbound platform."

In his beefy hand, a Snickers. He swallows a bite that causes a hitch in his throat. He lets me back through the turnstiles and we start labored communication through a small opening in the glass cage.

"What happened?" He's trying to sound interested but projects weariness, chocolate and nougat on the tips of his front teeth.

"Did someone just come through here? Big guy wearing a leather jacket? He had a beard and maybe a limp."

"You were mugged?"

Was I mugged? I paw my right front jeans pocket and feel the outline of my phone. My wallet is still in the right back pocket.

Not mugged.

"Your bag is open."

It takes a second for me to realize that he means my backpack. I turn around and see a few papers have scattered on the ground in the station.

Faith, having reappeared, has scooped up several of the straggling sheets. I turn back to the agent.

"Some guy nearly pushed me into the tracks. Can you call the police?"

"Nothing's missing?" He hates the idea of the bureaucratic time sink involved with reporting a non-mugging.

"You must have surveillance cameras." Maybe they got a good look at the falling mountain and me.

I turn to Faith, who stands just a few feet away, holding my papers. Part of me is wondering what she's doing, why she followed me, and where she came from, why she's wearing a skirt after dark in rainy mid-January.

"You must have seen him, Faith."

"You should sit down. You look a little green."

"I'm okay. I'll get it checked." I strongly suspect I won't. It doesn't take a former medical student to recognize I've got a head contusion and maybe a concussion.

"Your backpack has taken a mortal blow." She pauses. "Seen him? Who?"

"The guy who toppled me over. You passed him in the tunnel, or he passed you. You each appeared out of nowhere, simultaneously."

She looks momentarily stricken. "I'm sorry."

I need another approach.

"I usually don't interrogate a woman when I first meet her. Usually, it's a cup of coffee, or a beer, maybe dinner, and only then do I start treating her like a witness or suspect."

She laughs. "I wanted to make sure you were okay." For a millisecond, she lowers her brown eyes and then looks back up. She smiles reassuringly.

"What's on your sweatshirt? Did you get sick?"

I look down at the stain just above the left shoulder.

"Or did your baby get sick?" she asks.

What's with this woman? Does she know something about me?

"I've got a nephew," she explains. "When he was a baby, that's right about the spot where he liked to press his face when I fed him."

I look again at the splotch on my shoulder, and

feel light-headed again, momentarily unreal. This prescient woman is right. I've got feeding casualty on my shoulder. Isaac. My son. I'll see him again. I manage a smile. "Masticated avocado I bet. From the mouths of babes. Right onto my shoulder." Note to self: buy stain remover.

"I take it your baby is not in his or her twenties."

I feel my eyes mist. "Eight months, give or take. He spits up like an Olympian."

I cannot possibly be connecting with a woman, not now, not given my track record in relationships. I'm a romantic Hindenburg: promising takeoff, brief smooth sailing, splat. It's probably not the time to blurt that out, or disclose my dysfunctional personal life and worldview. I'm no longer with Isaac's mom, and he's with her. And I'm far from at peace with the whole thing.

"They're out of town. Visiting her parents."

"Who?"

Good job, Nat. Instead of confessing your romantic failings, you mutter non sequiturs. "Never mind."

"Anyhow." Faith hands me the papers she's gathered. "I've got to catch a cab and get home."

"Wait. Please." I'm coursing with a dozen questions, chiefly: What did Faith see? I ask her if she can spare five more minutes to help me deconstruct what happened on the platform. She acquiesces, with a light flavor of impatience, denoted by fidgeting fingers and diminished eye contact. She tells me that she bought a single-ride fare, made a quick phone call, then headed down to the tracks to get the K. When she arrived, she saw the huge guy fall

down toward me. She couldn't tell if it was deliberate or not, but she could tell it was a major impact.
"He squished you," she says.

It's not particularly helpful. And I'm definitely
testing her patience when I ask again if she doesn't
remember seeing the man or can tell me anything
about his physical demeanor. I observe that he was
clutching his chest as he departed; did she notice?
Was he limping?

Finally, I ask her about the piece of paper that fell
from the man's pocket, the one with my name on
it and the other name—Sandy Vello. Did she see it
fall?

She shrugs. "Maybe it's yours. Maybe it fell out
with all the rest of this stuff."

"Meaning what?"

"Your backpack droppings were everywhere.
You've got a mishmash of things. You took a pretty
good hit to your head. It can shake your sense of
reality."

She smiles, the same compassionate but sad smile
she gave the beggar when I first saw her at the turnstile. A beggar in the shadows. I'm about to ask another question, but she turns to go.

I blurt out: "Please take my card, in case you
think of anything about that guy. And can I at least
have your info, in case I need to follow up?" I tug
two business cards from my wallet.

She takes and studies one. It reads: "Nat Idle: By
the Word." She tucks it into her coat pocket. She
scribbles something on the back of the other card
and hands it back.

"Can I offer you cab fare?" I ask.

"I'm good. Take care of yourself."

She walks through the turnstiles and into the darkness.

I look at the ten numbers on the card.

Then I look at the scrap of paper I've been clutching this entire time, the one with my name and the other one, Sandy Vello.

I don't recognize the handwriting. It's certainly not mine. I know this didn't come from my backpack. Still, am I making more of this than it is? But, if so, isn't that my stock-in-trade? I've built a business and a life pursuing mysteries—little, medium and occasionally big. Just like Isaac, everything is a curiosity to be examined, touched, tasted, understood. I'm a toddler with a pen.

But there's something else: real anger. I could've died.

I indulge myself in that for a bit, but then my thoughts return to someone else. I'm wondering about this Sandy Vello. What if she's a target too? What if she has a kid, spouse, partner, or general desire to live?

I walk back to the top of the majestic stairs and pull out my phone. It's a first-generation iPhone, which in these parts makes me a Luddite, joke fodder, recipient of sad looks on public transportation. I call up an Internet browser and finger in Sandy Vello's name. In the customary minute it takes for the results to load, I watch a man on a bike pedal by, undaunted in the rain, a dog in his back saddle wearing a yellow slicker. Watching makes my knee ache and I wonder when I'll get back on a basketball court, my thirty-seven-year-old joints and weather permitting.

Google returns its wisdom, 171,000 related web pages' worth. Big help, Google.

I run the same search but for recent news. I get a hit. Sandy Vello has been in the news lately. Ten days ago, she was hit by a car in Woodside, a suburb in the hills half an hour south of San Francisco. She was killed.

I'm reading an obituary.

3

True to my business card, I make my living with words. Ideally getting $1.50 for each one. That's been easier since I exposed the plot to destroy our brains.

A year ago, I wrote a series of articles about how a venture capitalist with ties to the military was developing technology to store secrets inside fallow memory space in the human mind. The conspirators wanted to use brain capacity like computer disc space. The idea was to allow seemingly harmless humans (like the elderly or even children) to become stealth carriers of data, able to cross borders or military lines. Without knowledge of the carry or the suspicion of enemies. The brilliant conceit: the bad guys might know how to hack a password-protected supercomputer, but they won't be able to hack the brain of an eighty-five-year-old with dementia.

It's not nearly as farfetched as it sounds, at least in theory, given the malleability of the hippocampus, the brain's memory gateway. But in practice, the development of the technology entailed tinkering with and even destroying the memories of human guinea pigs, without their knowledge or permission. By happenstance, one of the guinea pigs was my grandmother, the iconoclastic octogenarian Lane Idle.

Grandma Lane's memory began fading in and out, failing precipitously, regurgitating memories not her own. I was scared, curious and then angry, and followed some leads. Story of my life.

Long story short: I wrote a story about the scheme, got some notoriety, banged out a string of freelance pieces about the impact of technology on the brain, scored periodic appearances on CNN, experienced the most intense work year of my life, won an award for investigative medical journalism and—trust me that this relates—now need to borrow a tie.

It's not that I don't own a tie, but it has big polka dots and probably will be seen as obnoxious at tomorrow's journalism awards luncheon at a private room at MacArthur Park in Palo Alto.

Sartorially, I remain unevolved, another late-thirtysomething unable to dress his age. But professionally, for the first time, I'm on solid footing. I even get a premium for my blog posts, $50 for some of them, having become something of a go-to journalist for investigations and wide-eyed tips involving neuroscience.

Which brings me to Sandy Vello.

According to her brief obituary in the *San Mateo Daily News*, the deceased worked as an administrator in the emerging neurotechnology division of a company called PRISM Corporation. She lived west of Burlingame, did regular volunteer work at the learning annex at the Twin Peaks juvenile hall, and enjoyed a modest fame in having been a contestant on an early episode of *Last One Standing*, a reality show that entails out-surviving other contestants over twelve weeks of humiliation and bug eating. There was no photo.

I haven't heard of PRISM Corp. I Google it and discover Pacific Rim Integrated Solutions and Management, a nondescript corporate web site, dark blue background with an image in the upper right corner of a ship on the high seas. A close look shows the ship to be constructed of thousands of ones and zeroes.

A section labeled "About PRISM" indicates the company makes software kernels that power "a range of consumer, multimedia and industrial products, from clock radios to home alarm systems." There's no mention of a neurotechnology department.

I find a handful of other references to PRISM. There's one PDF document filed with U.S. Immigration Services indicating that PRISM, a company with fifty-five employees, last year requested seven short-term work visas for foreign-born engineers. It's not out of the ordinary; virtually every high-tech firm, from Amazon to Yahoo, seeks visas for highly skilled software engineers from India and Turkey.

I'm baffled. I'm wondering what could possibly be the connection between a deceased former reality-TV-show contestant and me. The chief connection I can make is that I sometimes write about the brain and, at least according to her obituary, Sandy Vello worked on neurotechnology. And for a story, I once visited the juvenile hall at Twin Peaks, a salmon-colored prison, administrative building and learning annex for San Francisco's wayward teens where Sandy volunteered. The connection between she and I is, in a word, tenuous.

This is what preoccupies me so much that I nearly light my foot on fire.

I'm standing at the entrance to my office, having just barely sidestepped a mound of dirt with a candle sticking out of the top that sits just inside the door. I look up to see a handful of other such be-candled dirt mounds around the edges of the small office, forming a circle. In the center of the room sits my office mate, Samantha. She's got her arms crossed over her chest, her palms resting on her shoulders. She wears a peasant blouse and a patient smile.

"You almost made Mamma angry," she says.

"Whose mamma? Or should I say: who is Mamma?"

"Mamma Earth. She's helping drive away the negative detritus and the painful memories."

I look down at the mound of dirt. "You're allowed to stick candles in Mamma, but I'm not allowed to lovingly brush her with the bottom of my high-tops?"

She pulls herself to her feet. She smiles bemusedly, clearly dealing with a less-evolved creature. Then her full lips turn in, a slight frown. Slight. Sam can command a thousand complex emotions but for the sake of being straightforward with the universe, she tries to reduce them to three: mild displeasure, peacefulness, mild joy. She blinks.

"Whoa." She studies me. "Yellow with bits of orange."

To anyone who hasn't met Sam, this makes no

sense. But I've spent years having her read my aura, or Karmic glow, or whatever it is.

"Serious unresolved tension." She states the not-so-mysterious. She stands up, walks over to me, flips on the light by the door. "And green. Gross."

"What's green? My aura?"

"The throw-up stain on your shoulder."

"Isaac. Serious unresolved dinner."

She shakes her head, looks at me quizzically. "It's nearly ten." Maybe meaning: Why are you here and not at home?

I shrug. Half smile. She knows I can take refuge here since the breakup.

She leans in and kisses my cheek, tenderly, like a mom or big sister, which she is, in a way. She pulls back and holds my gaze, betraying sympathy in the wrinkles around her soft brown eyes. She's got a round face that I sometimes think of as a distant, wondrous planet.

Samantha Leary and her husband, Dennis, ten years my senior, are great friends, limitless sounding boards, and my veritable family, despite being two of the kookiest people in a city filled with their like-minded, soulful ilk. Sam is a masseuse, spiritual healer, and uncannily accurate reader of moods who has freed herself of all conventional wisdom in a search to feel peaceful and help others do the same. Recently, she spent two weeks taking natural hallucinogens in marathon sessions in a rain forest in Chile and claiming to get wisdom by talking to ancient plants. She is known to those of us who love her as "the Witch."

Dennis goes by "Bullseye," thanks to the time he

hit a bar waitress with a dart, ostensibly by accident. He's the Witch's polar opposite, a clinical, coldly logical thinker, and borderline autistic in his focus on math and all things computers. He says little, preferring to spend his time perched on a stool sipping an Anchor Steam at the Pastime Bar, which has long been our hangout. For the last six months, the Witch and I have spent more time at our joint office, which we decided to get when I started making money from journalism and she said she decided to treat her healing efforts more like a business.

She's got a way to go. Her business card is blank. She says people will find her when they need her.

It makes me wonder if she has different motives. She's been keeping a close eye on me. She says I'm working too much, am more likely than ever to see conspiracies and look for great stories, and then pursue them to obsessive end.

She avoids putting too fine a point on it but I know what she thinks: when things ended with Polly, the vivacious entrepreneur who birthed Isaac, I moved ever closer to the fine line between journalism and madness.

The Witch puts her hands on my chest and closes her eyes. Her palms are not just warm, but hot. She'd say that's because we're exchanging energy. Maybe. A different explanation for the heat, the clinical medical explanation, is that the hands act as veritable temperature controls for the body, the heavy blood flow to and from the palms allowing for feelings of hot and cold disproportionate to the rest of the body.

Samantha inhales deeply. I know she's trying to

shake something loose inside me, but I'm resistant, partly a skeptic, mostly a still racing mind. I look around our ratty one-room office, 120 square feet of yin and yang. On the right, my desk, a study in scrap heap: strewn papers and magazines, my laptop asleep in the midst; my only decoration a grainy picture of an embryo—Isaac at just a few seconds old, the first time I saw him—taped to the wall above my faux-wood pop-together desk of Scandinavian design.

To my left, Samantha's oak desk, with a single sheet of paper aligned in the middle. No computer. Her chair is a wooden stool, which she says forces her to focus on her posture, allowing energy to flow more easily in and out of her body.

Samantha's hair smells clean but flat, fragrance-free, and she's got a ton of it. I've never seen anything grow so quickly: thick, wild and relentless, a veritable bird's nest. One month, she shaves it to the scalp, the next it's a whirlwind of brown. I've wondered if she's got a variation of hirsutism, abnormal hair growth, all of it serendipitously placed on top of her head.

"Faith." The word pops out of my mouth.

"That's right. Have faith."

"No." I step back.

"Faith. The brunette from the subway."

For just an instant, the Witch grits her teeth, betraying frustration at the failed trance. But maybe it had its impact after all, and shaken loose a valuable revelation.

"I'm being played."

4

I close my eyes and picture the subway station. When I'd first entered the train station, I'd seen Faith, the brunette do-gooder, give money to a beggar.

I look into Samantha's wise eyes. "The beggar was the same man who knocked me over."

"What are you talking about, Nathaniel?"

"Maybe the beggar wasn't a beggar at all," I venture. "Maybe Faith wasn't giving him money, but just talking to him. Were they coordinating something?"

Samantha shakes her head. She's heard me do this before, begin stories in the middle, or the end.

"Let me get unloaded and I'll explain."

I take the short walk to my desk, dodging candles. I remove my backpack, noticing with a slight grimace the likely mortal tear to the black fabric. I've taken pride in its longevity, maybe like a construction worker gets worn into boots. I put the bag down. I look at the picture of Isaac, pink and crinkly. What a gift.

I gesture for Sam to join me on the blue futon that lies near a far wall and that she uses to give massages when I'm not around and to meditate even when I am. I tell her what happened at the train station, leaving out the part about the blow to the head. I imagine that Sam, hostile as she generally is to Western medicine, would pile me immediately into the hair on top of her head and fly me to the emergency room.

When I finish, she says: "May I risk upsetting you?"

"How so?"

"I'm going to tell you what the plants told me."

I gather she's referring to her Chilean visit and communing with the ancient vegetation. "The plants told you about what happened at the train station, or what was going to happen?"

"They told me that obsessing about mystery is a neurosis, a kind of pathology. Worrying about the unknown or anticipating an outcome is the biggest test to our true happiness."

"Getting run over by a train would be a true test of my happiness?"

"You weren't run over."

"So you're saying let it go?"

"Of course not. Call this Faith, or ask some questions about that poor woman who got hit by a car. But don't spin yourself into conspiracy theories. That's your way of—"

I finish her thought. "Uncovering vast international conspiracies." I smile.

"Of not dealing with your personal life. I should go." She stands. She's made her point. "Go home. Skip the late-night conspiracy spinning."

I notice she doesn't ask about Isaac. She seems increasingly reticent about doing so. I would never ask her but I think she regrets never having had children. She's professionally maternal, without her own offspring.

I drag myself to the hallway, where there is a full bathroom, replete with shower, accessible by keypad. We, the office tenants of the second floor, keep it locked to dissuade vagrants and the patrons of the retail shop that resides on the floor below us. It's a sex shop called Green Love that sells sex toys and paraphernalia that are made using sustainable and eco-friendly manufacturing processes and natural resources. Their tagline: Guilt-free 'gasms.

At the bathroom door, I key in Isaac's birthday, essential numbers, eminently hackable, my stand against an overly complicated world. I open the door and inhale mildew not fully overcome by the floral-scented candle the Witch set on the toilet.

In the mirror, I see the product of a long day, followed by a very bad night, mitigated by a decent haircut. At Samantha's prompting, I managed to get to a barber earlier this week, in time for tomorrow's magazine award luncheon. I look my age, give or take. I wonder what Faith saw when she looked at me; I've got symmetrical features and a prominent nose, looks that, I'm told, resemble some actor who regularly plays the ethnic-looking detective. I never had problems getting the girl. Just keeping her.

In the recessed medicine cabinet, I find Tylenol and take three tablets. I wash them down with tap water I drink from a plastic San Francisco Giants cup.

I twist my head in a variety of directions so that I can see the back of my skull in the cabinet mirror. This proves (obviously) impossible and absolutely comical, enough so that I actually laugh out loud when I nearly fall over trying to reflect the image of the cut on the back of my head off of an aerosol can so that I can see it in the mirror.

I return to my desk and snag my laptop. It's brushed stainless steel with the Apple insignia on the cover, a model that once was far outside my price range, but it's a cast-off from Polly, the ex in the astronomical tax bracket. I carry the computer to the futon, sit, and Google the symptoms for concussion. I know the answer before the Internet spits forth its wisdom—sharp impact, brief loss of consciousness, headache, nausea. But I also know the treatment: rest, fluids, watch for dizziness, changes in vision and, above all, get checked by a doctor.

I should do so but I can't stand the idea of spending hours in the emergency room to be told what Dr. Internet already told me. Besides, I'm almost an actual doctor myself. Almost, not quite. And I'm so tired. I'll just close my eyes for a second.

I dream of Isaac. He's sitting in a red train at the playground. He's got bouncy brown curls that he didn't seem to inherit from me or Polly and that I'm aching to run my fingers through.

"This train is bound for glory," I say, arms wide, aping to elicit a reaction. He grins a grin that could cure all ills.

I lean down and whisper with mock seriousness, "Little Man, I'm going to tell you a secret. Do you want to hear a secret?"

He nods, expectant. I lean in to tell him the secret, when I hear a woman's voice. "Time to go, lambkins."

It's Polly. She's standing in front of the train, prim in a blue business suit but with her straight brown hair cut at shoulder length, casual, irresistible. Suddenly, I'm filled with dread.

"Be careful of the train, Little Man!" I scream. "The train!"

Terrified, I jerk awake. Gray daylight floods the office, a horn blares from the street below, my mouth tastes of flour paste, my head thick. I've closed my eyes and slept all night. And I think: the train. Of course. So obvious. Just as my concussion doesn't require diagnosis by an MD, so my dreams don't require expert interpretation by Dr. Freud. I've nearly been run over by a subway and I dream of a train taking Isaac, his mother acting as conductor, or something like that. I can only hope my journalism is clearer and less clichéd.

I pick up my phone. I pull up Polly's number on the phone. I hold my finger over the touch pad. My digit trembles. I scowl and reach for my wallet, which sits on the floor. From it, I pull the piece of paper with Faith's contact info. Just my luck: the phone number is smeared from last night's rain but is sufficiently legible to allow me to make out four of seven numbers and have reasonable guesses at another two. I try several permutations, getting three wrong numbers, a couple of disconnected lines and one voice mail that asks me to leave my message at the beep but doesn't say who the number belongs to. Maybe it's Faith. I leave a short message asking her to get back to me, explaining that I'm the guy from the train station and that I hope I have the right number.

I am able to read Faith's email address, which is not as rain-smeared, and send her a note asking her to get in touch.

I also leave a message with a friend at the San Francisco Police Department. In the past, my stories have often put me at odds with the cops, but I've had a much warmer relationship with them in recent months. I attribute that to my career notoriety or, perhaps, career legitimacy. In my voice mail, I tell Sergeant Everly that I've had a run-in with a mountain dressed up as a man and would love to run it by him.

I feel the dull ache from the back of my head and finger the sticky wound, reasonably healing. I open my laptop, struck by an impulse: maybe somewhere along the line I've got a connection to the dead woman, Sandy Vello, that would make sense of last night's attack.

I find something odd. Two weeks ago, my anti-spam program filtered out an email from Sandyvello@hotmail.com. It reads: "Please contact me regarding a private matter." Then another, eleven days ago. Same sender. "Mr. Idle, contact me please regarding a private journalistic matter. This is serious. We have one month to stop the launch."

Launch?

Was Sandy Vello trying to reach me, and then she got killed? I do the math. The second note came the very day she was killed. Was someone trying to prevent us from connecting?

A quick double-check of her obituary reminds

me that she lived west of Burlingame, probably in the hills somewhere, and volunteered regularly at the learning annex of the Twin Peaks Youth Guidance Center. It's actually a jail for San Francisco's underage have-nots, pranksters in a minimum security wing as well as young men guilty of extreme violence far before their time, locked in cages that many in the city would be stunned to know share their pricey real estate. Next door is the annex, which I visited a few years ago for a story about the small organic farm the adolescent prisoners were tending in the yard.

I register the time, 10:30. I slept forever, I think, as an alarm bell rings inside my head. I've got an hour to be in Palo Alto, a forty-minute drive at least, to shake hands before the magazine award. I have to shower, find the tie and a clean shirt before composing my acceptance speech as I speed down Highway 101.

Then maybe a visit to the learning annex to see if I can justify the award.

5

I try not to envy other people. Andrew Leviathan, the man presenting me the award today, makes that very difficult. Where even to begin? The billions, the philanthropy, patents, brilliant anthropologist wife whose perpetual smile feels like an ignition switch to every man in the room, his apparently complete absence of pathologies, or the escape. How can you not start with the escape?

It was 1979, Romania, the cold war still in full effect. Andrew was a mere teen, and already on the cusp of being a singularly dangerous 21st-century cubicle soldier. The Eastern bloc, through its selection of the best and the brightest, had identified gangly Andrew as the preternatural math whiz who could make Mother Russia's supercomputers more super than evil America's. And he probably could have, but instead, given full access to their system, he introduced a noxious digital virus into Mother Russia's digital heart, like Luke Skywalker aiming lethal bursts into the Death Star. Andrew's was not a deadly shot, only nearly, and the young man got caught.

The morning he was to be hanged, the executioners came to his cell to find him gone. He'd bribed one of the guards by promising that, if he was set free, he'd hack into a Russian state bank and have $100,000 wired to the guard's family living in New Hampshire. That wasn't the fancy part. Once he was loosed, Andrew snuck into a local news station, got onto a computer, hacked into the country's central weather mainframe, and managed to set off a warning of a rare and imminent attack of cyclones. In the chaos, he piloted a plane out of the country.

The rest, in a nutshell: Italy, then New York, then Berkeley, where he got a PhD in computer engineering, then Palo Alto, where after a few entrepreneurial fits and starts, he created EDGE, the algorithm that helps you find things on the Internet and that is the kernel upon which Google and everyone else that really matters on the Internet builds their business.

He's now standing at a podium, the creator of the New Media Award for Public Service Journalism, telling a humble version of the escape story, minus anything self-aggrandizing, but it is plenty aggrandizing of me, embarrassingly so.

"I sat in that six-foot by six-foot dank Romanian jail cell, an atheist devoted only to numbers, and I prayed. I asked God for a journalist," Andrew says. "I prayed for someone who would tell truth to the world."

I look up at the three dozen tables filled with Friends of Andrew, faces held rapt over their pear soup. There is no way that I can follow this guy. I'm wearing rumpled clothes from the just-in-case bin I keep at the office, having taken a rushed shower in the bacteria-smeared bathroom in the hallway, and then bought a tie from the Green Love shop. If you look too closely at the faint horizontal image on the tie, you can make out a couple having sex standing against a tree. On the plus side, at a distance, the blue tie simply looks nicely patterned, and, plus, it's made of hemp. I pull my sport coat closed and button it over the tie.

"And we don't just need a free press that is permitted and encouraged to expose injustices big and small. That is not enough," Andrew continues. He's physically sturdy, a cyclist, I'd guess, with a fitness room in his basement, but with gray dominating his still-full hair, a presage of the frailty that will creep up on him in ten years. "We need individual journalists like Nathaniel who aren't afraid to take on the jailers of the truth."

He launches into my boilerplate biography: my upbringing in Colorado, my medical-school training, a summary of my stories about how digital gadgets can have an addictive quality that, if not managed, can lead to a short attention span and disrupt our ability to effectively create, and analyze, information. Affect our memory and our capacity to connect with other people.

As he makes me sound worthier than I am, I scan the room looking at the faces of the captivated. They are taking in the Silicon Valley icon, the immigrant who symbolizes the essence of the meritocracy that the region considers its defining characteristic, and someone who can write a check that in a nanosecond changes the fortunes of their start-up or foundation. They also, apropos of nothing, have the usual range of medical conditions. A woman in the front row in a smart blue suit can't suppress a deep cough consistent with the tail end of walking pneumonia, less throaty than bronchitis; two tables away, a retiree curled unnaturally over his lunch like a question mark looks to have camptocormia, a bent spine we now know to have degenerative origins, not psychological ones, as once thought. Across from him sits a rail-thin man with angular features and a bald head so shiny that I wonder about seborrhea, excessive secretion of the sebaceous glands. Oily skin.

And then there's the man in the doorway. It's not pathology that catches my eye, but the long, black leather coat, which seems out of place inside in midday Palo Alto, and, more so, the stare, the crew cut, like AstroTurf, covering the big, square head. Arms crossed, he's looking at me intently, right until I look back at him. He averts his eyes. He curls out of the doorway.

"Before I sum up," Andrew says, "I want to take a brief moment to do some unctuous politicking with the people who really set me free in this lifetime. To my beautiful and stalwart wife"—a few in the crowd coo—"thank you. And to my first Silicon Valley partner, Gils Simons, an operational genius, many thanks for turning ones and zeroes into a fortune, and for continued friendship."

I look at Gils. He's a fifty-year-old bland Boy Scout, tight haircut, sweater vest, the quintessential organizational guy who was the behind-the-scenes straight man responsible for the boring business side of early Leviathan Ventures while Andrew played mad digital scientist.

Andrew pauses. "Nathaniel, Nat, if I may," he then says after his beat, and I can feel him looking at me. I look back at him from my seat at the front table. "It has not been easy for you. You've fought through great personal and professional obstacles the last few years to remain devoted to your craft and to the pursuit of truth. While the rest of us have blindly embraced technology, me as much as anyone, you've shown us its limitations and even its potential dangerous side effects."

He looks at the audience, another pause, this time to reinforce the idea that he, one of the Internet's pioneers, appreciates a skeptic. I think: I wish Faith could bear witness—not Polly, I realize with some mild surprise, but the compassionate brunette from the subway.

"I give you Nat Idle, the recipient for this year's award in public health journalism. He is the essence of the journalist that I, a seventeen-year-old hours from being hanged, prayed to God to deliver."

As I stand, I feel no particular joy; this pomp and rhetoric is less about me than about Andrew reinforcing the value of an award he created.

The crowd claps as I shake Andrew's smooth, confident hand.

At the podium, I clear my throat. "When I was seventeen, I was a hacker too. I spent a summer trying to break into Jane Messersmith's brassiere."

Bad line, but big laugh from a sympathetic audience.

"Abject failure. If only I could've convinced her we were in for an attack of cyclones, she might've huddled with me on the couch."

"Andrew," I direct this to him. "We should work together in the future."

Smaller laugh. Time to get back to the prepared remarks, such as they are.

I thank Andrew and his wife, Catherine, and the audience.

"Hundreds of thousands of years ago, humans trolled the jungles, living amid the trees, running from tigers, and chasing rabbits," I begin. "Today, our jungle is a seventeen-inch monitor where we run from bad banner ads and instant-message interruptions from our bosses, sprint to keep up with tweets and Facebook status updates, use always-on connections to chase deals from mountaintops or even bathroom stalls."

Time for the numbers. I point out that the households in the United States consume on average 33.8 gigabytes of information, the equivalent of 100,000 words delivered in text, audio, video, graphics, constant bursts of data. I explain that one question driving my journalistic efforts has been a simple, dumb question: What does it mean that our environment has transformed virtually overnight into pixilated, liquid screens, delivering danger and opportunity every millisecond?

"We once adapted to the jungle by walking upright or brachiating." I launch into a stock line. "So how are we adapting to the digital jungle, for good and for ill?"

Lots of nods from the audience. I take them in

with a pause. I feel a wave of light-headedness, a lukewarm hot flash. I take a deeper breath. Andrew approaches the podium, and hands me water. I sip.

"I'm not accustomed to public speaking." I'm too close to the microphone, prompting an echo. "I try the old trick of imagining the audience naked, but then I get worried because I can't figure out where you'd all carry your iPhones if you don't have pockets."

Laughter, but thin—people are ready for their salmon. I thank everyone again, promise to spend my award money on a new flat-panel television with Internet access, then return to the head table. I sit between Andrew, who is listening intently to a blue-haired octogenarian talk about how much has changed in her lifetime, and Catherine, who leans in closely to me.

"I don't trust people who are comfortable speaking publicly, what's-his-name excepted." She nods toward Andrew. I smile, as she adds: "Are you feeling okay?" It's not the kind of question you ask in polite company, which means I must look terrible.

"Head wound."

"Really?"

"Just overwhelmed. Journalists are accustomed to being pilloried, so this kindness takes some getting used to."

I excuse myself and make my way around the crowd absorbed in lunch, silverware clinking on plates and voices mixing like a dissonant symphony. Out in the hallway, I expect to see the guy with the long leather coat, but no sign of him. I wonder if I imagined him before. I did see him, didn't I?

"Excuse me." A voice from behind me. I turn. I blink to focus on a man I vaguely recognize. It's the man with the shiny head I saw sitting near the front of the room. With bony fingers, he extends a phone.

"You dropped this on your way out." It's my iPhone.

"You okay?"

I nod and take the device. "Thanks."

I walk to the restroom and toss cold water onto my pale face. My body pulses with a dull ache, not just physical but also emotional: loneliness; maybe the absence of my son or someone to share this moment with. Instinctively, I lift my phone from the counter, and realize I've missed three texts from an "unknown" number.

I tap the screen. The first message is cryptic. "I got your message. Are you feeling okay? I remembered something."

The second message continues the first. "Something weird. Call me."

The third message is shorter. "Faith."

6

I hit send on the phone number provided in the second text.

"I can't talk," Faith answers with a whisper after the third ring. "In class."

Class?

"I can't talk either. In bathroom."

She laughs. "Nathaniel Idle? From the subway?"

"To be clear, I'm not in an actual stall."

"Call me later. Please." She clicks off.

I look in the mirror again, and see staring back someone who looks flushed by a schoolboy infatuation.

The rest of the lunch passes relatively quickly, the assembled having paid their homage to Andrew and, by extension, some rumpled journalist, and they need to get back to finding acquirers for their start-ups. As I walk out, Andrew approaches me just as he gets intercepted by an admirer, a small woman, fortyish, with a wave in her hair and thick glasses.

"Mr. Leviathan . . ."

"Andrew, please," he gently corrects her.

"Andrew, my son is Ralph Everson, from the second class at the Montessori. Your contributions have meant the world to him. He's still struggling but he's turned the corner."

"Ralph." He pauses, senses my gaze and looks up at me for an instant, a rare moment in which I've seen him caught off guard. Can he be expected to remember every child his contributions have helped? "I'm so glad he's benefiting from the program." He recovers. "Can we discuss momentarily? I want to bid farewell to our honoree, and give him a hard-earned check."

"Of course, Mr. Leviathan. I mean, Andrew."

He shakes her hand.

He steps toward me, leans in and near-whispers a self-effacing goodbye.

"Please forgive me if my speech was a little too much. It sounded less sentimental when I wrote it in the shower."

"Mine sounded a little funnier when I wrote it on the car ride down."

He gives me a firm handshake and a check for $1,000, which I take with a silent nod of sincere appreciation. It's new backpack time. He pats me once on the back in parting. He's a few inches more than six feet, mildly taller than me, but his gesture seems to come from high above, like you'd get from Dad or an elected official. I'd like to like him and can't identify why I remain on the fence.

I see his eyes gaze over my shoulder. "Gils, hang on a second." Gils, I notice, is sadly devoid of obvious medical quirks. He's a first-generation French immigrant but with the distinct lack of panache.

"I'm glad you came." Andrew smiles, as he walks over to his old partner. "Want to stay and grab a coffee?" Gils glances at me, aware he's being watched, then back at Andrew, then drops his gaze and shakes his head, uncomfortable, used to playing second fiddle. I have an instant sense of their clichéd dynamic: Andrew, the innovator, took up the stage, and Gils, the implementer, made sure the numbers worked. I wonder how many people get to say no to Andrew, even if just for coffee.

Andrew turns to find Montessori mom so I head to the valet to retrieve my car. Outside, I suck in fresh air and check my messages. Polly? Faith? Nope. A scan of daily news items. Equally unsatisfying.

I feel the valet behind me. He's jingling the keys to my car, or, I should say, to Polly's hand-me-down. She may have left me, but—after having great financial success in the start-up world before I met her—she left me with some good stuff. In place of the tattered, rollover-prone SUV I drove for a decade, I drive a three-year-old black Audi A6, which Polly told me without room for debate was safer for toting our precious cargo.

The car isn't Polly's only generosity. It is out of guilt, I suppose, that she's also given me the keys to her in-town loft, a major upgrade from my former apartment out in Richmond. I fall to sleep in it many nights not picturing Polly and Isaac in her Marin mansion, the two puzzle pieces of my nuclear family, nestling just fine on their own. I think about what I could've done differently to save us and whether the very act of creating Isaac, an accidental night of passion, was somehow both the flowering of deep love and its undoing.

"How old is your little one?" The parking valet extends the keys to me with a right hand absent the top quartile of his right index finger that I hope is an age-old accident involving a sharp object and not inflicted by someone else.

He's looking in the middle of the backseat at Isaac's car seat, which, with its straps and harnesses, seems safe enough to use on a space mission. My head pulses, the edges of the car seat fuzzy.

"Shy of a year. Isaac."

"The DustBuster phase."

"How's that?"

"They love the gadgets that make sounds and do crazy things like make dirt disappear from the floor."

I smile. Children are instant bonding. Complete strangers want to talk burping techniques and other toddler trivia.

I climb into the car, feeling an urge to quickly get away from the departing luncheon crowd and into a more comfortable setting, namely, asking subtle but intrusive questions; I'm headed to find out more about Sandy Vello.

I hit the gas and turn onto El Camino Real, a thoroughfare that stretches through Silicon Valley, when I see something that changes my immediate plans. A car length back, behind the wheel of a brown sedan, drives the man, he of the long, black leather coat. Hard to miss that long, square head. I move one lane to my right and he does the same.

I'm approaching a hotel and take a sharp right into its parking lot. He follows.

I pull into a parking spot near the green awning of the hotel entrance. It's too public here for anything too bad to happen, I'd like to think.

My shadower pulls into a nearby spot and steps out, a picture of cardiovascular noncompliance. Five-feet-eight, round belly where all the weight goes, besides his cranium. He's opened his black jacket to reveal a button-down white oxford tucked into shiny, stiff, dark jeans. No belt. A two-decade-old paisley tie and running shoes.

"Hello, Mr. Idle." His weary, high-pitched voice seems inconsistent with his carriage. "Congratulations on your award. Seems like you did a good thing."

I've seen this guy once before, prior to the luncheon. He was standing in the doorway of Green Love, one recent morning; I think I was whisking out of the office to get to an interview.

I've gotten out of the Audi, sprint-ready, though I'm too curious and tired to take off. He's in his fifties, and no physical threat.

"Have you had it checked?" I ask.

"What?"

"You roll your right ankle when you walk. I guess you've gotten used to it but you're stretching your ligament and sometime in the next decade you're going to hate getting out of bed."

"I got it tripping over a Labrador when I was chasing a deadbeat mom. Some banking exec." He looks down and rolls his ankle in midair. "That woman could fly."

Without taking his eyes from me, he reaches toward his back pocket with his right hand, deliberate. I flinch. He pulls out an elongated yellow envelope, official-looking. He extends it. I look at it but don't reach for it.

"You've been served."

He flips the envelope through my open car window.

"My work is done here." He delivers the stock line, and wanders back to his car.

Inside the car, I open the envelope. It's from the United States Treasury. I'm called into a hearing in four days. It says I've ignored repeated letters informing me that I owe "considerable" back taxes.

The letter offers few details beyond it telling me my hearing date is at 4 P.M. and, in all bold, that I may face criminal charges by failing to appear. Criminal charges.

It must be a mistake or joke. How does someone with my meager wages owe considerable taxes? And how could I not have seen the previous letters? Did I get them from the Treasury and ignore them? I am disorganized, I admit, but my chaos stops short of white-collar crime.

At the bottom of the letter is a phone number. I call it, reaching an automated phone menu that, when I follow it to its logical end—after inputting my tax ID number from the letter, and my birth date—I wind up getting an instruction to show up for a hearing with a revenue specialist on the date noted on the letter. Someday, some seventeen-year-old computer genius will destroy all the world's automated phone menus and have a national holiday named after her.

I look at the spot where the square-headed delivery man had been parked and is no longer. I wished I'd probed him a bit, maybe asked him how he knew to find me at the awards luncheon. But I'm also struck by the obvious answer: if he'd done any research on me, he'd have seen the event publicized in various spots on the web.

I toss the envelope into the back, watch it find a final resting place on Isaac's car seat, and I'm overcome with a wave of exhaustion.

I close my eyes for a catnap. I wake up with the sun still looming above one of the Valley's three-story office parks, feeling decidedly refreshed, ready to attack a mystery.

I call Faith. It again goes directly to voice mail.

Next up: a former reality-TV contestant named Sandy Vello. This approach I'll make in person.

7

Into my phone I punch PRISM, the name of the corporation Sandy worked for. It claims three campus headquarters. One each in South San Francisco, Berlin and Beijing. That's no surprise and maybe not true. Increasingly, companies establish several headquarters so wherever customers live they can feel local ties. I use Google Earth to eyeball the nearby address and find it located in an office complex near the bay, just north of the airport.

An hour later, I drive by the campus, such that it is. It's a single office building, six stories, glass and metal that feel as unwelcoming and lonely as the Holiday Inn across the way. The smattering of cars suggests the building is far from full, its engineers working typically odd hours or at home, or the company's presence here is small. Or maybe this company, like many on the Peninsula, provides bus service from San Francisco, ostensibly an environmental play to reduce traffic and car emissions, but also so employees can get the first wave of emails knocked out during the commute.

At the front door, I peer into a small, spare lobby. I press a buzzer on the locked door below a brass placard emblazoned "PRISM—Floors 4 and 5," with Chinese characters below it. Presumably, the receptionist is on the fourth floor. No answer. I try again, in vain. I wait for someone to come in or out, also in vain. On the wall beside the placard, there's a phone number for reception. I call. I get an automated phone system. It allows me to dial by name, which I do. A voice mail answers: "It's Sandy. Leave a message." Sandy Vello, at least, does, or did, work at this place. I hang up. I wait some more. But no employees show up, and none exit. No one for me to make an inquiry with, no string to tug.

This is pointless, and probably not the best way to announce my attention or intentions. I start the car and head north.

A half hour later, I'm at the entrance to a place equally uninviting but somehow more approachable, the Twin Peaks Youth Guidance Center. I swallow hard. I came here not long after Isaac was born—losing myself in work so as not to think about how Polly and I went wrong—writing freelance fluff for the *New York Times* about the organic tomato farm tended by prepubescent prisoners and supplying several gourmet restaurants in the city. It's the brainchild of a city supervisor who otherwise hates the free market.

As I pull into the visitor lot, I remember the layout. Three sections: a maximum security dormitory to the far left cordoned by a foreboding gate, a two-story administrative law building in the middle and, elevated on a hill just above the

lot, a learning annex. It's a single-story building that serves both inmates—the city calls them
"residents"—who prove themselves sufficiently able
to play with others, and a mix of lower-income kids
from around the city who get bussed in to do after-
school programs, learn tradecrafts, use computers,
read, perform one-act plays they write. The annex
itself actually has reasonably nice amenities, having
been privatized a couple years ago to offload budget
burden from a county starved of tax dollars. Still,
nice touches notwithstanding, the buzzwords here
are "basic life skills," a far cry from the buzzwords
"eventual Yale graduate," spoken at private schools
that are just blocks away and eons apart.

According to her obituary, Sandy Vello regularly
volunteered here.

As I kill the ignition, the Audi's fading dashboard
tells me that it's nearly 5, closing time. It's a tight
window for a long shot.

And something doesn't feel quite right. Two
cop cars, red lights flashing but unaccompanied
by sirens, sit in front of the high metal gate that
surrounds the dormitory section. Maybe trouble
inside. If so, I'm the only passerby taking notice.
Behind me, commuters crowd the adjacent artery,
not a rubbernecker among them. They're trying to
get home before the light drizzle turns more men-
acing. Dusk threatens.

In the annex area, there's not a soul in sight, I
follow a sign for "volunteer access" and trudge
narrow cement stairs to the entrance to a rounded
building resembling a high-school basketball gym.
I pull on the handle of the double-wide, thick green

metal doors. Locked, of course. Craning my neck, I try to peer through musty glass with wire mesh between its triple panes. I push the buzzer. I hear the door click. I pull it open and take in the peculiar smell of sweat and antiseptic.

I'm standing at the entrance to an anteroom bisected by a wall-to-wall heavy wood reception counter. Behind it stand two women engaged in conversation, neither of whom looks up at me.

"Not taking deliveries today. It's a lockdown." The slender woman now glances up. Behind her on the wall, a poster with its right edge curled from age displays a man with welding glasses and a caption: "Skills Not Pills." Beside it, cheap faux bronze framed, the portly head of the warden. He's got a comb-over, a rotten makeup job and, in the corner of his lip covering what I know to be his ever-present cold sores. When the county privatized this lockup facility, he got nominal oversight. The move mollified chagrined lefties who had been accused on conservative radio of acknowledging through the privatization the inhering failure of public projects.

"Doc Jefferson around?" The warden, nice guy for an anti-intellectual political hack who prefers a nickname instead of a title, had given me a tour of the farm to the right of the annex. I got too brief a tour of the annex itself, a maze of classrooms separated by those temporary, movable walls.

The slender woman looks up, tilts her head. "Building Two, but you'll have to catch him tomorrow." Her eyes tilt to the round wall clock: 4:55. "It's late and fighting broke out at the dorm."

"I'm actually here about someone else."

She's got short-cropped blonde hair that started as brown and my first impression is she cuts and colors it herself. "Don't forget to close the door behind you."

"Will do." Dead end. I turn around to go, then turn back with a flyer. "My condolences about Sandy Vello."

"Excuse me?"

"Sandra. I'm sorry about what happened."

"Is this a joke?"

"I just wanted to offer my condolences." I'm standing in the door. "I was a fan."

"I'm Sandy Vello. What do you want?"

8

At just this inopportune moment, I hear Polly's voice in my head. She's admonishing me for leaving in the sink a spatula, its tip gooey with cheese-omelet remains. I've done all the other dishes and walked away. Her admonition is playful but pointed: I overlook the finest details, she says, and kisses my ear. It's four months before she leaves me out of the blue, Isaac still *in utero*. "You'll teach our baking bean to finish the job," she says.

It's an instant flash to my failings. Is my head in the clouds? Am I an inexact romantic? Is this why everything went wrong? I feel my head pulse again and see Sandy Vello, a woman that I understood to be dead, glowering at me—short-cropped hair, long on attitude, very vertical given her alleged medical condition.

"You were on that survivor show," I say. Is this really her?

"What?"

Her obituary, or what I thought was her obituary, said she had been on a reality-TV show. Clearly, the obit was wrong in its most essential facet—i.e., Sandy Vello is, um, not dead—but maybe this fallacious death notice had some other facts right. I can't try to make sense of the overriding conundrum right now. My only goal: not alienate this person, who might yet provide answers. Avoid the direct approach. Not yet time to ask if she was trying to contact me. Let the conversation evolve.

"You were robbed," I say. No net now. "I wanted to offer my condolences."

"If you saw the show, then how come you didn't recognize me?"

"I did. I thought I did. I was too embarrassed. I shouldn't have said anything. I . . ."

"I *was* robbed. That Rodent Nuts Donovan made it look like I lied to Clyde. I'd never lie to Clyde. I'd trust that Marine with my life and, besides, he knows I'm tough but totally true to my values." She pauses. "What did your kid do?"

It takes a second to reorient. She thinks I've got offspring in lockup. I'm sizing her up too, and I instantly identify her pathology: IRC. Ideal reality-show contestant. Combative, self-assured, narcissistic, as desperate for attention as she is difficult to turn away from. Genetically tailored for TV. A doctor in Los Angeles actually came up with such a diagnosis, or so I read. This sufferer is leaning against the counter and I can see the veins in her heavily exercised forearms; she's got a narrow, birdlike head but also a charismatic, toothy smile, which she now is showing.

"No. Not visiting any residents. I've visited before. I thought it was common knowledge you did volunteer work—help kids. I took a chance you'd be around . . ."

She's blinking, skeptical.

I clear my throat. "I'm Nat Idle." I'm watching her face. She blinks, not with recognition, but boredom. The conversation just stopped being about her.

"Nathaniel Idle," I expand.

"I told you: we're in lockdown and closing."

She's got no clue who I am, which means she likely didn't send me an email overture purporting to warn me about some impending "launch." Launch of what? Would she know what that refers to? Is she as in the dark as me or, instead, one very good actress, far too good for reality TV?

I fight a rising temptation to tell her I'd heard a rumor that she'd been in an accident. Short of that, maybe I could ask her what she's doing now. It's a natural segue from her riff on someone named Donovan and someone named Clyde, and maybe an entrée into her job at PRISM, or Lord knows if she actually works there. But the rhythm doesn't feel right. I'm still in a mild state of shock.

"I've got a question."

"You want to know if they rigged the show, right?"

"That too. May I have an autograph?"

She looks at the doorway that leads to the back of the building. It opens. The smaller woman reappears.

"You should wait outside."

I'm not getting the impression that egocentric Sandy is someone who likes to volunteer with kids but maybe her work here conforms to her desire to be the most superior creature in the room.

"Perfect." I mean it. I've got a few minutes to make sure I'm not living in a dream world.

I walk the few yards to my car feeling a distinct chill, this one borne of weather, not shock. This part of San Francisco's microclimate makes the other foggy parts feel like sunshine. A few blocks later, I comfort myself, it'll be 20 degrees warmer. Thanks to our hills, valleys, stretches of trees and lush park that suddenly give way to swaths of concrete jungle, I live in microclimate central. This city's motto should be: Don't like the weather? Step to your left.

I sit in the car to extricate myself from the wind and pull out my phone. I call up the Internet and search for Sandy Vello. Again, as I had the night before, I get hundreds of thousands of responses. But none of the first ones is an obituary.

I start the search over, this time specifying her name and "obituary." Plenty of random search returns. None replicating what I'd found the night before. Same result when I put in her name and "bike accident."

Then I try Sandy Vello and "San Mateo Daily News," where I recall seeing the obit. There are a couple of hits. But both of them refer to Sandy as a "local woman" appearing on *Last One Standing*. I speed through one of the articles. It says the show took place in October 2008, filmed on an island off the coast of Washington in frigid conditions, and consisted of various outdoor survival feats. It ended for Sandy in an early episode and she accused one of the contestants of organizing the others to conspire to oust her. I guess that's the arch-enemy Sandy referred to as Donovan. It says Sandy's nickname was "the Perp," on account of her having spent some time in juvenile hall a decade earlier for reasons "sealed by the court." She's cast as a bad seed reformed.

There is nothing on the Internet suggesting this woman is dead and no evidence there ever was such a reference.

How is that possible? I know what I saw the night before. And the fact that the woman is right where I'd been led to believe I'd find her by the phantom obituary provides me some comfort that I didn't imagine the obit entirely.

But now it's gone.

I look up to see Sandy, standing at the window, casing the Audi.

I open the door but remain seated.

"Nice ride. After the show, Porsche put me in a Cayenne for a few weeks but it was too flashy for me."

"I thought you were a big road biker."

"On those shows, they blow your skills out of proportion so they can knock you down. But it's true that I've won my share of races for my age group, and don't you go asking what that is. So, yeah, I put in my time on the bike. It helps me feel centered."

"Isn't that dangerous? All that riding. Do you ever get in crashes?"

"Not a one. Knock on wood. How did you say you

found me? Not that I mind having fans. It's important for me to set a good example. I'm just curious."

Textbook narcissist; like a meth addict whose drug is attention and who burns through it every few seconds, then resents the need and its provider.

She's standing in the wind, arms crossed. I stand. "May I make a confession?"

"If this is some weird stalker thing, I'm going to call the guards." She sort of laughs.

"I'm a journalist."

She blinks a couple of times, discomfort. "Ha. I should've guessed." She looks at the prison. "This part of my life is off the record. I've been where these kids are, and neither I nor they need to have our stories reduced to a bunch of clever sound bites."

"I . . ."

"I don't want to be part of some humiliating 'where are they now' story. They warned us on the show we could be hounded the rest of our lives."

Yep, good suggestion: a story about where she is now. I clear my throat. "Guilty as charged. I'm following some of the recent stars to see how TV has changed them or their perspective."

"No thanks. Ask Donovan. Rodent Nuts craves the limelight."

"You keep up with him?"

"He's an investment advisor. But, get this: for kids! Doesn't that beat it? That duplicitous ape is selling himself to rich families in L.A., telling them he can help their children learn to understand Wall Street."

"I get it. The press can be obnoxious. I'm going

for something more thoughtful. It's a look into a life most of us can only dream of living. You've seen what it's like inside Hollywood. Inside the *machine*. I've heard that it can be a big disappointment—all the promises they make to people who come to it with good intentions."

"What did you say your name was?"

"Nat Idle." I reach into my wallet and grab a business card. I hand it to her. She makes an appearance of studying it. On her right hand, only her index fingernail is painted, light pink. She wears Levi's and a cotton T-shirt under her windbreaker.

"Who do you write for?"

"Various places—magazines, mostly, some online stuff. You know the drill these days. Work where you can get it."

She looks in my backseat.

"You've got a new kid?"

"Yup."

She's thinks about a second. "I've got to go. But I'll consider whether I want to do an interview. My time is pretty tight and my employer doesn't much like press."

"The prison cares about whether you do interviews?"

"Not them. This is pro bono." Without elaborating, she hands me a business card. It reads:

Sandy Vello
Student
Teacher

It's got an email address: 4ABetterWorld@gmail.com. For A Better World. It's obnoxious and, more so, it's not the hotmail address I received an email from before. I taste bile. Who does that belong to?

"You work for the government, as a teacher?"

"No questions. Email me and I'll think it over." She pauses, then says: "The timing could be interesting."

"How's this weekend look for you? Maybe for coffee. I'm under a bit of a deadline."

"Email." She walks across the small parking lot to a red BMW M3, a car lover's roadster. Hardly a step down from her Porsche. She's got money or a benefactor, but that's all beside the main point: Sandy Vello is alive.

I stand there, holding her card. Where am I versus where I was five minutes ago? A name was on a piece of paper dropped in the subway by a bum or a drunk or a would-be killer, and then I read on the Internet that Sandy's been killed in a biking accident. She—or someone on her behalf, or someone posing as her—reached out to me. Is someone playing with my head? Was the obit actually on my computer, or did I imagine reading it?

By way of getting answers, I can think of two things that need immediate inspection: the inside of my computer, and the inside of my head.

9

It's no wonder most people think of the emergency room as the ER. The initials fit and, perhaps more powerfully, the TV show spread the popular misconception. Most physicians actually think of it as the ED—emergency department. I think of it as something altogether different: Reason Number 4 I quit medicine.

I'm sitting in the ER/ED in a yellow plastic chair waiting to get the cut in my scalp checked. I'm flashing back to my second year of med school, on rotation right here, when I learned a painful lesson that helped redirect my professional aspirations. The teddy bear is a trap.

A seventeen-year-old redhead with pale skin, attended by her mom and clutching a stuffed brown bear with deep green inset eyes, comes in wailing from hip pain. The girl says it's been brutal since she careened off a mogul at Squaw Valley and hurtled into a tree. A surgical repair four months earlier left pins and a small metal plate securing her femur to her pelvis. She's run out of her opiates. She says the surgeon is located in Marin and not available to see her for a few days to refill her prescription.

The emergency-room doctor overseeing my rotation calls me aside and tells me we're witnessing classic behavior of an addict. As evidence, she points to 1) the teddy bear; and 2) the mother's arms.

The doc tells me that when someone over the age of about twelve carries a teddy bear, it's an unusually accurate sign of an attention-getting effort, or an emotional problem, or a prop. She also instructs me that if I study the mom, I'll find the thin skin, scarecrow teeth and, she speculates, the tracked arms of a heavy drug user. The doc says the girl is either sharing opiates with the mom or fronting for her.

The doc turns down the drug request and gives the girl a strong dose of over-the-counter painkillers.

I excuse myself and I stealthily follow mother and daughter to the parking lot. They have a terrible shouting match. As I stand in the shadows, mom tells daughter she wasn't acting sympathetic enough, then slaps her offspring.

I feel an arm on my shoulder. It's the attending doctor. She gently admonishes me for invading patient privacy, inviting a lawsuit, not trusting an attending physician, and wasting time.

She explains the emergency-room ethos: We stop the bleeding. She asks me what I'd have recommended we do with the mother-and-daughter drug seekers. I don't have a good answer.

I hate the ED. It's the coldest place on Earth,

the reductio ad absurdum of a medical profession, populated by generally well-meaning but worn-out doctors who in the name of expediency make tough calls, one after the next. It's the extreme version of why I left medicine, which I took to be too black-and-white, and so instead embraced the grainy and blurry world of journalism, where black is one side of the story and white is the other. I don't make the tough decisions anymore; instead, I comfort myself, fairly or not, that I give other people the information to decide.

Now, I'm waiting in the exact same ED for my head to be checked, two seats down from an obese woman holding her stomach, rocking back and forth, and mumbling. My money is on fast-food poisoning. Across the room, a large man in his early twenties watches the ABC *Evening News* on a TV mounted high on the wall in the corner. His rapid left-eye twitch suggests *blepharospasm*, a condition likely caused by stress, not pathology, which, oddly, may make it of little interest to the docs here even though the underlying causes are ultimately more dangerous than, say, stepping on a rusty nail.

Sizing up my fellow patrons distracts me from my dislike of this place and of hospitals, which has only grown since that chilly July night when Isaac was born at Pacific Medical Center. Crinkly and beautiful, he appeared three weeks early by C-section. It was a miraculous night, divine. But it was also the beginning of the abrupt end with Polly and my utopian visions for a perfect family.

"Nathaniel Idle," a woman calls from the reception desk.

She directs me to a cubicle where a nurse takes my vitals and temperature, and checks my eyes with an ophthalmoscope. He's looking for signs of papilledema, a swelling of the optic disc, which can result from brain swelling.

"Let's get you into a room. A doctor will see you shortly."

The standard ED room—with its reclining bed covered in relatively sterile blue paper, jars of gauze and Q-tips, cabinets filled with various bandages and swabs, and a monitor mounted in the corner that can be used to measure breathing or heart rate, among other things—offers me no entertainment value. So I keep the door open to watch conditions pass by.

My cell phone signal is weak, to say the least. And a sign reads: "No phone use in patient areas." But I dial Polly. Underscoring the bad connection, the ringing sound is intermittent but she answers on the third ring.

"Hello, mother of my child," I say, with manufactured cheer.

"Hello." Her voice sounds strange, garbled.

"Polly?"

"Hello." She can't really hear me.

"It's me. How's the nugget?"

The connection dies. I know from experience she's got bad reception on her end too. I dial again, without success. Maybe she'll send back a text, which tends to take less bandwidth than a phone call, and less interpersonal energy.

I catch a scent that I realize smells distinctly like the flowery aroma rising from steaming wonton soup. I look around the antiseptic room for Chinese food, seeing none, poke my head in the corridor and find only bustle. It's then I realize that what I might actually be smelling is a memory, a manufacture of my injured brain.

Polly sits across from me in a cubbyhole restaurant in Pacific Heights, tapping chopsticks, uncharacteristically nervous. Or maybe she's just trying to start working off the food. She's eaten voraciously. After the dumplings and wonton soup, she ordered mu-shu vegetables, kung pao chicken and fried noodles, but reluctantly bypassed emerald shrimp because shellfish and pregnant women don't mix.

She rests her left elbow on two folders she's been showing me. On the cover of one, a silver-haired man flashing dentures stands beside a sports car, a boat in the background. It's a prospectus for an investment fund Polly would like me to consider putting my nest egg into, all $19 of it. The other folder includes preschool applications. It's about three years too early to think about this for our unborn nugget, but her advanced planning might well average out my procrastination. In terms of life strategies, this beauty and I combine for a happy medium.

A waiter drops fortune cookies onto our table. He's got a limp in his left leg, my guess a meniscus tear from playing sports. I ask him. My diagnosis is wildly wrong. It's not knee but ankle. He hurt it tripping over a plate of fried duck a busboy dropped. As the waiter walks off, I ask Polly: How was I supposed to know that? Am I really supposed to be able to diagnose poultry-related leg injuries? I'm smiling. She's not. She's cracked open her fortune cookie. She holds it up. There's no fortune inside. Her lips quiver like she might cry.

Hormones, I assume. I gesture to the waiter to get another fortune. I look back at Polly. A single tear slides down her left cheek. Why do single tears seem so much more sad than torrents?

"Everything okay?"

"I need another fortune." She clears her throat. She forces a smile. Then she says, "We need to talk."

Back in the ED, I open my eyes, feeling woozy. I blink. Not for a second could I have imagined that my relationship with Polly was hanging in the balance that night—between the first fortune and the one the waiter would bring just a few minutes later. I blink again, squeezing my eyes hard. Much as I've replayed the conversation, I can't quite replay what we said or how things went so wrong in that unexpectedly pivotal moment.

I hear a knock.

10

Standing at the door is a doctor in his late twenties or early thirties, dark skin, glasses, closely shaven. He's thin to the point of an eating disorder. This is not an illness he suffers, but it's certainly a condition I remember well. It's the product of working seventy-hour weeks, including regular all-nighters, time usually spent walking or jogging from exam room to exam room, eating when time and a perpetually tight stomach permit. This is MRA, medical resident anorexia.

"I'm Dr. Sudanagunta. I'm the resident. I'll give you an initial check and then an attending doctor will see you. You hit your head?"

I give him the rundown of the moment and point of impact.

"I've been tired and groggy. I'd ordinarily ignore it but it was a sharp-enough impact that I'm wondering if I've got a punctuate hemorrhage." I smile to preface a joke. "I have that light-headed feeling that comes with a quadruple latte at Starbucks or a diffuse axonal injury."

I make light of my know-it-all-ness but by way of letting him know I've got some training. Why not just say so? Because it's just not done. It's the medical trade's own version of the "don't ask, don't tell" policy. In keeping with the strange custom, the resident's face registers only a small tic when he hears my use of the technical language.

Wearing rubber gloves, he prods the wound at the base of my skull, prompting me to wince.

"It's closing nicely. We'll obviously want to keep it clean. I don't think it needs a bandage."

He disposes of the gloves in a black hazardous-materials bin. He sits at the end of the bed and crosses his arms.

"Can I ask you a few questions? Basic stuff just to check cognition and memory."

He pauses, just instantaneously, and I can imagine him going down a checklist for the Mini Mental Status Exam—the basic concussion test. I feel for him, trying to remember and apply a range of triage techniques—from concussion in Room 2 to second-degree burn in Room 3—on the eight hours of sleep he's had for the week. But this exam, I know, is so often executed that it becomes rote.

He asks me to recite today's date and where I am, and asks if I know why I'm here. Then we move on to the more complicated questions.

"Let's start with memory. I'm going to list three objects. I want you to memorize them. In five minutes, when I'm done with the rest of the exam, I'll ask you to repeat them to me. Make sense?"

I nod.

"Here are your three: apple, tree and chair. Can you repeat those back to me?"

I do so. He asks me to repeat them again and I do. He tells me he'll ask me to repeat them once more in five minutes.

"Now. I want you to count backwards from one hundred by seven. One hundred, ninety-three, and so on. Or you can do three or eight if you want." He finally smiles. "We're not rigid."

"Sevens. I'm a traditionalist. One hundred, ninety-three, eighty-seven, eighty, seventy-three, sixty-six, fifty-nine . . ." I pause. I notice that he averts his eyes for a second.

"I missed one?"

"Ninety-three minus seven is eighty-six. Can happen to anyone. Let's try something else." He reaches for his clipboard, which sits on the sink counter behind him. He rips a standard admittance form.

"Take this piece of paper. Fold it in half, then in half again the other way to create a square. Then unfold it, and hand it back to me."

It's a test called a three-step command, which I perform ably.

"Good. Earlier I asked you to remember three words. What were they?"

"Piece of cake."

He looks at me with cocked head.

"Joke. Here ya go: apple, tree and high chair."

He looks up. "One more time, please."

"Apple, tree and high chair."

"You said 'high chair.'"

"I did."

"Apple, tree and *chair*."

"You're sure?"

He nods. "Do you have kids?"

"A son. Nine months. He's in the DustBuster phase."

"He likes to clean up?"

"He likes things that make noise and have buttons."

He nods. "Let's get you a CT scan."

The reason I know he's worried is that I wait a mere fifteen minutes to get my head examined by the massive white imaging machine.

The results come half an hour later from the resident and the attending doctor, a short woman with intense blue eyes and sandy blonde hair pulled back tightly in a bun, revealing tiny pimples dotting her forehead. Maybe rosacea.

She slaps the scan on a light tray on the wall. I know immediately what I'm looking at when I see the small white dots on a region of my brain that stretches across the front of the inside of my skull.

"This tells us to worry but not panic," she says. "The white dots show us blood spots, which is not good news. This is a serious concussion. But I don't see any evidence of hemorrhage or really troubling tissue damage."

"What can we do about it?" I ask, though I know the answer.

"As you may know, there's not much. Rest, but serious rest, not a lot of physical activity. I don't think we need to admit you. At this point, you're not looking at long-term damage but your short-term functioning could well be impaired. How much do you know about the frontal lobe?"

"It's what keeps me from acting like a two-year-old."

She smiles. "Right. Impulse control, and lots of other things. It's the last part of your brain to develop and it's essentially what lets you modulate everything else, the control center."

I nod. "I already tend to have an impulsive streak."

"In all seriousness, you should watch to see if you're feeling emotionally taxed, having trouble making decisions, more impulsive than usual. This is nuanced stuff to measure, but we'd want to follow up on that. How's your pain now?"

"I'm fine with Advil and a really soft pillow."

"Use it. Really."

I leave the hospital in the dark.

As I climb into my car, I realize I've had another short-term memory lapse. I've not gotten back in touch with Faith. I dial her and get voice mail. I ask her to call. From the trunk, I yank out my laptop. With it in my lap, I drive to a residential corner where I find a network connection I can Bogart. I log in and I search for "Sandy Vello," and "obituary," and lots of other variations that might give me the same information about her that I got last night and this morning on this same computer. But the obituary is not there.

It's absolutely official: the narcissistic reality-show contestant is not dead. Again.

For a West Coast-based journalist whose stories often have to do with technology, I'm remarkably not technology savvy. I'm the opposite of that. (For instance, I couldn't understand the need for instant messaging. What, email not instant enough for you?) In short, I'm not particularly sure where to look on my computer for the phantom traces of the obituary—to prove it was there, and erased, and, further, that I'm not imagining things.

But the traces must be there. After all, I don't really suspect I'd imagined the obituary because I'd have had no way of knowing that Sandy volunteered at the jail. And, beyond that, I've got a concussion, not a case of the crazies.

On my browser, I pull down the list of sites I've recently visited. There is no evidence of a Sandy Vello obit. I pull down the "History" menu and get a similarly unsatisfactory result. It stands to reason. I found Sandy Vello through a Google search, so my history shows my visits to the search engine and the terms I've searched.

It's just after 9 P.M. and I should absolutely be resting my brain and body. But I need to take my computer for a thorough diagnosis.

It's time to pick up a carnitas burrito, then visit Bullseye, the Witch's husband, a computer geek who doubles as a bar-stool statue.

Destination: the Pastime Bar, my regular pub and a black hole of San Francisco real estate that managed not to gentrify.

11

The foreboding thick wooden door, pockmarked with small nicks and cuts, looks like the entrance to a gulag. Inside, the low lighting, far from facilitating intimacy, makes it almost hard to see the details in someone's face. The jukebox plays vinyl. From the eighties. The black vinyl-covered stools hail from the seventies. Some of them are torn and duct-taped, others just torn.

Out front, there is an unkempt neon sign with the "A" and the "M" missing. So it reads: P STI E. The Pastime Bar, one of my personal seven wonders.

For years, it was my regular watering hole. I'd visit almost nightly when I lived a few blocks away, in Potrero Hill. It's an aptly named neighborhood, with such steep inclines that the Victorian row houses looked sloped to the side, particularly after a couple of pints.

But since Isaac was born and I gave up my old apartment to live in Polly's downtown flat, I've come less often.

"Idle!" Jessica the Bartender exclaims when I walk in the door.

Most of the smattering of regulars turns to look, all of them old friends or whatever you call a fellow bar regular. Family? Enabler? No one else joins in to remark on my first visit in at least a month. This is the Pastime. Such affection could cost you status, or, at least, emotional and physical energy.

At the far end of the bar sits Bullseye. When I first enter, I see he's sitting almost impossibly motionless, neck craned slightly up and to the right so he can stare at ESPN showing on the flat-panel TV, which is the sole reminder this bar exists in the current century. When the bartender calls my name, Bullseye, grudgingly, lolls his head to look my way. Unkempt brown hair hangs over his wide forehead, almost straggling over his eyes. His shoulders hunch. He wears a gray hooded sweatshirt, sans logo. He continues watching me, like I'm a zoo creature he's already bored of observing, until I'm sidled up next to him on the adjoining stool.

"You look like shit." He means this as an endearment. He and the Witch represent opposite sides of the same coin. Mother and Father. Nurturer and Go Screw Yourself. And I cherish his economy and lack of pretense.

"Where's Sam?"

He shrugs.

"Then I suppose we're bypassing the pleasantries?"

"I'll drink to that."

He nods to the bartender to set us up with a round. In the background, I hear someone smack the top of the jukebox to get it to play. The stubborn jukebox doesn't respond. I pull my laptop from my endangered black backpack. I put it on the counter.

"My computer is lying to me."

I see a flicker of interest in Bullseye's flat blue eyes. For him, computers are so much more interesting than most people. He can speak their language and, more to the point, doesn't have to speak at all.

I power up and tell him about the disappearing obituary. He listens impassively, partly because that's his disposition and partly because he's gotten used to the idea that I come bearing tales of coincidence and conspiracy. Maybe the Witch has already regaled him with the subway incident, my latest brush with the surreal. As I talk, Bullseye pulls the computer nearer.

"Log files," he says.

I sip my Anchor Steam while Bullseye deftly lets himself into my laptop's innards. He opens the browser, goes into the "View" tab, then clicks on a menu item called "Source." Hundreds of lines of computer code appear on my screen. The language looks to me like random strings of numbers and letters. Bullseye scrolls slowly down the list, stopping at one point halfway through, cocking his head to the side, and then scrolling down again.

"What time did you see the obituary page?"

I consider it. "Last night. Ten-ish."

He closes the file and the browser. Then he clicks on the file menu on the top of my main screen, scrolls down the menu and opens "System file." Another list appears of hundreds of lines of equally incomprehensible code. Bullseye scrolls down slowly, pausing at a couple of points. I'm struck that his intensity and manner come across much like the ED doctor looking dispassionately at my brain images.

The jukebox finally starts playing "Werewolves of London."

Bullseye scoots the cursor over to the left side of the screen, prompting a vertical menu to appear with my various programs, like Skype and iTunes. He clicks on the icon for "Google Desktop," which searches the computer the same way plain-old Google searches the Internet. Why hadn't I thought to do that?

He enters "Sandy Vello" into Google Desktop. The search engine returns no results.

"Hmm," he says.

"Let's hear it."

"There are three possibilities. One is that someone hacked into your computer and loaded a fake web page onto it. When you Googled this woman's name, a program directed you to a file kept locally."

"Rather than to the public Internet."

"Right."

"So is that local file still on my computer somewhere?"

"I suspect not. Any decent programmer would be able to program the file to delete itself after you looked at the web site."

"Which is why you didn't find it?"

"The second possibility is that someone was remotely controlling your computer and directed your search for Sandy Vello to a non-public web site."

"What do you mean, 'remotely controlling'?"

"They logged on to your machine while you were logged on to it, and at the right moment, inserted a link to a private web page that looked to you like it was on the public Internet. Do you use a Wi-Fi network at your office?"

"Yep. It's secured. Password is Isaac's birthday."

He shakes his head. "C'mon, Nat. Really?" This type of simplistic, easy-to-hack password is just the kind of thing that really gets Bullseye's goat.

"Sounds like a sophisticated attack." I know this may well not be true, but one of the most basic journalistic techniques is to play mildly dumb and put the responder in a position of authority.

"Sophisticated enough."

"You said there were three possibilities. What's the third one?"

He doesn't respond. He's looking at the TV again.

"Bullseye, what's the third possibility?"

"That you imagined the whole thing."

"How do you mean?"

"You saw a web page that doesn't actually exist. You've finally gone completely nuts."

"You're serious?"

"Not remotely."

"You're making a joke."

"I can be very funny." He almost looks me in the eye, then turns to Jessica the Bartender. "Can't I be very funny?"

"Not in my experience."

He turns his attention back to me. "I think I've got proof that it's one of the other two possibilities."

He opens the system file again and scrolls down the lines of code. About two-thirds of the way down, he stops at a line that has no code on it at all.

"This spot probably corresponds to activity that took place on your laptop this morning."

"But the line is empty."

"Which is what's odd. It looks like something's been erased."

We stare at it in silence. Then he scrolls halfway up the page—to another blank line of code. "This probably is the activity that took place last night."

"So there are anomalies in my computer at the time I looked for web pages. It seems circumstantial."

"Not to a computer person. This is pretty direct evidence of anomaly. Whoever did this is pretty good but either was in a hurry or sloppy and didn't totally cover their tracks."

"Would I find the same thing on my phone?" I ask. I remind him that I found the obit on that browser too.

He shrugs. "I don't know much about the phone system."

He takes a swig of beer and I do the same.

"What should I do?"

"Sleep is good."

"How does that help me find who did this?"

"Sam says you need to get some sleep. She says you're having trouble coming to terms with your . . ." He pauses—"with your personal life."

It's another unusually social thing for Bullseye to say, bordering on caring. I've suspected for a while that he's missed my regular visits to the Pastime and he blames not just Isaac's birth but also the struggles I've had dealing with Polly. I'm about to remark on his newfound empathy when my phone rings. I look at the phone and see a blocked number but I answer anyway.

"This is Nat."

"This is Faith."

She's speaking in a deliberately low voice, affecting the same tone that I used earlier.

She laughs. "You sound so serious when you answer the phone. Is that part of the journalist aura?"

I feel a slight rush, the neuro-chemical dopamine telling me this voice means something to me.

"Prepare to be grilled."

"You'll want to hear what I have to say first. I've got good info."

"Really?"

"About that big guy who fell on you."

"What about him?"

"I've seen him before."

12

I put up my finger to Bullseye, indicating I'll be right back. I stand, experiencing a head rush that is too strong to have resulted from a pint of Anchor Steam. I let it pass as the song "Night Moves" by Bob Seger and the Silver Bullet Band starts playing. Someone boos. I start walking to the front of the bar.

"Nathaniel?"

"You talked to the bum at the turnstiles. You gave him money."

"What?" I can't tell if she doesn't understand and can't hear me.

I push through the Pastime's thick and bruised wooden door and feel brisk wind when I walk out onto the desolate sidewalk.

I'm struck by a sudden change in strategy. I need to let Faith tell me what she's going to tell me before I offer her my theory or any helping hand. I don't trust her, particularly in light of the apparent revelation that she'd seen the burly bum.

"Can you hear me?" I ask.

"Hold on." I hear her put down the phone. When she returns, less than a minute later, she says: "Did I hear Bob Seger playing in the background?"

"The one and only."

"If you're listening to that, you really did take a blow to the head."

I want to return with a joke but I can only think she's smart enough to be dangerous and intellectually stimulating and I wonder if I can always tell which one of those traits is more alluring to me.

"I should have started by asking how you're feeling," she says.

I flash for a second on a curious bit of neuroscience done by chronic pain researchers at Stanford University. They found that intense feelings of passionate love can provide substantial levels of pain relief; when someone who is in love is subjected to painful stimuli—like having a hot compress put on their arm or leg—he or she reports feeling significantly less pain than someone not in an intense relationship. It shows not only the subjectivity of pain but also the intensely chemical nature of attraction. The researchers compared love to cocaine. Faith makes me feel like I've swallowed an upper.

"Been worse," I answer. "You said that you've seen the guy before?"

"Like you said, I gave him money. Upstairs, in the subway. A couple of dimes."

"I thought so."

"You thought so?"

A fair question. Should I tell her the truth: that she was so beautiful that she nestled immediately into my memory banks when I first saw her at the turnstiles? Instead, I tell her that over the last twenty-four hours I've spent some time trying to re-create the incident from the night before and that I thought I recalled seeing her and the mountainous man interacting.

"Why didn't you tell me about this last night?" I ask.

"Honestly?"

"That's what I'm looking for in a relationship. By which I mean a passing relationship with a complete stranger."

She laughs a honey drip.

"Honestly, I was pretty shaken. I was worried you were very hurt. I didn't really understand if you'd been in a fight or what was going on."

She sounds sincere enough. It's certainly possible that someone experiencing acute trauma would blank out on details. There's ample research that shows that when a fight-or-flight response kicks in and releases stress hormones, it overrides the short-term memory. But I'm also skeptical of the coincidences and of what feels like her careful use of language.

"When you said you'd seen him before, did you mean at the turnstile?"

She doesn't respond.

"Faith?"

"No." She sounds distracted. "At a diner in the Mission where I go for coffee. I've seen him hanging out."

I pause to make sure I've heard her correctly. I hear noise in the background. She says: "I need to go."

"Wait!" It's more threatening than I want to communicate. I soften. "Please. I suffered a concussion."

"Seriously? I thought you said you were okay."

"I feel okay but the doctor says it's serious. So I'm trying to understand what happened out there."

"Can we talk about it tomorrow?"

"No, I . . ."

"I'll show you, the diner—where I know him from." More sound coming from her background. Then a whisper: "I'll take you to the diner. Tomorrow." She hangs up.

I stare at the phone. I consider dialing Faith again but something tells me such a call would cause her a problem. With who? Boyfriend? Husband?

I tell myself: *Stop spinning theories. You lack the brain power to make sense of this.* As if on cue, my head pulses, begging me to sleep. I'll capitulate. I'll head to my luxurious downtown loft that is as hollow and empty as the emotions it stirs in me.

"Remember to pay the electrical bill or the sunshades won't open in the bedroom and you'll be consumed by darkness."

It's more than a year earlier, and Polly and I sit in the main room of the loft on the handsome maroon couch beneath a massive painting. The painting doesn't have any definitive image but I tend to see a fish kissing a laundry basket. Polly tosses me the keys to the loft.

"Polly, I can't take this. I don't want it."

"You can't live in your apartment. It looks and smells like Chernobyl. You'll eventually be arrested by the health department *and* child protective services. Our offspring cannot learn that it's okay to store food beneath the floorboards."

I loose a bitter laugh.

"If you weren't so generous, this would be a lot harder."

"Nat, life takes strange turns. We've talked about this. You can make this work."

"If I can keep the sunshades open."

She laughs her captivating laugh. She looks tired and I know how hard this has been on her but she's never shied away from pragmatics and her truth.

The memory slips in and out of my head as I put my key into the steel lock of the tall wooden door of the penthouse loft. I'm struck by a chill and immediately attacked.

It's Hippocrates, my loquacious black-haired cat, who welcomes me with plaintive meows and a whirl around my ankles.

I flip on the light and notice the pile of mail on the entryway table. I wonder if therein lies letters sent by the Internal Revenue Service, long ignored. I'll check later.

I inhale the antiseptic smell from the regular cleaning visits Polly paid for a year in advance. I hate this place. It embodies Polly's pragmatism, with the energy-efficient stainless steel appliances, and a collection of furniture that would be mismatched if it didn't work together perfectly. And it's devoid of Polly's romantic side, which I won't deny she absolutely had. It was once represented here by an eclectic collection of art—from expensive paintings and trinkets she'd picked up in her various travels to a mural that covers one wall on the floor below me and that depicts a little girl sitting on a bench reading a Nancy Drew book and waiting for a train. Only the mural remains. The rest of the stuff went back to Polly and some to her brother, a recovering meth addict.

I walk to the maroon couch that I once imagined would be central to our family hearth. Gone is the refinished antique brown coffee table that once stood in front of the couch. In its place, a red jumper for Isaac to bounce, bounce, bounce. There's a pack of blocks with alphabet letters, a gift from a magazine editor, that I've yet to open.

I plop on the couch and wish for the energy to make it upstairs to the loft. My wish is unmet. When I wake up again, still in my clothes, my phone tells me it's 10:15. In the morning. Another extraordinarily long sleep. A concussion can manifest as depressive symptoms.

The best thing for me to do is work and I don't want to do it here in this stately vacuum. I slug coffee. I pour myself into the shower and let scalding water bring me further to life. I shave, don fresh jeans and a plain light blue T-shirt. I pick up my tattered backpack, and the compromised laptop inside of it, and set forth for Sandy Vello.

But the other mystery woman intervenes.

As I approach my office on Polk Street, I see Faith standing under the awning of Green Love, avoiding a drizzle.

13

I'm half a block away from her when she looks up and, a millisecond later, seems to register that it's me. In that moment, her face changes—from pensive to warm, but manufactured.

"I know what you're thinking."

"That you must be pretty concerned to have taken off work and to show up at my office in person."

"That I'm not the sort of girl who loiters in the doorway of an environmentally conscious sex shop."

The line, though it feels pre-packaged, is delivered with enough poise to catch me off guard. She points in the window to a particularly well-endowed male prosthetic. Hung over it is a piece of string holding a sign that reads "BPA Free."

"Sure, it has no toxic plastics," she says. "But is it solar-powered?"

"Wind. You have to use it outside during a category five storm."

Her brown eyes twinkle and she smiles, then resolves it. To protect herself against the January morning chill, she wears a puffy brown jacket that says thrift, not fashion, and that sits high on her waist. Her white wool gloves, the fabric cut off the tips, show her slim fingers, nails unpainted. Her jeans hug her legs. I'm struck by an image; I can see her managing a staff at a nice restaurant, quietly controlling her environment, wielding influence, making something in her image. I want to meet her again under regular circumstances and take her out for a drink and feel weightless.

"What do you do for work, Faith?"

"You said you usually take someone out for coffee before grilling them." Another clever line, confident on its face, but she seems only to eek out the last couple of words. Under her eyes the thin lines of sleeplessness.

"Come on up to my office and let's talk about the burly man who tried to throw me under the subway."

She pauses, maybe trying to figure out if I'm joking.

"For just a sec. I don't have a lot of time and I want to show you the diner. Do you have a car?" I nod, a vague signal, approximating agreement. We walk upstairs in silence.

Inside, I pick up a narrow, manila-colored reporter's notebook and slip it into my back pocket. From my backpack, I pull out the Mac and set it on the desk.

"Faith, do you know much about computers?"

She's taking in my office. "Not really. Are you having trouble?"

Yeah, as in: someone hacked into my computer

and programmed it to tell me about the death of a former reality-show-contestant-turned-employee of PRISM Corporation. I look up at Faith, who looks at my futon. I see her glance at the Minnie Mouse nightlight plugged into the socket and wonder when I got afraid of the dark.

"Is this where you sleep?"

I ignore the question. "I ran into Sandy Vello."

She looks at me. "Who?" Genuine.

"Never mind. I need five minutes to check email. Pull up a futon."

A sound comes from Faith's jacket pocket. She extracts her phone. Her ringtone is Springsteen's "Born to Run." She sends the call to voice mail. "Do you have a bathroom?"

I show her to the hallway.

While she's gone, I call up my email. I type in my password, and while my messages load, wonder who else might be reading over my shoulder. This idea doesn't particularly startle me; on some level, I long ago accepted our Internet habits are a fishbowl being scrutinized by ne'er-do-wells—on a continuum from advertiser to nosy kid to blackmailer. There are creepy implications, no doubt, but most of what they'd discover is how mundane is our humanity.

In my in-box, there is nothing new, or at least interesting. I pull Sandy's contact info from my wallet. I scratch her a quick email. "Sandy, great meeting you yesterday. I'd love to hear your story, as would my readers. I'll respect all boundaries. You around tomorrow? Coffee or beers on me. Nat Idle."

I search under Sandy's name again, looking for something that might explain this odd duck. I try her name in various combinations with "criminal record," and "PRISM," and "youth volunteer." Empty, empty, empty. "Sandy" and "Youth Guidance Center" and "Twin Peaks." Empty, mostly. On the *San Francisco Examiner* web site, there's a mention of yesterday's group fight and lockdown at the juvenile jail, noting it's the most recent in a series of "behavioral flare-ups," according to warden Doc Jefferson. One twelve-year-old is hurt and hospitalized. But no mention of Sandy.

Faith has returned. She remains in the doorway.

I close my laptop. I used to tote the machine everywhere, but the iPhone lets me get my data on the go, when the signal works, so lately I've been less inclined to carry a Mac that can be stolen or weigh me down. For that matter, the iPhone, thanks to its bevy of apps, has proven a worthy replacement for lots of little investigative tools, not just a camera. I've downloaded a program that turns it into a flashlight, a ruler, a scanner. When it can write clichés, I'll be obsolete myself.

But today, my Swiss army knife of phones may not suffice. I drop the laptop into my frayed backpack and sling it over my shoulder.

As Faith and I walk in a relatively comfortable silence to my car, I recall a scientific oddity I'd recently learned from a researcher at Berkeley who studies the science of physical attraction. She said an unexpectedly big predictor in what causes mates to fall for each other is similar head size; the more alike the size and shape—as a ratio and proportion of the body—the likelier the physical connection. I blogged about this trivia in a brief post about the return of phrenology, the long-since dismissed science that valued putting a ruler up to the cranium. Is that what I find so irresistible about this siren named Faith? Is she a medium too?

"The diner's in the Mission. Potrero and Twenty-fourth," she says, climbing into the Audi. "You could take Van Ness."

She glances in back and sees the car seat. We each gaze for a beat at the blue-and-gray seat restraint. I notice I have failed to remove a rectangular manufacturer's warning still attached by a plastic band to the base; it warns me the company isn't liable unless the seat has been correctly strapped in.

"I told you about my nephew."

It rings a bell, though my memory of everything said the night of the subway accident remains fuzzy. I pull into light traffic on Polk, and turn onto Pine.

"Timothy," she continues as I take a left onto Van Ness, just sneaking through a yellow light. "He goes to school at Mission Day, and when I drop him off there, I usually stop at Glazed Over. That's the diner."

I don't respond. I'm looking in the rearview mirror.

"Nat?"

An aging black Mercedes guns it to make it through the light and follow my left onto Van Ness. I'd noticed the car double-parked a few spots behind me when Faith and I pulled into traffic. Correction: I hadn't so much noticed the car as its driver, and his familiar shiny bald head.

"The luncheon," I say.

"What?"

I don't say what I'm thinking: at the lunch where I'd received the magazine award, there was a man with severely oily skin, possibly seborrhea, and a thin strip of grayish hair over his ears that looked like wings. He sat at one of the front tables. He followed me into the hallway and told me I dropped my phone. Same oily skin and hair wings.

I slow the car so that he can't help but pull up close behind me. But I can't get a good look at him because he seems to catch my glance and look down.

"See that guy behind us?"

She turns. "In the Mercedes?"

"Do you recognize him?"

We're driving thirty miles an hour, the speed of the thickening traffic. To our immediate right is a delivery truck—white body, bold black lettering on its side and an image of some cute animals wearing red-and-black checkered bibs. I make out the word "catering." In front of it is a tan Lexus SUV.

"It's hard to see his face," Faith says. "Maybe he's texting."

I punch the accelerator and the horn. The truck driver slows, which is the desired effect. I squeeze in front of it, rudely and dangerously, jackknifing between it and the Lexus, prompting a chorus of horns. Once through, I again punch the accelerator so that I've effectively taken a sharp right turn onto Post Street. The Mercedes is locked in traffic behind me.

I pull into a loading zone in front of a neighborhood deli. I realize I'd at least half expected Faith to scream. She's sitting as far from me as she seems physically able, recoiled into the door, arms crossed.

"You've got a child." It's a condemnation what father would act so suicidal?

"Enough."

"What?"

"Enough, Faith!"

"Okay. Let me talk."

14

She looks down. I assume she's trying to escape the moment, but then realize she's glancing at the center-console cup holder. In it sits a days-old, half-drunk cup of coffee that has dribbled dark remnants down its side.

"Where are your wipes?"

"What?"

"Every parent has baby wipes in their car."

She swivels her head to look in the back.

"C'mon, Faith."

She nods and takes a deep breath. "That really freaked me out—what happened at the subway."

"And?"

"And I went to Glazed Over yesterday morning to see if he was there."

"The guy you suddenly remembered knowing."

"They said they hadn't seen him." I can't tell if she's tacitly acknowledging that her behavior has been odd or just ignoring my critical tone.

"So you're convinced it was the same guy from the diner."

She nods.

"What's his name?"

"Alan."

"How well do you know Alan?"

"I talked to him with some regularity at the diner. But he's disappeared."

"Since the subway incident."

She nods. She says that she got concerned because people who worked at the diner were concerned, having not remembered a day when Alan failed to buy a cup of coffee or at least linger at the tables out front among the sometimes trendy set. I can picture the kind of place and the San Francisco patrons, hybrids to the core in every aspect of their lives; they arrive in a Prius, loose from the back a labraschnoodle—one-third each chocolate lab, schnauzer and poodle—and sit with it outside sipping half-caf low-fat lattes. I'm not so different—well, substitute Isaac for the pup.

"Faith, I suppose I appreciate your concern for him but I don't get why you're taking such an interest."

She looks at me. "You think you're the only paranoid one?"

"Meaning what?"

"I looked you up. You get involved in some weird things."

"What in the world does that have to do with you? What were you doing at the subway, Faith?"

She looks out her window but remains silent. The dashboard clock moves from 11:12 to 11:13.

"Faith."

"He, Alan, asked me to be at the subway."

At last, a ring of truth.

"So you lied to me."

No response.

"Why, Faith?"

"Why did I lie to you or why did he want me to be at the subway?"

I smirk.

"I'm not entirely sure why he wanted me there. He said he needed my help getting your attention but I swear to you that I'm not sure why."

"You're not telling me the whole story."

"Help me find him so we can both understand the whole story. We're here. The café's just a block up on the left."

Her pause seems resolute. I'm making progress. I can afford to wait.

Here is Twenty-fourth and Potrero, which is not just an intersection but also a metaphor for one. This is where old-world, working-class San Francisco meets new money and tastes. Mexican groceries, tamale shops, trinket and clothing stories with piñatas and large inflatable animals dangling from their awnings anchor down a tenacious working-class culture. But they intersperse now with the occasional martini bar, an ice-cream joint that sells bourbon and-oatmeal-flavored organic scoops, and a café that seems to draw from both worlds, the Glazed Over.

Three sturdy wooden tables grace the front, with napkin holders and tins of sugar packets aligned neatly in their centers. At one table sits a woman in formfitting jogging attire and a wool hat, sipping a bowl-sized cup with two hands, braving the chill or inured to it by runner's high and caffeine. A leash attached to her right arm leads to her feet and an Australian shepherd with furtive eyes.

Through a big front window pockmarked with smudges, I see a setting no bigger than a studio apartment with a handful of tables. Behind the counter stands a stoop-shouldered Latina in her fifties wearing a hairnet, sipping an energy drink in a narrow can. And behind her, dozens of doughnuts lay in racks separating the front from a kitchen in back.

Faith walks to the counter, where I notice the barista has a thin haze covering her dark brown eyes. It might be early onset of macular degeneration, which would be consistent with the condition's higher incidence in Latin women; it's caused, I've read, by their disproportionate participation in working-class jobs—and their long hours, dim light, overall poor conditions.

Before Faith speaks, the woman turns, uses tongs to pick up a fragrant maple doughnut, whirls back and sets the doughnut on a napkin on the counter. "Coffee with enough room for extras?" the woman asks, lightly accented. Must be Faith's regular order.

"Thanks, and one for my friend," Faith says. "But first, I wanted to ask about Alan. Big Alan."

"I didn't see him, like I told you. Not for two days. He's usually here when we open." She places the top on Faith's coffee.

"Maybe he's out of town," Faith ventures.

"I work with Alan," I interject. "We're on an important project and I haven't been able to reach him by phone. Do you know how I might get ahold of him?"

She shrugs. "Maybe Tony knows." She walks around the racks and pokes her head into a doorway to the kitchen. Faith looks at me. "That's the best you can come up with?"

"Award-winning investigative journalist in action."

We watch through the doughnut racks as the barista talks in Spanish to a man in back holding a large ball of dough. She returns. She stamps her feet in the doorway, sending up a light dusting of cake flour.

"You work with him?" she asks me. "On computers?"

I nod. Good information. "I'm really stuck."

"You work with him but you don't know where he lives or how to reach him?"

Checkers just became chess. I'm contemplating which piece to move when Faith reaches into her front pocket. She extracts a twenty-dollar bill. She puts it on the counter. The woman shakes her head.

"The truth is that I'm worried about Alan. He's sick," I explain, then pause. I'm woozy, looking for my words. "I like to drink."

"What?" Faith says.

"I mean, *he* likes to drink," I correct. "Alan's a drinker."

"Are you okay?"

I nod. I'm fine. But I'm surprised myself by my slipup with pronouns. The barista blinks a couple of times.

"I know you can't stop people from drinking but you can try. You have to try."

"He lives down the street," offers the barista without a smile. "In an apartment over the phone store. That's what Tony says."

A line has formed behind us. The barista turns and snags a second maple doughnut and sets it in front of me on a napkin. She takes Faith's $20 and walks to the register. She deposits the money but doesn't return with change.

Faith and I exit. She turns to the right, walking with purpose. "How do you know Alan's a drinker?" she asks.

"A hunch. But that was more of a sympathy play than anything else. Is he—a drinker?"

"She took the bribe, after all."

I sidestep a woman pushing a stroller, exiting a shop. I pause long enough to see her baby, wearing an oversized red sun hat. I want to tell the mother that it's okay for the baby to get a little Vitamin D, especially with the sun hanging low in the sky this time of year. Haven't I tried to tell Polly that Isaac needs more sun?

"Nat?" I feel Faith's arm on my elbow, nudging me along.

A block and a half later, we cross in the middle of the street as I feel doughnut sugar tickle my brain.

Next to a phone store, there's a stoop and a stairway to apartments located above. I walk to the intercom laid into the red brick wall. I see among the ten apartments two that might belong to an Alan. "A. Parsons" and, simply, "AM." I press "A. Parsons," prompting a buzz. There is no response. I buzz again. Nothing. I press "AM."

It buzzes. A woman answers with a hello.

"Alan, please."

"Who?"

"Alan. Big guy. Lives in the building. I'm worried about him."

"You and me both," she responds.

"You know him?"

"I'll be right down."

I look at Faith, who shrugs. Moments later, the doorway fills with a tall woman in her early thirties dressed from the Banana Republic catalogue. "I'm the landlady." There's education in her swagger and my impulse is her parents bought her the apartment building five years ago and she's managing it. I introduce myself and so does Faith. The landlady studies Faith for a second because, well, how can you not?

"I assume you buzzed Alan."

I nod.

"I've sent him two emails asking him to fix my router. Nada."

Another reference to Alan's skills.

"You're obviously not solicitors," the landlady says.

"Friends," Faith explains. "I work with Alan."

The landlady turns around and starts to walk away, holding open the door. We follow her up a flight of stairs covered in low-cut maroon carpet, the sidewalls painted with care in complementary beige. The landlady stops on the top of the second flight and walks to a door labeled "2C." She bangs a brass knocker that resembles a lion's head.

No answer. She knocks again, forcefully. Faith steps forward and reaches an index finger toward a white button to the right of the door.

"Ringer's busted," the landlady says, pauses, adds: "Broken infrastructure means I have the right to peek in to see if everything's okay."

She reaches onto her belt loop where I notice both the ring of keys and the pronounced blue veins on the back of her thin hands. It's not a medical condition but a genetic bonus; plump, visible veins give nurses easy access for intravenous lines. She extends a key from her ring and unlocks the door.

She pokes her head into the apartment.

She screams.

15

I instinctively nudge Faith away from the door. The landlady's still peering inside, frozen.

"Alan. Mr. Parsons!"

I move the door open and gently put my hand on her shoulder. She flinches. I nudge her to her left, causing the door to open most of the way. A large man lies facedown. The soles of his heavy boots face us, the heel of the right one graced by a circle of dirt-encrusted pink gum. His beefy corpus stretches along a hallway nearly too narrow to accommodate him. His head rests at the foot of a square table stacked neatly with mail and magazines. Blood pools around his shaggy hair.

Even from here, I recognize the man from the subway, decidedly felled, and fetid. It smells of infant feces and rotten food, just like a dead person.

"What's going on?" Faith asks. She brushes against me, and then whispers: "Oh my God."

I want to look at her to see if I can trust this reaction but I can't take my eyes off him. I step inside.

"Wait." The landlady produces a phone.

I walk to the body and squeeze along the wall trying not to touch Alan. I kneel by the head. The death smell commingles with aroma from the frothy vomit near his mouth. The scent saturates my blood-brain barrier. I wobble. I cover my nose and mouth with my right hand.

"I said 'wait,'" the landlady repeats.

"We have to see if there's anything we can do." I'm muttering through my fingers, knowing damn well we can't help Alan unless we've got a time machine to go back more than thirty-six hours ago.

And bring a nitroglycerin tablet.

Despite what the landlady might think from the sticky pooled blood, I'm looking at a heart-attack victim. The blood, matting his forehead and beard, didn't flow from anything sinister. It came from a laceration just beneath his right eye, right on the orbital bone. It's where, as he fell, his face smashed the corner of the table.

His head, flattened on the cheek, is turned to the right and for the first time I see his eye. It's open. Red from hemorrhage floods the corner. I can still make out the dull blue retina.

My own vision flashes sudden light. When did I last see a dead body? I inhale and taste his decaying vomit. It's edgy and sharp, like battery acid. Where am I? I'm dreaming. My legs weaken. I fall to my right knee, then my left.

"The police are coming," a voice says.

I blink.

"He's too young," I say.

"What?"

"Give him his dignity," I hear myself plead. I

manage to put a foot beneath me, even as a voice inside my head screams: lie down. But there's another voice, the journalist, the overly curious and aggrieved, the father nearly turned subway smoothie.

"I'll get a sheet," I muster.

"Please get out."

I stumble into the apartment. I make out a doorway to my left and two to my right. I peer into the one to the left. Just a couch. Covered in blankets. It faces a wall bearing a huge TV. Pinball-like, I bounce to the doorway on the right. Kitchen. Sink stacked with pots and dishes. I glance at the fridge. No magnets hold pictures or phone numbers. I stumble to the second door on the right.

"Get back here!"

"Coming." I'm not sure if I say it aloud.

The last doorway is shut. I pull it open. Bedroom. Spartan. There's a queen-sized bed, piled at its foot with a comforter, along with two plastic fifths with red labels: vodka, I guess. Both are empty. Then I see the desk, sitting along the right wall. It's jerry-rigged; cinderblocks stacked on each side holding up plywood. Atop it stands a computer monitor, big, maybe twenty-six inches. In the bottom right corner, a light blinks green. The monitor's getting power but the screen is dark. Where's the computer it's connected to? Where's the . . . my head pulses. I focus. I see for the first time the stack of papers and folders to the right of the monitor. I walk to the desk. Scribbled notes and phone numbers cover a yellow-lined sheet on the top of the stack of papers. I pick it up and stuff it into my back pocket. I see a folder beneath it. It's labeled with two Chinese characters.

"Did you have something to do with Alan—with him dying?" I hear the landlady behind me. "Did you know he was hurt?"

I turn to see her standing in the doorway.

"I was looking for a sheet to cover him."

"On his desk? Tell it to the police."

Her arms are crossed. Resolute but frightened. I would be. I am. "Where's Faith?"

"Who?"

"Where's the woman who came with me?" I practically roar it.

She points down the hallway. "Gone." I walk toward the landlady, gaining momentum as I reach her. I'm clearly going to push past her. She moves. "They'll get your fingerprints." She glares at me.

I chase Faith.

16

I tiptoe past the body, fly down the stairs, pause at the building's stairwell, look left and see a man in a cap carting boxes piled high on a dolly slide into a grocery. No Faith in sight. I look right. I see her. She's in a demi-jog, turning a corner two blocks down. I start sprinting.

I cross a street against a red light, prompting a tinny toot from a cyclist. I take two more quick steps in the direction Faith disappeared, and then stumble. I put my hand on a parking meter and am struck that the top of it looks like a face, frowning, melting. "Are you okay?" I'm not sure where the voice is coming from.

"I lost someone," I say or think.

I put a second hand on the meter. It's cold and damp.

"You had me fooled there for a second," I mutter to the meter, my head clearing.

"Are you okay?" I hear the voice again. I turn to see a lumpy lady in a baseball cap.

I start walking again. I reach the corner where

Faith turned. I look down the street. I don't see her. It's not immediately clear where she might have disappeared so quickly. The street is residential, with just a couple of pedestrians and one jogger paired with a large dog. Halfway down the right side of the street, a crew of three stands on scaffolding, retrofitting a three-story house, the tallest one on the block.

Maybe Faith disappeared between two houses, or climbed into a car or maybe I was disoriented longer than I imagined, giving her ample escape time. Escape from what?

My head pulses. I look behind me. An ambulance pulls up outside Alan's building. No sirens. Paramedics hate dead bodies. No adrenaline rush, just paperwork.

I pull out my phone. I dial Faith. It rings once and goes to voice mail.

"Faith, it's Nat. Talk to me or the police. Your call."

I hang up and think: stupid. Faith's reaction to seeing Alan might well have been natural. Is death why I left medical school? The loss? I guess I understand why Faith might flee, but she keeps leaving the scene.

I'm unsure what to do when I feel a familiar urge to check my email. It used to be I'd require a ping of an incoming message to prompt my curiosity, but now I've internalized the ping. I'm the dog without Pavlov's whistle and I know psychologists know why. Email provides one of the greatest of addictive properties in that it's randomly reinforcing. You never know when an interesting email is going to come so you feel compelled to check constantly, even though most of the stuff is worthless. It's not a phone; it's a pocket slot machine.

This time, mini-jackpot. There's a message from Sandy Vello: "Sure, let's meet. How about 2night? Call me to cordinate. My terms. No paparazzi!" She includes her phone number.

So she can spell "paparazzi" but not "coordinate"; that's everything I need to know about this woman's personality. But what are her secrets? What do they have to do with dead Alan and disappearing Faith?

I walk back in the rough direction I parked my car, having trouble placing which side street we parked on. The path takes me kitty-corner to Alan's apartment building. The ambulance remains parked outside. Now there's a squad car too. A little crowd has gathered. Still moving, I look over my shoulder to see the landlady wander out front and confer with a cop. He looks up and down the street. I drop my head.

Around the corner, I lean against a wall painted with a wilted cigarette nearly my height and spewing smoke, the progressive antics of an anti-smoking tagger. I reach into my pocket and withdraw the notes I took from a dead man's desk. Stylistically, they look like they were written by a busy engineer—the handwriting precise, the letters written in small block font. Yet, various words and numbers are written at different angles across both sides. Scratch paper filled with artful scribbles.

On the front, there are two phone numbers. One in the 650 area code, which means Palo Alto and its surrounding cities. Next to it, a name: Kathryn Gilkeson. I thumb the number into my phone but don't call it. The other number is in the 415. I recognize it; it's already in my phone. It belongs to Faith.

On the top right corner of the yellow-lined sheet are five sets of numbers: 8:47, 9:06, 9:11, 9:35, 9:50.

Times. I make this assumption not just because of the obvious syntax but also the phrase just below the numbers. It reads: "Dr. Jurgenson—7:45–8:40."

Dr. Wilma Jurgenson. I flash on her image: thin, praying mantis-like in the crooked way she collapses her long legs beneath her when she sits, plain face, straight black hair, prematurely aged hands from hyperthyroidism. I got together with her at 7:45 the night of the incident at the train station, just a few minutes before I nearly died on the subway tracks.

I feel another light-headed flash, warmth flooding across my brow, an acid scent in my nostrils. How does Alan Parsons know my schedule?

I'm having trouble focusing on the piece of paper. It's not my eyesight; my hand is quivering, like I've got late-stage Parkinson's.

I start walking down the block, away from Alan's apartment. I pause next to a Mexican bakery. I'm trying to remember where I parked my car. I again picture Dr. Jurgenson. She's a brain specialist, friend and a great journalistic source who has been invaluable in helping me understand the human mind. But I can't seem to remember what Wilma and I discussed when I last saw her. It was nothing special, I think, not substantive at all, not much science, maybe about family, more catch-up than interview.

I shake my head. I remember where I parked the Audi—on a lightly trafficked street just off the main drag, two blocks from the café. A few minutes later, I climb inside. I place Alan's scrap paper on my knee. In a carefully etched box on the left of the paper there is a list of groceries: "Oreos, bacon, Tater Tots, soy milk, Tylenol PM." So he's a bad sleeper, maybe lactose intolerant, not a health nut.

To the left and a few lines below the list, there are math equations. At the top is the dollar amount $14,000, from which he's subtracted $3,500, and then, from the $10,500 that remains, he's subtracted $1,500. The figure that's left is $9,000, and it is, in turn, multiplied by 1,000. It leaves $9,000,000, which is circled several times with neat zeal.

It's a neither here-nor-there sum, maybe big for an individual like Alan but small for a corporation or a major conspirator. In Silicon Valley, money is measured in billions, with a B.

On the other side of the paper, there are two Chinese characters. I've seen them before, I remember, on a manila folder on the dead man's desk. As I look at the characters, my eyes glaze, the character outlines getting fuzzy. One looks like a horse with wings and the other like a piano standing on a mouse. Beside the characters, there's what appears to be a date: "2/15."

It's February 3. The fifteenth is in two weeks. My first thought is that Valentine's Day falls on the fourteenth; I picture Polly a year ago in fishnet stockings. My head pulses. I need to rest.

One thing to do first. I should wait until I'm clearheaded to bull-rush into this evidence, the 650 phone number, Palo Alto.

I dial.

17

The evidence remains inconclusive that radio signals cause tumors. Believe me, I've looked. I got obsessed with the idea after Isaac was born at a hospital built under the shadow of Sutro Towers, the huge radio and TV transmitter poking totem-like through the fog on Twin Peaks.

But my real paranoia came from the phones. I picture Polly, her BlackBerry nestled by her head. She looks like a baby bird taking manna from the maw of the device, or maybe it's the other way around. She once told me she favored headsets because the psychology of deal making could be undone by poor sound quality, like wind gusts. For a brief period, I couldn't get it out of my head that a barrage of radio signals was hurting her head but my foray into that investigative realm came up empty. Over the years, the cell phone makers, terrified they'd be sued for killing everyone on the planet, moved the radio chips nearer the mouthpiece and away from the part of the headset closest to the brain. No critical mass of science had yet given a plaintiff's lawyer enough to mount a reasonable case.

Still, the old fear surfaces as I bring my phone to my ear. After the third ring, I hear it answer.

"Hello, this is Jill." For a second, I can't tell if it's an actual person or her answering machine, a confusion that happens to me more often lately. Once, during happier times, I launched into a full-throated romantic poem before realizing I was talking to Polly's voice mail.

"Hello," I venture.

"May I ask who is calling?"

Split-second decision. "Hey, Jill." Always repeat the name. "I'm about to make a complete fool of myself."

"You're in good company." She laughs. "Can I help you?"

"I'm not a telemarketer. I'm a journalist. Nathaniel Idle. I promise: not selling."

"Okay." Wary.

"I might have the wrong number, though. I'm looking for Kathryn."

Silence. Then: "You're joking." Mildly alarmed.

"I . . . Kathryn Gilkeson," I stammer, reading the name from the piece of paper.

"You're a mean man."

"No, I'm . . ."

"I know who you are. I can find you."

"Find me?"

"Your number's on my caller ID. I'm in the middle of something. Please don't bother me again."

"I want you to find me. I want to find you. I . . ."

"I'm getting off now." Click.

I droop my head. What the hell was that? And what was I expecting? My forethought was nonexistent. Maybe, no surprise; a concussion stuns the frontal lobe, the part of the brain involved in planning and setting priorities.

Time for a different tack. I etch out a text. "It's Nat Idle. Again. Sorry for foot-in-mouth. Have ? about Alan P. I'm on up-and-up. Google me."

I look at it. If this person is bad news and associated with dead Alan, it'll come to her as no surprise that I'm Nat Idle, the journalist, trying to track her down. She'll dump the text and that'll be that.

If, on the other hand, she's completely uninvolved, I'll do no harm by sending a text referring to Alan P.

But if she, or someone named Kathryn, has some indirect role in any of this, I might pique her curiosity and prompt her to answer my phone call at some future point. In other words, I send the text and risk putting her off, or don't send and risk that I already have.

I hit send. I stare at the phone, conditioned for immediate response, but knowing that none is forthcoming.

I consider my hasty decision to call the phone number on the piece of paper, and the bouts of wooziness. I picture Alan's body, squeezed into a hallway, likely felled from natural causes but who knows?

People are dying—and being reported as dead in fake obituaries—strange happenings to digest even if I were in my right mind, which I'm not.

Still slumped in the car, I peer out the driver's-side window. On the foot of the stairs of a faded purple Victorian, a toddler stuffed into a winter coat draws on the ground with a piece of chalk nearly as thick as her arm. The girl puts the green chalk in her mouth and looks up at a woman sitting on the stair above, expecting or seeking admonition. But her mom is fiddling with her cell phone, too distracted to engage. The girl looks my direction, perhaps sensing my gaze, and starts drawing again. I think back to Polly. Even when we were together, she spent so much time on her phone. Was that the problem? She ultimately didn't want to or couldn't fully connect with me?

I shake my head to send the memory scurrying. I look at the dashboard's digital clock. It's almost two. I'm both nauseous and craving something salty.

Brain blank, I drive back to my office. Three doors down is a hole-in-the-wall pizza joint where the dyspeptic Chinese proprietor with a world-class comb-over and perpetual laryngitis doubles as a holistic healer, offering five-minute neck massages in a chair near the brick oven for $10. In Hollywood, everyone aspires to be an actor or writer. In San Francisco, a healer. I've run into a lawyer doubling as a yoga instructor and a schoolteacher who spends her weekends organizing silent retreats in frenetic Union Square, the idea being to learn to listen to yourself amid chaos and, apparently, shopping.

For his part, the pizza guy's subspecialty is shiatsu pressure points. I've never experienced his handiwork, but I find his mushroom and pepperoni to have spiritual properties.

I plop onto a cheap metal stool at the ancient

yellow Formica counter. Heat from the brick oven makes this tiny place unforgivably hot on many days but is just right today with foggy chill seeping into everything. Steam smudges the glass door and the waist-high windows where I can see passersby passing by. From my pocket, I pull the paper I found on Alan's desk and spread it on the counter. I gesture to the proprietor, who is half glancing at a TV airing a reenactment of a sea battle between two ancient ships, the story subtitled in Chinese.

"Can you read this?" I turn the paper his direction.

He leans near, stares at the characters, blinks. "The second one means 'computer.' The first one makes no sense."

"It's not a Chinese character?"

"It's like three squeezed together." He traces his finger underneath it. "It looks like the word for Earth and the word for clown lumped together."

"Like at the circus."

He half nods.

I consider this, take a step back. "So all together it means 'computer earth clown'?"

He shrugs. From the smoldering brick oven, he brings my slice, which suddenly looks revolting. He takes my money and returns to his show.

I take two bites of the pizza as I walk to the office, and toss it in a trash bin outside my building.

Upstairs, I sit on the futon and call Sandy Vello. She answers on the first ring and gets right to the point. "How about 5:30 at the Ramp?" Thanks to caller ID, I think, no one says hello anymore, they just launch right in. "Do you know it?"

I do. It's a bar with a patio situated on the bay fre-
quented by functional alcoholics who excuse their
afternoon drinking on the grounds that they're just
getting some sun. I look outside. It's going to be
cold and maybe wet. "Sure."

"No paparazzi." She hangs up.

I fall asleep with the phone in my hand, picturing
corpulent, dead Alan. Something about the position
of his body troubles me. I wake up two hours later,
just shy of my meeting with the reality-show contestant. It's already getting dark. I pull from the closet
a full-length wool jacket and walk into the cold to
head to the Ramp. I'm thinking about the Chinese characters, and something I remember about
PRISM, Sandy Vello's employer. It's got headquarters in Beijing. I'm wondering if this mystery just
jumped the ocean—when my phone buzzes.

On it, a text: "I looked u up. I'll tell you about
Kathryn, God rest her soul, but I can't imagine why
you're interested. Jill."

I click on the text, which brings up the sender's
contact information. I dial.

"That was quick."

"Thanks for the response, Jill. I . . ."

She interrupts. "Why are you interested in Kathryn?"

"I'm honestly not sure."

She pauses. "I'm her mother. I was. You do really
interesting stories. You won an award from . . ."
She pauses again, then rephrases. "You won a fancy
journalism award."

"Kathryn is . . ." Now it's my turn to pause.

"She died twelve years ago. She was seven."

"I'm sorry, Jill. I really didn't know. Was she sick?"

"No. She . . . car accident, a wreck, an accident, something. I've never been able to find the right word. But I don't really want to talk about this by phone and I still can't understand why you'd care at all about it."

"Can I come see you?"

She doesn't respond.

"It so happens I'm going to be in the area." I'm using a common tactic to suggest it would be convenient for us to get together.

"How do you know my area?"

"Your area code. I assumed Palo Alto."

"Not tonight. Tomorrow. Menlo Park. Between two and four, I'll be at the Woodland Learning Center on El Camino, near Kepler's bookstore. You know the area?"

I know it. We hang up. A dead girl. I wonder what a former reality-TV star knows about it. And where is Faith?

18

Wraparound sunglasses, name-brand windbreaker, and a vacant smile that communicates she feels herself in control of the situation, whatever it is. These are the first of my second impressions of Sandy.

She sits at the end of a long, wooden outdoor table in a light wind and drizzle, dark sky mitigated by a weak patio light. The rudimentary ambience at the Ramp suits the post-college Greek system crowd, which suggests Sandy's chasing hipness. Twentysomething San Franciscans brim with confidence they've found Mecca here until they have their first kid and realize they can't afford housing AND private schools, and then move.

The deck extends over bay water a half mile from AT&T Park, home to the San Francisco Giants. I wonder, looking into the misty fog in the direction of the ballpark, whether AT&T realizes that half the expletives uttered during games are directed not at the visiting team but at the fact that AT&T's iPhone service doesn't work there.

"Wimps." Sandy looks through the window at

the after-work crowd toasting with plastic cups. "But we can talk privately out here. Some things I'll tell you about the show are off the record."

She removes her glasses and winks.

"Do they have anything stiffer than beer?"

"I drink water. I got you a Bud Light. What's your kid like?"

I tense but don't respond and she doesn't need much of an opening to get on her soapbox. "I'd love to have a kid. It's important to pass down life lessons."

It's all about Sandy. Good. The challenge tonight isn't getting her talking but getting frostbite when I can't shut her up. I sit, feeling dampness; wish I'd worn something thicker than my T-shirt under the coat. She pushes a plastic cup filled with dull yellow liquid at me. I bring it to my lips, sip. Awful.

"He's got an oral fixation." I feel a pit in my stomach at the idea of sharing anything about Isaac with this woman. But I have to give to get. Take my time moving from me to Sandy the TV contestant to Sandy the PRISM employee, which is the reason for this ignominious meeting. "Puts things in his mouth, tastes them, senses the world that way and tests his boundaries. If his taste buds are any gauge, he's curious like his dad."

My brain bounces; I think for an instant about the new science around the oral fixation. Freud had us think it was psychological. But the infectious-disease specialists suspect kids put things in their mouths to train the immune system what to react to. The innocuous things, like chalk, get ignored. The bacteria-laced Styrofoam cups found on the ground prompt an immune response.

"There was an episode where they made us eat bugs." Sandy smiles, taking back the limelight. "It was a joke. Clyde told me he knew from his Marine training that the bugs they chose couldn't make us sick. Lots of protein. Whatever."

"Clyde."

"Robichaux. From the show. Tough-ass Marine."

"He's . . ."

"Lives in Redwood City. Don't go there. He shoots trespassers. The main thing is, I'd trust him with my life."

"Right, I remember but . . ."

"Aren't you going to write this down?"

"Is that okay?"

"I'll tell you when it's not."

I pull a notebook from the inside pocket of my coat. My head pulses from concussion and the pain of this interview. What thoughtful conspirator could possibly make use of this narcissist? Am I being decoyed? Let the source ramble, I remind myself as coldly as I once dissected bodies, and it will reveal its nature. And that of PRISM.

Suddenly, she's off and running with her story. She tells me how she had a rough childhood but became a triathlete, double-majored at a community college in child psychology and fitness, moved to Los Angeles with dreams of doing life and nutrition management for children of movie stars and other wealthy people who grow up facing "more stress than young people should." She got some big-name clients, who she lists but I've not heard of. One of them, a big soap-opera actor, got her a casting call on the reality show.

"The cliché is that you make your own luck. But I say you *fake* your own luck. You act and feel lucky and the world bends to your will." She looks to make sure I write that down.

"You're always moving forward."

"What do you mean?"

"You didn't get hung up by the nonsense on the show. If I can speak honestly, it must have been tough, what happened—getting the boot—and yet, boom, you moved on."

This is a key reporting technique; say something that sounds just mildly critical—but ultimately is not—because it implies growing intimacy. Like, We're tight enough that I can take a chance on being frank.

"Bingo. What else do you observe about me?"

There are various carvings on the old wooden table: hearts and filthy overtures. If I had a camping knife, I could whittle, "My Intellectual Curiosity Died Here."

"I observe you've got some lessons to pass on, like you were saying earlier. The stuff at the youth center . . ."

"Stop."

"What?"

"Thank you. Thank you." She starts to applaud. It's a condescending act, followed by, "I've been waiting for you to reveal yourself."

I put my hands up.

"I will tell you why I volunteer at the youth center but it's off the record. You cannot use it—not under any circumstances. I will sue you. That record is sealed."

I'm trying to make sense of this gamble. She's so dramatic about her purported criminal record that, I'm thinking, it can't possibly be that interesting. But if it is central to some conspiracy, I'll find a way to write about it.

"Off the record." I want to tell her that muckraking is an honorable tradition of exposing truth but why bother.

She eyeballs me. "I came from upper-middle-class money, and neither of my parents drank—alcohol—so who knows why? But I took my first drink of whiskey from my uncle's bar when I was nine. I never felt so great. I was a closet drunk by twelve. When I was sixteen, I stole my dad's Buick and drove it into the plate-glass window of a Gap."

She pauses. This is the truth.

"You crashed because you wanted to get caught."

"Some people have addictive personalities. I've wrangled mine to the ground. Discipline. Fitness. Inner truth. I don't crave."

This part is neither true, nor, I think, material. She's, in fact, an addict—of attention. "Lots of people make mistakes," I say.

"My mysteries belong to me. I disclosed it all to the producers. And they agreed they could reference the fact I had a dangerous background but leave the details to me. Actually, it was their idea, and I felt it was a fine compromise."

A few things fall into place: she loves appearing more dangerous than she is. She loves her aura. Her volunteer work could well be ancillary to the reason I'm here. I need to get back to whatever mystery this egoist is involved in and away from rambling preamble.

"Back on the record?" I ask.

"That'll be my call."

"What's the message? How did you parlay the reality-TV stuff into a new great gig?"

"I eat the bugs that scare other people."

"Bugs?"

She says that one of the benefits of doing a reality-TV show is that they agree to plug your skill set, in her case: nurturing kids. When the show ended, she got contacted by a company looking for help pushing innovative products to young people to help them better themselves.

"What kinds of products?"

She smiles. "That's stealth. Stay tuned."

"Oh, give me a break," I gag out feigned desperation. "This is so fascinating."

"Stealth," she repeats.

"You can't even say what kind of work, generally?"

She shakes her head. She takes off her glasses and eyeballs me, a practiced look of quasi-interrogation or challenge I can picture her using effectively on camera.

I pause. "What do you mean 'bugs'? You said you'll eat bugs other people won't. What does that have to do with your new gig?"

"I see what you're doing."

I don't say anything, hoping she'll explain. She doesn't. Her light blue eyes wander aimlessly at the sky behind me. A blast of wind hits the patio. Sandy locks eyes with me and seems to have transformed into a worthier adversary. She reminds me of addicts and alcoholics I've known, drug seekers who come to a hospital under the auspices of needing a prescription for severe back pain. They are plain in their needs but savvier and more manipulative than they get credit for.

"I need a full picture, Sandy. Your life didn't end when you left the show. That's the whole point I'm getting at. You're the ultimate survivor, right?"

"What are you asking me?"

"Nothing intrusive. I just want to paint a picture of what you're doing now."

No response.

"Sandy, you mentioned when we met at the jail that this might be a good time for an article about you. What did you mean?"

"Off the record."

Jesus. I nod.

"All cards on the table. I might be looking for a new gig soon and it's good to have the clip. You make your own luck, see."

"You're leaving your job?"

"Project coming to an end. May lead to something else, may not."

"What kind of project?"

She considers this. "Marketing." The word comes out flat, hard to read.

"Of? I mean, in general terms."

"Not for print."

"Absolutely not for this article, not until I get the go-ahead. We'll find language you're okay with. I just want a sense."

She pauses. I'm about to confess that I did a little digging and tell her that I know she works for PRISM, up the stakes, when she smiles.

"Tiny jugglers."

I shake my head, hopefully expressing my lack of comprehension.

"That's an awesome image, right?"

"Well, yeah, but I . . ."

"I work for some of the smartest people in the world. They've figured out how to use computers to make people smarter. Kids. Way smarter."

"By teaching them to juggle?"

"To juggle data."

"Sorry, Sandy. I'm just a journalist, I'm not a technical person, so I . . ."

"Let me see your phone."

"Why?"

"You're so defensive. You're like Deacon, on Season Two. Just let me see your phone and I'll show you."

I hand her my phone. She holds it so I can see the screen.

"Texting, emailing, calls, Skype, a million apps, and so on. There's so much information coming at you. And the biggest consumers are kids."

She launches into a presentation I sense she's given before. She tells me that one recent study found that adolescents consume 7.5 hours of media a day. With rampant multitasking, she says, young people will soon be consuming media for more hours than they sleep or are in school.

I get the point and wave her on to continue.

"Their brains can't handle it all." She meets my gaze, wanting me to clearly understand this point.

But it's not a revelation. Since the 1950s, it's been clear to researchers that the human mind can't simultaneously process two streams of information, let alone make decisions about them. Our brains can't do two things at once; rather, they try to rapidly switch between the tasks, often at the expense of harming the performance of the individual tasks.

I picture newborn Isaac with ones and zeroes flying around his head. He swats them away with his tiny hand.

"Hello," Sandy interrupts my conversational vacation.

"So we've got a way to make it easier for a new generation of children to keep up." I recover.

"Think: juggler." She says this like it's a punch line. "The juggler," she repeats. "Great image, right? We've got dozens of digital balls in the air. Who can catch them? Who can keep adding balls without dropping any?"

"I'm still not following."

She laughs. "I'm not either. It's complex stuff. I'm still learning. Anyhow, let's move on."

Something about Sandy does not add up. The blowhard has turned sophisticated communicator. Unpredictable. Were I a TV producer, I might have picked her too.

"So is this stuff available on the market? Can I see the kinds of products you're talking about?"

For a second, she holds my stare. It's subtle but revelatory. This woman lacks self-awareness but she's no fool, and a tiny distant light turns on for her; she senses I'm homing in on something but she's not sure what or why. She looks away.

"Earth clown," I venture.

"What?"

I'm thinking about the weird Chinese characters: Earth clown. "Sorry, rambling. It's something I heard about from Jill Gilkeson, Kathryn's mother."

She blinks three times, seemingly lost.

"Look, Sandy, I know you work at PRISM. I found it online."

She takes it in. She shrugs. Maybe, she thinks, this is possible. "So why pretend you didn't know what I'm doing, Mr. Reporter?" She doesn't seem disturbed by this revelation.

"I don't know what PRISM is. It looks like some software mill, some modest real estate here, headquarters overseas."

She laughs. "It's the new thing, blending American know-how with this crazy work ethic they've got over there. They're dying for a piece of what we've got. They want to catch up." She pauses. "Off the record!"

"You're doing all this marketing, the tiny jugglers, for PRISM?"

She shakes her head. "I told you as much as I can. You know how these non-disclosures work. But stay tuned. I'll definitely get you in the loop as soon as we're ready to announce anything. It'll be a great scoop."

We sit there looking at each other, an impasse coming on quickly.

My phone rings. She's still holding it in her open palm. On the caller ID, I can see the word "Faith." Sandy looks at it.

"I should take this." I snag the phone and put it to my ear. "Hi, it's Nat."

"Can I trust you?"

"Of course."

"I need help. Now."

19

I stand and hold up an index finger to Sandy, indicating I'll be right back. I walk to the edge of the deck.

"Where are you, Faith?"

"He's following me."

"Who is?"

"I'm near your office. There's a pizza place where they give massages. Do you know it?"

"Who is following you, Faith?"

"The man with the Mercedes. The bald man from this morning."

A vicious wind whips in from the bay. Frothy waves smack against the pillars of the deck below me. I cup my fingers over the mouthpiece.

"Where's the man now?"

"In his car, a block away, double-parked in front of a head shop."

"Does he know you've seen him?"

"No." She pauses. "I'm an actress."

The sentence strikes something deep in me. It feels both like a bit of a non sequitur and the single most honest thing Faith has told me.

"Order a slice of the mushroom and pepperoni."

"What?"

I feel something on my shoulder, like a tap, but it's another burst of wind passing over the deck. My knees go weak and I have this sensation I'm going to turn around and find Polly standing behind me, Isaac in her arms. I turn. There is no one. Not even Sandy. She's no longer sitting at the table. I squint through the drizzle into the restaurant/bar, seeing only a smattering of young revelers. Maybe Sandy's gone inside but I figure she's taken off, the phone call giving her an easy exit.

"You want me to order pizza?"

"Yep. Avoid the massage. I'm coming."

I case the parking lot outside the Ramp and see no sign of Sandy or her car. I dial her as I climb into my Audi. The call goes directly to voice mail.

Traffic is not accommodating. It's clogged by the tail end of rush hour and rain; everything in the Bay Area moves fast—ever faster by the year—except for drivers in the rain. For some reason, the slightest drizzle seems to stymie this population, leading to agonizing jams. We don't need GPS; we need hybrids. I hop onto Third Street and take it toward downtown, against the commuters, angry less about the overly cautious drivers than the two mystery women in my life.

Sandy says she is marketing new technology designed to help children cope with the onslaught of information in the computer age. On its face, that's not necessarily noteworthy. But the company's parent is Chinese, like the characters written on a piece of paper left beside the computer of dead Alan Parsons.

And someone duped me into thinking Sandy Vello was dead. You don't have to be a modern-day, mild-mannered blogger to toy with going old school: grabbing the narcissistic reality-show contestant by the lapels and shaking her until she comes clean. Or maybe I just need to keep pumping her with unctuous questions until she looses a revelation I sense she's holding just under the surface.

Or, just maybe, she's less fool and more fatale than I'm giving her credit for.

Why did she disappear from the Ramp? Were my questions, or her answers, making her uncomfortable?

And what to make of Faith? With her, the lapel shaking should come sooner rather than later. Why did she disappear from Alan's house? What's she doing back in my neighborhood? Does she have some connection to Sandy?

Who is following her?

My phone, which is nestled between my legs, buzzes and hops a millimeter off the gray leather upholstery. Incoming text. The sound and sensation catch me sufficiently off guard that I, though traveling only a few miles an hour, slam on the brakes. In neurological terms, the digital stimulation is called a sudden onset; the primitive parts of my brain react to surprise, overriding focus on other activities, like not crashing. Behind me, a horn blares. Then another.

I look at the phone. The message is from Sandy. "U still here?"

With traffic inching ahead, I balance the phone on the wheel and tap out: "You disapeard so I lef."

A second later, a text returns. "bathroom. guys r so impatient. u coming back?"

I'm about to tap out a response when she texts again. "Nevr mind. Ive got plans. I was going to TELL ALL. Ha."

I look up again and realize I'm well down Pine Street, the thoroughfare where I need to turn left to get to Polk, my office, Faith and the shiny-headed man in the black Mercedes. The phone slips from my hand onto the floor as I pull a hard left, narrowly making the turn and avoiding the curb. Sandy and her texts are proving unpredictable and dangerous. I'm reminded of the popular bumper sticker: Honk if you love Jesus, Text if you want to meet him.

Pine Street flows smoothly and ten minutes later, I find a parking spot a block from Polk. I pick up the phone from the floor and dial.

"Where are you?" Faith asks by way of answering.

"A block away. Parked. Is the man in the Mercedes still there?"

"Yes. Are you coming?"

I hear a tap on the driver's window and I jump. A woman holds a tattered black umbrella over her head with her right arm. Tucked under her left arm is a small, scruffy brown dog, curly-haired, pink tongue extended between the teeth. Its eyes are blank white, like an albino. It's blind. I grit my teeth, girding myself against an instant of horror and then a wave of nausea. I look up and into the sunken eyes of the gray-haired beggar. She's got a tiny square stud piercing her right nostril. I pause on it; the chief nurse who delivered Isaac had one just like it. I look back at her eyes, and she returns my unintentionally hard gaze. She blinks, looking startled, like I've frightened her, and takes a step back. She shakes her head, as if to say, "I'm not interested in your money."

"Nathaniel!" It's Faith, from the phone. Her bark brings me back to reality and realization: My concussed brain remains on the fritz. I feel like my thought process and focus keeps slipping off the tracks. "Are you coming or not?"

I clear my dry throat. "He asked you to come to the subway. Alan."

"Yes."

"Why?"

"I'll explain. It's straightforward."

"Do you know Sandy Vello?"

"Who? Nat. This isn't funny."

"Kathryn Gilkeson?"

"What is this about?" The recently revealed actress sounding baffled.

"What are you doing in my neighborhood, Faith?"

"The man in the car started following me at Safeway, an hour ago. I didn't want him to follow me home. Are you coming to the rescue or not?"

To the rescue. I nearly laugh. How can I resist?

"Faith . . ."

"What?"

"I'm tired of being the one person in this mystery who is not holding any cards."

"I told you I'd explain."

That's not what I'm getting at. I tell Faith that there's a café next door to the pizza joint. It has a back door that leads to a small alley. I want her to go to the café, order a large coffee, sit down at a table, spend five minutes hanging out, and then go into the back as if going to use the restroom. Instead, she's going to escape into the alley, where I tell her that I'll come to meet her.

"Doesn't the pizza joint have a back door?" she asks.

"Yes. But I don't need pizza. I need coffee. Black, please."

"Nat. This is really serious. I'm scared. Why do we need to go through this charade?"

"Trust me."

Because I need time. I'm formulating a plan. It's half-baked, like my concussed brain. But I've got to try something. I've got to try to turn the tables.

20

Across the street from where I'm parked is a small grocer that carries the staples of modern life: bread and canned goods, cheap liquor and tobacco, and cell phones. A plump woman standing behind the counter, prematurely wearing dentures, sells me a Motorola phone that a decade ago would've been among the most powerful mobile computers on the planet. The computational zing wrapped in its dime-a-dozen metallic clamshell would've been housed in a block-long warehouse, a veritable state treasure. Now it's near the lowest rung on the technology ladder—so much so, it's displayed behind the counter next to boxes of condoms and antihistamine. And it costs only $35, provided that I also load it with one hundred minutes of pre-paid talk time for an additional $23. I don't have to sign any contracts or sign up under my own name.

I unwrap the phone and then stand momentarily stymied where to toss the disemboweled packaging. Into the black trash bin, the blue recycling one, or the green container for compost? Trash, I conjecture. I turn on the phone. It's got some battery life, but not much. I offer the woman a dollar if she'll let me plug my new phone into the wall outlet for five minutes. She shrugs.

"You're not the first," she says.

Five minutes later, I'm back in my car with a new pre-paid phone and a meager plan. I tuck the new phone into my pocket and use my existing one to call Faith. When she answers, I say: "Are you ready?"

"With a tall cup of No Doze with your name on it. Let's go, please."

"See you in the alley."

To avoid driving past the man in the Mercedes parked on Polk Street, I drive around the block in the other direction. I slide into the alley behind the café. The alley—lined with dozens of the holy trinities of state-approved garbage, recycling and compost cans—is such a tight fit that Faith must squeeze sideways to get into the car. As she twists her body, I glance at the short brown skirt that comes only to her knee, slit up to her thigh, not the least bit practical unless Faith was expecting a summer day to suddenly break out or she wants attention focused on her legs.

She hands me the coffee. I take a big slug, grimacing as the scalding liquid scorches the roof of my mouth.

"It's even more exhilarating if you pour the whole thing on your head." She smiles and my heart skips a beat—either from caffeine or the stimulant created by Faith's proximity. Maybe it's the same neurological mechanism.

I'm about to make a comment about the fact that it's strange to me that Faith is composed enough to joke even though she's allegedly being stalked, when she says: "Thank you for the rescue."

I swallow hard. I put the coffee into the center console and drive in silence to the end of the alley. I take a left, drive half a block, take another left and drive two blocks, then take another left heading back toward Polk. Just before the intersection, I park in a red loading zone in front of a neighborhood bar called Leap Year. I feel Faith watching me. I turn to her and then back to Polk; half a block up the street, double-parked as it has been, sits the black Mercedes.

"He's going to see us." The anxiety is back in her voice.

"We're behind him. No streetlight shining on us. If he sees us he'd have to turn the car around and we'd be outta here." But I'm irritated that maybe she's right. "You have any tips, Faith?"

"Tips?"

"On doing surveillance. You seem to have the knack."

"I don't want to do this. I want to be somewhere safe."

"You're free to go at any time."

"You know he'd see me."

"Then we're stuck with each other—for now."

She doesn't respond.

"Aren't you curious who is following you?" I turn to look at her. Her eyes glisten with tears. "What's going on, Faith?"

She sniffles once, then takes a deep breath. With

the tips of her fingers, she wipes moisture from under her right eye. She looks at me, suddenly composed.

"So he's dead? Alan."

"I think he had a heart attack. I don't think he was . . ." I don't finish because I'm not sure whether he died of natural causes. He'd seemed hurt when he fell into me. Maybe his heart was already giving out. Or maybe someone drugged him, before or after our collision.

Faith interrupts my introspection. "Are you sick too?"

"No, why . . ."

"When you saw Alan, you . . . passed out."

I don't respond.

"Then it touched a nerve," Faith says. "You've lost someone."

I think: Ain't that the truth. My first true love, Annie Kindle, drowned five years ago in a lake in Nevada. My paternal grandmother, Lane, though still alive, suffers intensifying dementia. Polly, who was going to make it all better, left me. Things I love die or go away.

"I was disoriented." I finally offer my explanation. "I've got a concussion." So, yeah, I think, sick, in a way.

"It's not my fault."

"Why would my concussion be your fault, Faith?"

"I was just doing him a favor. That's it." She sounds just a tad defensive but maybe fairly so; a man is dead.

"Hold that thought."

The man in the Mercedes steps out of the car. He's tall and thin, more leg than torso. He looks in the direction of the café where I picked up Faith and cocks his head. He closes the car door and starts walking to the café: gangly, awkward strides, long arms, pink head, birdlike. He's favoring his left leg, but at this distance in the dark I can't settle on a diagnosis. Maybe lower back pain.

"He knows I'm gone," says Faith.

The man disappears into the café. I can imagine he's looking around, checking the bathroom, then asking the tattooed dude behind the counter whether he's seen a brunette in a brown skirt. At some point, he'll realize Faith disappeared through the alley or he'll wonder if he lost focus and missed her wandering out the front.

"There he is," Faith says.

"Turkey vulture."

"What?"

"He moves like a bird."

"Absolutely does. The way he cocks his head, a buzzard. You know your birds of prey."

Back at his car, he finds a ratty-haired man in decrepit full-length coat looking through the back window and scratching his arms. Crack addict. The buzzard pulls out a wallet. He extracts a bill. He holds it up so that the druggie can see it. He drops the dollar onto the ground behind the car.

The addict shrugs and bends to pick up the money. As he starts to stand, the buzzard launches a soccer-style kick at the druggie's head. Just before he's about to make contact, the gangly attacker pulls back, sparing the druggie a terrific blow, causing him to fall to the street in a ball.

"Oh God," Faith says.

"Mean buzzard."

He climbs into the Mercedes. No sooner does exhaust start to come from his tailpipe than he is off. He peels into light traffic, cutting off a diminutive European smart car made for parking, not surviving crashes.

I pull out to follow. The Mercedes is separated from us by the smart car and an old-model sedan coughing exhaust.

"Take me to my car," Faith says.

I don't answer.

"You're kidnapping me."

"You think this guy is just playing around?"

"I . . ."

"Help me find out what's going on so that we can both feel safe."

Faith crosses her arms across her chest, resignation. The Mercedes takes a left onto Bush Street, a thoroughfare that heads in the direction of downtown.

"At least tell me what we're doing."

"I'm following him to see where he goes and you're going to continue telling me how you happened to observe my almost murder by subway."

I take the left onto Bush. I'm now separated from the Mercedes by only the sedan, a Buick. But I doubt he would be able to see us in the darkness and drizzle. The light turns green. We continue toward downtown.

A few blocks later, the Mercedes takes an abrupt,

illegal left turn onto Grant Street beneath an enormous green gate with an orange dragon on the top. Chinatown.

I hear a honk and realize I've stopped in the middle of the street. The Mercedes is half a block away now but moving slowly; not surprising given Chinatown's narrow streets and the challenge of navigating a handful of jaywalkers, the very last of the night's produce, and shoppers toting bags.

The Mercedes's taillights disappear over a slight hill.

21

I hate this place. It's always had a hold on me—not the mysticism of the hole-in-the-wall herbal dispensaries, the wrinkle-faced trinket sellers in their comically costumed conical hats, the bloodied chickens hung by their feet from the rafters of the Chinese butchers. That stuff I love.

It's the parking. This is the place where parking Karma goes to die. Tiny spaces, seemingly never free, with what seem to me to be the most arcane rules in a city of arcane parking rules. Here, a sign might read: NO PARKING 8 TO 5 OTHER THAN FIRST TUESDAYS AND THURSDAYS OF MONTH AND AS OTHERWISE NOTED. Why not add: PENALTY IS DEATH. Two spots away, a different rule.

I work through a small crowd and crest the hill in time to see the Mercedes slide into a spot. I can't tell whether it's legal, but it nevertheless puts us in a pickle. I can't stop and double-park in these narrow streets.

"Duck," I say.

"What?"

"Lower your head."

She understands. We're about to pass the buzzard. She bends to the left so she's lying on the seat, out of sight. To stabilize herself, she reaches across the center of the car and her fingers brush my knee.

To avoid having him see me, I instinctively contract my neck, trying to pull my head inside my body. I also slow to keep from getting too far ahead of the Mercedes, but even at this pace, we're a full block ahead of our prey. Faith sits up.

"He's just sitting there." I report. "Lights off."

I hit a stop sign at an intersection that marks Chinatown's innards, the place where tourists gawk but no longer buy. The shops here cater to Chinese restaurateurs and residents. At the corner, a thin Chinese man in a suit holds an umbrella, its outline framed by the neon sign in the window of the dessert shop behind him.

I flash back to the reason I hate Chinese food.

I'm sitting across from Polly at Golden Lucky Duck. It's the night she got an empty fortune cookie. Cracked in her hand, it looks dry, like an egg without an embryo. She tells me she's got something important to discuss. Uncharacteristically, she stutters. Polly, the polished entrepreneur with the Wharton street cred, can't get her presentation out.

"Say something, Polly."

The waiter returns with a replacement fortune cookie. Polly takes it and smiles sadly. "Let's open it and find out our fate."

Back in the present, I hear a voice: "Nathaniel?"

I look up at the neon dessert sign and it looks like it's bending. I exhale through pursed lips.

The man with the umbrella crosses the street. After he passes, I pull over to the side, essentially parking in the crosswalk. I feel Faith's gaze on me as I turn around to look at the Mercedes.

"Start talking. You said Alan asked you to come to the subway. You did him a favor."

She sighs. "He asked me to make sure that you got his message. That's it."

"Message?"

The buzzard in the Mercedes opens his door and extends out a long leg but doesn't get out. He's getting air, or can't decide his next move.

"He told me you were a journalist," Faith continues. "He said he wanted to get your attention."

"Why didn't he send me an email?"

But as I'm asking, I'm struck by a theory. Maybe he tried to send an email. Maybe he had originally tried to contact me using a fake account under the name Sandy Vello. On my computer, I'd found several emails from the address Sandyvello@hotmail.com. But the emails went to spam, or I ignored them. So did Alan then jack up his efforts?

Then another theory. On the piece of paper I found on Alan's desk, I'd seen the date 2/15. That's two weeks from now. But it's a month after I received an anonymous email from an account bearing Sandy Vello's name. And that email had read, "We have one month to stop the launch."

"Faith, what's happening in two weeks?"

"What do you mean?"

"What's happening February fifteenth?"

"I don't know. And to answer your other question—about why Alan tracked you down in the subway: I got the sense he wanted to reach you anonymously but also that he thought you were more likely to respond to dramatic overture."

"Like getting pushed under a subway?"

"I didn't expect that. I thought he was going to hand you something or whisper something to you and then run off. I was supposed to . . . intercept you . . . to get your attention so you didn't follow him."

I'm looking at the shops and buildings around the Mercedes. Why did the man come here? Is he merely looking for authentic take-out dumplings or something else? What's interesting around here?

"It's an awfully big favor you did. You must have known him well."

Directly next to the Mercedes, on the same side of the street, a trinket vendor closes up for the day, using a pole with a hook on the end to remove inflatable dragons from an awning dripping with drizzle. To the shop's right is a thin three-story office building or apartment complex, or maybe a combination. Its windows are dark, except for one on the second story with blinds. To the shop's left is a storefront with a banner written in Chinese with some English: Safe Happy Travel Agency.

"I didn't know him well. Just a little from the café." Faith turns in her seat so now she's facing me and the Mercedes. I glance at her silhouetted profile.

She explains that over the last year or so, she often saw Alan hunched over his laptop, intent, sometimes even muttering to himself, not with insanity but intensity. One day, a few months ago, when they were at adjoining tables, he struck up a conversation by offering to bet her a doughnut that he could guess what she wanted to do with her life.

"It was funny, not sleazy like you sometimes get." Left unsaid: she often gets hit on. "His guess was that I wanted to be a meteorologist."

"Not a bad line."

"I bought him a doughnut. My first mistake."

I turn to look at her and find her looking right back. Shade darkens the left third of her, as if lit by a bad movie director wanting to suggest her inner darkness.

"You want to predict the weather?"

Her face softens. She blinks and smiles with her cheeks and eyes, her lips barely moving. Even in dim light, they look full and pink.

"I filled in on Channel 4 for a few weeks when the meteorologist was sick. Alan also guessed that I wanted to be a singer, which was close too. I wanted to be an actress. It kind of took it out of me when I did a few commercials for bug spray. I was supposed to be a dispirited housewife with a cockroach infestation."

"Faith . . ."

"He called me Valerie." She explains she reminded him of a younger Valerie Bertinelli, the actress from *One Day at a Time*. She says Alan liked the reference because it reminded him of his efforts to stay sober—one day at a time.

"So you are an actor."

"A hobbyist. I make my living as a transition specialist."

"Explain."

"I help people make transitions—one job to the next, one life situation to the next. It's a bit of a New Age gig but it paid well when things were booming here. People wanted to assess their options and make sure that they made the right choice to fit their goals. When the economy tanked, I helped people come to terms with lowered expectations."

"Paid well, past tense."

"Things aren't booming. In fact, they're so dead that people can't afford to cope with lowered expectations."

"You liked him. Alan?"

She clears her throat. She pulls her jacket closed. "He seemed to know a lot about me. He was uncanny that way."

"So you followed me because he was nice and geeky and lonely and needed a favor."

"No. Because he promised to pay me one thousand dollars and I need the money. And he kind of freaked me out, because he knew so much about me. He presented both opportunity and a subtle kind of threat; I can't fully explain it, but it's the truth. I'm obviously not getting paid and I don't care. I'm sorry this happened, that you got hurt, and I'm very sorry that I just want this to all go away and to not have this man bothering me, or . . ." She pauses, and then stops altogether.

"What's an Earth clown?"

"What?"

"Kathryn Gilkeson? Who is that?"

"I have no idea."

"Alley."

I'm looking across the street from the Mercedes. There is a butcher's shop closing up for the day and a Chinese bookstore already closed. Between them is an alley with a man standing at its entrance, cupping his hands around his mouth, maybe blowing in them to keep warm. Next to the man on the side of the alley is a sign that is too distant for me to read, if it's even in English.

The man scopes the street and takes two steps backward and disappears into the alley.

We fall into silence. I want her to continue the story but it feels like she's said her peace or maybe we're just tired or comfortable. Five minutes pass, then ten, more. I'm wondering why I'm not cold. I should be cold but I know concussion can mess with internal temperature regulation. We watch our buzzard. The already thin sidewalk traffic thins further. The butcher turns off his light.

I'm shaken by a buzzing noise. Faith reaches into a small purse and pulls out a phone. She looks at the bright green-and-white square of the screen, her caller ID. She clenches her jaw. She hits a button, sending the caller to voice mail. "It's almost eight." She puts the phone back in her purse. A second later, it buzzes again. She ignores it.

"Do you need me to step outside so you can take a call?" I'm looking at her in the pinkish light from the neon sign on the dessert store.

She cocks her head. "You're kind."

She leans forward, pauses, then she kisses me on the cheek. I'm flooded with a sensation that moves from the top of my concussed skull to my Achilles' heels ragged from basketball and then zips up and settles in my loins. She pulls back, reorients slightly, and she kisses my lips, lightly, like the brush of a fingertip.

"I trust you." Her words hover just above a whisper.

"Faith . . ."

"I just wanted to get that out of the way."

But I'm thinking about something else. The buzzard is out of the car and walking to the alley.

22

We watch in silence as he disappears into the alley.

"Faith, may I wax melodramatic?"

"Wax."

"It's now or never."

"That is melodramatic. But what's it mean?"

I'm surprised to hear myself laugh. It's both a real emotion and a desire to connect. I shouldn't. She's a gigantic question mark with full lips and deep eyes and no obvious medical condition.

From my pocket, I pull the pre-paid mobile phone that I purchased an hour earlier. I tell Faith my plan: I'm going to walk by the Mercedes and put the phone onto the car windshield. When the man returns, he'll find the phone and we'll give him a call and try to elicit some information. Who is he? What does he want?

"That's the plan?" Faith sounds surprised, in an underwhelmed kind of way.

I half nod.

"What's to keep him from throwing away the

phone or ignoring our call or hearing your voice and tossing it?"

I don't say: 1) I want him to feel like he doesn't have all the cards; and 2) her questions are all spot-on and I don't have the answers.

Instead, I say: "Now or never."

She puts her hand on my arm. "What am I supposed to do?" Implicit in her question: what is she supposed to do if something happens to me?

"Get in the driver's seat in case."

"This makes no sense."

From a compartment between the seats, I snag a black pen and reporter's notebook and stuff them into my back pocket. I step out of the car into a light drizzle, San Francisco mist. It's momentarily refreshing, then chilly. I consider opening the trunk to grab a sweatshirt but there's no time. I walk a few steps, then jog toward the Mercedes, hewing as close as I can to the buildings, imaging somehow I'll become invisible if I can blend into the grayish stone exteriors of Chinatown in the dark.

As I jog, I'm squinting at the mouth of the alley. But for a second, I see the inside of my brain. I imagine blood pouring into the sensory cortex, supporting my vision, and dopamine cascading into my nucleus accumbens, my pleasure centers, giving me a rush. I see the little white spots on my frontal lobe, the concussion, which might explain the slightly blurred vision. Or maybe that's just an effect from the drizzle.

I am standing at the Mercedes. I whip out the pre-paid Motorola phone from my front pocket, nearly fumble it, have to bend down to catch it. I stand, look at the mouth of the alley. No buzzard sighting. No one else on the street.

I glance at the intersection where I've parked. I can't see my car. I squint. Blood to sensory cortex: where is my car?! Then I see it, just where I left it. Had it disappeared, ghost-like, then reappeared, or was my brain flickering on and off?

I pull out my iPhone. I scramble through dozens of apps I've downloaded; a game where I shoot birds at buildings, a program that turns my phone into a mirror, a calorie counter. I find the flashlight app. I click it open. Lights blasts from the phone. I direct it to the passenger window and look inside the Mercedes. On the leather passenger seat, there sits a to-go container, open, half-eaten onion rings inside. Intrepid investigator. I've discovered the reason he has oily skin. In the cup holder in the center console, there sits a pack of menthol cigarettes. The backseat is empty. I peer at the mouth of the alley. It's empty too.

Frontal lobe to Nat: Do something and then run away?

I place the pre-paid phone on the passenger-side windshield. I look at it, gathering drizzle. I lift the slippery wiper blade and place the phone underneath. On an impulse, I put my hand on the passenger side door handle and pull up. It's unlocked. I open it, causing the inside light to go on. I snag the damp phone, wipe it on my shirt, toss the phone inside, onto the onion rings. I start to close the door. My eye catches a receipt taped to the outside of the food box. I pull it off. Scrawled on it, "buffalo burger, onion rings." Circled in pen, the word "Bill." The buzzard has a name.

"Buzzard Bill," I mutter.

I peer at the alley mouth. I sense movement. The light is changing, playing with the shadows, something or someone emerging from the shadows. In one motion, I push the car door shut and fall to the ground. Thankfully, the car's inside light goes off instantly.

I don't know if the movement was Buzzard Bill, or someone else, or my imagination. Where to escape? I look at the sidewalk behind the car. It's unlit but wide open. Exposed. I look to the front. Same bad news, and then some worse news. At the intersection ahead, I see taillights ignite. My taillights. The Audi pulls out and disappears to the right. Faith has left. Again. For good reason this time? Did she see Buzzard Bill and freak? Did she get a mystery call?

I look directly behind me at the darkened stairwell with shiny, wet steps that bisect the storefronts.

Crab-like, I hustle to the stairwell. I press up against the wall. At the stairwell, I pause; if I slink up the stairs, I'll be fully exposed. I listen to my heartbeat, fast and regular, comforting me, weirdly, a reminder that I'm largely intact. I take two slow breaths to slow down my heart and my mind.

I hear the Mercedes door open. It closes hard and heavy. Buzzard Bill is in a hurry. I hold my breath and crab-scamper up the stairs. The engine turns over. Car in gear, tires on wet pavement, he's out.

I remember the reporter's notebook in my back pocket. Hadn't I planned to write down the license plate? I feel self-recrimination that, suddenly, dissolves into laughter. A momentary outburst. Relief. I'm safe. More neurotransmitters flooding my brain. Neurological goodness. What would be great would be to feel this way all the time—the feeling of escape, and completion, but without the near-death antecedent.

I glance around. I'm on the top step of the entrance to an apartment building. An intercom system hangs just below eye level with a list of residents, lit dimly from an internal light. Most of the names are in phonetic Chinese, like Chu, some with native characters.

The rain has picked up. I hope the buzzard has reached for a soggy onion ring and found a mysterious phone. He's deciding whether to pull over and find something telling about it—the owner, address book—or to toss it out the window, maybe figuring it for some kind of surveillance device that tracks his whereabouts, or, alternatively, gunning it back to Chinatown to find whoever put it there.

I'm also trying to imagine what happened to Faith. Why not ask? I pull my own phone from my pocket. I call her. The phone rings and rings. No answer. I leave a message. I contemplate calling the pre-paid phone but decide it's too soon. He may come right back here before I can get my bearings and make sense of this place.

The phone's clock reads 9:10. I sit down. It's quiet enough that I can hear the drizzle. I'm not sure of my next move, so it's as good a time as any to reflect on the events of the last twenty-four hours:

A gangly, oily-headed man sits in the audience of

my awards presentation, then hands me my phone. Had it really fallen from my pocket, or had he somehow taken it and tinkered with it? The next morning, he shows up at my office, trying to follow me and Faith. We evade him, then discover the corpulent corpus of Alan Parsons, the mountain man who nearly felled me at the subway. On his desk, the phone number for a woman with a dead daughter. And a second reference to February 15. Hours later, after I've met with still-living narcissist Sandy Vello, the man appears again, this time ostensibly drawn there following Faith.

Faith is beautiful and cautious, scared and confident, irresistible and unpredictable. Why did she kiss me?

And what does any of it have to do with Chinatown? There were Chinese characters on a piece of paper I found on the dead man's desk. The words have something to do with computers, and so does Sandy Vello. Does it relate to a dead girl named Kathryn Gilkeson? And do all these roads lead to the alley across the street?

One way to find out.

It's 9:15. I take deep breaths to let a few more minutes pass and make sure the street is as quiet as it seems, and to see if Faith has returned.

9:20. The street is quiet. My car has not returned. I've lost Faith.

9:23. I look across the street, at a restaurant on the corner with a pair of enormous chopsticks hanging in the window. It's a tourist trap, and an emotional one. I flash again on my fateful dinner with Polly, the night I associate with two fortune cookies changing the course of my life. I picture the waiter, his limp left leg, the first empty fortune cookie cracked like an empty egg, water condensed on the outside of Polly's glass. She's not sharing my Tsingtao; she's pregnant. I picture the red table-cloth, damp around the bottom of the water glass. Polly's smiling a sad smile. She says she wants to tell me something. But I can't quite remember what she said, or how she said it. I grit my teeth. I look down at my phone.

9:28. Enough.

I stride onto the sidewalk, then across the narrow, empty street, my steps lit intermittently by storefront neon. I reach the mouth of the alley. On the wall next to it, I see the plaque I'd been unable to read earlier from a distance. On its top, Chinese characters. Beneath, a translation: CHINA-US HIGH-TECH ALLIANCE.

I can't tell if it refers to the dark-windowed office to my immediate right, or something located in the guts of the alley.

I peer into the dark maw.

I see the red glow of a cigarette tip.

23

"Who are you?" The voice is accented, the "r" swallowed.

A hefty man steps forward. He's half a head taller than me, square cranium that's a bit too large for his body, short-cropped hair, flat nose consistent with his Asian DNA but squished to the right. The right edge of his upper lip looks crooked, a jigsaw puzzle. Big head, slightly exaggerated nose and mouth. I almost gasp from mild thrill. I've never in person seen a case of acromegaly, a chronic disorder caused by too much growth hormone.

"You walk like someone who has fame or money." He reaches to his mouth, pinches the cigarette with thick fingers and flips it against the wall. "Are you famous? If so, I'd like to know you."

"Not famous." I half step backward.

"Then it's the other option."

"What?"

"You've got money. I like money."

Before I can react, he grabs my shirt. I pull back sharply, extricating myself. But I slip. I fall backward, bracing my hands beneath me. I land, feeling a pop in my elbow.

I feel hands on both my feet, pulling me into the alley. I can't resist him. My arms, awkwardly bent behind me, prove no match. I cut my losses and put my hands under my already fragile head, skidding.

Then I see lights. A car appears to our left, bouncing along the uneven, one-way street.

When I look up again, I realize I'm lying just inside the alley entrance, the man having slid up my torso, knee on my chest. He rips at my jeans, going for my wallet?

I say: Take whatever you want. But I'm trying to figure out how to hit his solar plexus or the nerve-rich hollow above his collarbone.

He raises his balled right hand, a beefy flesh hammer. He cocks it. It arches downward. I at once buck against his weight and cover my face with my hands. I picture my concussed brain, like an infant, curled up, vulnerable.

"I have a son," I mutter, or think.

The car lights get closer. A horn blares. The man's hand crashes down. A supernova explodes inside my skull, then swallows itself.

24

"I'm seeing phosphenes," I say.

I sit on a ledge next to infant Isaac. He looks different than I remember him, more teeth and hair. We're thousands of feet in the air, cloud level. He wears white overalls with alligators on them. I picked them out at a Babys"R"Us in South San Francisco with sticky floors a few months before he was born. Between us on the ledge, a white plate holds two fortune cookies. One is cracked open and is empty.

"I realize you have no idea what I'm talking about."

"Of course I know about phosphenes," my tiny son responds. "I'm little but I'm not stupid."

"You can talk?"

He puts his adorable index finger on his nose and wiggles it absently, an infant discovering his personal space.

Phosphenes are the product of electrical static inside our brains. When neurons fire—which happens pretty much all the time—they are accompanied by electrical signals. The signals throw off static, just like any electrical signal, a veritable neurological white noise. If you've ever closed your eyes tightly, you can see a matrix of light; that's the static. You can see it too with your eyes open, often against a black backdrop.

At this moment, I'm seeing phosphenes in spades, my brain murky and white with static, like I've blown a circuit.

"Isaac, am I going to die?"

"I dunno. I'm just a baby. But I do know she's been lying to you."

"Who?"

He doesn't answer.

"Faith? Sandy?"

"Yes."

"Which one?"

"And you're lying to yourself."

"About what, Isaac?"

No answer. I look down at the brown cookies on the plate, understated little bows of pastry and pre-science.

"Wake up, Daddy. Before the damage is irreversible. Besides, she's calling out your name."

"Nathaniel, you're not serious."

"Again."

I open my barely cracked eyes and see a tacky white ceiling, cheap square paneling. Then hair. It's light brown, long and loose, strands tickling my forehead.

Faith sits astride me. A sheet covers her shoulders. Behind her, on a bureau, sits a cheap television set, flat-panel, from the 1990s, a CRT. I'm in a hotel—no, motel.

"How about if we take a break and get you to the hospital?" the nymph asks.

I shake my head. No. I hate hospitals. "Am I dreaming? I was just dreaming."

"You're awake. And you're having real, live, great sex. Apparently again."

I try to lift my head but pain and drool keep it pasted it to a pillow. I smell starch and taste glue.

Fighting pain, angered by it, I sit upright. I feel momentarily refreshed, alive, and then intensely dizzy.

Dim gray light comes through the edges of closed curtains covering square windows to my right. A brass-poled lamp stands in the corner. Beneath it, a stiff patterned-cloth recliner is piled with clothes. To my right, on a faux wood nightstand, a square plastic stand holds an advertisement for Roger's Motel at Ocean Beach. It shows a picture of a motel with a red awning offering "free Wi-Fi" and "free coffee and donuts 7–9." It instructs: "Dial 0 for the best motel service in San Francisco." The scuffed and boxy beige landline phone sitting beside it looks like it was bought from a garage sale a generation ago.

My phone sits next to it, looking by comparison like a spacecraft from far in the future.

I look straight ahead, at the bureau with the TV.

Behind it, there's a rectangular mirror with a note written in red lipstick:

back soon.
drink water.
f.

I elongate so I can glance to see myself in the mirror. My right eye is puffy and half-closed, flooded with blood-carrying cells to rebuild the hammer-fist-struck tissue. My elbow aches with distended ligament.

I turn to the side of the bed and I dry heave.

I have no memory of how I got here or when. I'm pretty sure I remember having sex. I called it therapy, and so did Faith.

I slide my feet onto the floor. I stumble to the bathroom, and fumble to extract a paper cup from its sterile paper wrapping. I gulp tepid water, refill and repeat. Even without turning on the light, I can see in the mirror light streaks of red on my chest and arms. Fingernail marks. Faith doesn't mess around or, rather, she does and with more animation than I might've guessed.

I hear buzzing coming from the other room. I wade back through my fog to the bedside, lift and look at the phone resting in the palm of my right hand, notice the screen go briefly out of focus. If I didn't have a concussion before, I've got one now.

A notification tells me I've got a voice mail. More brain radiation, I think, as I listen to the message.

"I can tell you more about the juggler thing. Back at the Ramp tonight? Same time."

It's cryptic but recognizable. Sandy Vello. The juggler thing. Something having to do with technology and kids.

The motel door swings open. In the doorway stands Faith, breathing hard, her hair wet and flat on her head. She holds a cardboard tray with two coffees and a pastry. I realize my first reaction is not curiosity but hunger.

"Pants," she says.

"Pastry first, then explain what you mean."

"Get dressed or you're going to have to run to the car naked."

"You're even kinkier than I remember."

"He's coming." She reaches onto the chair by the door and tosses me a ball of my clothes.

"Who?"

"Let's go. Now!"

27

I slither into my clothes as she sprints over and kneels by the bed onto a dull purplish carpet the color of an interred spleen. She peers and reaches under the bed and retrieves a charm bracelet.

I lean down and snag the coffee and high-tops. Hustling back, she takes my hand and pulls me toward the door. She looks at my shoeless feet. "They'll dry. Let's go."

She opens the door to show the washed-out light of mid-morning in wintry San Francisco—fog central, punctuated by a drizzle. We're on the second floor of a two-floor shithole, blue chipped paint covering the floorboards and railing. I have a vision of being here before that feels something like déjà vu and something like nausea. I'm seized by extreme vertigo and I wobble, looking down at a parking lot with a single car—mine.

"Let's go, Nathaniel." With a free hand, she grabs me and starts to walk quickly to the stairs.

"The sprint of shame."

On the stairs, I feel a sharp pain on my right

foot, a splinter nicking my slippery arch. I'm hobbling two steps behind Faith when we reach the Audi.

"Where and who is the mysterious stalker forcing me to leave the warm and dry place?"

"I'll drive." She pulls out my keys and clicks open the doors, we climb in. "Faith . . ."

"The Mercedes guy. I don't know how, but he found me when I went out for coffee. I took a couple of quick turns and got away from him and came back for you." She starts the car and pulls to the exit, looks left, pulls onto the street. "Maybe I should've left you and come back later. He's lurking."

"Take the one to the 280."

"What?"

"South."

We don't speak until we hit the exit for Pacifica, a lower-rent coastal town on a hillside that waits patiently for global warming. When it comes, the fog-soaked apartment complexes will become shoreline properties and their long-suffering owners and Al Gore will be vindicated.

"Pull off," I say.

"I thought you said . . ."

"Please."

She exits the highway. I gesture with a nod of my head to stop by the side of the highway. I open the heavy Audi door and I dry heave. I sit with my elbows on my knees.

"I should take you to the hospital."

I pat the tender skin around my eye. If the orbital

bone is broken, there's not a damn thing I can do about it other than trying not to continue to use my head to deflect things.

"Earth clown?" I mutter.

"What?"

I inhale coffee—instant energy, semi-clarity. A deep breath, more caffeine. I reach into my back pocket and I pull out the paper I found on Alan Parsons's desk. On it, I locate the Chinese characters the pizza maker couldn't quite make sense of.

I pull out my phone and call Bullseye, barmate and personal IT guy. Predictably, he doesn't answer. He loves using devices, just not to communicate with other human beings. I leave a message. "I've got a mission for you. Text me a place I can fax you something."

I bring up the menu of my voice mails and return a call to Sandy Vello. She doesn't pick up either. I text her. "c u at the Ramp."

A text pops onto my screen. It's just a number, with no pleasantries. Bullseye's fax. When I get a chance, I'll send along the Chinese, and let him scour the Internet for an explanation.

In my phone directory, I call up the number for the offices of Andrew Leviathan. I wonder if he has any idea of the identity of a man with a sleek bald head who attended the awards luncheon, cocks his head like a buzzard, circles like one too.

I dial. A curt woman answers: "Mr. Leviathan's office."

"Hi. My name is Nat Idle."

"Yes."

"I'm a journalist who . . ."

"I'm sorry to cut you off but I refer all journalist calls to . . ."

"And I'm sorry to cut you off. Andrew just gave me an award and instructed me to call him if I had any questions." I leave vague whether or not I am referring to questions related to the award.

"Yes, Mr. Idle. Let me take a number."

I give the info and we hang up.

"Not to the hospital, I take it," Faith says.

"Menlo Park."

We drive in silence, in drizzle, unless I'm going nuts and seeing only phosphenes—lots of them. Consistent with a down economy, the highway isn't crowded; it's only bumper-to-bumper here during midday stretches when venture capitalists are funding start-ups faster than they can come up with clever names. A solid fifteen minutes pass before I speak.

"What are you doing, Faith?"

"Driving you to Menlo Park, like you asked."

"Why are you with me right now? What could possibly be compelling you to join in a goose chase with a near stranger who keeps getting into extremely bad situations and has suffered two head wounds?"

"Your memory is really that bad?"

"It's seen better days."

"You don't remember what we talked about last night?"

I remember getting slugged, going black, experiencing a drunken state, sweaty and light, realizing I was having sex—for the first time since Polly.

Faith waits for me, then continues. "You told me the man in the Mercedes is dangerous. You told me there was a connection between him and Alan, and a big Chinese company and some reality-TV burn-out, and that your computer had been hacked into. You said I'm not safe and shouldn't be alone."

"One of my cheapest-ever pickup lines."

"I don't like being taken advantage of."

"I didn't . . ."

"Not by you. I make my own decisions about who I sleep with. You're right about being unsafe, and I don't like being taken advantage of by whoever is making me feel that way and I have just as much of a right as you to figure out what's happening as you do."

Fair enough.

"Did I say anything else of value or interest?"

"Ouch."

"What?"

"You said 'ouch.' I got a little aggressive with my fingernails."

She smiles. It would seem shy, demure, if not for the subject matter, which she's raised.

"Sorry." She laughs lightly. I look out the passenger-side window at the blurring greenery on the hillsides of Atherton. I don't want her to see the degree to which she has me off balance.

"Next exit," I say.

She pulls onto Sand Hill Road, a freeway exit that can't but help make you feel poor. Literally seconds from the off-ramp stand a series of modest, nondescript offices that house this region's barons, the investors who seeded Google and Facebook and the rest.

"What happened last night, Faith?"

"I told you."

"How did we wind up together at the world-class motel?"

She explains that she watched the bald man come out from the alley and climb into his Mercedes. Fearing he'd see her, she took off, intending to return for me. And she did, but it took longer than expected because of the one-way streets in the area. Plausible enough. When she finally pulled up, she says, she saw me knocked down. She honked and watched a husky Asian man disappear into the alley.

"When I got to you, you were mumbling stuff that didn't make sense."

"About conspiracy?"

"About Isaac. You said you were sorry for hugging him too hard."

She helped me to the car. It was her idea to go somewhere we couldn't be easily tracked. She says it didn't dawn on her until we got near the motel that I was definitely not all there.

"You talked about the first time you'd seen a dead body."

In the present, I look out the car window and see we're passing the Stanford Shopping Center.

"Take a left on El Camino."

I have a vague recollection of telling her about my first anatomy class. The woman whose body we dissected had died at eighty-six years old with an interesting backstory. She'd suffered bone cancer and intended to take her own life by parachuting from a plane. Before she climbed into the airplane, she took a sedative, went to sleep and never woke up. It shook me that death can be so cruel that, even when you plan to embrace it on your terms, it can wrestle away the upper hand.

"Why would I tell you about that?"

"You were telling me you understood why I got so shaken when I saw Alan's body."

We pass a bookstore, a furniture store, a salad place I've been for a work lunch where they pride themselves on serving sixteen variations of lettuce. They frown upon the use of salad dressings, which, the menu notes, dilute the fresh, earthy flavors of the greens.

Faith says: "You don't remember."

I shake my head. "We're going two blocks up on the right."

Traffic's thin. Faith drives cautiously; she uses her blinker to switch from the middle to the right lane, even though the nearest car, a beige Jaguar, is four car lengths ahead of us. Dull sun peeks through light clouds, a temperate winter day in the sixties.

"What did *you* tell *me*, Faith?"

"I revealed all. You don't remember my extraordinary revelations?"

I manage a laugh. "Refresh me just a little."

"I told you about my fascination with going to the zoo, and with the anteaters."

"This I absolutely don't recall. You're sure you were talking to the guy with the head wound?"

"They can suck up thirty thousand ants a day. Nature's vacuum."

"That's why they fascinate you? Bad experience at a picnic with ants?"

She clears her throat. "Because everyone's got a purpose. No matter how different they seem."

Oddly, something does ring familiar about the zoo, maybe because the motel was directly across the street. There's something deeply familiar too in the way we're talking, an emotional accord.

"I'll give you a recap later. Do you remember telling me about your ex?"

I shake my head. Does she mean Annie or Polly?

"You told me about the night she ended it—over Chinese food and two empty fortune cookies."

I wince. The night my life careened off the rails at a restaurant in Pacific Heights. I can see the waiter with the injured ankle limping back to our table, holding a big white plate with a fortune cookie. It's Polly's second cookie, the first having been devoid of a fortune. Polly, usually so composed, has tears in her eyes. I shiver at the thought of the ensuing conversation, and because I can't remember describing it to Faith.

"Take a right here."

Set back off El Camino, there's a gated building made of fashionable concrete and steel. It's accessible from the side street we've turned onto. On the gate, a stately sign reads: "Woodland Learning Center." In the yard stands a woman, arms crossed, studying me.

28

"Please pick me up in an hour."

Faith pulls over. She puts the car in park. "I'm joining you."

"Nope."

She blinks several times quickly, and bites the inside of her cheek. I smile tightly, trying not to betray how much I want to make her laugh or feel comfortable. Based on my track record with the opposite sex, whatever is going on with this enigmatic beauty, it ends very badly.

"An hour."

"Don't use your cell phone."

"What?"

"Last night. Did I say anything about how someone might be monitoring our calls and emails?"

"Something to that effect."

"If you need to call me, or someone, speak in generalities."

I'm thinking about the evident surveillance skills of whoever hacked into my computer to suggest the premature death of Sandy Vello and, also, the man in the Mercedes. It should just be common practice nowadays: assume someone is monitoring you and act accordingly.

I step out of the car. The woman in the yard now holds open the gate. She wears a dress with flower patterns, something modest but from a bygone era of feminine attire. She's got shoulder-length blonde hair and a tic in her right eye.

I hear Faith pull away. The woman's eye twitches three times. She juts her chin toward the street. "That's where Kathryn died."

I walk into a yard that looks like the miniaturization of an Ivy League campus. A stone walkway bisects grassy patches, the one on the right planted with a massive oak. On the side of the two-story school grow vines that are at once overgrown and chaotic and pruned to look this way. It's no wonder this elementary school harks to hallowed institutions; in Silicon Valley, parents expect kids to matriculate directly from sixth grade to Harvard or Stanford, or else.

Jill gestures for me to sit on a bench cut from stone. It looks out on the street.

"We're a pair." She sits. "My nervous tic and your black eye. Did you upset someone with tough reporting?"

"Journalists are the most distrusted profession, after lawyers. It's really not fair. Lawyers get paid so much more and can afford reconstructive eye surgery."

The crow's-feet beside her eyes crinkle with a

slight perfunctory smile. She smoothes her dress and folds her hands on her lap.

"I've read about you and I trust you. But there's not very much to tell and I can't imagine why you or anyone would care after all these years."

"Would you mind indulging me? I'd be much obliged."

"She walked into the street."

I don't respond. It's one of the hardest skills to learn in journalism: waiting through the moment a source wants to be prodded to the more important moment when they start to express themselves on their own terms.

"Volvo," she finally whispers. "I never cared about cars. I could barely tell one from the next. But I had this idea that I'd like a black Volvo. They looked so sleek with a spaceship dashboard and they have this reputation for being so safe, so heavy, filled up with air bags. But that was the catch, I guess."

I wait.

"It came around the corner. It wasn't even going that fast." She swallows hard. "They're just so heavy."

"Volvos."

"This wasn't a school then. It was a private home. Kathryn's girlfriend lived here. They were playing. They weren't chaperoned but the mom was inside, generally keeping tabs, and they were plenty old enough to know not to run into the street."

The picture starts to form in my head and I'm both fascinated and desperate to push it away. As if she's at a far distance, I hear Jill's voice, faint, describe how seven-year-old Kathryn opened the swinging gate of the white picket fence, then ran into the street. A witness on the corner said the girl was laughing, carefree.

"As near as we could figure out, it was a totally impulsive act, like Kathryn was a baby again." Jill looks at me. "You know how little kids can be, just acting on a whim, exploring their space, totally unaware of the consequences. They can take on the most terrible risks with such complete innocence."

I feel a terrible weight on my chest, like I could suffocate. I see the phosphenes—dancing static.

"I got to talk to her before she died," I hear Jill say. "I mean, she was alive in the hospital, but not conscious. I'm sure she heard me."

I feel a tear slide down my right cheek, then one on my left, and I let them be.

"Are you okay?"

"I haven't been getting much sleep."

"There wasn't anyone to blame. The family who lived here was so devastated and apologetic they moved to the East Coast, their own penance. The Volvo driver, a nice young man studying engineering at Stanford, refused to drive for years. There wasn't a bad actor. Maybe that's why my marriage fell apart; Hank and I had no common enemy, no proverbial fall guy."

"I'm sorry." I look down and see my fists balled tightly.

"Maybe some good came of it. This school, after all."

"School?"

"It's done wonders helping kids in this area who

don't have the same resources as the ritzy set. I'll put a fine point on it: the children from East Menlo and East Palo Alto get world-class instruction, generally a free ride, and the first batch have gone on to colleges. It's been a success story. We all couldn't be more thankful to Andrew."

"Andrew. Sorry, I'm having trouble keeping up."

"I thought that's why you were here."

"Sorry, I'm . . ."

"Oh," she says with some recognition. "Maybe you don't realize the connection. I'd been working for Andy, Andrew, about two years when Kathryn was killed."

She studies me and can see I'm still lost. A look crosses her face that suggests she's getting lost too. My lack of comprehension is starting to unnerve her.

"Andrew Leviathan."

"Andrew," I repeat. "You worked for him when Kathryn . . . when it all happened."

"I was an executive assistant. Maybe overqualified for the job. But he paid so well. He became a mentor to me, really to all of us."

I'm swimming, the miasma of concussion mixed with shock. How did Andrew Leviathan become part of this mystery? How does the magnate who just gave me a magazine award connect to a woman and her run-down daughter and to a dead man who nearly shoved me in front of a subway?

My phone rings, a timely interruption. I look at the screen; it's a number in the 650 area code, nearby.

"Go ahead." Jill waves a hand.

"Hello, this is Nat."

"Hi, this is Andrew. Leviathan. Sorry for the delay in getting back to you."

I hold my breath, miasma swirling.

"Nathaniel?"

"Hi, Andrew." I look at Jill as if to say speak of the devil. "This is a long shot, but I'm in the area and I'm wondering if I might have a few minutes of your time."

"Everything okay?"

"Just ten minutes would be great."

He pauses. "I get my afternoon mocha at Peet's on University. I'll be there a little after three. What's it about? Did my check bounce?"

I force a thin laugh. "I just need to pick your brain for a story. It'll be quick and painless and you'll feel like your brain was hardly picked."

"That's remarkably vague."

I laugh again, this time genuinely. "Being obtuse is part of my award-winning technique."

"See you there."

I turn to Jill. She looks at me with concern. "I hope you won't make a big deal of this with him, with Andrew. He's built a half dozen schools but he's modest about his work. So if you wind up writing about his contributions, please don't make him out to be a hero. He hates that kind of thing. Is that what you're writing about?"

I nod, albeit absently. I look across the street. Faith sits in the Audi, reading something in her lap. I glance at my clock phone. It's 2:15. Plenty of time to get to Andrew but there's a stop we need to make first.

I stand. "Can we play the name game?"

She shrugs, not sure what I mean.

"Alan Parsons. Know him?"

She blinks twice, rapidly. She scratches her right shoulder. She bites the inside of her cheek.

"It rang a bell for a second but I can't place it." She cocks her head. "Maybe it'll come to me. When I start talking about what happened here—the accident—it tends to override the rest of my brain."

"Totally understandable. May I contact you again?"

"Of course."

I turn to her, as she stands. "Can you remind me when Kathryn died?"

"Two thousand. March eleventh."

"And how long after that did the school open?"

"In the fall. Remarkable, right? Andrew makes up his mind and he can change the world."

She takes a few steps and opens the gate for me. "You never quite feel like you're out of the woods—with kids."

"How so?"

She's distant and doesn't respond.

"Jill?"

"Those suicides—over at Los Altos High School."

"I don't know about . . ."

"Three kids last year—copycats, I guess. They stepped in front of trains."

I remember reading the speculation that the children, coming from highly educated upper-middle-class families, couldn't cope with the intense pressure to succeed.

She says: "When I saw it, I thought: as a parent, you can never pause to celebrate. You never know when they'll do something . . . childlike."

She looks away. This is too much for her.

I turn back to Faith. She glances up, catches my eye, then looks down herself. I'm surrounded by people who cannot look me in my darkening, purplish eye. I doubt it's because of the oddity I've become, with the swelling.

It's because too many people in my life are lying to me, and not for the first time.

29

My first true love, Annie, was an illusion. I met her just after medical school. She professed to cherish me with abandon, to get lost in me the same way she became overcome with emotion when she saw a puppy on the street or a baby elephant at the zoo. She hooked me completely. But true connection petrified her and she made a folly of it. She left me without even saying goodbye.

Then along came Polly. Unlike Annie, her self-confidence and zeal for life were real. She could be vulnerable but she ran her relationships with the same efficiency she ran her start-ups with, things mapped out and executed. Life was an exciting enterprise, growing quarter after quarter. Until it didn't.

"You're going to be fine and Isaac's going to be fine," she told me with the utmost confidence when it became clear that things were coming to an end. I was sitting on the edge of her bed, looking not at her, but through slats in the shades as traffic passed by.

What a lie.

"You're going to get yourself run over."

The voice shakes me back to the present. I'm standing in the street next to the Audi. Faith studies me like I'm some bizarre creature from the deep that she's watching on the Nature Channel. I wonder what lies she's telling me.

"Your eyes are glazed over and you're standing in the middle of the street."

"I'm fine."

"And I'm an African princess who can make you millions of dollars if you email me your social security number."

I walk around to the passenger side and climb in.

"I need to get to an Internet café."

"Who is that woman?"

I see Jill standing at the gate, glazed over, like me.

"She's mysterious clue number seven."

"What does that mean?"

"You tell me, Faith. Who is she?"

Faith punches the accelerator and the powerful Audi practically jumps twenty yards onto El Camino, the thoroughfare. Faith puts on a left blinker. "Usually I'm communicating better than this with someone when I start sleeping with him."

I swallow my retort: So why did we spend the night together? What are your motives, Faith?

Her phone rings. It's sitting in the cup holder between us. I pick it up. The caller ID says "Carl_L."

"Ignore it, please," Faith says.

I replace the phone. Faith takes a sharp right and

pulls to the curb. We're sitting in front of a cubbyhole of a café. In the window, a teenager sits at a
counter, tooling away on a computer.

"I'll wait here." Faith picks up her phone as I step
out of the car.

Behind the café counter, a man in his fifties cradles a book about quantum physics. He's probably
one of the overqualified engineers that this region
can periodically thrust into low-paying jobs when
the start-up economy tanks.

He looks up. "Shatter the orbital?" he asks.
Diagnosis-wise, he's quick on the draw, a rare out-
flanking that makes me feel flush. I decide not to
mention the hunch in his shoulder that I suspect
comes from a mild case of kyphosis, an outward
curvature of the spine. I order a large coffee and
twenty minutes of Internet time.

I also ask to use the café fax. The man shows me
an antiquated machine in a cubicle near the back
where there is a stapler, hole punch, copier, and a
sign: "Business Center." From my back pocket,
I pull the piece of paper I found on Alan's desk. I
make a copy of the Chinese characters. I fax them
to Bullseye.

At the front of the café, I settle in next to the
teenager locked in eerie focus as he shoots cartoonish birds from a slingshot at a target, the casual
game *du jour*. For a moment, I imagine what his
brain must look like, coursing with dopamine, the
sensory cortices lit up.

I settle my hands over the smudge-stained key-
board and look at the thin screen, as if preparing

to mount a horse. Into Google, I call up a Chinese-English translator. I spend a couple of minutes trying to figure out how to enter in the Chinese characters but find myself stymied. I'll let Bullseye handle this part of the goose chase.

I return to Google. I enter "Alan Parsons" and hit return. Big shock: I get infinite hits, many for the rock band of the same name. I try "Alan Parsons" and "Computer," and get an equal number of responses.

I need my bad guys to have very unique names, or at least not be named after popular eighties rock bands that, adding insult to injury, I always disliked.

I try "Alan Parsons" and "Andrew Leviathan." There's nothing of interest. I'm fishing.

"Andrew Leviathan" and "Sandy Vello" come up empty, and so does "Andrew Leviathan" and "PRISM," the corporation where the reality-show star works.

I put in "Andrew Leviathan" and "China." Tens of thousands of hits. I click on the first several, which are news stories from local newspapers, and one in the *New York Times*, in which the Silicon Valley icon has commented on the importance and challenges to technology entrepreneurs of breaking into the Chinese market.

"It's the Valhalla, the ethereal empire beneath the sea," he says of China. "It's the promised land, but you can't figure out how to get there, or if it's even real."

Andrew is a peculiar breed of source that journalists love. He is a "quote monkey," someone who can be counted on to say things in such a pithy and accessible way that the quotes elevate a mediocre story to a compelling one.

And yet, for a quote monkey of such brilliant success, Andrew is relatively sparsely quoted. He's picked his spots carefully. Perhaps not surprising, though. The biggest venture capitalists and others here follow a predictable course in their relationship with the press: they court journalists when it serves their ends in growing their first businesses, grow bored and squeamish of the relationship with media when their businesses boom and when reporters start asking tougher questions, and then, when they are so big that media can no longer harm their efforts, reestablish ties with a few reporters they trust.

It's this last bit of the evolution that fascinates me; they establish close ties with the media again because they want, more than anything else, a legacy. The riches—the stately house in picturesque Atherton, the $140,000 electric car, the co-owned jet kept at the Palo Alto Airport—all start to feel empty and they chase instead history's stamp of approval.

But Andrew is so infrequently quoted that I wonder if he's the rare success story who doesn't want or need ultimate validation from the media. Or maybe there's some other reason he's cautious about having intimacy with the press.

Outside the café, Faith sits in the car, talking animatedly on the phone. I've let her waltz into my life—rather, I've pulled her without reservation onto the dance floor—and aside from her beauty, she's a blur.

Across the street from the café, two moms and their toddlers file into a bookstore. A cutout of Winnie the Pooh hangs in the window.

I glance down the list of Google hits and something catches my eye. It's a reference to Andrew Leviathan and the China-U.S. High-Tech Alliance. It's a press release from four years ago announcing that Andrew has taken a board seat on the alliance, which, the press release explains, is aimed at "fostering ties of mutual interest."

The China-U.S. High-Tech Alliance—the placard on the outside of the building in Chinatown. Right before I got slugged in the face.

Back to Google. I try various other ways to connect the lines between the Chinese alliance and Andrew. I get one hit. It's another press release—from a year ago. It's just one paragraph that notes Andrew has resigned his board seat. The release reads: "Mr. Leviathan has been replaced by Gils Simons, a prominent angel investor who provided key early funding and counsel to eBay, Google and PayPal."

Gils Simons. Andrew Leviathan's early right-hand and operations man, the bland bean counter who had been at the awards ceremony. Interesting. Maybe. I wonder why the press release doesn't mention the connection between them.

Maybe a subject I'll ask Andrew about when we meet for coffee. I look at the clock on the computer and realize I've got twenty minutes to get to the nearby Peet's to see the programmer-turned-entrepreneur-turned-billionaire-turned-mystery man.

Into Google, I try one more search: "Andrew Leviathan" and "charity" and "school." Up pop tons of mentions about his investment in a half dozen well-regarded schools in the Bay Area that help low-income kids. It's all part of the man's vibrant philanthropy, hailed by educators and parents and scholars. But rarely by Andrew himself. The few stories I call up make note that the genius philanthropist prefers not to comment but, rather, to let his charity speak for itself. And, the articles note, the charity speaks loudly to a single point: Andrew, the immigrant genius, has become the champion of American children, committed to world-class education.

I'm trying to make sense of any of it. Andrew builds his school just a few months after Kathryn Gilkeson, his administrator's daughter, walks into the street and gets killed. Sounds innocuous enough. He found a cause, became wildly acclaimed for it—big deal, right? So why the dead man from the subway, and the bizarre Chinese connection, and the weirdo reality-show contestant? Why won't my brain work? Why can't I piece any of this together? Does it fit together?

And Jesus, that girl, that poor, poor Kathryn, who impulsively ran into the street and turned her mother into a shell.

I look up and out the window.

Then I see it. Or, rather, him.

Across the street, on the sidewalk in front of the bookstore, stands a boy. He wears overalls and a jockey cap.

Not just any boy. It's not possible.

He takes a step toward the street.

"No!"

I scramble to my feet. It cannot be. I'm at the doorway of the café. I'm on the sidewalk. The boy takes a tentative step off the sidewalk, into the street. Not just any boy.

"Isaac!"

A car comes screaming from the right. It's heading toward my son.

I sprint across the street. I fly. I'm practically in midair, my feet only touching the ground, my vision narrowed to a point, head screaming. I hurl myself in the path of the car; it screeches, swerves. I lope and gasp toward Isaac. I scoop him up with one arm.

He screams.

"It's okay. It's okay." I cradle him. I look into his face. I see blue eyes filled with terror, quivering lips, the round heaving nostrils filling with snot bubbles. Tender features, innocent and beautiful, but not ones I recognize.

"Henry. Henry. Come here. Come to Mamma."

It's a quavering voice pushing the limits of the vocal cord, a protective lioness poised to pounce.

"What's wrong with you?" she accuses me.

"He . . ." I start, then pause, then see Faith approach, quickly, darting from across the street.

"Your son looked like he was going to walk into the street," Faith says to the boy's mother.

"I had him under control."

Faith takes my hand and leads me away. Before we reach the car, I withdraw from her, willing myself for objectivity and clarity, about her, about everything.

30

I slip into the driver's seat and coax the keys from Faith.

"It's off-limits."

"What's off-limits?"

I don't answer as I take a left from El Camino Real onto University, a swanky commercial strip. Here, entrepreneurs with full hearts sketch business plans to fill garages first with start-ups and then with BMWs those start-ups eventually afford. Back-of-the-napkin central.

The energy here is so vibrant and so enervating. The entrepreneurs reject propositions that aren't "game changers" or aren't "fundamentally disruptive," then turn ones and zeroes into dollar signs, then, upon realizing their dreams, settle into a stifling and predictable suburban lifestyle; they raise children who can feel like failures if they don't take full advantage of the advantages. At the main high school in Los Altos, there was a suicide and two copycats by accomplished students, all heading to the best colleges. Now I remember. When their peers were asked why, they responded: every time we accomplish something it feels mostly like a doorway to the next test.

"What's off-limits, Nat?"

"Isaac. My family, such as it is."

"Okay, but . . ."

"No."

"We already talked about him." Muttered.

I assume she is referring to the idea that we, apparently, spoke about Isaac during the blur that was last night. No more—no more blur, no more offhand or concussion-fueled personal revelations, the information exchange now goes in only one direction. I'm laser-focused, I tell myself. I'm in total control of the only thing I've ever been halfway decent at, pulling up rocks people don't want unearthed. My personal rocks will remain entrenched.

"That's him." I gesture with a nod.

"Isaac?"

"Andrew Leviathan."

He sits at a table in the sun at a corner café. As we pass, he sips a drink and flips newspaper pages.

I take a right on Cowper and pull into a parking spot.

"Give me fifteen minutes."

"No." Faith's arms are crossed. "Do you remember hearing about Timothy and the music triangle?"

I have no idea what she's talking about. With a locked stare, she reminds me that Timothy is her nephew and that she and I had discussed him briefly last night.

"I told you about the argument he got into with

a music teacher who said Timmy wouldn't stop hitting the triangle. He's got Asperger's. They know that. The teacher grabbed him by the arm and shook him."

"I remember." I don't, mostly.

"To Timmy, that kind of discipline comes out of the blue. So I went to the school, to the teacher's office and I took her by the arm to show her what it feels like to be physically handled when we don't understand what's going on."

"And so you're not willing to wait fifteen minutes?"

"I'm here to protect myself and my family, not because you're a great lover. If you want me to keep waiting for you then you need to start telling me what's going on in these mystery meetings."

"You're after information."

"Aren't you?"

"I'll tell you about my meetings and you tell me more about Alan Parsons, and about whoever keeps calling you on your phone, and what is motivating you to stay so close to an investigation that seems to be making your life more dangerous, not less."

"Fifteen minutes."

I open the car door.

"Nathaniel." She forces me to catch her eye. "Even with a head wound, you are, in fact, a really great lover."

The main thing that this brunette is fucking is my head.

In the half second between the moment that I reach Andrew Leviathan and he looks up to greet me, I realize I have absolutely no plan.

"Nathaniel." He seems unsurprised and to slightly recoil, the *Palo Alto Daily News* open on his table.

"I figured you for an iPad."

"Too much of that stuff will burn out your brain. What happened to your eye?"

"Fell down the stairs."

He blinks, furrows his brow, purses his lips—the pantheon of mildly disbelieving facial expressions. He wears a stark white-collared polo shirt that shows biceps I'm guessing were sculpted by a personal trainer.

"You want to grab a coffee?"

I shake my head. I pull out a chair, seeking conversational footing.

"I was mugged. Maybe someone heard I won the journalism award and figured I was carrying a bunch of cash."

"Mugged? C'mon."

I tell him the truth; I got slugged in Chinatown.

"Just a random attack?"

"I'm being followed."

He looks at me, then around us. It's a natural reaction, and I follow his gaze. Parked cars line the street. None of them a black Mercedes.

"You're being followed now?"

I shake my head. "Earlier, last night. By someone who was at your awards luncheon."

He takes me in.

I tell him there was a man sitting at one of the front tables at the lunch. He stuck in my memory because he had a shiny bald head and an interesting, elongated walk. I explain that I noticed him twice outside my office, and then he followed me in a black Mercedes.

"How can I help, Nathaniel?" He must be used to getting all manner of weird questions from people who work for him and think he has the power to change their lives.

I tell him that I'd like to get a list of attendees, particularly anyone whose name he doesn't recognize.

"I'm not sure I'm comfortable with that." Before I can respond, he adds that he'll look into it. I doubt he'll be much help, but it's not really, or exclusively, what I'm looking for in this meeting. I'm here to look into his eyes.

"Andrew, to your knowledge was there anyone at the lunch associated with ties to the Chinese government or any Chinese investor groups?"

He tilts his head.

"I ran into a guy the other day named Alan Parsons. He wanted me to look into a story about some interesting technology coming out of China. I wonder if it's connected to the guy who is following me."

I'm mostly making this up or experimenting with logic. Andrew's pupils constrict slightly, indecipherable.

"So some guy that wants to see what reporting you're up to follows you into an awards banquet? Why not wait outside?"

"Maybe he heard they were serving salmon."

"What?"

"Never mind." I'm not sure why I stepped on my own interrogation with a bad joke. Maybe I'm not asking a fair question, about how someone with ill intent could get into the lunch. After all, it was essentially open. It even served as easy hunting grounds for the rotund process server who chased me down to let me know I somehow owe back taxes.

Andrew shrugs. "Can you tell me more about the story you're doing?"

"I wish." I laugh, mostly genuinely. "This is one of those backward stories."

"How do you mean?"

"Someone seems really upset at the idea of me learning something. I'm working backward from that point. The theory being that the more someone doesn't want you to know something, the potentially more interesting it is."

"But you don't know what something you're looking for?"

I let his question linger, then hear a buzzing. From a pocket, Andrew extracts a BlackBerry, looks at the screen, pauses, gives his device the thousand-yard stare. Is he thinking how to respond or using the opportunity to strategize about our conversation? He taps something back.

I have a sudden visceral reaction that I don't want to overplay my hand, not yet. I'm deciding not to broach the issue of the dead girl and his charitable work with the schools, or Sandy Vello. I need some cards for future conversations with Andrew, and I'm feeling at this point there will be more. I've got him engaged, curious, even if he's playing me too.

"Are you feeling okay?"

I realize I've been floating, mind wandering, my gaze resting on a newspaper rack.

"Dandy."

He nods, lips pursed. "Off the record. Okay?"

I nod.

"You ever have your arms lifted behind your back?"

I shake my head.

"The first night when I was in prison, in Romania, two beefcakes spent the night pulling my arms over my head, proving their mettle by trying to tear off the scrawny arms of a computer geek."

"That's off the record?"

"I pissed myself. I was delirious with pain." He clears his throat. "I had this plan to break out by getting help from one of the guards by promising I'd hack into a bank and wire his family a hundred thousand dollars. But the problem was that I got so delirious I couldn't tell which guard was most likely to go for it. The question was, Which guard would show pity on me and which would more likely turn me in for a slightly larger apartment with a river view?"

"How'd you figure it out?"

"You know how computers make decisions?"

I shake my head.

"Simple math. Probabilities. Sure, the fancy ones, like Deep Blue, mix in some algorithms that calculate, if you will, the unpredictability of a human behavior. They factor for chaos. But it's still ultimately about the numbers. What is the best probability of effecting a certain outcome?"

"Okay."

"Do you know how children make decisions?"

I feel suddenly warm. Don't talk, Nat, let him ramble.

"Their frontal lobes aren't developed yet. So they can't make long-term calculations. They don't think in terms of goals or priorities, certainly not numbers. They react to primitive emotions, like what interests them on a sensory level, or what seems like a safe or trustworthy situation." He pauses. "Or person. So as I'm sitting in my own piss, I tried to set aside a lifetime trying to think like a supercomputer and tried to think like a baby. I asked myself, which man feels to me like he'd be the best dad? Which would feel most comfortable for me to turn to were I his child?"

"And?"

"And I chose the other guy. I figured the guy most likely to care for his family would take the apartment with the river view. The other guy would see the situation more coldly."

He doesn't finish the story. History has shown he chose the right guy.

He stands. "Sometimes it's hard to tell the good guys from the bad guys."

I let his allegory wash over me.

"Especially if you're delirious." I give voice to his apparent lesson. "You think I'm delirious?"

He smiles, all white teeth and trust, charisma incarnate, the friendly genius, the omnipotent, warning me that things don't seem right with me.

"You're an investigative journalist. Isn't delirium an occupational hazard?"

He extends his hand. We shake, firm, but he avoids eye contact.

"I'll be in touch," he says.

Back at the car, I find a parking ticket on the windshield and Faith asleep in the passenger seat. A ribbon of brown hair cascades across her face, moving slightly with each exhale.

I gently open the driver's seat door; she stirs but doesn't wake up. In the cup holder, I spy her cell phone. At this point, all's fair; with one eye on sleeping beauty, I lift her phone to explore her recent communications.

31

I scroll through the recent calls. What stands out are the calls from "Carl_L," including two last night after midnight. There also are two calls this morning from Mission Day School. If memory serves, it's the school her nephew attends.

Faith stirs. I lower the phone. She settles back down, and I lift the device again. I check her voice mails. She's cleared all but one—from last night from "Carl_L." I lower the phone's volume, and hit play on the voice mail.

A male voice says: "Stop playing around, Faith. You're running out of time." The caller hangs up.

I play it again. I can't gauge how stern the warning sounds. The hostility of the words, and their brevity, suggest something very threatening, but the voice sounds plaintive, even desperate.

Faith stirs, and rolls toward me, curling into a quasi-fetal position. I feel an intense urge to close my eyes, put my head next to her, wake up on an island.

What or who is haunting you, Faith? Who are you? Why are you running out of time? To do what?

I put down her phone but leave it open. I reach for my phone and into it copy the number for "Carl_L" and hit send to initiate a call, then quickly end it. I close Faith's phone.

I reach into my wallet. I pull out the number for a different phone—the one I'd placed on the windshield of the Mercedes while it was parked in Chinatown.

In the compartment on the driver's-side door, I find some old earbuds among the compact discs. I plug them into my phone.

I start the car, drive ten minutes up University Avenue until I wind myself back to Highway 280. At the on ramp, I pause at a yield sign and punch into my phone the number for Buzzard Bill. I roll onto the highway and hit send.

The phone rings and rings. I end the call and hit redial.

It barely rings once when someone picks up. A voice says: "How was Peet's?"

The café where I met Andrew.

"Fine, but their French roast has too much aftertaste."

"You didn't order coffee."

"You were there?"

"We're everywhere."

We.

I look in the rearview mirror. I'm sloping up a hill just past the exit for Atherton, struck by how rural this area can suddenly become. City and suburb one second, endless stretches of Golden State the next. Here, peaceful terrain and powerful sports cars.

I see only one car in the distance but can't make

it out. To the right of the highway, there's a sharp drop-off that levels off, then widens into a meadow green with tall grass, and then the green terrain begins a gradual climb into the foothills. To my left, a steep ravine covered with bushy green heritage trees opens onto the northbound highway. Peaceful indeed, but if I had to make a quick maneuver on this stretch, I could easily torpedo off the edge.

"Who are you?"

"Like you want my name and stuff?"

"Bill, right? I'll settle for what you want and why you're following me."

"I want you to make sure to get some rest."

"Buy me a pillow."

"You really have no idea, do you?"

"I really don't."

"You're not seeing things clearly."

"Come out in the open and things will get clearer."

"Okay."

I check the rearview mirror. The car behind me is gaining. Faith sleeps. I'm nearing the crest of the hill. "Do you work with Alan Parsons?" With a toe tap, I push the car from sixty-five to seventy.

"No. But I liked his style."

"Liked?"

"As you know, he's deceased."

I cruise into a shallow dip that curves right and then begins a long slope upward. The car in my rearview mirror is a sports car, maybe a Ferrari, exploding over the hill, then passing me with ease to my left.

"Did you kill him?"

"Of course not."

"But he discovered something. He stumbled onto some information. He wanted to give it to me, or maybe he gave it to me. It's information you don't want me to know or make public."

"It doesn't take an award-winning journalist to figure that out."

"What does he want me to know?"

"That's your job. Not mine."

"What's your job?"

"To protect you."

"Protect me from what?"

"Mostly yourself."

I reach the hilltop. Behind me, I see a flash of light, a silver grill, reflecting sun. The car seems to leap over the top of the hill, one lane to my left. I swerve hard to my right. The car, a sport utility vehicle, speeds past me. A gas guzzler, not Bill.

I hear and feel gravel beneath the tires and swerve hard left to straighten the car and avoid sending me and slumbering Faith to our deaths. I watch the innocuous SUV disappear ahead of us. False alarm, high-risk paranoia at high speeds.

"Mr. Idle?"

"Do you work for Leviathan? Does this have to do with the girl who got hit by a car a decade ago?" I pause, working out my thoughts. "Was it not an accident? Was Leviathan somehow responsible? Is he involved in something with the Chinese? Maybe involving Gils Simons, the old team back together again?"

"You're confounding things. You're all over the place. Pointedly, you're not stable."

I look down the ravine into the southbound lane. A pack of a half dozen cars pass, tightly packed. Human nature abhors a gap.

"Getting attacked twice in one week has a way of doing that."

"True, but you haven't been the same for months."

"Cut the bullshit."

"Not since . . ." He pauses.

"You know you've got a skin condition. It's why your scalp gets so oily."

"Not since your family fell apart." He matches my non sequitur with one of his own. A hot sensation courses through my body, sizzles my brain in an instant of light. I blink. I'm swerving again to the right onto the gravel at the highway's edge, and pull the car back to the left.

I feel a hand on my knee. I look down to see Faith, waking up but still half asleep, alarmed.

The man says: "You're dangerous now—to yourself and others. You need to focus. You've lost the ability to trust or to know who to trust. Are you honestly trusting that trollop?"

"Who?"

"To get what she wants, she'll do anything, with anyone."

Faith sits up, rubs her eyes, looks at me, like, what the hell is going on?

The man presses on: "Can you honestly tell me that your brain is working correctly? Can you tell me you've seen things clearly since your utopian fantasies were set ablaze? It's why you see Wilma, right?"

Wilma. Dr. Jurgenson, a friend and source. I get together with her periodically to talk about life, stories, whatever. What's she got to do with this?

"Leave my family out of this." I want it to sound like a threat but it's plaintive.

"Mr. Idle, you've completely lost your grip on reality. You can no longer tell the good from the bad."

Another hot flash. Isn't that just what Leviathan said while we were having coffee?

I don't respond.

"Vello," the buzzard says. "She's the key. Find her. Immediately."

"The key to what?"

"Whatever you do, don't print anything until you talk to me. I want to help. I'll be watching, or call me on this phone. I can be a good source but if you print lies you'll do the world a great disservice, and you'll make us very, very angry."

"Us?"

"Vello. Twin Peaks," he says, "and one more thing."

"What's that?"

"Wave."

I look in the rearview mirror. No cars. I hear a honk. I look down on the northbound lane. A black Mercedes flies by. The phone goes dead.

I look to my right and see the exit for Edgewood Road. I slam the brakes, fishtail violently, but manage to make the exit.

"Nathaniel, what the hell are you doing?" Faith demands.

I take a quick left at a stop sign, cross under the freeway and speed onto the highway going south.

32

"Who was that?"

"Who is Carl?"

I'm flooring it, southbound, chasing a phantom. He's nowhere to be seen.

The speedometer sneaks to ninety.

"Slow down."

No sooner has she said it than I see the flashing light in the rearview mirror, a quick end to my high-speed chase. I pull over, put my hands on the wheel, wait for the cop to lumber to Faith's window. When he pokes his beak through, I see the quarter-inch pink surgical scar across the center of his thick neck—from the removal of a mass of some kind. He asks for my license and registration.

Faith interjects: "It was my fault. I'm so sorry."

He looks at her. Demurely, she lowers her eyes, then glances up at him, touches her fingertips to her lips. It's like physical double entendre: on one level, contrite; on another, raw erotica.

"Your fault?"

"I . . . I'm embarrassed."

"I've heard it all. Tell me." She's got him.

"I told my brother I had to pee, badly." She glances at me, then back at the cop. "When I start pleading in the little girl voice, it can be tough to ignore me." She smiles, then lowers her eyes again. The cop takes my license and registration, pretends to give a long look, doesn't bother to check his on-board computer, and leaves me with a stern warning.

"There's a rest stop a mile up," he says to her. To me, he adds: "Lighten up on the accelerator." He walks to his car and pulls off.

"I really do have to pee."

"You're dangerous."

"I'm not the one chasing ghosts at high speeds."

No longer. Ghost long gone. I pull onto the highway.

"Who is Carl?"

"You've been going through my phone."

"He called while you were asleep." Small lie.

"Did you talk to him?"

I shake my head.

"He's an ex."

"Ex-boyfriend, ex-lover?"

"More or less. I don't want to dwell on the past."

"If he's still calling, it doesn't sound like it's in the past."

I see the sign for the rest stop. I decelerate onto the ramp. Just to the right, there's an enclave nestled against trees with a public restroom in a bland concrete building. I park. Faith grabs her phone and hops out of the car.

I watch her disappear. My head throbs. I unfurl the vanity mirror to see how damaged I look. A folded piece of paper slides from the visor. I unfold it to find a picture of Polly that appeared more than a decade ago in a magazine published by the Wharton School. Polly had been featured among female graduates of the business school with a headline, "Attacking The World With Style." In the picture, Polly wears that smile of hers that seemed to say: Today, I ran a triathlon and founded an Internet start-up, now let's go make love all night and don't you dare tire out on me.

I feel stung with a sensation well beyond sadness.

The door opens, startling me, and I drop the picture on the seat. I look at it, so does Faith.

Where did the picture come from? Did I leave it? Someone's fucking with me. I toss the picture into the back.

"I'm not interested in dwelling on the past either."

"Nat." She kneels on the seat, facing me.

"Sandy Vello."

"What about her?"

"That's our present and our immediate future. Give me your phone."

"Why?"

"I can't use mine. I want to call Sandy."

I'm using Faith's phone because I'm worried that someone is following my activities on mine. It's also why I'm not using my laptop. Still, I'm sure it can't be hard to track me. I must continue to assume we're not alone. Faith hands me her phone.

I plug in Sandy's number and hit send. As I wait for an answer that doesn't come, Faith puts her hands on mine, holding my shaking fingers.

"My sister's a collector," she says.

I withdraw my hand and end the call.

"A collector of what?"

"Everything. Stuff she buys on the shopping channel, or gets at garage sales, junk mail, containers from places she gets take-out food, everything. In her flat, you literally have to wade through crap to get from room to room."

I start the car. Faith untucks her legs, sits, fastens her seat belt. Time to head onto the highway, heading north again, in the direction of the Twin Peaks Youth Guidance Center, where some buzzard turned self-proclaimed guardian angel has urged me to track down a TV diva. Beats dwelling on the past.

I've heard of this psychological collecting condition, if not a neuro-chemical one. They tend to believe that the things they collect might someday come in handy and so they don't toss anything. The condition, like so many that humans suffer, isn't that hard for most of us to connect to, if we really think about it. Who among us hasn't struggled over whether to hang on to an old wallet or ragged T-shirt, wondering whether it might provide some future use?

I hit the accelerator and we pull out of the rest stop.

"Why are you telling me this?"

"She, my sister—Melanie—has trouble taking care of her son, my nephew, Timothy."

"Okay."

"Pull the car over." Pointed.

"Why?"

"I'm trying to tell you something."

"So tell me."

"I'm trying to tell you about me."

"I need to pull the car over for that?"

I do the opposite, I merge onto the highway. She doesn't speak for a moment. I look over at her, head slightly hung, exasperated. I feel at once like I'm on my first date with this woman and like I've dated her for years. I can read her emotions, and feel desperate to connect to them. And just as desperate to escape them.

I look in the rearview mirror at the thickening highway traffic. Where's Bill? Does he have a crew, a team? In the yellow roadster? Or the pickup truck jacked two feet off the ground, or the white van with tinted windows and no front license plate?

"Faith?"

"You don't trust anything, or anybody."

I laugh. "You set me up at a subway, haven't been totally clear on why that is or how it happened, lead me to a dead man, then manage to be lingering when I get knocked unconscious, pick up the pieces and seduce me into saying and doing who knows what while I'm still half dead."

"Jesus. What happened to you?"

"What's that mean?"

"What happened that you lost all your trust in people?"

The blood drains from my face. I can feel it, the cells slipping from my ears and cheek and neck and draining into my aching stomach. I want to tell her to fuck herself when I feel my phone buzz.

"Hold the wheel."

"What?"

I withdraw my hands from the wheel and pull out my phone. Faith takes the wheel and I read my text. It's from Bullseye. It reads: "Chinese characters = interesting."

I tap back: Means what?

I take back the wheel. "How's that for trust? I let you drive."

She sighs.

"Nathaniel, when I first saw you on the subway you looked at me and I thought: Encyclopedia Brown."

I glance behind me at the cluster of cars. The van with the tinted windows flies out of it and passes me. Its side reads: "Broom Town—Floor Care Specialists." Maybe.

"You've got curious eyes, passionate, but they're boyish and innocent. Even if I'd not been asked to intercept you, I'd have wished we'd met. Every woman wants to meet a man who wants to understand her and will dig deep to do it."

"You're an actress with an unusual relationship with someone named Carl."

"I'm a transition specialist who is low on work."

I take the exit into Glen Park, a former working-class-neighborhood-abutting-the-freeway-turned-trendy-San-Francisco-enclave. I turn up O'Shaughnessy, heading to Twin Peaks and Sandy. As we wind tree-cornered hillsides on the city's southern edge, patchy cloud cover gives way to a foggy carpet.

"You think you can't trust an actress? I've done a few commercials, and do you know why I started acting?"

It's rhetorical, but I shake my head. She says that when she discovered her nephew's struggles with learning, she did a bunch of reading and learned the best way to focus kids is with pretend play. The idea, it seems, is that kids get so entranced in a pretend world—whether acting like they're tossing a ball to one another or pretending to be animals on an adventure—that it teaches the brain to stay on a single subject and develops neural networks accordingly.

She decided to take an acting class. A director who would drop in occasionally spotted her and asked her to be in a commercial.

"Yeah, well, we could use an actress right about now."

"What?"

"Can you play a delivery driver, or an aggrieved mom so desperate to see her incarcerated son that it distracts the guards and gets me inside this place?"

We're at the entrance of juvenile hall. To our left, the high-gate of the maximum-security entrance, a cop again parked out front. To our right, the driveway to the learning annex, dominated by a white wide-load delivery truck lurching just in front of us. It continues through the parking lot, along an access road that abuts the right side of the annex.

I park between a roadster with a roadrunner painted on the door and a school bus, probably ferrying students to afternoon programs here.

"Where are we?"

Figuratively, we're at the point where I take Sandy by the neck and start to demand answers. I step from the car, smooth down my shirt, a reflexive maneuver I imagine enhances my professionalism. I pull sunglasses from a shirt pocket and don them.

"I'll stay in the car."

"Join me."

Faith sighs. She steps from the car, lips pursed. Each time she accedes to go along with me, I trust her less. But this time she's going to come in handy. She can be partner and decoy to allow me to find and focus on Sandy.

Just then, a better option for breaching the learning annex presents itself. The building explodes.

33

A siren wails.

I orient. Black smoke swirls in the form of a twister from the back of the annex.

"The delivery truck."

"What?" I can read Faith's lips but can't actually hear over the siren or stunned eardrums.

I sense movement and turn to see a police cruiser and a van careening up the driveway behind me, followed by the din of another oncoming siren.

I run up the concrete staircase leading from the lot to the heavy annex doors. As I near them, they swing open. A mousy woman I think I recognize from my previous visit bounces out, blinking, waving. "I'm sending them this way." I don't take her meaning until the first boy juts through the doorway. Then another, then a stream. Most in their early teens wearing blue uniforms. Hooting and hollering. Mingled with them, a few younger kids in street clothes. No Sandy. Something tells me she's in there, in the back, where smoke mingles with gurgles and pops.

I press myself against the open door, avoiding the scrum. Waiting for my moment. It comes shortly, a lull in the dense parade. I head into the stream, and the annex. Inside the doors, ordered chaos. The mousy woman directs a thinning group of boys to safety. Their diminishing numbers, coming from a set of double doors that lead to the inside, suggest most have cleared out already.

The mousy woman looks at me. Then her eye catches an oversized teen carrying two cans of paint—arts-and-crafts class, I think—but she clearly sees the tools of imminent prank or vandalism and, comically, snags the boy's huge arm in her own wiry talon. I whisk by her, skirt a handful of blue-clad boys, slip into the guts of the annex.

Temporary walls and smoke. A long hallway, beneath the cavernous ceiling, bisects classrooms separated by some cheap material, rollers at the bottom that give the place a hollow, tinny feeling. I peek into the room on the right. A library. Books on the walls, the floors, a bookshelf yanked down. I'm about to turn away when I see the boy. Under a table, rocking, a book in his lap that he's reading or cradling. "Hey!" No recognition, his eyes remain down. I take a half dozen steps to him. He looks up. Says something.

"What? You've got to go."

"It's mine." He pulls the book to his chest. An illustrated *Treasure Island*.

"You have to get out. It's all yours. Take it with you."

I cough, once, twice, a couple of more times for effect. The thickening smoke will be dangerous in another few minutes.

Then: Boom! A mid-sized explosion comes from the back of the building. Like an appliance erupting, something localized. The boy crawls out, stands, sprints past me, clutching the book. I follow him back into the hallway. He heads to the exit. I head the other way, now not a soul in sight. Smoke pours from a room near the back. And within it, a figure, walking, emerging. I blink. Is it a boy? He looks translucent, an apparition. Isaac?! I blink again. The image is gone, just my imagination coming out of the smoke. I wretch out a cough. A thin carpet of gunpowder-colored smoke coats the high ceilings, resolving into a gray fog as it floats lower to the ground.

I'm about to pass the next room on the left. Better check. Inside, a small kitchen, refrigerator, microwave, bag lunches on a folding table, a break room for the staff. No boys. Move on. A few steps more down the hallway, the next room on the right. An open doorway. Inside, folding tables and chairs, easels around the edges, pails on the tables filled with pencils, pens and markers, paint cans in the corner on a drop cloth. No boys. Nothing to see here. But then, my eye catches something on the outside, through the windows. A hulking figure, a stout man wearing a blazer, carrying a briefcase. He looks out of place. I know his actual place: an alley in Chinatown. The man who blackened my eye. He's moving by the window, quickly, looks up, must sense me, staring in my direction. Can he see me? He semi-smiles, cocks his head.

There's another explosion.

The stout man propels forward, like a projectile, but still on his feet. He's not felled, not even thrown, just accelerated, toward the front of the building, like a bad special effect in a 3-D movie. I duck to avoid a smattering of shattered glass. I reorient, not really in danger, the explosion having come from the outside, the back of the building. I'd bet my fees for a hundred blog posts that's where Sandy is.

I scramble back into the hallway. I sprint into the darkening air to the last two doors on the right, covering my mouth. I ignore the heat wave growing by degree with each step. I reach a door two rooms away from the one pouring the lion's share of the smoke and now, I can see, licks of orange flame.

"Help!" A voice rises over the gurgles and pops. I blink away the heat and peer through the door. Sandy stands at the other end of a room. Trapped.

Between her and me is a wooden desk, or what remains of it. It's fully enflamed. It's on its side, blocking her path to the door. Outside, more trouble. A burning delivery van, white and wide-load, like the one I saw driving up here earlier, pressed against the building. Its nose is smashed into a gas pump. A diesel pump. The explosion explained? Instant guess: bad man from Chinatown drives van into pump?

I focus back on the narrow room where Sandy stands. It's separated from the one next to it only by the shattered remains of a glass wall. It dawns on me what I'm looking at, and standing in the doorway of: an observation room. The glass wall allowed whoever sat in this narrow room to look at whatever

was happening in the much larger room just to my
left, the one that is consumed with flames. I squeeze
my eyes shut to protect my retinas, dispel the heat.
I open them and look at the enflamed room and see
only a puzzle of images: long cafeteria tables with
lines of burning laptops on top of them; on the far
end, a pile of handheld devices that look from here
like portable video game players; walls painted with
murals, going up in flames, including an image of
an imposing but smiling ninja juggling a half dozen
balls, his black ponytail curling up in flames. Below
the Ninja, tinged with flames, I can make out the
painted words: "Masterful Juggler."

A computer at the far end of a table pops with
a mini-explosion. On the floor, in the far corner,
a freestanding little kids' basketball hoop burns. It
looks like a scarecrow, demonic.

I pick up a scent, something unnatural.

Chemical fire. Something powerful and deliberate. The smashed diesel pump a decoy? An osten-
sible accident and an excuse for a fire?

I look back to Sandy.

"Are you okay?" I shout. She gives me a "what
the fuck are *YOU* doing here" look. She turns away
from me. She lifts a chair, like she's going to clear
away the jagged glass left in the window so she can
make her escape, then drops the chair. She looks at
me. "Save yourself!"

A minute ago, she yelled for help. Now she's
showing she's got it all taken care of, bravado in
front of a journalist, even now. I hear sound coming
from the hallway behind me, voices, feet. Friend or
foe? Before I can check, Sandy lifts the chair again,

spins it through the jagged window glass, creating a wide berth. She's got an exit. She's not taking it. Instead, she's throwing a metal storage box out of the observation room. Then another. They're filled with folders.

Sandy looks at me.

I feel a hand on my shoulder.

34

I whirl around. I'm met with a firefighter, a woman two inches taller than me, decked out in a flame-retardant brown jacket with yellow racing stripes. Freckle-dotted face, blurred skin on her upper neck near her right ear from a burn graft.

"Easy." She puts a hand on my back.

I look back at the narrow window in the observation room. Sandy's disappeared.

"I need to get in there."

"I don't think so."

She takes my right arm with a firm grip, not hostile. I pull out of it and step inside the observation room, but I'm actually looking inside the eerie computer-center-cum-recreation-room. Sandy had told me previously the company was teaching kids to multitask. If that's all this was, why the fuss, or the deliberate fire?

I peer inside, through intensifying smoke turning from gray to black. I make out a pile of cell phones on the corner of the table, glowing with fire, maybe explaining the metallic odor. On the floor, next to the table's edge, burns a train set, the wooden bridge somehow having escaped the fire. I can't take my eyes from it, when I feel the grip again on my right arm, stronger now, and then one on my left. Two firefighters. They practically pick me up and turn me around.

One of them puts a mask on my mouth and I inhale fresh oxygen. I gulp. The mask is pulled away, and they march me back down the annex hallway. The smoke starts to clear, giving way to chaos. Outside, men in uniform are corralling excited youth, seemingly with success, though one firefighter holds a sulking kid in a headlock. The female firefighter at my side offers me more oxygen. I greedily accept.

"What's your name?"

I pause. "Nat Idle." Instantly, I think: I shouldn't have given my name. I can't think. No telling how much new damage I've done my brain by depriving it the full measure of oxygen the last five minutes.

"Can you take a deep breath for me?"

I do. I cough but not excessively.

"You're going to be okay. Can you spend a moment talking to an investigator?"

It dawns on me that she's not checking my health status, at least not exclusively. She's wondering what I was doing at the origin of the fire. Maybe, or I'm being overly sensitive; my ability to make sense is flickering.

"Sure. Of course. May I have water?"

She nods. With a hand on my back, she gently pushes me toward the top of the stairs that lead to the parking lot. A few feet from the top of the stairs, a gaggle of emergency personnel gather around equipment and a snoozing Siberian Husky. I scan for Faith. Not among the kids being marched down the stairs. Not among the cops and firefighters milling and working at the front of the building. I crane to see down into the parking lot. Clumps of people, cars making their exit. No discernable Faith.

"Wait here." The firefighter makes sure I'm looking at her. I nod. Amid the group near where I'm standing, one firefighter says something to another, then they both laugh. From their relatively calm demeanor, I sense this isn't a calamitous fire. It's localized in the back, controllable, but still doubtless to get a lot of press attention given the setting. The firefighter who escorted me walks a few steps away, presumably to get me water or find an investigator or both. With her back to me, I take a few tentative steps down the stairs that lead to the parking lot. I run.

Seconds later, I'm at the Audi.

Still no Faith.

She's resourceful. Right? Got herself to safety. Or did she flee? Again?

I manage a five-point turn amid emergency vehicles and point the car down a long entrance road that seemed innocuous on the way in. At the far end of my only escape route stands a cop directing a handful of others trying to depart to park on the side. No one exits without an interview.

I pull down the visor and glance in the mirror. I look like a coal miner. I hear a tap on my window. Outside stands a cop with a rosy nose. My options stink. I can ignore him and try to zip past the car ahead of me, fly onto the road, attempt to outrace any officer who might not like that idea. Lose.

I roll down my window. I reach for my wallet and pull out a press pass. It identifies me as a freelance writer for the *San Francisco Chronicle*. It's long since expired. I'd asked for it two years ago when I did some semi-regular blogging on medical issues for the business section of their web site, SFGATE. I'd asked for the press pass mostly because I wanted something quasi-official to put on my windshield if I was ever in a parking pinch. The only two times I tried to use it for that purpose, I got parking tickets.

"Nat Idle. I write for the Chron. I'm late to file."

He glances at the pass. "You ever write about the Giants?"

"I wish. Great beat. You get free hot dogs."

He takes in my sooty face. "You were in there?"

"Trying to get a look."

He's lost interest. To him, this situation is bad luck, an annoyance that may keep him from getting home in time for dinner, not a conspiracy. I look at the maximum-security wing. It looks intact, not impacted by the localized explosion. "Pull over to the right and the guys will ask you a few questions and you can go."

"Got it."

I watch him wave to the cop ahead of us to let me through to another little grouping of cars awaiting exit interviews. I pull between a station wagon and a bus. Their drivers prattle on their phones. No one comes to interview me. I look over my shoulder. No one's watching. I slide into drive, slip between the cars, hit the open road, accelerate, don't look back.

I feel tightness, smoke inhalation and something I can't name—not physical—an emotion, or lots of emotions, threatening to explode out of the sealed Ziploc bag that is my chest. I look in the rearview mirror. No cops. But still. I'm acting with wild impulse, like the little girl in Palo Alto who walked into traffic. No wonder, maybe: I've taken a serious beating to my frontal lobe. I'm responding, reacting, darting from whim to whim, following bright lights and curious clues, being led around by my nose, without filtering anything through a mature and experienced brain. I'm playing a serious adult's game with a seriously regressed brain.

I turn left onto Market, thinking I might lose myself on a side street. But more impulse. I take a left onto Twin Peaks, the winding road that leads to a 360-degree view of this majestic city, and of one seriously powerful brain beam. Just to the west, the Sutro Tower, a looming radio transmitter that delivers us our virtual lives via radio and TV and that, near as any responsible scientist can tell, doesn't also deliver brain tumors as I figure it must in my most muckraking moments. Shy of the top of Twin Peaks, I pull into a gravel road marked "No access," and take a turn so I'm out of view of the main road. I step from the car and I wretch.

Dark smoke curls in the sky to my left, above the learning annex and prison, blocked from sight by a half mile of mountain and rolling topography. Dead ahead, the Golden Gate Bridge. To my right, the Bay Bridge. Escapes everywhere I can't take because

my brain—not geography or even circumstance—
holds me captive.

I glance at the Audi's passenger seat, at Faith's
knit hat. Is she right that I have no idea how or who
to trust?

I glance in the backseat. At Isaac's car seat.

I drop my head back and I loose a guttural yell, a
jumbled cacophony of energy, a deformed baby universe exploding from charcoal lungs.

I try to yell again, let out whatever is in there, but
it feels forced. I close my eyes, think, open them.

I pull my phone from my pocket. I scroll through
the address book until I find what I'm looking for. I
put the cursor on her number, and I hit send.

"Hello," a woman answers.

"Polly?"

"Who?"

"Goddamn it, Polly. Please."

"Did you call earlier?"

I don't recognize this voice.

"Where's Isaac?"

"What?"

"Where is my son?"

"You've got the wrong number. I've told you
before. Please don't call here again."

The phone goes dead.

I'm staring at the device. Hot tears on my cheek.
Where's my son? I can't believe Polly would do
this. I can't believe she'd change the number. Not
now. Or did she do that earlier, and I forgot? Why?
What could I have done to have deserved this humiliation? I can't let go, right, is that what she'd say?

I treat relationships like stories, pulling and tearing at them until I've left nothing but scorched Earth?

And is this why I can't trust—because Polly took everything from me without warning? Am I right not to trust?

I cock my arm back, device in hand, ready to fling it down the mountain. It rings.

"Polly," I answer.

"I'm sorry I lied to you," a woman's voice says. "My heart is true."

Not Polly, Faith.

35

On the downward sloping hillside in front of me, a white rabbit takes two awkward bounces, pauses, bends its neck down and licks its leg, hurt. Behind it, in the distance, rises downtown, gray and white buildings like a mouthful of crooked, dangerous teeth.

"Where are you, Faith? Lied about what?"

"I'm fine. Check Mission Day."

"Mission Day?"

I hear a shuffling on the other end. A male voice says: "See, she's okay." I recognize the voice. It's the man from Chinatown. "But she need your help." He leaves the "s" off "needs."

"Who is this?"

Laughter. "They're going to think you started the fire."

"I'll let the police know where to find you in Chinatown."

"Tell them to look for the Chinese man. That should make it no problem."

"What do you want?"

"Did you get those files?"

Files? Does he mean the ones Sandy has?

After a pause: "I got them."

"I need them."

"Did you kidnap Faith?"

Deep laugh. "Kidnap? This one does whatever she wants. But let's make a trade. Two hours?"

"I'm not sure what you're proposing. What kind of trade?" Faith for the files? What are they? But I'm trying to buy time.

"Meet at Baker Beach."

"Let me talk to her."

"Two hours. You know the place?"

"What? I can't hear you." It's not true.

"Baker Beach!"

"My phone reception gets very shaky in this area . . . and I . . ." I hang up.

It's impulsive and it won't buy me more than a few seconds. I need even those. What was Faith talking about when she said "Mission Day"?

Using my phone, I Google the phrase. It's an elementary school, fancy web site, private institution advertising the "Growing intellect through imaginary play." The school where Faith's nephew goes. Timothy, right? So?

I study the web site, struck by another simple possibility. Faith is trying to tell me to watch out for her nephew. She's told me that she tends to care for him because her sister is unreliable, kooky. Maybe Faith's sending me simple code; she's innocent and merely worried about a loved one.

But if she's so innocent, what did she lie about?

The phone rings. It's Faith's number again. I pick it up.

"Hello? Are you there?"

I hang up, feigning poor reception, buying more time, keeping a modicum of control in this uneven relationship. The phone rings again. I send it to voice mail. Less than a minute later, my phone beeps, letting me know that I've received a voice mail. I listen. "You don't have the files but you'll get them. You have until tomorrow morning or say goodbye to your Faith."

For a dude speaking broken English, he's stumbled into some solid wordplay.

But is the threat real? Will he hurt Faith, or is she helping him? Is she kidnapped or complicit?

Sandy, did you survive and take the files with you? What's in them? Did it relate to that surreal computer lab burning inside the learning annex? Maybe Sandy was targeted for her work at PRISM or maybe for her work at the prison, or both.

I call the main number for the prison. I ask for Doc Jefferson, the warden, who obviously is not available. I leave my name, number and affiliation: the guy who did the freelance story for the *New York Times* about the organic farm. He'll call me back at half past never.

I look out at the field, and let my eyes glaze over. The sun has begun to set. It's chillier than I realized. I feel the all-over body ache that adrenaline has been masking. My head pounds. I sit in the driver's seat. I close the door. I turn on the engine, put on the heat, tilt my seat back.

Reclined, I let my mind drift and I find it settling

on a June day a year earlier when I was nearly felled by a stuffed turtle. Polly and I stood in an aisle at Target in South San Francisco, looking at car seats. I wore Bermuda shorts, which would be suitable for June anywhere on the planet except for damp, gray San Francisco, where summers come to die. Polly glances at my attire and shakes her head.

"You'll dress our son for the weather, not the calendar." She smiles as I walk toward her to take her hand and assure her that I'll dress our son accordingly. A projectile comes flying through the air. Instinctively, I duck out of the way. Polly nearly doubles over with laughter. When I get my bearings, I see I've dodged a stuffed green turtle that lies on the floor next to me. A humiliated mother stands next to her four-year-old son, who'd thrown the furry critter.

"His dad's been teaching him to play catch." The woman scoops up the stuffed critter.

Polly looks so sad.

"What's the matter, Polly?"

"C'mon, Nat. You know. Things don't always work out the way you dream they will."

It's the last thing I picture before I fall asleep in the front seat of my ex's ex-Audi. In my dream, I'm sitting at the restaurant with Polly. She has something important to tell me. But there's something odd about her that takes a moment to place. She's wearing a costume on her head. It's an elaborate rubber dinosaur mask. She's a triceratops. I know this because I've recently bought a book for our unborn son and fantasized about memorizing the names of extinct beasts, like I once did with my dad.

The waiter with the rusty ankle limps over, carrying a white plate with a single brown fortune cookie. He's replacing Polly's first cookie, which was empty of a fortune.

"This one will be better." He puts down the plate.

Polly puts one of her beautiful, slender fingers on the table. She lifts the cookie.

"We should talk," she says. Or that's what I think she says; it's hard to hear under the mask.

"Open it, Polly." I'm so excited.

She cracks open the cookie. Inside, a tiny dinosaur. It smiles, like only a baby dinosaur can, with tiny, perfect teeth. "Hi, Daddy."

I reach out to grab the little guy. I want to brush the spikes on his tiny little head. I'm startled awake by ringing. It's dark outside. I'm suffocating from car heat. I notice the dashboard says 6:30 P.M. I reach for my phone. It's Bullseye.

"Want to know what the Chinese characters mean?"

36

"No." I sit up. Woozy. Shake my head for bearings. He doesn't respond.

"Not on this phone, Bullseye. Meet me Where the Sun Don't Shine."

He pauses, then says: "Now?"

"If not sooner. Please. Bring a laptop."

"Fuck you." He'll be there.

I hang up. One Sunday five years ago or so, I had tickets to a San Francisco 49ers game at Candlestick Park. I offered to take Bullseye. Samantha, his wife, my witch, implored him to go because, she said, he needed to explore light from some source other than the bar's televisions.

"Get some Vitamin D. It'll improve Ida and Pingala." Those aren't people, she informed us, but rather, energy centers associated with the Chakras. In plain old English, she wanted him to get some sun.

"Are you kidding?" Bullseye muttered. "Candlestick is the place the sun don't shine."

She laughed. "I always thought that was your wildly hairy butt."

For years, it became a joke at the bar. Candle-stick, frigid and wet, like the city but more so, was the place Where the Sun Don't Shine. "Shove it Where the Sun Don't Shine," someone would mutter and someone would say, "Bullseye's hairy ass?" and someone else would say, "Candlestick!" Begetting another round.

Groggily, I start the car. In the sky, I discern no residue from the fire. No dark cloud over the area of the juvenile facility.

On my way to the highway, I pass the Youth Guidance Center. In front, five cop cars and two fire trucks. No lights and sirens. It's inert here. I drive back down O'Shaughnessy, and turn on the radio. I try the various AM stations to hear vari-ous iterations of the same brief report about the fire at the Youth Guidance Center. Authorities say it was an unfortunate accident but a small, localized fire that injured no one and did modest property damage. Sandy must have survived.

I enter the highway. Minutes later, I detour through the drive-thru at In-and-Out Burger, order a double-double animal style, fries and a chocolate shake. I inhale them and ten minutes later, exit the highway again just south of San Fran-cisco. Just ahead, on the edge of the bay, looms a football stadium majestic in its setting and outdated in every conceivable way, structurally and in terms of its amenities. But it serves my purpose now in that it's devoid of humans, lonelier than after a loss to the Cowboys. I pull into one of the gravel over-flow parking lots and leave on my fog lights. Five minutes later, Bullseye pulls up in his baby, a meticulously restored 1972 Cadillac with crack-free red leather seats, an impeccable eight-track tape player, and dice hanging from the mirror.

Knowing that Bullseye likes to exert as little energy as possible, I unhook my seat belt and walk to the Caddie. I'm met with an unpleasant surprise. Samantha sits in the passenger seat. Her shoulders are wrapped in a ceremonial Indian scarf. She holds a deck of cards.

Bullseye opens the door a crack and shrugs, a kind of apology; he knows that I can't deal right now with Samantha's witchery, or the filial worry that seems to accompany all of the recent attention she's given me.

"Hi, Witch. No time for tarot."

"Solitaire." She smiles warmly. I doubt her words; she wouldn't be here if she didn't have some healing plan up her sleeve.

Bullseye steps from the car and pulls the seat forward so I can climb in back. Samantha looks at my scared and charred face, now bathed in the car's interior light. Her smile disappears. She looks down at her cards. What does a big sister tell a little brother who keeps screwing up?

"Let's hear it, Bullseye."

He sits back down and shuts the door, reaches under the front seat and lifts a razor-thin Apple laptop. It's open, the rectangular screen projecting a grayish green light in the car. He hands it to me, and I settle back with it in the seat. I see a graph.

Along the left are six Chinese characters and so too along the bottom. In the middle of the graph there are words to describe the intersection of the characters. I think I get that this means the interpretation of these symbols depends on the meaning of the individual Chinese characters, which themselves may have different meanings.

"From the Net?"

"Hacker friend from Beijing." In his tone, an atypical pride.

I look more closely at the possible meanings. At the bottom left of the graph, the meanings are so bizarre as to be worthless. The first reads: "Circle Haircut," then "Round Hemisphere Clown." One in the middle reads: "Fast Turtle Balance." They take only slightly more meaning as the graph moves to the right. The one on the farthest tip means "Brain Balance Drug," and "Earth God Drug."

I pause from reading when I sense movement in the car. Samantha steps out of the front seat, pulls it back, climbs next to me. She puts her right hand on my forehead, as if taking my temperature. She holds it there.

"What's interesting about this, Bullseye?"

"The gestalt—something my friend explained but that I didn't write down."

I wait for him to go on, and after a beat, he does. "It's a potent drug."

"What is?"

"He said if he had to interpret these characters, aside from what they denote, they seem to symbolize a transformation. Something that changes people."

"Like a psychedelic?"

"Like something that turns you into God."

I clear my throat, thinking.

"The hacker told me: picture a giant brain balancing the Earth."

"Balancing," I mutter. Then, just a bit more loudly: "Juggling?"

Bullseye shrugs.

I'm feeling warm. I look up. Over the red leather top of the front seat, he extends a yellow Post-it. On it, he's written a phone number and address in Palo Alto.

"Where you can find the hacker."

"In Beijing?"

"He's doing security work in the valley, on an H1-B." Temporary work visa.

I take the note and notice the letters and numbers he's written look fuzzy around the edges. I blink hard.

"Why do you encourage him?" Samantha asks her husband.

"I find it entertaining."

"He's broken."

"Chasing things is how he heals himself."

"Hey. I'm right here."

I expect Samantha to respond to my protestation with something like, Yeah, but you're not really here. You're not *all* here. You're not dealing with your life. It's not just the concussion, and the black eye, the black face, the urgency of investigation, not trusting. It's the void, she'd say, that black space inside your head, pulsing with orange and red on the outside, not caused by concussion. But something else, or the absence of something else. C'mon, Nat, you know what I mean.

Why did Polly change her phone number?

I look at Samantha, who I notice now has one hand on each side of my head, cradling it upright. Energy work.

"So chase," she says.

I nearly manage a smile.

"What?" she asks.

"Did you just mind-meld me?"

"I have no idea what you're talking about."

I wriggle my head to get it out of the Witch's grasp. "Okay. I'll chase."

I know where to start. It's not at the hacker's house. I look at Bullseye. "Can I take your Mac?"

He shrugs his ascent. I need it because I need to find the address of my next stop. And I need to set a trap.

37

Bullseye's taillights disappear. In my mind's eye, I see that void again, the black one surrounded by orange-and-red fire that the Witch planted, or exposed, or that I allowed to surface. I blink so that it'll recede again. Whatever I'm chasing will lead inside that void.

And I think: how melodramatic.

I walk to the Audi, open the trunk, pull out my own laptop. I power it up and sit in the front seat. I open a browser, then realize that, unlike with Bullseye's computer, mine has no Internet card. That's relatively easily solved, I hope, by one of the handful of restaurants and homes on the hillside near the ballpark. I drive less than two minutes to a diner, the Niner Diner, and luck into an unsecured Wi-Fi connection called "FIRSTNTEN." I sit in the lot. A lone night owl sits in the diner.

I log in and I search for "Budget hotel Marin, CA." I find a link to a site advertising nine hotels under $44. This turns out not to be true but it's beside the point. This is just a head fake. I click on two of the hotels, choose one, then put its address into Mapquest. Then I ask for directions to the hotel from "my present location." I get a map. I close the computer.

I have no intention of following the directions. But I suspect someone else will.

I have ample reason at this point to believe someone is monitoring my phone or computer activity. Or multiple someones. It's a reasonable assumption given the fact that I'm dealing with someone who managed to get my computer to post an obituary for the very-much-alive Sandy Vello.

I open the computer again. I need to give whoever is watching reason to believe I'm unaware of the surveillance. Into the browser, I type: "Faith Aver." I get the usual thousands of hits. One seems relevant. The link connects me to a San Francisco agency booking "local talent" for TV commercials/billboards/print ads. The web site features a dozen head shots, including one of Faith. I click on it to get a brief bio: "Get Faith. This versatile brunette can play a vivacious girlfriend or alluring young wife or mother. Suggested for use in advertising restaurants and bars, home-care products, or in office settings. Quick on her feet, Faith has experience with improv and can flow on the set. Resume on request."

Left out: scene stealer, scene-fleer, can play vixen or victim.

I click to ask for her resume. It brings up an email box. "I'm interested in hiring Faith to do some commercial work," I write. "Please send her resume." I leave my email.

I close the computer. I can't afford to sit too long, now that, thanks to Mapquest, I've given whoever is watching me "my present location." Besides, maybe they already know my location from my phone, which I power off.

I open Bullseye's computer, which I doubt anyone's tracking or peering into. Into Google, I type "Sandy Vello" and hit return. The third link is for a page with cast bios for *Last One Standing*. I click the link and get brief biographies and photos of a dozen of the Season III "personalities."

The first belongs to "Donovan," a guy who evidently is too cool for a last name. Sandy mentioned him. He's got long brown bangs but short-cropped hair on the sides, which taken together looks like the work of two competing stylists, one from the eighties and the other from the fifties. He's sneering. His bio says: "Donovan graduated cum laude from Princeton, spent four years on Wall Street, earned enough to buy a mansion in Northern New Jersey, then moved west. In Season III, he was the runner-up, after pulling out of the dramatic finale with a leg injury."

I click on "Where is Donovan now" to learn he's founded Silver Spoon Investing. It's an investment firm that promises to help families invest their fortunes while teaching their kids how to think about investing in one-to-one seminars.

I'm going down a digital rabbit hole. I click back two screens to get back to the main bio page—when I'm startled by a skidding sound coming from outside the car. A monster-sized SUV pulls into the diner's gravel lot. It passes me, pulls around the left side of the building, skids on gravel as it stops outside my view. I turn on my own car's ignition in case I've got to make a quick exit. I wait.

No one appears. The driver, I'm guessing—maybe a regular or employee—has disappeared through a side door. My head pulses. I dim the light on the computer monitor, thinking maybe my concussion has made me more sensitive to the crisp resolve of the backlit screen against the darkness of my surroundings.

Car still on, I study the bio page. At the bottom, alphabetically, I find Sandy Vello. I'm about to click on her bio when I'm struck by another of the show's "performers." Clyde Robichaux. I recognize the name from my conversations with Sandy. What did she say about him? I can't quite retrieve the memory.

From his picture, Clyde seems out of place. He looks kind, almost apologetic, big dark eyes—soft and watery—with the thick jowls and puffy cheeks of someone with a large head. He wears a suit that his neck bulges through, like a tree puncturing sunbaked soil. He's got light brown skin, an ethnic mix of white and something Asian or Latin American. Pock scars dot his upper cheeks, a residue of adolescent acne I always associate with creating humility—in a good way—in adults who once suffered it.

His bio describes a former Marine who saw action in the first gulf war and a "survivalist" who worked as a cameraman for another reality show called *Wild Man*, where the host and one-man crew visited remote areas and documented a month living off the land. In the third season of *Last One*

Standing, it looked like "muscle-bound Clyde might hook up with fiery Sandy Vello until, in one of the show's most dramatic moments, she was caught double-crossing her would-be beaux."

I'm momentarily appreciative of the seductive nature of the language. It's like the reality-TV producers have done for words what McDonald's did for burgers and fries—made them irresistible at the expense of substance. Made them appealing and provocative on the most primitive level. And the competition for attention on the Internet has sharpened further the skills of these 21st-century chefs of pre-packaged sound bites. It's fast-food for language.

I click to find out where Clyde is now. "Clyde joins adventure travel groups as a photographer and videographer through WildPhotos.com. When not hanging from cliffs with his camera, he lives the simple life in Northern California."

I click on his web site. It features dozens of extraordinary pictures—a woman white-water rafting, a man with rifle leveled at a tiger, and a family of four standing on a rock outcropping so high up that I can see the clouds hundreds of feet below them. Beside the photo, there's a smaller inset image of a man hanging by harness attached to a sheer cliff by rope and caribiners. A caption says: "Clyde goes all-out to shoot the Cohens in the Klamaths."

I look for contact information but the only option is to send an email.

I open a new browser window. Into the address line, I type "whois.net." The site lets you check who registered a particular web site, often giving contact information. Since most web site registrants don't realize the information is public, they tend not to mask their contact info. So the site can be a bounty for the otherwise stumped journalist.

Indeed.

The registration for WildPhotos.com lists Clyde's address in Redwood City. I put the address into Google Maps. As the location of his residence appears on the screen—in the hills above Silicon Valley—I hear another car approaching on the diner's gravel driveway. Instinctively, I duck. I turn my head to see what's approaching and find my gaze too low to see out the back. Instead, I'm looking dead into Isaac's car seat. Somehow, a piece of Styrofoam peanut packaging has lodged in the side of the seat, maybe, remarkably, from when the seat was still new.

The peanut's shape looks a bit like a single hippocampus—half of the hippocampi, which is the gateway to memory. It's a region in the middle of the brain where neurons form when we have new experiences. The neurons are the seeds of new memories that, with passing time, spread out to the rest of the brain, encoding the new experiences as long-term memories and learning. I stare at the peanut until it becomes blurry. I feel something tugging at my own memory centers, more than tugging, pulling, demanding my attention. My head pulses in beats, arrhythmically, with the sound of the car skidding along the gravel.

It's like I know something so important but I can't remember what it is. It's in that void inside my head, surrounded by strange colors.

I close my eyes. I picture a rat. It's this pudgy gray fellow with a long rat tail and pink around the eyes. On its head, it wears electrodes. I saw it when doing a story about memory research at the University of California at San Francisco. The researchers measured electrical activity in the brains of rats. They were watching new neurons form and travel to different parts of the brain. The researchers discovered that when rats have new experiences, they can only encode long-term memories—the only way those new neurons travel to the rest of the brain—during substantial periods of downtime. It was both a revelation and a confirmation of the obvious: when a brain doesn't rest, it doesn't have time to record memories.

I need to rest. Have I been chasing ghosts and irrelevancies at the expense of remembering something critical?

It feels like my brain flickers on and off, like Wi-Fi or bars on a phone.

Do I know some truth and can't remember it? What is it? A connection between Andrew Leviathan and Sandy Vello and a little girl who walked into traffic, and PRISM and a God drug, and Faith?

Is my chase leading me to truth?

Or is it obscuring truth by denying me downtime to record my own memories, my own truth?

Or, as Bullseye and the Witch suggest: Is chasing what heals me? Is this all nonsense, cooked up by a concussed brain?

I sit up. I look at the newly arrived car, a late-model pickup, its brake lights still gleaming. Two men sit in the front seat conferring.

I don't have the answers. Sandy Vello has some of them, at least.

I look back at the web site with the address of the registrant for WildPhotos, Clyde's address, presumably. There's a phone number. I dial it.

At the first ring, someone answers. "Hello, Clyde?"

I catch my breath. It's Sandy's voice.

I hang up.

I put the car in drive.

38

After a twenty-minute drive south on a darkened Highway 280, I glide past the Farm Hill Road exit, which leads to the residence of a former Marine and reality-TV wannabe. Before I stop there, I've got more traps to lay.

I drive five miles farther south to Sand Hill Road, the exit for Palo Alto, feeling the property values rise with each tick of the odometer. I pull off the highway, pull out my own laptop, and cruise around the tree-shrouded office complexes just off the highway. I stop every few offices to see if I can find an unsecured Wi-Fi access point. I find one outside Mercurial Ventures, which, nearly makes me smile; it seems like a refreshingly frank name for an investment firm throwing hundreds of millions of dollars into the wildly swinging tech market.

From my wallet, I pull out the yellow Post-it note I'd been handed by Bullseye. It contains the home address for the Chinese hacker. He lives in a tree-lined area of Palo Alto once catering to Stanford scholars called "Professorville." I call up his address on a map. I have no intention of going there. But I hope someone thinks I intend to—maybe the shiny bald buzzard or the stout pyromaniac, or whoever is monitoring my computer activity. I pause on the map in hopes of letting the image sink in with whichever miscreant is watching over my shoulder. I close the browser but leave the computer on to let the additional misdirection set in.

I want to close my eyes, but find myself looking at the surrounding venture-capital firms, struck with another question. I pull out Bullseye's laptop, open it, search for Andrew's former business partner Gils Simons. I get a mountain of hits. He's celebrated as the canny operational guy who knows how to turn cutting-edge technology into gold. It's no small trick, by the way; there are countless stories in these parts of savvy engineers who came first to the idea of online auction sites, or Internet search engines or online booksellers, but got crushed by eBay, Google and Amazon because those companies coupled the technology with business smarts.

From his bio on Wikipedia, I learn that Gils grew up outside Normandy, attended the Sorbonne, dropped out, came to the United States, paired up with Andrew Leviathan in the early 1980s as Co-employee Number One of Leviathan Ventures, left the company in the late nineties to pursue his investment interests, and likes sailing and climbing. There is no reference to the China-U.S. High-Tech Alliance.

Wikipedia lists Gils's current investment firm as Alps Partners. I visit the web site to find an image of a snowcapped mountain and little substance. A blasé formulaic section describes the firm's determination to find "break-out" companies and market-moving ideas with international potential. Same old blah-blah investment rhetoric. I look down the list of his strategic investment partners. One is Baidu, China's equivalent of Google. He's got a hit on his hands. The other is Trans-Pacific Limited Partners, described merely as a leading Chinese investment firm.

There's a contact link. I click on it and am surprised to find an email address: GSimons@Alpspartners.com. I noodle my missive only briefly before writing: "My name is Nat Idle. We sat across from each other at the luncheon at MacArthur Park. I'm interested in writing about your latest venture. Want to meet and discuss?"

I leave my phone number. It's cryptic enough to suggest much more knowledge on my part than I've actually got and, as a result, perhaps lure him into a conversation. It's meaningless enough that, should Gils have no involvement in whatever it is I'm chasing, I can easily explain the note away by saying I wanted to learn about his latest business dealings.

I search for information about the Twin Peaks Youth Guidance Center and the learning annex. Various wire news reports repeat what I heard on the radio: pretty much nothing of value. I look at some of the history of the place. When it was re-built in the late 1990s, it was intended by county authorities to be a model of modern rehabilitation. Huge cost overruns ensued. So the learning annex got privatized into a place where the county pays monthly fees for learning classes, supplies, volunteers, but far less than it would pay to take care of the entire building and pay the mortgage on it. It's a classic taxpayer abdication but one that has gotten kudos from around the country, particularly from economists and right-wing think tanks. Through all kinds of classes, the learning annex has taught youngsters basic employment skills, including short-order and pastry cooking, maintenance of things like air conditioners and furnaces, "manners," email etiquette, computing.

Computing.

I search on this specific area. I'm looking for connections to PRISM and Sandy Vello to something called the Juggler. I find little. There's a brief mention in a filing from a year earlier to the Board of Supervisors of the City and County of San Francisco of a pilot project at the facility aimed at teaching residents the latest media techniques. It is passed unanimously without comment.

A handful of searches about the learning center gives oblique notifications of other partnerships offered and accepted. From what I can gather: a major coffee chain has contributed espresso machines to teach both coffee making and maintenance of the fragile devices; tutors in computer support give technical certificates for learning the ins and outs of Windows software; a medical conglomerate has donated an old-generation magnetic resonance machine so teens can learn to be medical assistants.

It's all both heartening, I guess, and self-serving by the private partners, who develop brand-specific line workers. The tech-savvy lower classes of the next century.

I look at the clock. Nearly thirty minutes have passed since I parked here. It's just before nine. I close and turn off both laptops and start the Audi. Moments later, I speed onto Highway 280, and after five minutes more, exit again, this time on Farm Hill Road. The directions on Bullseye's computer guide me up a steep, narrow road that climbs a Silicon Valley hillside. On some of these hillsides reside the swankiest estates, $3.5 million at a minimum. Not this one. Smaller houses, fixer-uppers needing serious cosmetic surgery at a minimum. I drive by one ranch-style house that has been expanded on one side with a room-sized tent, the kind that might accommodate a wedding party. Here the houses are bargain-basement, costing only around $1.5 million but, to fit in, need a complete overhaul and requiring BYOA—bring your own architect.

Clyde Robichaux's house looks like it belongs in that bargain-basement bin, maybe at the bottom. It's a narrow three-story house, a fixer-upper that feels perched almost precariously upon the ground-floor garage. A wooden-slatted staircase, also shrouded in darkness, extends up the right side of the house to the entrances on the second and third stories.

It's poorly lit, but for what looks like dancing orange flames projecting in a surreal fashion from the picture window on the top floor. Someone is home and they've got the fireplace working.

I roll slowly by the house on the single-lane gravel road, which is rutted, sloping upward to the right, entering an area even denser with trees, the opening scene of a children's book about the secret lair of bears. To my right, a sharp drop-off into a shallow gulley, protected by a thick line of firs. To my left, I'm hugging a steep hillside thatched with foliage and thick-stumped eucalyptus trees protruding at a slight angle.

I wince with each squirt of gravel popping beneath my tires, announcing my whereabouts. It is so quiet. What the houses here lack in modernity, they make up for in acreage; I still haven't passed another residence when, thirty feet ahead, I see the road widen slightly on my left, sufficient to create room for a car parked tightly against the hillside.

I recognize the car. It's a red BMW M3, one of the sleekest cars on the road, one Polly once dreamed of having. This one belongs to Sandy Vello. I saw her climb into it at the learning annex where I first realized that, no, Sandy Vello is not dead. From the presence of her car, I'm guessing she's still not dead. I'm guessing she's upstairs. Maybe protected by a Marine.

39

Another thirty feet ahead, a small driveway appears on the right, protected by a rickety metal gate and a sign: "Private Property." Ideal.

I put the car in park, slip out of the driver's seat and walk to the gate, hearing the small loose stones beneath my feet. The thick metal gate swings open with a creak, cool and damp in my hands. Beyond it, the road doglegs right so that I can't see what house lies in the pitch black.

I drive through the gates and park to the far right, tires nearly teetering into another gulley. I kill the lights. I shut the door gently, acutely aware of every sound amid the crickets. I'm cold, not from the air, which I'm guessing is not much below 60 degrees, but from something deep inside. I trudge between two trees, slide into the gulley, and then walk up the other side. I can see the house lights but discern nothing further, obscured by half a football field of distance, rolling terrain, and a phalanx of trees.

My phone buzzes, and I jump. I pull the device from my pocket and look at the screen. It's a reminder that I've got an upcoming appointment. With Wilma. It takes a second to picture her, the straight black hair, prematurely aged hands, posture like a long-legged insect with her legs folded beneath her. There's a note with the calendar: "Do homework for Wed meeting with Wilma."

Homework. Homework? Am I supposed to be preparing questions? What story am I working on with Wilma?

On the phone's calendar, I see that I've got another appointment, for tomorrow. "Tax evasion hearing, civic center courthouse, 4 P.M." I have to think hard to picture the portly server who, after the awards luncheon, handed a letter requiring my presence at a hearing alleging tax irregularities. I wonder why I've written tax "evasion" hearing. Did I evade taxes? Or was that shorthand?

I also remember the letter stating that if I didn't show for the hearing I could face criminal penalty.

I've got more immediate issues.

On the touch screen, I tap the number for Sandy Vello. It rings twice, then goes to her voice mail. I leave a message. "It's Nat Idle. Are you okay? That was so strange today."

I wait for her to listen to it. I guess I want to set up an alibi, for her not to suspect me, just in case. I turn off my phone, and am struck with wonder that I didn't do it earlier. If the buzzard or the kidnapper is following my movements on the computer, he's probably also doing it—even more easily—by triangulating the signals on my cell phone.

I consider my options. I can walk to the narrow house, hope that Sandy happens to come to the door, not chaperoned by her reality-TV buddy and former Marine, and that she's forthcoming with her spirited files and other secrets.

I'm struck by a better option. I start running.

Moments later, I'm standing in front of Sandy's BMW. I peer through the window. Or try to. It's black dark, forest dark, a sliver of moonlight barely cutting through an opening in the branches extending over the road. It's just enough to let me make out two boxes in the backseat, and to see they are empty. No files here. In the trunk, maybe. But I doubt it.

On the hillside next to the car, I rummage through the soil with my hands. I feel for a rock, baseball-sized. Too small. I reach for another. It's jagged and oval, bumpy, like the moon or the surface of the brain. I raise it. I slam it against the windshield. It doesn't crack. It rolls off the front of the car. I pick it up again. I close my eyes and I picture Polly. She's telling me that she loves me and that everything will be okay. Her eyes look so tired, crow's-feet in the corners, watery. She wears a blue gown, resplendent even in the hours before she gives birth. Even with our split imminent and my visions of nuclear-family bliss dashed.

I slam the rock down on the window.

The thick glass cracks in the zigzag shape of a fault line. The car alarm splits the night air. My ears ringing, I sprint into the trees across the road, impulsive, like a little girl running into the street, about to be crushed by a Volvo.

My whole plan is that impulsive. Nothing this risky could be well thought out. Or maybe it's just deliberately stupid. I'm willing to risk everything to find out what I'm chasing.

My hope is to draw out Sandy, or maybe the Marine—somehow get Sandy alone, and discover files she may have taken into the house.

I hear a voice on the stairs. It's Sandy. I can't make out her words. She appears, striding down the steps, a phone to her ear.

"I can handle myself, Clyde," she says. She pockets her phone. She walks purposefully down the stairs.

I don't have much time.

40

Sandy turns back into the house, and disappears. I wait. Less than two minutes later, she returns. She's cradling a long, thin object in her arms, walking with purpose, confidence. Near the bottom of the stairs, she pauses. Starved of light and clear vision, she must be trying to use her sense of hearing to determine what dark forces lurk in the trees. But the wailing car alarm owns the night, and would mask the sound of feet on fallen leaves.

I can now discern that she cradles a shotgun. She shifts it into her left arm. She wears running tights and windbreaker. With her right hand, she reaches into its pocket and withdraws something. Keys, maybe. The car alarm continues to wail. If she wants to turn the sound off, she's going to have to get closer, even using a remote. Shotgun held in front of her, she walks down the gravel path.

I squeeze against a tree not fifty feet from her. I feel pain sting my left shoulder, at the edge of my chest. And an image floods my brain: Faith astride me, fingernails digging into my skin, right where the bark's digging.

She collapses on me, and whispers, "Catharsis."

"What do you mean, Faith?" I remember asking her.

"I'm moving on."

"From what?"

She looks away. "Post-coital interrogation. You're kinky."

"What are you moving away from?"

"A lie. Are you moving on from yours?"

The memory turns static, fades out. What lie is Faith moving away from? I look up to see Sandy move cautiously through a bend in the road. In just a moment, she'll be far enough away that I can make my move. I hold my breath and I wonder why I can't stop thinking about Faith, and what she meant, and whether she's safe, and then I'm cursing my own brain, such as it is.

Research suggests that people who are capable of great focus, like great athletes, tend to have thicker myelin sheaths, a coating on their neurons. So they're less distracted by extraneous information. I wonder, knowing it's totally impossible, if my sheaths, such as they are, suffered when I hit my head—first at the subway station, then against a sledgehammer fist in Chinatown.

Focus, Nat. Sandy disappears around the corner.

I run across the gravel road. I hug the door of the garage, then find myself at the base of the stairs. I glance into the darkness. I hear the blaring car alarm in the distance as I look up the steep concrete stairs, many of them, leading to glass-door entrances on two floors. I sprint up.

I reach the first glass-door entrance. Inside, it's dark. I try the handle. In the darkness, inside, I see a nondescript baby's face. It's an illusion, I know. I blink and it's gone. So much to lose. I open the door. I peer inside. I can make out a small room, fitness equipment—a home gymnasium, smelling of disinfectant. Not what I'm looking for.

The car alarm goes dead. It's momentarily dead quiet before I hear the crickets. Not much time.

I sprint up another dozen stairs to the top floor. Inside is bathed in light, a wide-open floor plan. To the right, a kitchen. Folksy, tidy, from another era. An upright toaster, polished to the point of gleaming, sitting on a seventies-style Formica counter. The counter divides the kitchen from a dining room, with an ice-clear chandelier and flame-shaped lights hung low over an empty table. A floor of outdated tile in the dining room gives way to a single step down and fluffy beige carpeting of the family room. Sleek couch covered by a blanket, glass coffee table, worn leather recliner.

Then, all at once, all the atmospherics become ancillary, tertiary, totally fucking irrelevant. In the middle of the floor, in front of a fireplace, I see what I've come for.

Files. Folder upon folder. They're lying on the beige carpet. Most of them, at least. A handful lie on the stone fireplace stoop. And I can make out the remains of manila inside the fire, behind a metal curtain. Embers too, and a brief whisk of orange from dying flame.

I stop and listen. Nothing from outside. Maybe Sandy's exploring. Maybe she found my car. I shut the door. I hustle to the living room. I juke around the coffee table and skid to a stop next to a pile of folders that represents the only unkempt spot in this Marine's tightly-kept quarters.

Woozy, I bend over to grab the folder on the top. Affixed to it, near the right bottom quarter, there's a white label with a long number, maybe ten digits. I open the folder.

I'm looking at a brain.

It's a grainy printout of an MRI. The image shows a side shot of the front upper quartile of the brain, the frontal lobe. Along the left side, a scale bar indicates the size of the image. It seems relatively small, maybe belonging to a toddler or child, if my currently concussed memory of neurology is accurate. But beyond that, I couldn't begin to explain what I'm looking at. I'm not sure even a seasoned radiologist could discern something of value from this murky reproduction. Some areas of the printout seem darker than others, and, in a few spots, there are whiter splotches. This might indicate different regions of blood flow or activation. It might mean someone has a lousy laser printer.

I pull open the manila folder, hoping to discover something to explain this image. But there's nothing else. As I fumble, though, I notice some scribbling on the back of the piece of paper with the MRI image. It reads: "Group II," and "62 percent."

I fall to my knees and begin scrambling through the folders, opening, exploring, tossing, looking for something to make sense of this. More folders with more numbers and more grainy pictures of brains and more percentiles on the back. I swirl to the bottom of the file, seeking meaning. I throw a file toward the fire, then another. I reach the bottom, finding no explanation. I look up at the dying embers and feel the violent pulsing inside my head. I'm so royally pissed off, sitting in this unkempt stew of meaningless brain images, helpless, stirring and swirling evidence that has no meaning.

When do I get some fucking answers?

Then I hear the footsteps.

Sandy's back.

I snag a couple of the grainy brain images, fold them haphazardly and stick them in my back pocket. I make a minimal effort to pull the strewn folders into a tighter pile. Sandy won't expect someone to have broken into their house. She'll think some random act of violence or nature befell her car.

I turn on my haunches. I see what I'm looking for. Beyond the dining room, there's an open doorway. I suspect it leads to the living quarters in this narrow troll house. I hope it leads to inside stairs and the exit that will lead me outside to drive away to freedom with the curious evidence I carry in my back pocket. And I've got something to trade Faith's kidnapper, or cohort.

I quickstep to the opening. At the doorway, I discover a short hallway, in the shape of a *T*. Three doorways, one each a few steps to my left and right and a third, the same distance, dead ahead. No staircase. Maybe behind one of the doors. I choose the one to the right. I reach it in two strides. It opens toward me. Closet. Linens and toilet paper, meticulously organized. I push it shut, realizing as I move to the middle door it didn't completely close. It's a minor hitch I don't have time to remedy, as I open the middle door. Bathroom. I pull the door closed.

As I open the third door, the one to the left, I know I'm not going to find a staircase. The architect of this troll house means to see me caught and crushed. My intuition gets confirmed by moonlight peering through slats in the window shades lightly illuminating a bedroom.

I hear the front door open, then close.

I need to muster the courage to walk out into the troll house, explain myself to Sandy, make this situation much more rational. She's not nefarious, just narcissistic and in trouble. She needs a friend and I just need to think through my approach. But how nice, I think, to just lie down on the queen-sized bed, facedown, come what may.

I take two steps to the right and, quietly as I can, pull open the right side of a two-door closet. In the center, a shelf holds sweaters and shirts stacked neatly. To the left and right, shoes line the floor, pants hung on a low bar, nicer shirts hung on the upper bar. I step inside.

I push aside pants and shirts on my far right. I press myself against the corner. I pull the door closed.

I extract my phone and put it on mute. The only rational thing I've done within the hour. I close the phone. Then my eyes.

Inside my closed eyelids, I see Polly and the fortune cookie, the night that my life's roads diverged and somehow I was led to this closet, a dead end, serious peril, and, I realize, some nagging sense that I'm not sure I care anymore.

41

"**A** boy."

Polly's eyes glisten, which I assume mean she's sad. But she's also wearing this smile, a 60 percenter. Polly's got the fullest range of smiles of anyone I've ever met. She's like the Baskin Robbins, but with smiles. She can take investors and customers on a stock-market ride of emotion, guide them just where she wants them by turning her lips up and down by infinitesimal degrees only the heart can measure.

When she nears 65 percent, I see the residue of Willow Tree mushroom from the mu shu vegetables in the corner of her mouth. Why can I remember this and not, precisely, the rest?

"Fungus. On your lip."

She wipes it off. She turns the smile dial down to 45 percent. This is not good news. I see the condensation on her water glass, the damp stain on the red tablecloth, the cracked empty shell of the fortune cookie on the small white plate. In the corner of my eye, I see the waiter with the left ankle limp plodding our direction with the cookie's replacement.

"Boy?" I know what she means and I can't believe it.

"You're having a son." She's up to 70 percent but the eyes still glisten.

"I thought we weren't going to . . ."

"You know I'm more organized than that."

I know she is. Of course she was going to find out. But I'd have thought it would be a joint decision. It's not like her to find out without me. The limping waiter nears, extending the white plate with care befitting royalty. My majestic woman, my queen mother, deserves nothing less.

"That's amazing. Amazing. Amazing! I will immediately get baseball mitts and have someone teach me how to teach him to throw a slider. I peaked out at curveball. Though you know that you shouldn't learn to throw junk before the age of one. It can hurt development of the wrist."

The waiter sets down the second fortune cookie in the middle of the table. Polly eyes it and dials it back to 28 percent. For Polly, this is a frown. She reaches for the cookie and covers it with her hand.

"What? Is he . . . is the boy healthy?"

She picks up the cookie. She cradles it. "Completely. Gestating beautifully. Five months of crinkly perfection, currently snarfing sixteen pounds of digested lemon chicken."

"Then we should drink. I'll drink for three." I look at her face, looking at the cookie. "What's the other shoe? Drop it, already."

"Nat, we've always been . . ." She's still looking down. "Different kinds of people."

My heart drops a thousand feet from the apex of news about my unborn son. "So. And?"

"There are lots of different ways to raise a family."

I'm frozen. I don't want to ask her what she means. I want time to stop. That's because I know Polly. And I know that she doesn't bring subjects up for discussion. By the time she raises a serious issue, she's already figured out how to resolve it. Whatever she says next is going to make me very unhappy.

She looks down into her hands. With two thumbs, she cracks the second fortune cookie. We look down at it, stunned by what we see there.

"I'm so sorry." Her smile has dipped below zero.

"What?" This I whisper aloud. In the present. "You're leaving me."

Standing in the closet, I open my eyes. Then close them again. I can't seem to remember how the rest of the conversation goes. I close down and I look at the cookie she's opened and I can't believe my eyes either.

I hear a noise. It's coming from the present. I open my eyes. The closet door swings open. I see a burly former Sandy Vello, the very-much-not-dead reality-TV wannabe, holding a rifle.

I say: "What did I do wrong?"

42

"Journalist?" I very nearly laugh when Sandy says it because it sounds like she opened the closet and saw a totally random animal species, maybe armadillo.

She steps forward, gun very much aimed at my chest. She's half in darkness, dimly lit across half her face by the moonlight peeking through the slatted shades.

"You packing?"

I assume she's asking me if I'm armed and again, despite the myriad forces working against me, I also nearly laugh at her deliberate and dramatic language. She's playing to a nonexistent audience.

I hold up my hands, surrendering.

"I can't risk that you're armed. Turn around."

I do so. I feel her left hand pat my pants pockets, front and back. I like my chances if I whirl around and tackle her at the knees. She'd be unable to shoot me given the angle and size of the weapon. For that matter, I'm not sure she has the willpower or desire to shoot me, or anyone. She's a narcissist, not a killer. But narcissists have extraordinary powers of rationalization.

"Don't think about it. I'm well within my rights to shoot you." She smacks the butt of her rifle against the back of my head. The blow is meant as more of an admonition than an effort to knock me unconscious. But it's a sufficient surprise that I buckle against the shelves and start sliding to my knees. I blink, orient.

Instant message to self: don't underestimate Sandy.

"Journalist. Where am I now? Isn't that the story you said you were doing?"

"I can help you, Sandy." I'm still facing away from her. My hands brace loosely against a pile of neatly folded sweaters. I pull myself up.

"Where I am now is pointing a gun at your back. That's where I am. You can quote me."

At rifle-point, she marches me to the dining room. She watches me closely as she moves to the other side of the table, turns a chair around so that she's straddling it, sits. She rests the rifle on the dining-room table, finger laced through the trigger.

"We printed out pictures of Donovan and pasted his picture on the tree and Clyde taught me to shoot."

"Donovan?"

"Stop playing stupid. I've never bought that act from you."

Donovan. The guy from the reality-TV show.

"Clyde says I'm the best shot he's ever seen for a beginner. He says I've got the kind of focus that could've made me a sniper."

"I can help you," I repeat.

"I don't want any press. And I'm not just some volunteer teacher, a guidance counselor at juvy. And if you print that, I'll come after you with lawyers. This is a stepping-stone."

I look at her, trying to make sense of the situation. Does she have any idea what she's involved with?

"You work for the men from China. You're supposed to test me," she says.

I shake my head. "Which men?" I see Sandy's index finger tighten on the trigger. It's a good reminder of the reality I face. Under other circumstances, I might be able to manipulate Sandy, but she's pushed well beyond her limits. She's got red skin around her eyebrows and at the edge of her hairline—without a doubt where the fire at the learning annex singed her. She's likely plenty scared, or should be. Scared plus narcissistic equal danger.

"Look at my arm, Sandy."

I start to push my jacket up on my left forearm. My captor lifts the rifle. I hold up my hands, surrender. I explain I want to show her my own wounds. I remove my wool gray jacket, lay it on the floor. I hold up my arms, palms down.

"You need to do forearm curls," Sandy says.

"It's my own fire damage."

The hair on the back of my hands has been singed to curly nubs. I brush my left forearm, causing some of the dried brush to flake away.

I start to talk.

I explain that I'd come to talk to her more at the annex, arriving just in time to see her nearly engulfed in flames. Obviously, I was beyond piqued, so I looked back through my notes, found her references to Clyde and then tracked down his house.

She fairly interjects any number of plausible objections, such as why I would have then smashed her car and snuck into the house.

"I'm a freelance investigative journalist."

"Bullshit."

"I got a tip that something strange was going on at PRISM."

"Tip?"

"Donovan."

"Bullshit."

"He's obsessed with you, Sandy. He can't stand the success you're having. He still wants to bring you down."

Sandy cocks her head. She starts to laugh.

"Donovan?"

"Rodent Nuts."

"How stupid do you think I am?"

"Sandy."

"They bring people like me onto reality shows not because we're good-looking or physically fit. It's because we think we're more important than the next guy and the way we prove it is by calling out their bullshit and trying to humiliate them more than they humiliate us."

It's surprisingly solid self-awareness.

"I'm calling your bullshit, journalist. Start saying something true or I'll exercise my right to shoot you on my private property and then turn it into an awesome interview with Nancy Grace."

I take a deep breath. "Alan Parsons. He wanted to bribe Andrew Leviathan."

I'm surprised to hear the sentence come out of my mouth. I'm not sure if it's true or just sounds right or how, in either case, I made the connection.

"The rich Silicon Valley guy? What's he got to do with . . ."

I cut her off. "Alan tipped me off about you and PRISM. You know Alan? Big guy, drinker. He found out about the technology, but needed me to get him more information."

I watch her eyes carefully when I mention his name again but she indicates zero recognition. She doesn't blink or avert her gaze. She doesn't know him.

"Alan was working with Faith."

"Damn it, start making some sense."

I continue. I explain that Alan suggested I look into a story involving Sandy and PRISM and some dangerous new technology. She clenches her jaw. I wait for her to say something but she doesn't. I try to think about what I actually know and what I might surmise. I start thinking aloud, trying to put any of the pieces together.

"It's technology for kids. So they can do more multitasking, juggling, like you told me."

"It's a huge market. So what?"

"Sandy, you're misunderstood."

"What do you mean?" She loves any sentence revolving around her.

"You got hired by PRISM because you understand people and how to communicate ideas to kids. They wanted you to work with kids at the learning annex to get them to test the technology. They thought you could reach the kids, be a good entrée, 'cause you've got some notoriety and had spent some time in jail yourself as a youngster. They ultimately want to see what it does to their brains. But they also thought they could get you to keep dirty secrets. That's not your way of doing things. You've got your own code."

She chews on this.

"It's a joint effort between the Chinese government and Andrew Leviathan."

She doesn't respond.

I continue thinking aloud. "He built some amazing software, and PRISM is building the hardware. It's a classic relationship; the software gets made in the United States, and low-cost Asian manufacturers build it, import it, pay licensing fees to the American innovator. In this case, the technology is marketed as a way to help kids multitask, to make their brains stronger so they can deal with the onslaught of data in the digital world. Text messages and instant messages, Facebook status updates, phone calls, tweets, all of it. The idea is to build better brains—21st-century gray matter to digest all the machine chatter.

"I told you that already. It was off the record."

"But it has a side effect." I'm building steam. "It actually . . ." I pause to let myself think before I mutter it. "It retards development."

I think about the pile of files on the ground in front of the fire, the MRI of the frontal lobes. I can't tell anything from the grainy pictures that have no other identifying information than a few letters and numbers on the back.

From anatomy class eons ago, I picture the

frontal lobes. They're beige but with a grayish tinge if soaked in formaldehyde. Like the rest of the brain, they're deeply contoured, tiny hills and valleys of essential gray matter. But they stand apart from the rest of the brain. They make us human by allowing us to organize information, set priorities, establish control over our lives, or try to. They let us, to borrow Biblical language, establish our dominion over our world. And they develop last, often not fully formed until people are in their thirties or even forties. Without them, we remain impulsive, childlike, likely to have trouble establishing priorities. It's no mystery, I think, I'm acting somewhat irrationally given a concussion that has temporarily set back my frontal lobe a few development cycles.

"What happened to your eye?" Sandy asks.

The question hardly sounds maternal but it's curious in a way that suggests she's softening.

"I went to Chinatown to follow a lead and got clobbered by a thick guy with a crooked smile. He looked like a bouncer at a prison nightclub."

"Steve."

Steve. "You know him?"

"Not really. He hired me, and ran interference with management at PRISM. Kept the parents from being a pain in the butt. How much is he paying you? He pays well."

"PRISM isn't running this operation?"

"I report to Steve. I think you do too."

"I swear to you, Sandy. He's my enemy."

"He's always talking about security breaches and how he used to deal with them in rural China.

Likes to use the word 'electrodes,' and sounds stupid when he says it. Clyde says I shouldn't buy a word of it. But it wouldn't surprise me if he put you up to this to see if I'm violating my confidentiality agreement."

"He tried to set you on fire. And me."

I hold out my singed forearms. She looks at them, unconvinced. I know that look, something like pity and skepticism. I feel like I engender that look more than is healthy.

We're at an impasse.

"I see a counselor."

"What?"

"Her name is Wilma. I see a counselor named Wilma." I'm now talking for Sandy's benefit as much as for mine. My sentences feel just shy of revelation. I'm remembering that once a week I go to Wilma and, after many months of sitting across from the gangly counselor in a high-backed chair in a boxy office, I resigned myself to lying, cliché-like, on a stiff couch. But I can still sense Wilma's looking at me with pity and skepticism when I recite the goings-on of each week. I remember my latest homework assignment for her: I'm supposed to define the word "loss," or some inane exercise like that. How has this memory eluded me the last few days? What else have I forgotten or misunderstood or misplaced since Alan Parsons slammed my head onto the subway pavement? Didn't it happen when I was heading home from Wilma's office?

"Admitting you see a shrink—is that supposed to make me sympathetic? Just because you're weak doesn't make you an ally."

"Go fuck yourself, Sandy."

She smiles, a kilowatt grin. It's the kind of raw response she craves.

"Clyde returns tonight, in a few hours. He's been in Wyoming shooting photos of some rich family on a luxury camping trip."

"Good for you."

"Should be home anytime and he won't hesitate to shoot you. Actually, he probably won't shoot you but he will blacken your other eye."

"I won't give him any reason to do so. Besides, I don't see why it's a big deal that you basically ran classes at the learning annex. It's why they recruited you. They knew you'd be good with this population."

She stands up, still training the rifle on me. "I want a share of the movie rights."

"For what?"

"Do you agree?"

I nod. I have no idea what she's talking about.

"Don't you dare print that I just do volunteer work at the learning annex. That's slander, or libel or whatever. It's a bigger job than that. Otherwise, why would they have tried to burn the place?"

"But it sounds like you were just monitoring the kids, babysitting, essentially . . ."

"I knew something weird was going on," she cuts me off, as I'd hoped. "I told Clyde. I told him it was more than just keeping those kids entertained and product refinement."

"What product?"

She says: "You honestly won't believe how cool this is."

43

Sandy takes two steps back from the chair just as I feel my phone buzz. I'm not sure whether to answer when it becomes clear that Sandy has picked up my distraction. She tells me to pull out the phone and put it on the table. She watches the movements carefully. The phone buzzes again, jumping lightly on the table, then stops.

"Interesting," Sandy says.

"Why?"

"Usually we don't get reception here, unless you stand on one foot near the window in the downstairs bathroom." She smiles at what feels to her like a clever line. "You probably just got a text."

From the phone's abbreviated buzz, I'd have to concur. She reaches forward and pulls the phone nearer. It's a surprisingly painful invasion of my personal space. She clicks with her thumb and she says: "I remember Alan Parsons."

"You do?"

"That's what it says."

She slides the phone toward me. I start to raise my hands.

"Leave them on the table, palms down." Sandy's playing a part she once saw on TV. I have a vision of Faith being held somewhere at gunpoint, just like this.

I look down at the screen of the phone. It reads: "I remember Alan Parsons. Call me."

It's from Jill Gilkeson, mother of Kathryn, the girl who ran into traffic.

"It's from a woman who works for Andrew Leviathan. Can I call her?"

"You can't call anybody."

She reaches forward and she pulls the phone to her edge of the table. "What's it mean?"

"It means that another piece of evidence suggests that whatever you're involved with—whatever we're both involved with—points to one of the most powerful industrialists in the world."

"Movie rights."

I want to throw up. But I'm liking the way the psychology is unfolding; Sandy's paranoia is giving way to her narcissism, which is the easier of the two of her prevailing traits to manipulate. And she's feeling taken advantage of by PRISM or her Chinese handlers and humiliated that the world will see her as merely a volunteer teacher. Still, even as I try to keep her gaze, I'm glancing around for some escape hatch—a weapon, sharp object, fire extinguisher, anything I could use to throw or wield, distract, not harm or injure her so much as facilitate my exit.

Rifle trained on me, she takes two steps backward, bumps into the chest-high counter that separates the kitchen from the dining room, feels her way around its rounded edges until she, without taking her eyes from me, winds up in the kitchen. She slides open a drawer, looks down. I reach down at my feet and lift my untied sneaker with my right hand. It's a hapless projectile I drop when Sandy returns and I see what she's holding aloft: a black plastic device that's shaped like a cross between a portable video-game console and a small baseball mitt. It lies in her right palm, attached by a strap that encircles the back of her hand.

"Meet the Juggler."

My head suddenly goes light. I picture Polly holding up an empty fortune cookie poised to lay something heavy on me. I cough twice, sharply, begetting a dry heave. I raise my head, eyes watery, trying to keep a grip. Reality, memory and mystery have begun to collide. Everything feels scrambled up inside my gray matter, an omelet of imagery and emotion and I can't seem to separate out the ingredients.

I recall where I've seen this device before. Piles of them sat burning at the learning annex on a long cafeteria table.

"It's obviously a prototype." Sandy moves to the edge of the counter to my left. She sets down the rifle but not in a way that offers me any particular advantage. She's ten feet away from me, not close enough. If I tried to attack or flee, she'd have ample time to take aim.

Eyes still on me, she reaches to her left and lifts a second device from the drawer. It's identical to the first. She slips the second one onto her left hand and she holds up the two Jugglers, palms facing me. I can see now in the center of each device a rectangular video screen slightly larger than the screen on a mobile phone. On each screen shines an image of a juggling ninja, an image I recall seeing on the mural inside the burning learning annex. Above their hands, these cartoonish, macho Ninja juggle tiny little clouds, not balls. What strikes me is the image quality. It's more vivid than I've seen on any television or even movie-theater screen. It's not just the colors but also the way they seem to leap from the screen like they're combusting with the air. I can't take my eyes from them, to the extent I'm wondering if I'm imagining it.

Sandy lightly lifts the device in her right hand. Into the air pops a high-definition image of the number 1. It arcs in the air and it lands on the device in her left hand. She holds up the device in her left hand so that I can see the screen; on it is the number 1. The image has traveled, wirelessly, from one device to the other.

She then starts moving the devices at the same time, as if she were juggling them, though they remain in her palms. But the air starts popping with images of ones and zeroes. They travel in neat little arcs from one device to the next. It's a digital air show, 21st-century wizardry, something from the hands of a supernatural creature in a Harry Potter story. But even as I stare in wonder, I know this hardly is science fiction. It's well within the realm of software.

"Data juggling, literally?"

"Have you ever seen anything like it?"

Her hands have stopped moving. In the air, above the devices, a static image appears: ninja jugglers with their hands beneath an arc of tiny clouds.

I shake my head.

"It's infrared and wireless technology, Bluetooth, twelve hundred hertz image refresh, basic stuff." She knows she's got me. "It captures body motion like the Nintendo Wii system. I don't even know all the technical terms. But this is just the sizzle, not the steak."

She has grown more impassioned, her mouth slightly agape, lips moist, lost in presentation.

"You should see how excited the kids get."

"How many kids?"

"Fifty overall, give or take. But only twenty on any given day. A totally captivated group. Taking care of struggling kids is really the wave of the future in forward-thinking communities. This is where we start building the middle class from people who might otherwise get stuck at the bottom rungs." She's reciting from a manual. "There's one kid, Samuel. He's ten, I think. Robbed a convenience store. Cutey. Loves me. Gets what I'm about. He spends hours with the Jugglers, and so fast. He can whiz through the data."

She reaches with her right thumb and swipes the side of the device in her palm. She starts moving the device again, literally in a juggling motion. This time, a maze projects into the air; on the end of the maze near her left hand is a virtual piece of cheese while on the other hand is a mouse. She starts moving the fingers of her right hand, prompting the mouse to move in fits and starts through the maze. It's awkward, either bad design or she's just not very good. All of a sudden, the device in her right hand beeps. A cat appears and begins chasing the mouse, and is just about to catch its virtual prey in the maze when her left hand beeps.

"Level Two," she says.

The maze seems to leap such that it now hovers only over the right-hand device. Over the left device, a new maze appears. It's got a different configuration, this time with a tiny egg on one end of the maze and a dinosaur on the other. She starts glancing back and forth between the mazes, trying to move the creatures simultaneously—the mouse to the cheese and spiky-backed dinosaur to the egg.

Between the two mazes, there's a bridge, projected about two feet in the air above her hands. A cacophony of beeps commences, marking the appearance of new images. Beep. Mouse. Beep. Cheese. Beep. Cat. Beep. Dinosaur. Beep. Bigger dinosaur chasing smaller one chasing egg. She lowers her hands, prompting the images to waver, then disappear.

"Samuel can switch and switch and switch. He's a genius. He's going to run the twenty-first century." She pauses and laughs. "Just so long as there are no food trays."

"Huh?"

"He's incredible when he's on the device. But when he's not using this thing, he's a little tyrant. Can't sit still. In the dormitory, he climbed onto a table, started throwing food trays. He started a riot, got a black eye and then detention. I'd have been more upset but it honestly reminded me of myself as a little kid, raised in a tough environment."

I take it in.

"There are a dozen games. The older kids can do the hard ones but even the younger kids can do better than I can. The boys get so focused on the firefighter game. No tension between them, the anger and all that just melts away when they're Juggling. They . . ." She trails off.

"Sandy?"

"Watch for yourself."

She pushes a handful of buttons and a scene appears over the pair of jugglers. It's a high-tech, translucent video. I'm watching footage shot of the learning annex. A boy wearing the devices moves his arms in fits and jerks, a controlled spasmodic, sending ones and zeroes flying through hoops and tunnels.

Click.

A small boy—shaved head and syrupy-thin arms—spins three holographic balls down three holographic bowling lanes. He alternately grimaces, smiles, focuses, his face a bubbling landscape of the turmoil within. I feel like I'm looking at the physical correlate to the chaos going on inside their brains.

Click.

Five boys in a semicircle, juggling, captivated, at once completely active and utterly inert.

Click. The static image appears, the ninja jugglers and the clouds. *Click.* The image vanishes.

"Clouds?"

"The Cloud."

"Juggling the cloud?"

"C'mon." Impatient with my evident stupidity. "We're moving into the cloud, all of us. This next generation, they're the cloud warriors, the digital ninjas. I guess we've got lawyers getting a bunch of different trademarks."

Before I can follow up, she switches directions. "They obviously lied to me."

"Who?"

"The brain images. Something's not right. I know that. They say they're giving the kids physicals, full consent from the county and the parents whose kids get bussed in and all that. They say they're making sure that playtime builds better kids. But it's obviously not that."

The brain images. "What do you mean?"

With her right thumb, she clicks off a button on the device in her palm. She pushes it onto the counter. She seems suddenly defeated.

"Everything I've told you is true."

"I know that."

"I've been there less than a year. They wanted a celeb to reach out to the annex and inspire the kids to use the Juggler. Y'know, get them thinking that if they followed my lead, maybe they could get on TV, stuff like that. A lot of the parents are heavy TV watchers or first-gen Americans, some right-off-the-boat support staff. They like the idea of having me as part of the mix."

"Okay."

"I can tell you, without any reservation, these kids are getting smarter with their devices. And I honestly don't see what the big deal is; sure, this is

great technology, but it's just an amped-up version
of portable video games and mobile devices with
some of the brain-game technology mixed in."

"Then why did Steve try to burn it down?"

She shrugs and drops her eyes.

"It was an accident, I'm sure."

I give her the "give me a break" look.

"I think you're the one who's lying. You're doing
corporate espionage, just like they warned me
someone might do. You want to know how it works,
how it works so well with their brains."

"I'm a journalist."

"Then do what modern journalists do and wait
for the announcement."

I shake my head, not understanding.

"It'll all be public soon enough. Ten days. The
marketing and product launch."

"At PRISM?"

"Chengdu."

I shake my head again. Am I hearing correctly?
My ears feel like they're ringing. Two weeks. The
launch. What I'd been warned about.

"Huge city in China. I guess they're all huge.
They've got a zoo there. They're going to have
clowns and, of course, jugglers."

"China." I'm surprisingly staggered by this piece
of information. It doesn't conform to the picture
I've been forming. And I can feel the wary gears of
my overtaxed brain trying to adjust. "Why test it in
San Francisco? When is the U.S. product launch?"

"Never. That's the big thing. They did some
refining of the software here, for obvious reasons.
Smart engineers, U.S. know-how, and all that. But

they don't want this product to come to the U.S. Not ever. Or at least not until they establish control over the intellectual property."

"Why not?"

Sandy's eyes go wide. But she's not looking at me. She's looking at the front door of the house. I follow her gaze. I don't see anything. Then I do: some movement, a whisking in the shadows.

She raises the rifle.

44

With Sandy's eyes averted, I reach for my iPhone. I lift it from the table, undetected, then slip it into my pocket.

"Clyde?" Sandy directs her shout at the door.

It's not. At the door, a figure appears through the glass, not Clyde. He peers inside. He sees the shotgun and recoils. I can't see what he does next but I infer that he slinks a step or two down the stairs, and pastes himself against the outside wall. He's thin, tall, with a rounded head that, near as I can tell from the partial darkness, is bald. The buzzard.

"I know my rights." Sandy squeezes the trigger, prompting a blast and then an explosion of glass.

A rectangular window next to the front door seems to ripple, a slow-motion effect, then its puzzle pieces start to fall to the ground. The door itself looks lightly peppered with buckshot and punctured on the far right, just above the handle, with a hole the size of a baby's fist.

I slide to the ground and peer through the legs of the dining-room chairs at the doorway. No movement. No fallen body. The whole thing feels both violent and almost comical; melodramatic Sandy Vello makes her last, loud stand.

"Call 911," Sandy orders.

There's a pause, then a sound from the outside, the buzzard making some kind of noise near the front door. Hurt? Taking aim? Suddenly, an object flies through the shattered window. It's making a wailing sound, like an alarm.

"Bomb!" Sandy yells.

I flatten myself and cover my head. I think: Isaac. I see an image of my crinkly baby. Pink, then pale, then blue. Not breathing. What's wrong with him? He's so still. I'm paralyzed. Is this how it ends?

I hear footsteps. They're coming from the outside, shuffling, maybe down the stairs. Definitely down the stairs. Our attacker in full escape; I thought he said he'd protect me.

I look up. I can't help myself. I should be retreating. I should cover my head but, impulsively, I look up. I peer at the object that flew through the window. The supposed bomb on the floor, between the entrance to the house and the dining-room table. It's small, wailing like an alarm clock. And it's not a bomb. Not even close. It's a cell phone. Not just any cell phone. I know it. I bought it. It's the cheap-ass Motorola phone I put on the seat of the black Mercedes.

"Not a bomb," I yell. "A phone. A diversion."

"What?"

I get an idea. I pull on my sneaker and say: "It's just a cell phone with the alarm going off. He's getting away."

"Fleeing like a little girl." Triumphant.

"Not if you get a shot at him from the front window."

She doesn't respond.

"Sandy, what's to stop him from going back to his car and getting some actual bomb, or whatever, a gun?"

She starts moving. Peering between the refinished legs of the table, I see her feet churn toward the front of the house. My cue to move. I slink around the back end of the table. I lift my head to see her absorbed, pushing aside a rocking chair that sits beneath a square window at the front of the narrow house. I snag one of the Jugglers from the countertop. Sandy sets down her shotgun, then looks back at me. Just before she sees me, I lower the Juggler and lift my phone. Into it, I shout, "Intruder." I mouth to Sandy: "911."

Sandy turns back to the window. She opens a lock on the side and begins to turn a crank at its bottom. Her hand slips, betraying nerves. I can imagine the collision in her brain of neuro-chemicals and ego, the ego compelling her to show her moxie, the chemicals urging her to fall to the floor and remember she's not a super-secret spy but a physical-fitness devotee caught up in something well beyond her resolve.

The window pops open. I start moving quickly to the door. I reach it and twist the door handle, my silent hopes answered when it turns, unlocked. Sandy lifts the rifle, fumbles it, and seems to hear my movements behind her. My own mordant curiosity—some preternatural inquisitiveness that the Witch would say borders on a death wish—prompts me to pause and see what Sandy decides to do, rather than duck from the window. She starts to raise the weapon in my direction, then hesitates. I do not. I step into the darkness.

Keeping my head down, I fly down the wooden stairs slippery with night, trying not to fall and pretending I may not get shot. Within seconds, I'm on the ground, beside the garage. Then: *Bang!*

Sandy's pulled the trigger. I look up the side of the house. I'm nearly directly below her, but slightly around the corner of the house. I doubt she's aiming at me. The angles don't work. So what, or who, is she aiming at? I peer across the road into the mini-forest. Tall trees, dense, underbrush. No movement. I'm guessing Sandy isn't shooting at anyone at all. She's announcing her presence.

And doesn't she have to reload? I sprint across the road into the underbrush, duck beneath a leafy limb, step onto a rock and feel my knee twist. I stumble forward, drop the Juggler, demi-dive after it, find myself lying on the ground, my head nestled beside a puddle.

I pause. I wait for the pulsing pain to pass. I listen. Silent night. I picture Polly, teary-eyed, holding the fortune cookie, and Isaac, pale in the delivery room, chaotic sounds and nurses and doctors circling, a cacophony of shouting but, for me, everything going terribly silent. My baby boy born, Polly prone on the delivery bed, pale, my dreams on the cusp. Something's gone terribly, terribly wrong.

I stand. I don't look back. I stop listening. I don't

care. Shoot me, Sandy, if you will. Capture me, buzzard, if you can.

I sprint in the direction of my car, then stumble, sprint, stumble, sprint, the Juggler somehow in my hand, slippery, the grainy brain images in my pocket.

I reach the Audi. I climb into the car. I whisk it in a tight circle. I pull up to the metal gate, step out of the car, open it, am about to climb back into the car when I hear it. Rustling. To my right, in the darkness and trees. I see it, don't I? An angry red light. It's the tip of a cigarette, ten feet deep in the trees, held head-high. I flash on an image from a few hours earlier; a packet of cigarettes in the front seat of the car of the buzzard. In the present, I don't bother to strain to make out the face behind the cigarette—or to discover if I'm imagining things or not. I drop into the driver's seat and I gun the car, fishtailing through the gate, then swerving more as I pull a hard left onto the main gravel road.

Seconds later, I pass the house, again without incident. I'm free. Has the buzzard sprung me? Or taken pity?

I pull out my cell phone and, numb-fingered, dial, my brain bursting with questions and theories, not just about the Juggler and the conspirators behind it, but about the reasons my life fell apart. My cozy dream shattered, in a moment over an empty fortune cookie, the pieces strewn over the last agonizing nine months. The phone rings. I picture Faith, the compassion of a nurse, nubile movements of a dancer, the fraudulence of a stage actor. Still, I'm feeling something. It's deep. It's affection, a genuine crush. It's the first time I've felt it, maybe that I've felt anything, since . . .

My thoughts are interrupted when a man answers my cell.

I say: "I have what you're looking for."

45

From his groggy silence, I infer skepticism. Maybe I'm projecting. I actually don't have what he's looking for. Not all of it. But I have a reasonable bluff. "Brain images," I say. "And the Juggler."

"Tomorrow night."

"Now!"

"Too late."

The dashboard clock reads 12:30.

"Then I'll go to the police." Another bluff.

"I'll call you back."

Click.

The tires jitter. I've moved too far right and I'm sloping down on the slanted edge of the gravel road, pointed at the stump of a once proud redwood. I swerve left. Righted, I gun the car and I exit the rural subdivision, leaving behind Clyde's fixer-upper, Sandy, maybe Buzzard Bill, a mess of clues I'm starting to connect, I hope.

When I hit the paved road, I take a sharp left. I'm headed in the direction of Highway 280 North, and home. As I reach the highway, the on-ramp appears to split into two unfocused ghost images. For an instant, I can't tell which of the two ramps is the one that leads me home and which is a blurred vision borne of exhaustion that will lead me to slam my car into the wall.

I pull the car hard to the left. I need sleep. Now. I cross under the highway interchange, still not seeing any other car lights. I keep my trajectory west, heading toward the sharply rising hills that separate the highway from the Pacific Ocean. It's even more rarified real estate here; big lots peppered with ancient trees, some with grazing deer and fenced horses, accessed, like the house I've just escaped, by narrow gravel tributaries.

It's one of those off-roads I seek.

Less than a mile up the canyon, I find the one I'm looking for. It's a turn to the left over a creek bridge onto a road that serpentines up a hillside. But I can see as I slow, nearing the turnoff, that, just beyond the bridge, there's a spot to park. It's just barely visible from the road, and only if you happen to be looking closely for, say, a slumbering journalist. I pull into the spot, turn off the car, and then, nearly, the phone. I don't want to be tracked here. But with my finger poised to power off the device, I remember one last task.

I read the text from Jill Gilkeson: I remember Alan Parsons. Call me.

It's too late for that. It's nearly 1 A.M.

I type: "Sorry 4 delayed response. I'll call in morning."

I hit send.

I start to power off the phone. It beeps with an

incoming text. "Im up." I hit send to initiate a call, trackers be damned.

"I haven't slept well in years," she says by way of answering the phone. I blink back a tear. In my exhaustion, I feel connected to this woman.

"Alan Parsons."

"An amazing teacher. A genius."

"Of computers."

"Right. Andrew was so good to him but, if I remember—and please don't quote me on this—Alan just couldn't keep it together."

"Back up. I'm having trouble keeping pace."

She laughs, like, of course. "By the way, why are *you* awake right now? I guess journalists get focused on their stories, but this isn't all that interesting. Is it?"

"I've experienced loss too." It's out of my mouth before I realize I've said it. I wonder if I'm establishing empathy as a tactic, or something rawer. In the brush, I see movement. I flinch. Is it a deer or my imagination?

I kill the fog lights. I don't know if I want to see what's out there before it visits me. Come what may.

The defeated woman on the other end of the line starts talking. She takes me back to when Andrew Leviathan started building new charter schools on the Peninsula. His goal, she says, was to give opportunity to at-risk students but also talented teachers who the public school system might not embrace. Alan Parsons, she says, was one such teacher. He was a computer whiz, engaging, bright, and thirsty. A drunk, he wound up dropping from Stanford's computer science PhD program, where he'd been a favorite among undergrads he taught. There was some chatter that Alan did a bit of corporate espionage and hacking to support his booze habit and that he tended to get playful when wasted. He could be a recreational hacker and a devastatingly good one. There was a rumor that Alan, virtually joyriding on gin, once hacked into Pentagon computers and made it look like a warhead had gone missing.

Andrew, the tech-savvy savior, came to the rescue. Andrew hired Alan to do tech support at one of the first charter schools. And, so long as he remained sober, to teach one class.

"How to multitask?" I ask.

She laughs. "That word barely existed then. But, if it did, Andrew wouldn't have allowed it in the school."

"What do you mean?"

"Andrew wouldn't even let computers into class. I only remember this because it seemed so odd. He said the school could teach the *logic* of how computers work, programming skills and capabilities, but wouldn't allow screen time."

It rings familiar. Polly mentioned at some point in our discussion of future school options for Isaac that some Montessori programs keep technology at a distance. But it doesn't sound consistent with the Andrew I've been learning about. He's been pushing heavy technology use; it's in his blood, and maybe that blood is bad. I'm hypothesizing that he's been simultaneously developing insidious Juggler technology on the sly while creating a public face that limits use of technology in schools. Why?

"Jill, was Andrew involved in the Juggler project?"

"Haven't heard of it. But I didn't know Alan all that well."

She says that, as far as she could recall, Alan couldn't stop drinking. He was fired. But the two men kept up their ties. She says that she seems to vaguely recall Alan's name coming up recently; she thinks Andrew might have contacted him again.

"If you're looking to do a story on Andrew's generosity, I think you could include the part about Alan."

"Alan died recently."

She doesn't respond. She can't stand hearing about death.

"I need to go," I say. I really do. I can't see for exhaustion. And, I realize as the adrenaline starts to fade, I'm ravenous.

"Get some sleep."

"Jill?"

"Yes."

"May I ask you one more thing? It's about your daughter."

Silent ascent.

"Did she ever have contact with Mr. Leviathan?"

"What's that supposed to mean?" Alarmed.

"Sorry. Terrible turn of phrase. I meant: was he generous with her too, in terms of his time or his commitment to education?"

"Oh." She pauses. "Not really." Another pause. "Other than the after-school program."

"Program, like . . ."

"Glorified babysitting, for kids of employees. Board games and computer games. Early ones. The kids got to play with all kinds of toys the big brains in R and D were developing."

Internal alarm bells, a burst of adrenaline. I let it pass so I don't betray the zeal of my curiosity and frighten her. She fills in the silence.

"She must've gone for near two years. She really craved it, hanging out with the other kids. It was a little wonderland. It brought her alive, in a way."

"How so?"

"I'm really not comfortable talking about her. Suffice it to say, Mr. Leviathan's a saint. Now, I've got to try to get some sleep myself."

End of interview.

"Sleep well, Jill."

Click.

My phone beeps. I look at the screen. There's a notification: tomorrow afternoon, I'm due at the courthouse to meet with tax authorities.

I turn off the device. I drop it into the center console. I trade it for an energy bar that I devour. Dinner, breakfast, whatever it is at this point.

I recline. I close my eyes, craving sleep, seeing puzzle pieces. I form a picture: Andrew Leviathan, through his partner and intermediary, Gils Simons, has sold or is otherwise exporting to China some technology that entertains kids and professes to help them multitask, turn them into cloud masters. But it actually hurts their brains. Does it hurt development of their frontal lobes by overloading them with data? They're not mastering the cloud, or successfully juggling it, they're winding up in one.

I suspect Andrew had been testing the technology for years.

Recently, Alan Parsons stumbled onto their plot and he tried to blackmail Leviathan, his former benefactor. He first tried to reach me by a fake email address for Sandy Vello. I overlooked or ignored or didn't see it. So he used Faith to help seduce me into his efforts. But why? Why did he need my help? Was he afraid Leviathan would come after him, and is that exactly what happened?

Where does Buzzard Bill fit in, and the stout man with the crooked smile in Chinatown? My guess is that each is acting as muscle but exactly for what and whom?

And what more is there to Faith? Is she safe?

I see a memory fragment. I've awakened in the hotel room with her, after a night of feverish sex in a concussed state. I open my eyes to find her staring at me, eyes glistening, real emotion. In my mind's eye, in the present, her face transforms into Polly, eyes glistening, sitting over an empty fortune cookie. "I have something to tell you," she says. "Brace yourself."

I bite the inside of my cheek to shatter the memory fragment. I feel a sob deep inside my chest, rising. I see its origin: a black void inside me, creeping from my head into my body, a fast-spreading emotional malignancy, like a fresh bloodstain.

I fall asleep.

I wake up with a start when I hear the tapping on the window.

46

My first thought: someone needs an endocrinologist. My second: that someone is a cop.

He stands at the driver's-side window. Blue and brown uniform, no cap. And no facial hair. Zero. His face looks ice smooth. It's a relatively rare hormone imbalance, low testosterone, unless he shaves every forty-five minutes.

Nonchalant, he holds a black baton in a beefy right hand that does not lack in testosterone. I open the driver's-side door. Behind the cop stands his motorcycle, sun bouncing off the black gas tank.

"Not a cool place to sleep one off." His voice matches the detached coolness in the air. He's not picking a fight, just giving both my first and last warning. A bird chirps. In the tree above us, a gray gnatcatcher stops on a leafless limb, then darts upward into a crisp, cloudless morning. From the angle of the sun, it might well be ten in the morning.

I swallow hard, tasting foul, lumpy paste.

"I'm sorry, officer. I worked late, got too tired to drive 280."

He cocks his head. I look at the underside of his nose, a likely spot to see hair growth if his face is capable of it. No little sprouts. He clears his throat, wanting my attention undivided.

"You need to get home to your family."

"No family, officer."

He furrows his eyebrows. Those he has. I see him look in the backseat and I turn. He's eyeing the car seat.

"I could give you a field sobriety test."

"I'm sorry. I'm sober. One thousand percent. I'm . . ." I run out of words. "You're right. My family needs me."

"I'll be back in five minutes to make sure you're gone."

I turn on my phone, which tends to be the first thing I do every morning for the mini adrenaline burst, a wisp of dopamine roughly equivalent to a whiff of coffee, right before the first sip. With an impolite beep, the device lets me know that the battery is low. And there's one voice message. "Tonight. More instructions later." It's spoken in the choppy tonality and grammar of a non-native speaker.

I turn off the phone to give it the rest it needs.

I curl my head in a circle, feeling the crackling in my upper vertebrae, the awakening crinkles of the folds of skin around my neck, the paraspinal muscles and fatty tissue at the base and sides of my neck.

I feel a peculiar sensation. I pause, head leaned at three o'clock, to make sure I'm not mistaken. I'm not. I feel lucid. Clearheaded. I look outside and see colors as vivid as I've seen in days. I take in the brown pre-spring nubby leaf buds on the tree branch, and the dusty red bricks stacked at the base of a wheelbarrow near a wooden gate. I'm seeing the world in high-definition again.

A hollow, urgent sensation grips my intestines. Hunger. And then a more demanding pressure just lower down from my bladder. I need to pee and eat.

I angle down the rearview mirror so I can stare back at myself. I know that look. I'm rested. And determined. Nine hours of sleep have done some healing magic that no medication could do for my concussed brain. I can imagine the white spots that dotted my frontal lobe beginning to dissolve. In their place, healthy tissue and priorities. Time to tick the first item off the to-do list.

The Mission Day School stretches a half block, a stately and brown brick facade, then cuts sharply and handsomely off on each end so that the building forms the shape of a U.

A string of neatly aligned trees, transplanted from some forest north of the Golden Gate Bridge, ornament the shallow front lawn behind an ornate black metal fence.

A plaque next to the front gate reads: "K–8, Curriculum Vitae. For Life."

The stately edifice is out of place in a part of the city, the outer Mission, where everything is out of place. Worn concrete-surfaced playgrounds surrounded by chain-link fences abut trendy small-plate restaurants serving $16 finger food abut $2 million three-story stand-alone hipster pads abut the barred windows of "deluxe" low-rise shoebox apartments renting for $625 a month to single moms, Mexican day-workers and their families, and slam poets.

In the idle Audi, parked across the street from the Mission Day School, I gulp a three-shot espresso drink called a Depth Charge and an egg-and-cheese croissant sandwich from a nearby hole-in-the-wall café. I've closed Bullseye's laptop, which I used to visit the school's web site. In a nutshell, Mission Day is an elite school, regarded as one of the best in California at using alternative teaching methods to "foster a generation of 21st-century leaders." This is Andover and Choate, San Francisco style, costing parents $30,000 a year.

This is where Faith's nephew goes to school. It doesn't add up. Faith says that her sister suffers a mental disorder and lives a disheveled life. And she says that her nephew has inherited some emotional instability. I recall his name is Timothy and she described him as having Asperger's syndrome and as being disruptive in class. How does the family pay for tuition at Mission Day? It seems doubtful that the nephew has earned a scholarship if he's a source of in-class tension.

I initially wondered if Andrew Leviathan had anything to do with the school but can find no evidence on the Net that he has a relationship to Mission Day. Is he connected to Faith?

Meantime, I do see a different connection between Mission Day School and the events of the last few days. In glancing at the roster of the school administrators and finding the name Carl Lemon. "Carl_L."

He's a former corporate lawyer turned director of admissions. There's an image of him but it's not a picture. It's a caricature that was drawn, it says, by one of the school's students (all of the administrators' images are caricatures). The one for Carl makes him look mid-thirties: close-cropped curls on the top of his head, maybe light-dark skin, a loose tie, a thin smile. He likes giving out tardy notices in the hallway.

From my glove compartment, I snag a notebook and a pen. I see a little boy walk through the front door. I look back at my car seat. I picture Wilma and hear her give me my homework assignment: focus on the image of the nuclear family you romanticized. Let yourself mourn its absence and passing. Think about "loss."

"You're getting somewhere," I recall Wilma saying as I exit the last time. "See you next week."

It's the last thing I remember clearly before I head to the subway on the fateful night this mystery began to unfold. I vaguely recall standing on the subway platform, picturing how Isaac might view the entrance to the subway, how my little guy might view as intriguing the ominous black subway tunnel glistening with condensation.

I flash back further, months earlier, to the night of the Fortune Cookie, and the revelation from Polly that changed my life. "Nat," she says, her smile at 40 percent, "I have something to tell you. Brace yourself." In the present, her words sting so much that I instantly blink them away. The memory feels more vivid than it has felt in days, like the colors outside the car where I woke up this morning. I can't think about this now. I'm close to answers.

I spring out of the car, leaving the empty car seat behind me.

I stand in the pristine hallway with smooth arches sloping to form a high concave ceiling. A stern-looking woman in her mid-fifties approaches. She wears a sleeveless blouse with a sweater tied around her waist.

"*Peux je vous aider?*"

I shake my head, confused. My best move is to go on the offensive.

"I'm heading to administration." Purposeful, just shy of angry.

"It's French Day. We ask parents to participate." I'm being scolded.

"*Gracias.*" The only non-English word that comes to mind.

She points to the right and shakes her head.

Carl Lemon's brass nameplate identifies his heavy brown door. I knock, causing the slightly ajar door to open. Behind a desk sits a man wearing suspenders and who has been flattered by the caricature on his web site. His brown curls have begun to recede, foretelling an eventual sharp widow's point in the center of his spacious forehead.

"Mr. Lemon."

"Do you have an appointment?"

"I'm here about Faith?"

"You'll need to make an appointment."

He looks down again at whatever he's working on, summarily dismissing me. He's serious to a fault.

"I'm with the press. On a big story involving your school."

"If you don't leave, I'll call security." Still looking down.

"I relish the opportunity to talk with them." Now he looks up. I continue. "Where is Faith? What have you done with her?"

He blinks.

"So get security."

"Come in. Shut the door behind you."

47

"Who are you?"

I realize my arms are crossed, an emotionally defensive posture, which is not the message I'm looking to send. He needs to feel like he's backpedaling, mostly because I've got only bluster, not information. If he feels threatened, he might start offering a confession as part of a conditional surrender. I've seen it work in interviews before. I've also seen it miserably fail.

I lift an expensive brown wooden chair from its perch near the wall to my right and carry it to the edge of his desk. I can feel its leg dragging, bunching the image of the African women carrying the swaddled child that is woven into the area rug beneath me. He winces. Why on Earth would Faith want her nephew to attend school here?

I drop his gaze to situate myself in the chair, letting the silence stir up inside him. I look at him, then glance around the room, playing a role of confident interrogator that, even in my most officious moods and with the most inane corporate-relations flacks, feels manufactured. He's got a couple of diplomas on his textured white walls and a picture of a beached whale being encouraged by the cheers of children.

I tell him my name as I pull from my wallet my driver's license and business card. It's intended to show I'm unafraid to reveal myself. I tell him that I tend to do investigative pieces and that he can look up online my recent award to get a sense of the kinds of stories I write. He doesn't much study my license and business card, which I generally find to be a sign that he trusts what I'm telling him. Or maybe he knows who I am already, but I doubt it. In either case, he's ready to bargain.

I pull my notebook from my back pocket.

"What do you want?"

"Where is she?"

He shrugs. "I have no idea. Did you say this is for an article? Which publication?"

Already, in an instant, I can feel the momentum shifting against me. I've got little to go on.

"She's worried about her nephew, Timothy."

He clenches his jaw.

"You're using him." I'm being deliberately vague.

He averts his eyes slightly to the left.

"Did you mess him up with the Juggler? Is he part of the testing?"

His gaze hardens, then he looks at me quizzically. I've overextended myself.

"Alan Parsons sent me."

Several rapid eye blinks. It's not that he knows about Alan Parsons. Far from it, I realize. Rather, he senses I'm either a fraud or someone on a fishing expedition who cannot rightly threaten him. Something bad happened between him and Faith, but I've got no clue what that is.

I stand. I lean forward on the desk. For the first time, I peer through the picture window behind his desk. I'm looking into a large grassy play area, the courtyard, with serpentine brick walkways, a wooden playground in the far corner anchored by what looks to be a large sunken ship, and dotted in spots by benches. I can't take my eyes off a boy sitting alone on a bench, holding a toy airplane in his right hand, pretending to make it fly over his head.

I pull my gaze back to the bureaucrat. I'm seething with anger but with little way to channel it. A gut impulse strikes me. Where logic and rational argument fails, I need to use emotion. I need to appeal to something rhetorically irrefutable.

"I'm also Faith's boyfriend."

I deliberately lean another millimeter forward, like I just might jump over the desk. "Cut the merde."

"What?"

"It's French Day, asshole."

The crazy-guy look in my eyes must perk him up. It can't be my pronunciation. He holds up his hands, palms out. "*She* came on to *me*."

I feel prickles. Revelation coming. I let my body recede that extra millimeter to suggest I'm willing to listen.

"That's not how she tells it."

"This is not for an article. It's off the record. And I know the distinction between off the record and 'for background.'" He uses air quotes around the words. "She used me."

"You're going to hate losing this job."

"Her nephew doesn't belong at this school. I told her that. We owe it to our families to make sure every student contributes to making this the most competitive learning environment, and creative one. I gave him a chance and he's squandered it."

I remember hearing his voice and words on Faith's voice mail, telling her she is running out of time. Demanding, threatening.

"That doesn't give you an excuse to threaten her."

"You're her boyfriend, so you know exactly what she's about. She picks at weak spots and exploits them. But that's beside the point. By the time I was . . ." He pauses, looking for the words. "By the time I was spending time with her, I'd already agreed to give her nephew a chance and to provide a scholarship. He needs a chance too. Our relationship, brief as it might have been, has nothing to do with the issue of her nephew's education."

I'm scrambling to stitch together his clues. I can almost picture my resource-starved working memory, my little closet filled with precious near-term intellectual capacity, churning like the engine room in the *Titanic*. An idea starts to form, and it's darn simple: Faith seduced this guy in order to get her troubled nephew admission and a free ride into the best school in the city. This doofus happily went along for the ride, then got pissed when the ride ended, leading to threatening phone calls.

I try it out on him. I act surprised, a little hurt. I ask him whether Faith started sleeping with him as a way of getting her nephew into school? And, now that he's in the school, she's withdrawn?

He doesn't answer. But he seems to indirectly accede by asking: "So you're here as boyfriend, not journalist?"

I ignore him. I think I've begun to understand Faith's secret, or at least the first part of it.

"You told Alan Parsons about this? You gave him ammunition to use against her."

"Get out of my office."

Another insight. He didn't tell Alan Parsons. Then, another silent A-ha. He has no idea about Alan Parsons. Alan was a hacker who got to know Faith at a coffee shop. Alan needed Faith's help to seduce someone else—namely, me. So he hacked into her email or computer or whatever, and figured out Faith had her own weak spot, something to exploit: she had slept with a school administrator to help her nephew. Alan essentially blackmailed her to help get my attention on the subway platform. If she didn't go along with it, he'd expose her seduction of this imbecilic dean of admissions.

It's a theory, at least.

The doofus reaches for the landline phone. I lean over and I hold the receiver in place, daring him to turn this into a physical confrontation.

"If you kick Timothy out of school, I'll . . ." I pause. I don't like the gravity and clichéd nature of the threats poised on my tongue. I can't say them and mean them.

"You obviously don't have kids, Mr. Idle."

I blink, stung. I drop his gaze and glance out the picture window behind him. On the bench, the boy flies the airplane over his head, amused, captivated, free, healthy, alive.

"My son is Isaac." A whisper, or maybe I just think it.

"If you had kids, you'd understand that you should let this go. Faith is a big girl looking out for her nephew. Your threats aren't helping him or her. But I'm willing to let this go. End of story. Okay?"

"Excellent decision, Carl."

I look again at the boy with the airplane. I suddenly can't breathe. I take a step backward, let myself out the door. And then I'm running down the hallway. Sprinting.

It's the most lucid I've been in days. It's the first time my head has cleared. I can see the memory fragments now, talking to Polly over the fortune cookie, then discussing that night with Wilma, the therapist, getting my homework assignment. Focus on what you've lost. Blink, I see the hospital, Isaac born, tiny, Polly so pale. The chaos and the doctors.

I'm outside, down the path, between the out-of-place trees on the front of the out-of-place school. I'm sitting in the Audi. I pull out my phone, turn it on, hear the urgent beep demanding it be plugged in. I dial.

"What do you want?" the voice answers.

"Now."

"I told you: tonight."

"Now, or I go to the police. And the press. I know everything."

He doesn't respond.

"Twin Peaks?"

"No." He doesn't continue.

"Where?"

"Mount Davidson. Rainy now. No one will be there. At the cross. Thirty minutes." The phone dies.

I'm sure he'd prefer a nighttime exchange. Faith for my information, and the brain images and the Juggler. At night, it's dark, free of witnesses, easier to dispatch us. During the day, I've got a better chance.

Don't I?

Do I care? No.

I can see clearly for the first time since my head smashed onto the subway platform why my life has come undone. No, I can see it clearly for the first time in much longer than that, maybe eight months.

I've got to outrun the memory. I'm willing to die trying.

48

Fog so dense it requires windshield wipers greets me at the foot of Mount Davidson. It's more of a huge hill, really, accessible by a cul-de-sac at the edge of St. Francis Woods, one of San Francisco's ritziest neighborhoods. The mansions here defy the urban space limitations elsewhere in the city.

A ten-minute winding-trail walk up the mini-mountain leads to the top. There, when the fog permits, you get a splendid view of downtown and the East Bay. But the bigger payoff is the massive cross looming over Mount Davidson, an unlikely and imposing 103-foot concrete crucifix built in the 1930s, its upper edge popping just above the high trees on San Francisco's highest hill.

In the late 1990s, it was nearly felled by city residents who disliked the church-and-state implications of a massive religious symbol mounted on public lands. It was preserved through a deal with the Armenian Church, which rewrote the narrative to make this not just any cross but a memorial to Armenian genocide in Turkey.

And in the 1970s, Clint Eastwood nearly died here at the hands of a serial killer in the first Dirty Harry movie.

If it was good enough for Clint, it's good enough for me. Not a bad place for an agnostic to meet his own end.

I park in the cul-de-sac in front of a home with a massive oval front window. I push open the heavy door of an Audi I have no business driving, or, rather, that I certainly can't afford. Not on my own. I see the nick in the driver's-side door, just below the handle, where, just a month before Isaac was born, Polly got woozy and hit a cement wall pulling out of a parking lot. It was the last time I remember her driving this car, or any other. I look in the backseat at the car seat, empty.

I should be coming up with a plan. I should find a sharp stick with which to defend myself. I should figure out how I'm going to confront Andrew Leviathan and Gils Simons. There are a thousand things I should do.

I open the back door. I slide in next to the car seat. From the tag still hanging off the side I can see that it's made by Graco. The plush gray fabric is so clean, unstained, pristine. There's a rubber band still around the clasps that would hold in place my precious cargo.

Would. In theory.

This car seat has never been used.

I lean my head next to it. I close my eyes. I see Polly sitting at the Chinese restaurant, her smile at 40 percent, sad, poised to tell me something, holding her empty fortune cookie. I shake my head, making the image disappear.

I pull my phone from my pocket. I know it is almost dead for wont of a recharge. But I push the power button anyway. An Apple emerges onto the screen. Then it beeps and shows me an image of a battery near empty with a red sign, indicating five percent left.

Five percent may be all I need.

From my contact list, I call up Polly's phone number. I press it to dial. I put the phone on speaker. I hear the phone ring only once. It answers: "This number is out of service."

The phone dies.

Out of service. The last time I called, when I was at the hospital getting my concussion checked, a woman answered and didn't recognize my voice. She asked me to stop calling. She must be tired of me calling her, asking for Polly. She finally put the number to bed.

I exhale and lay my head against the side of the car seat. I feel the plastic edge press uncomfortably against my temple. I ignore it. I close my eyes and I see Polly. She opens the fortune cookie and discovers it is empty inside. She manages a bitter half laugh.

"How appropriate," she says. "My future looks bleak."

"Señor." I hold up my hand to the waiter with the gimp knee. "Another fortune cookie for the fine lady."

He nods and disappears into the kitchen.

"I have something to tell you, Nathaniel."

Polly looks down. I follow her gaze to the water-stained tablecloth beneath her glass, seeing the damp trail as it bleeds slightly into the two folders Polly has brought to dinner, one with preschool applications and the other aimed at helping me set up a 401(k).

"I have a tumor."

I push my neck forward. I'm not sure I've heard her correctly.

"You know how I've had trouble sleeping, the headaches, that mistake I made in my presentation last week at the investment conference . . ."

"That's just the pregnancy, the hormones."

"The baby is fine, Nathaniel."

"Stop it."

"You're going to be a father. You're going to be a great one. You're going to teach him how to throw and catch and make great but judicious use of adjectives and, you've got to promise me, to also add and subtract. He's going to need some practical teaching along with your romantic leanings."

"Polly . . ."

She looks at me now, square. I know this look, the one she gives investors when she's reached her bottom line.

"It's in my brain, and its Stage Three and it's inoperable, at least until this bundle is born, and they can't do chemo because it could . . ."

Almost as if from a distance, I hear myself say: "We can make another baby, another time. We have a lifetime. When the life of the mother is at stake, the baby takes second position."

"There's a chance we'll both survive, a reasonable chance. We'll schedule an early C-section so I can get care as soon as possible."

"How can you be telling me this now!" Less question than accusation.

"It happened so fast. I found out two days ago. I've been in disbelief and denial." She shakes her head, almost bemused. "I wonder if you're right: maybe all the deal making on my cell phone radiating my brain. Don't let our baby boy press the device to his head."

The limping waiter appears with a plate bearing a second fortune cookie. I wave my hand. We need privacy. I hate this man, the bearer of the empty fortune cookie.

He sets down the plate and scurries. Polly reaches for the cookie. She's got tears rolling down her cheeks. She cracks open the fragile brown pastry.

She holds it in her hands. It's empty. Just like the first.

"Bad batch." She smiles a smile I've never seen before. It looks 90 percent effervescent but, at the same time, terribly empty, a 100 percent black void.

In the present, I see only intensifying drizzle, the foul San Francisco fog, the shroud of death, weather just like the night that Isaac was born.

I picture the ambulance unloading Polly at the emergency room after she's passed out in the family room of the loft I later inherited. They rush her to labor and delivery for a C-section a month earlier than planned.

"Isaac," Polly says as she goes under, then goes terribly pale. She gasps. Beeping, shouts, I'm pushed aside.

I went to medical school. I should be able to do something. I'm not just a writer, not just a romantic, a chaser of conspiracies and weaver of disparate ideas, a synthesizer, blogger, storyteller, seducer of sources and readers. I'm not just a neurotic who can identify medical conditions like some *Jeopardy!* savant. I should be able to do something. But all I can do is diagnose Polly's cardiac arrest, and watch in slow motion.

After that, it's all a dream. Isaac appears, crinkly and pink, but not pink enough, white, if I'm honest. I touch his pale arm, waiting for the wailing. A nurse gently pushes my arm away while sterilized hands and blazing figures in blue and green scrubs bob and weave and take the fight to the death. In the midst, helpless with my medical degree, a chronicler of life and conspiracy, I pull out my phone. I snap a picture of Isaac's first and only moments on Earth. That is my helpless act, a memory, I tell myself, to share with Polly when the world rights itself.

There's a knocking sound.

I spring upright.

The man with the crooked smile stands at the window. He wields a knife he's been using to tap the glass. In his T-shirt and off-center San Francisco Giants cap, with his crooked smile, he's the devil-may-care.

Polly is dead. Isaac never had a chance.

What can this man possibly do to me now?

49

I open the door. At his silent urging, I reach into the front seat and snag the Juggler and hand it to him. I stand. I pull the brain images from my back pocket.

"There's more," he says.

"Of course. But not here."

Knifepoint aside, he's more genial than I remember, stocky, but an ambler, like a guy trundling to get a beer from the fridge.

I walk a step in front of him, hands jammed in pockets, where I feel my keys and the phone they mingle with. Weapons? Hardly.

It's anger that wonders these things, not hope. The future no longer matters.

I walk up a modest grade, soil and chunky rock beneath my feet, trees becoming denser as we ascend Mount Davidson.

"Where's Faith?"

"Safe and very comfortable. Comfy." He's trying out the vernacular. "She spent the night at the Mandarin. Keep walking."

The Mandarin. One of San Francisco's nicest hotels.

I trudge, my feet sinking slightly into the damp soil, winding up the hill into what is becoming a veritable rain forest, surrounded by thickening English and cape ivy and blackberry bushes. It's the lush green, primitive San Francisco that lies beneath the crisp green money and the organic lettuce. My vision glazes over but in my mind's eye I can clearly see the whole mystery, not the mystery involving Leviathan, Faith, Alan Parsons, the girl killed by the Volvo, the Juggler—that remains hazy—but my own mystery.

Polly died the night Isaac was born. Isaac died hours later. I plummeted into disbelief and grief. I poured myself into work. I became surrounded by sympathy, even from the cops who once hated my zeal for undoing authority. Every compassionate touch felt like a burn. I can see now the Witch pleading with me to come to terms with my loss, trying everything. That's why she wanted to share an office with me, so she could monitor me, cajole me, albeit gently and with her witchery. She lit candles, offered temple massages and patiently, without comment, took down the picture of Isaac that I'd emailed myself from my phone and printed out and, inexplicably, tacked to the wall.

Finally, relenting, I agreed to see Wilma, a therapist. Less Witchery, more Freud. I said I was going because I just didn't feel like myself.

For months, I wouldn't talk about Polly. Our relationship was so brief that she never really happened, we didn't happen, Isaac hadn't really come into this world, just stopped by in transit, so what was the point in talking about it?

But in the last few weeks, right before the subway incident, I started to feel something different. Grief. Raw emotion. I started to see Polly and Isaac not just as another dream deferred but as a connection severed, one I'd spent a lifetime trying to make. I left med school because the practice of medicine was too barren and impersonal. I'd pursued writing, a lifetime of poor-man's poetry through prose. And I'd found my muses in Polly and Isaac.

Then I got smacked in the head. Concussion. The fresh wounds of realization paved over by blunt-force trauma. My new neurons of grief commingled with nine months of denial, giving rise to a twisted fiction in which I'm separated from Polly, living in her former house, driving her car, but somehow still connected to her and Isaac, whose toy bouncer remains unused on the floor of my living room.

I hear voices—from the present.

I'm standing at the crest. I hear the man with the knife only a step behind me. In front of me, ten steps away, stands Faith. She wears a puffy jacket but still wraps her arms around herself to ward off the chill. Next to her stands a man who looks vaguely familiar, but I can't quite place him. Then I can.

Looming above them, the monster cross. We're at its feet, supplicants and sinners.

"Gils Simons," the man says. He takes two steps forward, extends a hand, as if he might shake.

I look back to Faith. She's unshackled, evidently not a prisoner. Is she here of her own free will? What is real?

I look out in the distance to the far edge of Mount Davidson. Soft fog, weather's most passive-aggressive state, blankets what could be a majestic view of downtown and the bay. I close my eyes. I wobble. I picture myself juggling all the lies and half-truths, the ones that I'm being told and the ones I've been telling myself. I've juggled at the expense of experiencing something real, and static, and true. I cannot juggle anymore. I fall to my knees.

Faith says to the two men: "Would you mind if I handle this?"

50

When her hand touches my shoulder, it releases a memory, her hand on the same shoulder, we're naked, clawing and releasing. My head remains down, neck exposed, like the night we made love in a beachside motel. Faith has transformed from seductress to executioner.

I'm coming, Isaac.

I hear her crouch next to me. I open my eyes to see her knees, clad in jeans, hit dirt.

"Nothing funny," one of the men says, voice nearly swallowed by the wind. Head still bowed, I can see the two men's feet, one wearing worn work boots with frayed shoelaces pulled tight on the tongue and Gils Simons's brown loafers, tasseled and as out-of-place as he seems to be.

I feel Faith's eyes on me. She shifts from my side so that she's facing me, her knees only modestly indenting the hard, wet earth. She reaches for my hands, held limply by my sides. I withdraw them at her touch.

I see one of the work boots step forward.

"Can't you see how hurt he is?" Faith says. "He's no threat to you."

Faith reaches for my hand again and I relent. She cradles my fists in her palms. She says: "They need to make sure that you've not given away their secrets."

I don't say anything.

"Nathaniel, you need to assure them of that."

"I'm not comfortable with this." The voice belongs to Gils Simons, deep and resonant, accustomed to being listened to.

I look up. Faith and the man with the crooked smile have turned to Gils, the French-born right-hand man of Andrew Leviathan. With our attention directed at Gils, I feel Faith slip something into my right hand. It's cold and blunt, metal, with ridges. It might be a pocketknife. In my fist, I can conceal all but its tip. A weapon?

"Stand up," Gils says. "This is ridiculous. This is Silicon Valley, not the old West."

"How do you execute people in Silicon Valley?" I manage to speak. "Shot at dawn by teenagers trained on the Wii?"

"Execute?" Gils sounds surprised or bemused. "We threaten lawsuits, Mr. Idle. We bring lawsuits. We ruin reputations. We guard our trade secrets very carefully. We can even use our influence to have criminal charges brought if it looks like someone has used illegal means to steal our intellectual property. The AG here loves to brag about putting away people who undermine American competitiveness."

I look at the man with the crooked smile and a knife.

"Lawyer? Is the knife his copy of the Constitution?"

"It's gratuitous and he'll put it away. But it's understandable that Steven wanted it for defensive purposes, Mr. Idle. You've shown yourself to be impulsive and dangerous. The way he remembers it, you attacked him in a dark alley, and, at least according to my sources in the police department, are being sought in connection with a fire at a juvenile detention center."

"Don't forget how I started global warming and shot JFK."

"Your zealous efforts to steal our intellectual property and expose our marketing plan have crossed the line well beyond even the most generous description of free press and investigation journalism. Look, Mr. Idle, I don't understand why you've come undone, I just know that it's a complete and tragic unraveling."

I wince. He's right. I'm suffering an acute case of post-traumatic stress disorder. I lost my son and his mother and my vision for the future. I've been chasing ghosts. My hold on reality is thin enough that I'm wondering if he's making sense. Did I invent a conspiracy and pursue it because I've, as he said, come undone? But I feel the object that Faith snuck into my hand. It's a tangible reminder that I face a real threat or, at least, a mysterious and dangerous situation.

"You've developed technology that makes kids dumber," I mumble. "The Juggler. If I expose that, which one of us will the jury convict?"

"He crazy." It's the man with the crooked smile.

"You blew up the learning annex."

Gils steps forward, asserting himself. Until this moment, I've been too bewildered, too fatalistic, to bother examining him. Now I notice the non-descript visage of an accounting type, his don't-notice-me short haircut and outdated windbreaker, frugality and conservatism incarnate, the money guy behind Leviathan's empire. He hates whatever he's gotten himself caught up in.

"I don't want to listen to any more of this non-sense, Mr. Idle. The Juggler, which, by the way, is an embargoed trade name, helps kids navigate the modern world. They can become masters of the cloud. It's cutting-edge, *bleeding-edge*, technology. And more than that, it's fun. We're going to introduce it first, on our terms, into an overseas market, then see where we go from there. By the way, this is all off the record. And, besides, you've got much bigger problems right now."

"Like which publication I'm going to sell the brain images to—the ones that show the degraded frontal-lobe capacity of test subjects in a juvenile jail. That is a serious problem. Just think of the competition for the . . ." I feel Faith's hand on my arm, squeezing. I'm pressing my luck.

"First of all, the way we read the images, they are inconclusive," Gils says. "The real-time MRI tech-nology has its limitations and the neuro-chemical blood testing remains primitive. We'd hoped they'd offer proof of the neurological value of our work so that we could responsibly market the benefits. But we will choose our words more carefully in our ad-vertising. We absolutely will not go further in our claims than the research allows, and on that point, Mr. Idle, you may someday get permission to quote me."

I'm having a lot of trouble following and as much trouble caring. This has been the neurological rhythm the last few minutes; the recognition of my loss of Isaac and Polly anchors me in a pit—complete capitulation to the world and its forces—and then I poke my head up and out, prompted by some primitive impulse.

"The explosion at the annex," I say.

"Nearly killed my support staff. After all we've given to that place. The diesel pump was faulty," Gils says. "We've already expressed our grave concern with the annex. Can you imagine what a lawsuit would do to their already faltering finances? We're all just so glad no one was hurt."

"Uh-huh, and Faith kidnapped herself."

"This is absurd." Gils is now just dismissive.

"They didn't," Faith says. "I went of my own accord."

I look up at her, bewildered. "Outside the jail? After the explosion? I don't believe that."

I look at Gils. "You're in cahoots with Chinese investors. You test software here, manufacture the Juggler abroad and sell it in the East—China, Japan—then bring it to the U.S."

"And? That's some kind of conspiracy?" The executive-turned-investor bends on his haunches. "You really smacked your head. Am I right?"

I don't respond.

"Faith told us about the subway. You suffered a major concussion. You're totally out of touch. It's robbed you of your common sense and your ability to discern truth from imagination. You're making connections and seeing things that aren't there."

"I'm bringing Leviathan down."

I see Gils' body tense at the mention of the name of the man he once partnered with to build one of Silicon Valley's most iconic companies.

"He has nothing to do with this. If you print that, you can't imagine the pain you'll suffer."

"From a lawsuit."

"Why are you doing this?" Gils is truly exasperated. "Nathaniel, this is the future. We're giving the next generation great tools, facilitating an extraordinary new world. We're doing in Silicon Valley what we've always done."

"Getting rich."

He shrugs, as if to say, And your point is . . . ? He stands. He turns to the man with the crooked smile and the knife, now tucked in his back pocket.

"Make sure he gets someplace warm."

"Count on it."

Gils brushes his hands against his pants and starts walking down the mountain.

51

We wait a minute in silence.

"Which one do you think is his?" asks the henchman.

Arms crossed, he's looking through the trees at the St. Francis Woods mansions. This is where Gils must live. So we met here because it was convenient for the executive, and not because it was a secret execution spot?

"I'm freezing," Faith says.

"Then go."

"We can go?" she asks.

"It's a free country." He half laughs. He likes saying this.

He turns and starts walking south, making crunching noises as his boots hit the concrete at the cross's base. Presumably, he parked at some other access point. He pauses and turns back.

"I'm sorry I hit you so hard. I thought you were trying to steal from the company."

It feels coached. He disappears into the wind.

"Let's go," Faith says.

I try to swallow and nearly choke from dryness. "Nathaniel. It's cold."

A pigeon swoops from the treetops and pecks at some unseen snack at the base of the cross. It sails off again, its off-white feathers blur with the sky behind it and I wonder if the concussion is beginning to reassert itself. Then I realize why I'm so blurred. It's not my brain but my eyes. They are filled with tears, blazing hot grief. A drip, a stream, cascade. Sobs.

I see Isaac, pale, bundled, not bundled, actually, shrouded. His weakened mother could not sustain him *in utero*. I'm in a trance when they show his lifeless body to me and wonder if I'd like to say goodbye. I look down at him and then at the nurse, clenching her teeth, holding it together, much more than I'm able to do.

Time passes, drizzle comes in and out, Faith finally speaks again. She says she needs to check on her nephew, Timothy. I stand and I find myself straining to look at her. It's not that I don't trust her, though I don't. I don't want to make full contact with her because it will mean acknowledging that I'm part of this world still, that what I'm experiencing now—the loss—is real.

She tries to take my hand and I neither resist nor embrace her. I stand. I turn. I feel a muddy patch beneath my feet, the ground indenting, my heart with it. I know the symbolism of this walk, back to the inherited Audi, on with life. Polly got two fortune cookies, both empty, like her future and Isaac's future, our future. The one I embark on with my next step.

"Please tell me what's going on," Faith says.

In my right hand, still clenched, I feel the metal object that Faith handed me and that I've forgotten about entirely. I open my hand and see, as I'd expected, a pocketknife, a modest weapon that Faith had imagined for who knows what purpose. It falls into the mud.

I take the next step.

52

"May I drive, Nathaniel?"

I click open the car and climb into the driver's seat. Warm air blows from the dashboard vents.

"I'll take you to Timothy."

"I slept with the admissions director at his school."

I don't respond.

"He sought out my advice because he was thinking of getting out of his job. He seemed, frankly, pathetic. I honestly just needed some release and I dated him. It was his idea to take Timothy into the school, or maybe I planted the seed. When I broke it off, he said he might force Timothy out of the school."

I slow the car to allow a woman to cross the street. She has the same crazy, lazy look as her muzzled pit bull.

"I don't know how Alan figured it out but he essentially blackmailed me. It was gentle. Not an outright threat. But he said that if I helped him get your attention, he'd pay me $1,000 and help me with my problem at school. Reading between the lines, he was suggesting he could make my problem with Mission Day School worse too. Carrot and stick."

"Hacking."

"What?"

"You said that Alan seemed to know a lot about you. Of course he did. He might've monitored your email, or hacked your voice mails. He knew what was going in your life—my life."

"Why? What is all this?" Stricken, understandably.

I turn left onto Market, one of the city's arteries. In a veritable monotone, I tell her: I had a pregnant girlfriend named Polly. She contracted brain cancer, a particular kind called anaplastic astrocytoma. Stage Three. It comes on fast and it doesn't quit. It weakened her so severely she couldn't nourish the baby. And it created a deadly conundrum. Starting chemo would kill the baby, but removing Isaac prematurely came with its own severe risks. In the end, there was nothing modern medicine could do.

I take a right onto Clipper, a steep slope downward into Noe Valley, then the Mission, the fog lightening slightly.

A whisper: "I'm so sorry. I lost one too. A very late miscarriage, a very early marriage."

I let her revelation sink in. "They kidnapped you," I finally say.

"It would be hard to prove."

Something compels me to look in the rearview mirror. A few cars back, I think I make out the Mercedes. It disappears to the right, onto a side street.

"At the fire at the annex, the man Steven asked me to go with him. And I said I would do so. Actually, I told him that if he touched me, I'd scream.

He said: 'Please, I could use your help.' I obviously knew he wasn't that helpless but the way he asked made me realize that I could . . ." She pauses.

Silence.

"Faith?"

"I'm not stupid. I'm aware of the effect I can have on people, specifically, men. I guess I like the hurt ones because I know they need something besides a trophy kill. I've become expert at discerning injury, emotional need. I see it everywhere. Where it's absent, I run."

"That bully is hardly vulnerable."

"Maybe not physically vulnerable, to a man. But I could see that, if necessary, I could manipulate him. I wanted to know the answers too. You were acting like a crazy man."

"Where did they take you?"

"To the Mandarin Hotel. I met Gils Simons. We called you, and then they gave me a room and my cell phone to call Timothy and whomever else I wanted. I think they must have drugged me. They told me I could go, but I fell asleep and I slept hard."

"You gave me a pocketknife."

"To use against Gils Simons. He, by contrast, has no emotional needs. He's like a calculator, a computer, an adding machine with a toupee."

"That's a toupee?"

"Might as well be. The guy's a mannequin."

In spite of myself, I laugh, albeit lightly. My first half laugh of the new era.

"As near as I could tell," Faith says, "they are excited to launch some new product. It's some new toy or video game they're testing here and they're beginning to sell in China, with the blessing of the government there. Steven is the liaison to the Chinese. He takes that role very seriously. He thinks you're ruining the launch or stealing the secrets or something like that. Are you?"

I shake my head no. I don't really know the answer to her question.

I take a slow right onto Folsom. A block back, the Mercedes materializes. I lose sight of it around the corner and it doesn't reappear as I head straight on Folsom past the clumps of day-workers gathered on the corners.

A few minutes later, I've arrived at Mission Day School.

Faith hustles to unbuckle her seat belt and open her door. "I'm going to figure out how to pay the tuition, if I have to go even further into debt. Timothy's thriving here, in a relative sense. But I've got to get out from under this jerk."

She stands at the door. She kneels down. She looks at me until I relent and meet her gaze. She blinks her brown eyes and I realize that, even though she senses her power to connect, physically and emotionally, she doesn't know its depths. I want to make her smile. And she wants to say something. She opens her mouth, only a tad, then pauses, her perfect lips hung in space. Maybe she's waiting for me. I'm waiting too. I'm waiting to say what I know I feel: give me a few weeks and then let's get coffee and a doughnut and see what we can do about having an honest connection, the first I've had in nearly a year.

I have the feeling she wants the same thing.

"Goodbye, Faith."

53

"Are you having a threesome with state-sponsored terrorists?"

This is the question that greets me when I get to the entrance to the office. Rather, it's the question on the meticulously hand-painted sign in the window of Green Love, the politically correct and eco-friendly sex shop that never fails to remind me I'm not nearly the weirdest tenant in the building.

I can't help but read a flyer in the window below the provocative question. It explains that some "mainstream sex lubricants" use petroleum-based oils that can "line the pockets of Middle East terror states that treat women as chattel." The flyer goes on to urge the use of sex products "sold here" from certified fair-trade communities in Latin and Central America and also from local artisans.

If I ever get horny again, I'm pretty sure I'm not going to be looking for lubricant made in someone's bathtub in Sonoma County. But then, how could I ever look myself again in the mirror over the bed if I wasn't making love, but terrorism?

I look over my shoulder and I see no sign of the bald buzzard or other lurkers. And a minute later, I've trudged up the stairs and see that the door to my office is ajar.

Almost without a pause, I push open the door. Inside, I see the one person who might pose the biggest threat. At least emotionally.

Samantha, my Witch, my sister-in-arms, sits cross-legged on the floor. Her head is back as if looking at the heavens but her eyes are closed and, even if they were open, the most exotic or mystical thing she could see is a water stain on our ceiling that looks vaguely like a tarantula eating a strand of spaghetti.

She's in deep thought, or a trance, something I've learned not to interrupt. Not that I want to. Seeing the Witch means poking the wound I've just discovered.

I start to walk to the futon. I'm going to lie down on it and then get up again when I'm struck by any urge of any kind that seems more powerful than the urge to lie on the futon.

But, then, I've forgotten the lure of my mobile phone. En route to the futon, I remember that it—my iPhone—is dead for wont of a charge. I beeline to the desk to plug it in, genuinely rueful at the inescapable need to attend to my device. I find the power cord plugged into the wall behind my computer. I insert it into the device. I see the picture of Isaac on the desk. It's the one I took with this self-same phone, the image I emailed to myself and printed out, wanting, perversely, to keep alive some memento of all the things I lost. Equally inexplicably, I kept tacking it to my wall, no doubt one of the many small missteps I made that allowed me to create a virtual reality, concussion enhanced, that left me believing that Isaac never died.

I pick up the photo.

I turn around. The Witch stares at me. With her hands folded in her lap, as in the shape of a cup, she looks like a statue you'd see in some comically peaceful Asian rock garden. Water should be flowing from her lips into her hand cup.

I take the picture and I lay it on the desk. Facedown.

This elicits no discernable reaction from Samantha. Maybe her eyes soften. Maybe I'm projecting. She tilts her head back and looks up in the direction of the water-stain tarantula, then closes her eyes.

My phone chirps, suddenly juiced, coming to life. On it, the clock reads 12:05. What day, though? Then the phone, as if reading my mind, beeps again. The calendar pops up, reminding me I've got an appointment in three hours. It's the tax hearing.

I wonder if I'll make it.

I plod to the futon. I plop down. I fall asleep. I don't dream.

I feel warmth on my hand. I open my eyes. The Witch sandwiches my fingers between her palms, bringing me to life as if an anesthesiologist gently awakening a cardiac patient from a post-surgical haze.

"Your phone says you've got a meeting at three," she says.

"What time is it?"

"Twenty minutes until your meeting."

I sit up and prop my back against the wall.

"I'm glad you've stopped running."

"Yeah, maybe."

She cocks her head. I imagine she's seeing all kinds of different Karmic colors swirling around me.

"What if I'm running to something, instead of away from something?"

"Are you?"

I stand up. I walk to my desk and I pick up my phone.

"Nathaniel, have you ever?"

"May I say something important?"

"Please."

"I hope you and Bullseye aren't using lubricants that support radical extremists."

She laughs. "I saw that sign. Don't worry. Our love oils are certified organic."

Outside, I climb into my car and see a familiar face or, rather, two. Sandy Vello and boyfriend, Clyde. They sit across the street from my office in a pickup truck—Clyde's, I presume. When I stare at them, they first pretend not to see me. Then Clyde starts the truck and speeds off.

I suspect they are no threat, though I'll need to deal with Sandy again at some point. Not when I've got a date in court.

54

The magistrate wears a pantsuit and a grim visage. Making sure to alternately make eye contact with me and a mousy man with a small head and a full beard sitting across an oak table from me, she explains she's not a judge but a state-appointed arbiter. Do we have any questions about that?

Just: Why am I here?

"I'm not being cute," I say. "I got served two or three days ago."

"You know about your responsibility to pay taxes," says the man, the Internal Revenue Service rep.

The magistrate holds out her hand, nun-style, urging calm. Her hair is pulled so tightly into a bun, I see scalp.

Overhead, one of the filament lights blinks out, making the boxy bureaucratic room even dimmer.

The magistrate looks at me. "This revolves around the estate of Pauline Sanchez."

I nod. Of course. I clear my throat. "How much is she in arrears?"

"Not she," the mousy man says. "You. Nine hundred and fifty thousand dollars. Plus penalties. We'll not settle for a penny less."

I shrug. Okay. "Why me?"

"Is this guy for real?"

The magistrate cautions him again with her hands, palms down. "Mr. Idle, you understand you have to pay the estate tax on what you inherited."

"On the apartment and the car. I'm sorry, I . . ."

The mousy man seems to soften. It dawns on him that I am not merely playing ignorant.

"You're the journalist," he says.

I nod.

"You obviously know you've got to pay the tax not just on the hard goods but also the liquid assets." It's not confrontational anymore, a tonal olive branch.

I shake my head. "I don't . . ."

"The cash," the magistrate interjects. "Several million dollars in . . ." She looks down at the file. Something seems to dawn on her too. "It was in a trust but payable to you in the event of . . ." She trails off.

"You're aware of the inheritance." The tax man blinks rapidly.

I'm aware, vaguely. Even before she died, I had already moved into Polly's house and started driving her car, all at her behest so that I'd be ready to take care of Isaac. Subsequent to their deaths, I'd been contacted on several occasions by an executor with regard to Polly's estate but I'd asked him to take care of it, figuring she had her own cadre of money people. I recall him telling me I was in line to inherit a substantial sum of money. But, I kept thinking, for what? For being the helpless guy who watched the whole thing fall apart, who sat on the sidelines with the medical degree and the reporter's notebook?

I'd asked him to give the money to Polly's brother. I seem to recall that the executor had told me that, given the brother's substance-abuse problems, Polly had wanted the lion's share to go to me.

I remember getting letters from the lawyer and some from the IRS. I piled them up on the end table at the front of the flat I inherited and never quite took ownership of.

The magistrate clears her throat. "I'm going to order a continuation, Mr. Idle. Get yourself a good accountant."

I nod.

"I'm sorry." She puts her sun-cracked hand on my arm. "No one should lose a child."

I put the Audi into drive and take a right out of the lot. No one should ever lose a child.

I pull to the side of the road, next to a yellow-painted curb, which, if memory serves, means I can be fed to piranhas if caught parking here. I pull my phone from my pocket. I dial Jill Gilkeson.

"Hi." She's lifeless in a way I now get.

"I'm sorry to bother you. One more question regarding all the fine work that Mr. Leviathan's done."

"Shoot."

"Were there any others who worked with you early on at Leviathan Ventures, people who could attest to the germs of his efforts?"

She asks for a second to think about it. She starts listing names, thinking aloud. She promises to get me contact info for the ones she can find. She asks if she should just email me the names and contact info and I say sure. I'm fishing for something, not really sure what, when it leaps onto my boat.

"I'd appreciate if you didn't call the Gearsons. Lena and Erik."

"Sure. They don't get along with Mr. Leviathan?"

"Oh no, not that. They just lost their son. He was friends with Jill, my daughter. A long time ago. He died earlier this year. He was one of those kids at Los Altos High School."

"Sorry, I'm not following."

"They had three kids who jumped in front of a train. Anthony, I think that was his name, he was the first. Then two copy cats."

"Anthony Gearson."

"Please don't bother them."

"I promise." Deep exhale. "No one should lose a child."

"Do a nice article. Andrew has given his life to make the world a better place."

"I will."

Click.

I sit bewildered, five minutes, ten. The phone rings.

I answer and hear: "It's Doc." I don't respond, uncertain which ghost this voice represents. "Doc Jefferson. Sorry it took so long to get back to you. It's been crazy, right?" Then friendly laughter. It's the warden from Twin Peaks juvenile hall, the

nominal administrator of the learning annex that
went kaboom. "You're one hell of a journalist."

"How's that?"

"Snooping around before an explosion. Great in-
stincts."

He knew I was there. Must have heard my name
from the firefighter.

"I'm not sure what you were doing there but you
nearly got an incredible scoop," he says.

Revelation forthcoming?

"Our diesel pump exploded. We're going after
the pump company. Cost us our whole computer
lab but it's going to be rebuilt—and NOT at city
cost. You can quote me on that."

"They were experimenting on those kids."

"Who?"

"PRISM, Sandy . . ."

"The reality-TV gal? Are you kidding me? We're
committed to training our young folks and we're
going to get right back to it. We'll have a new computing lab built in no time. Everything else you
need is in the press release."

I'm mute.

"Gotta run," Doc Jefferson says. "Stay in touch,
big guy."

Forty minutes later, I'm passing Peet's Coffee on
University Avenue. It's the same place where I
met Andrew a few days earlier when I wasn't sure
whether he was friend or foe. Now I'm sure.

It's nearly six o'clock, darkness falling in that
eerily temperate Palo Alto way, the suburbs 2.0.

I park and turn off my phone. I pull my laptop

and Bullseye's laptop from the trunk. I find a spot inside Peet's with a free power outlet. On the table next to me, three Stanford MBA candidates speak in a whispered shrill about an idea they have, to bring "greater efficiencies" to television programming guides by making them more accessible through mobile phones.

It's not quite time for the confrontation. It's time to set it up.

I plug in Bullseye's laptop, the one I believe is not being used to track my whereabouts, take a huge slug of acidic coffee, and start writing.

55

Bullseye, please don't read this unless you haven't heard from me for a few days. Seriously. And if you do hear from me, delete this. I'm likely to want to refine it. I should never write anything for public consumption when this heavily caffeinated.

Bullet point: Andrew Leviathan, Silicon Valley icon and tech and education investors, has in parallel and in secret been developing technology with dangerous neurological implications.

Bullet point: Over the last decade, he's built the engine for a handheld device called the Juggler. It's technology that marries the hologram with the Nintendo Wii, using motion capture and vivid high-definition imagery to turn multitasking into a high-octane video game and, ostensibly, a high-tech learning tool.

Bullet point: It's about to be sold in China. The marketing of the device will promise to teach kids how to become better at switching among tasks. It'll prepare them to be 21st-century navigators of data, supertaskers who can switch from one mental challenge to the next, ostensibly giving them over-lapping capabilities. The Juggler will allow kids to balance two or three or who knows how many tasks. Email, PowerPoint, Skype, video production, brain games! Don't let your kids be left behind! Let them master the cloud!

Bullet Point: The cloud is where we keep all this data. The cloud is a complex array of millions of servers scattered across the globe, congregated in data centers, connected through wires running under oceans and through mountains. Servers, with their multiple processors, can ably juggle data. The human brain cannot. In fact, when we try to juggle, we may crash.

Bullet point: In actuality, the Juggler will retard the development of kids' frontal lobes. This slow-developing portion located right behind our fore-heads traditionally serves as the control tower for our actions, the thing that makes us human by al-lowing us to establish dominion, if you will, over our impulses. If someone feels a tickling sensation in his nose while standing onstage during a wed-ding, his frontal lobe may keep him from sticking a digit in a nostril to scratch it; if someone's senses come alive at the smell of doughnuts, her frontal lobe might help her choose a healthier alternative. If someone sets about to write a business plan or a love letter or a book but keeps being inundated by the ping of a cell phone, the frontal lobe helps keep his brain focused on the longer-term goal, for better or for worse.

Sometimes, there is no better.

If someone sees a bright color or flash of light

across a street and feels an impulse to run to explore it, the frontal lobe helps her pause and say: wait, am I supposed to run into the street?

That, I believe, is what happened to Kathryn Gilkeson. Somehow, in some way that Andrew Leviathan has to answer for, her heavy use of the early Juggling technology eroded her impulse control. She acted like a child whose sensory impulses overrode not just her training but the maturity level her frontal lobe should otherwise have achieved.

Bullet point: Kathryn Gilkeson may not be the only victim. There were other children, at least one. Evidence suggests that Anthony Gearson, a young man from Los Altos High School who recently took his own life, may also have suffered from long-term effects of early Juggler technology.

I pause in my writing. I drink more jet fuel. I am appreciating my sudden focus. I attribute it to the fading effects of concussion and the increasing ones from caffeine but also something else: when I'm writing, I'm less susceptible to all the outside forces, insulated somehow from the attentional whiplash my curiosity compels.

I almost begin to type again, when I'm struck by a strange parallel between the effects of the Juggler and my concussion. The last few days, with my frontal lobe not at full strength, I've acted with, even for me, intense impulse, abandon, outright stupidity. It's possible that my erratic behavior helped uncover a conspiracy but also highly possible I could've gotten much of this information without running headlong into the apartment building of a dead man, dark alleys, fists, shotguns, and fires. I've been in my own neurological cloud. Waxing a bit: Is that where we're sending our children? Under the auspices of helping them rule the modern world?

Bullet point: I hypothesize that Leviathan perfected the Juggler technology, and then decided to export it to China. Why? I can only, for now, speculate: he hated the authoritarian Cold War regime that nearly had him executed and so he wants to harm China, another, albeit much less authoritarian, non-democracy.

Bullet point: He got Gils Simons, his former (???) business partner (current silent partner???), to be his point man in contact with the Chinese through companies involved with the China-U.S. High-Tech Alliance. Gils sold it to his Chinese contacts as a great new device for kids. He took on a hapless thug named Steven who helped deal with Chinese contacts and small-time errands here. For instance, he hired Sandy Vello, whose work he'd seen on a reality-TV show and who he naively felt could appeal to parents, to volunteer to teach multitasking at the Twin Peaks learning annex but where they actually tested the latest versions of the Juggler. See: blown-up learning annex and destruction of evidence.

Bullet point: It's all feeling too complicated. What am I missing?

Bullet point: Alan Parsons was a drunk who used to work for Leviathan. He uncovered Leviathan's plot and the connection to the death of Jill Gilkeson. He wanted to blackmail Leviathan. But he couldn't put the whole thing together, couldn't make all the pieces fit. So he came to me. He wanted me to follow the trail. He tried to email me but I didn't respond or see his overture. Then he essentially used my innate curiosity and a woman named Faith to draw me in (???).

Bullet point: It's all still feeling too complicated. Time to find out what I'm missing.

Bullet point: *Bullseye, you know how much I hate to use a cliché like this: but, to repeat, if you've read this far, I'm probably no longer around. Send the police after Andrew Leviathan (see above). I don't have a will. Let this serve as one. I've inherited some money from Polly. A lot of it. Keep a chunk for yourself and Samantha. Make sure to pay the taxes. Oh, and get yourself some season tickets to Where the Sun Don't Shine. It's good to occasionally go outside.*

I open my email account and send the file to Bullseye as an attachment. In the body of the email, I beg him again not to open the email unless he hasn't heard from me for three days. He's likely to go along.

I close the laptop and remember a story I once heard about Palo Alto. Researchers parked a relatively new convertible by the side of the road here, leaving the top down. They did the same thing in a poor urban area on the East Coast. Within hours, the car on the East Coast had been stripped for parts by vandals. The car in Palo Alto went untouched for days, until it started to rain. Someone drove by, stopped and put the top up on the convertible.

I put Bullseye's laptop on the floor of the booth where I'm sitting. Someone will pick it up and make sure it gets back to him.

I turn on my own laptop and my phone. I walk

out the front of the café, inviting a modest chill. I take a seat on the patio, alone. I wait.

Twenty minutes later, he shows up. The shiny bald buzzard pulls up in his black car and parks across the street. He rolls down his passenger-side window and he looks at me, at least I gather in the dark, and I at him. He rolls up the window. I wait.

Ten minutes later, a Jaguar sedan pulls up in front of the café. The car is an older model, elegant but worn. Andrew Leviathan rolls down his passenger window. He smiles thinly. "Where are you parked?"

I point a half block away.

"Follow me."

We wind up the Palo Alto hills. Leviathan in front, me, the buzzard. Eerily, like a funeral caravan. We take a right onto a dirt tributary, wind along the gravel road, through the increasingly dense trees, to a place well beyond help. I expect we'll reach a house with a towering black gate, maybe a sentry, a moat or a stone statue. But when Leviathan slows, it's at a rustic fence. With help from the headlights, I can see two retrievers rush to the gate, barking their approval at our arrival.

The ranch-style house spreads wide across the horizon, blocking a view of the bay behind it that I imagine makes it worth whatever Leviathan paid for this understated place, and whatever it took to amass the fortune.

He parks in a roundabout in front of the house, and lumbers out of the car. I, with just the slightest hesitation, do the same. The buzzard stays put. Leviathan nods his head to the right, where I see a stand-alone structure, maybe a home office or guest house, cut into a break in the trees. He starts walking toward it.

I look in the doorway and see Leviathan's stunning wife, arms crossed, wearing a bathrobe and a grim look. I look down and away, as if embarrassed.

Leviathan disappears into the trees, heading toward the guesthouse.

I follow.

56

Boxy but distinct. The square edifice stands two stories, the gently sloped and white tile roof extending a foot over the edge of the house, like the brim of a sun hat. Separated by a grove of trees from the main house, accessible by an inlaid stone path, it also projects a less-rustic character, a home office maybe, with the emphasis on office, not home.

The nerve center of a dark plan.

Leviathan, still a few steps ahead of me, walking in silence, pulls open a heavy door and walks through it. I'm struck by the plodding character of his gait, and mine. The two of us head without relish toward an inevitable confrontation. It strikes me that I'm not the one already feeling defeated.

Inside the door, I'm greeted by Richard Nixon. His painting hangs on the wall to the right of a ponderously heavy wooden staircase that bisects the entryway. I can't help but pause at the former president's brooding visage, downturned eyes, holding a pen suspended over some document as he sits in the Oval Office.

"Hubris," Leviathan mutters, halfway up the stairs. He plods upward. Then he says "on" and the upstairs lights ignite. I plod after him. I follow his path into a room directly across from the top of the stairs.

When through the door, I nearly lose my breath. The view.

Through a window that stretches most of the length of the backside of the house, Silicon Valley materializes. I inhale the majestic view of an airplane at low altitude. In the foreground, the hills give way to the flatlands stretching from Burlingame to San Jose, and then the three spans leading to the East Bay and the rest of the world: the Dumbarton, San Mateo and Bay bridges. From the mind of Leviathan and a handful of true pioneers, semiconductors and software roll out from here across the Earth.

"God and his creation," I say.

He pulls out a chair behind his antique desk and sits, his back to the view. He gestures with an open palm for me to sit on a worn cloth love seat that looks like he picked it up for free after reading an ad on Craigslist.

"That chair survived the bombings at Dresden."

"Another reminder from history, like Nixon?"

"Overextension comes at a price."

The love seat sits a few feet in front of floor-to ceiling bookcases that line the walls. As I sit, I see the gun. It sits in the middle of the desk, where I might have expected a computer. The black handgun looks inert, small, a toy thing from a movie set.

"We could do a modified interview style."

"What's that mean?"

"I ask you a series of questions and then when you feel I've overstepped the boundaries, you shoot me."

He grimaces. He's not the sort of bad guy who seems to enjoy the role.

"You obviously discovered the Juggler. Tell me what you know and I'll fill in the rest."

I look at the gun again. I can't help but flash on the night that Leviathan as a young man spent in the jail cell in the Eastern Bloc, anticipating his execution. He plotted with all his might to survive. By contrast, I'm going so quietly.

I could run, I suppose. I could yell "off" and command the lights to extinguish, then dive for the door. But run to what? How far would I get? They can track my movements. I knew what I was getting into when I drove here. I wonder if I'm destined to see Isaac and Polly on the other side of some spiritual barrier I'm not sure I believe exists.

"I wrote a file that will be widely distributed in the event of my disappearance. One way or another, the world will know about what you've done."

"Maybe."

I don't understand and shake my head.

"You're a great journalist, I mean that. But you vastly underestimate the ability of even modestly talented hackers to invade your devices, use them to do surveillance on you, control your digital output, and so forth. If you left a file to be distributed by email, I could probably kill or modify it."

"So I probably shouldn't have let on."

"Tell me what it says and, like I said, I'll fill in the rest."

"What do I have to lose?"

"Honestly? Nothing I can calculate."

I tell him most of what I've surmised, concluding that the Juggler, scheduled for imminent distribution in China, slows development of kids' frontal lobes, making them more impulsive, less able to focus, indulgent like children years their junior. "When it comes to frontal lobe development, age ten is the new seven and seven is the new five."

"See, that's much better wordplay."

I tell him I don't understand the mechanism that allows the technology to take a neurological toll. After all, I note, the Juggler doesn't seem much different from a lot of the high-intensity phones and game machines.

"I'm not entirely sure myself of the mechanism," he says.

As a matter of substance, it's not helpful. But it is an admission I'm on the right track.

"May I pace?" I ask.

He nods.

I walk on the thin area rug past his desk, pivot, make another pass. I tell him that I suspect Gils Simons, his old chief operating officer, passed the technology to the Chinese through the High-Tech Alliance. I pause from my walk and look at him, struck by something.

"You and Gils aren't exactly on the same page."

"What makes you say that?"

"Different henchmen."

"Go on."

"You're tracking me with the tall bald guy. Shiny head makes him tough to miss." He starts to ask who I mean, and then just nods, a silent appreciation or, maybe, endorsement of the description. I continue: "He, Gils, has a closer relationship with the Chinese guy with the crooked smile."

Leviathan waves his hand, urging me to continue.

I tell him I suspect that Alan Parsons learned of the plot and tried to blackmail the group. But, I say, Parsons couldn't quite piece it together and somehow needed my help. I'm walking again, a bit lost in my own thoughts. This is where things get shaky for me. And, in addition, I'm not quite sure how to play this next bit. Do I come right out and say that I know about the death of Kathryn Gilkeson? And the recent suicide of the kid at Los Altos High?

My reservation, I realize, is I don't want to provoke him unnecessarily. I may be going gently into that good night but I'm not going to actually shove myself.

"May I go out on a limb?"

"It's a bit late to ask."

"You've hated authoritarian regimes since you were a boy. You want to poison a generation of Chinese kids, I guess, as a way to make a political statement. But it just doesn't seem like you, to be honest."

Smirk. I'm not sure how to read it.

"Fill in the blanks, Andrew. First tell me about the girl," he says.

"The girl."

"Cut the crap. The girl. The one who died."

Something in the room begins to change. I'm watching the famous Leviathan composure drain from his face. In its place, a look I've never seen from him and, rarely, from anyone. It's the sheer falling away of a mask. The cheek muscles go limp, eyes droop, a cascade of cells rinses downward like gravity or the final layer of base makeup washed from the face of the clown.

"The girl," I whisper.

He rests his hand on the gun. "Tell me what you know."

57

A hot flash seizes me and an image of death creeps into my mind's eye. It's the stick-thin doctor in blue scrubs telling me that Polly will not make it. "Sit here as long as you like," she said when I looked at her with shock and silence.

Oddly, I felt for her at that moment, not me, or Polly or Isaac.

And in this moment, I feel a bit like the doctor, in the position of delivering painful news. For a journalist, this is supposed to be exhilarating, the gotcha moment. But I've never particularly liked the handful of times when I move from discovering a truth to confronting a bad actor with it. It's beyond anti-climactic. It's sad. The death of someone's dark dream. And my own realization that my success in solving a mystery, the arrival at some analytical Mecca, has not made me whole.

"She ran into the street," I begin.

I tell him what the girl's mother told me. I tell him what I only suspect: that the girl had been among a handful of test subjects he'd used to develop the precursor technology to the Juggler. The girl must have grown increasingly impulsive, I speculate, unable to focus, and then one day the technology pushed her still-fragile frontal lobe over the edge.

"She acted like someone with the brain of a three-year-old, running in front of the Volvo. Maybe she saw a dog across the street she wanted to touch, or some blinking lights." I pause, then add: "I can only imagine how much more dangerous the commercial version of the technology will be."

He stares at me.

"Care to comment?"

He stands. He picks up the gun. It hangs in his hand. He turns his back to me and he walks to the window. Below, tens of thousands of houselights burn, creating a collective glow to rival the darkness.

He extends the hand with the gun at the window. He's pointing slightly to his left, in the vicinity of Menlo Park.

"You can see it," he says.

"What?"

"That's why I built this place."

I start walking to the window. He turns and I jump back, wondering if he's about to shoot me. Wondering too: maybe I'm not ready to die?

He turns back to the window. "You're right: I hate authoritarianism. I'll give you that."

He's switched topics on me. I'm still not sure what he was pointing at but he appears to want to take the conversation in another direction and he's the one with the gun.

"Hence the beef with the Chinese kids."

He shakes his head.

"Nope. Will you grant me some literary license? About literature? About Orwell and Huxley."

I shrug, not following. Is he going crazy?

"George Orwell and Aldous Huxley depicted distinctly different views of how the modern world could crush the human spirit. Orwell presaged the mortal dangers of authoritarian regimes. Roughly speaking, it was the kind of thing the Eastern Bloc represented."

"Or China."

"But in *Brave New World*, Huxley identified the problem not so much as the state but our own frailties. We could succumb to our own ravenous desire for entertainment, truth subverted to triviality. We could become awash in bells and whistles."

"Okay."

"It's been said many times in a very flattering light that I created one of the Next Big Things. But I created the Brave New World."

I consider it.

"The Juggler entertains us into a stupor?"

"It's so much worse than that." He turns to me. A deep-set wrinkle like a river on a map trails across his forehead. "The technology I helped build, the algorithms meant to serve us have tapped our worst demons, our most primitive impulses. In that respect they are so much more powerful than I ever dreamed."

"You wanted this?"

"No. God no."

He gestures again out the window with a jut of his chin.

"I'm not sure where you're pointing."

"See the tall building, with the smattering of lights on the upper floor? It's west of the Dumbarton Bridge and a bit to the left."

"It looks like a law firm?"

"That's the one. Now look two blocks further left."

I see a smear of residences. It dawns on me.

"That's the street Kathryn Gilkeson ran into."

Silence. Then: "When I built this house, a year later, my dear wife couldn't understand why. We have plenty of space. I've never been a particularly materialistic person and certainly not fixated on real estate."

"You wanted to be able to see where she died." I whisper it. I'm wondering: Is Leviathan some kind of sociopath, a serial killer who has created a view to his kills, a virtual collector with a window through which to ogle his conquests?

But then, in an instant, something else replaces that thought.

"You didn't mean for her to die."

"It has crushed me, Nathaniel. Destroyed me." It seems his voice might break but he clears his throat. He tells me that he introduced a new generation of multitasking software to the kids, like little Kathryn, who came to free day care and after-school programs at Leviathan Ventures. He jerry-rigged handheld devices, nothing fancy and commercial like the current Juggler. But the devices were years ahead of their time, combining crisp video and motion detection to allow the kids to move from one task to the next. The kids were entranced. He thought he was preparing them for the future.

"I used to sit in class and marvel at their immersion. It was like watching baby kittens bat balls around—endlessly excited and with preternatural dexterity. I could see their reaction times increasing. But they were moving data, refining their multitasking, becoming more competitive, not less."

"So it worked."

"In one respect. They did show increased visual acuity. They could pick up amid the clutter of images the ones they needed to focus on. At least that's what I could discern through my unscientific observations. And research has since backed me up on that." He pauses. "Then it turned dark."

"When Kathryn got hit by the car."

"Months before, the kids started getting agitated. They hated disconnecting. One kid hit another. A few parents started complaining that on the days after, their kids came acting like they were back in the terrible twos—impulsive, unwilling to take direction, highly susceptible to being startled."

He says the teachers looked at whether they were serving too much sugar, providing insufficient rest time. The complaints never reached Leviathan. But after Kathryn's death, he started asking questions and surmised that something wasn't right.

"I buried the technology."

"You knew it was problematic."

"I suspected."

"More than suspected. You built a bunch of charter schools. You became a firebrand for improving education. You . . ." I pause, thinking it through;

Leviathan's schools limited the use of technology in instruction. I look at him. "But the technology resurrected."

He nods grimly. "That's what I needed you for."

"Me?"

A sound comes from the direction of the stairs. I look up to see Leviathan's wife step into the room. She stops, and looks at her husband, stricken, as if suspended mid-step, a horrified puppet.

"Please no."

"My fair lady."

"A gun."

"It's over, sweetheart."

"You don't have to do this, Andrew."

"I've already done it."

58

She blinks, and she suddenly smiles. She walks toward me. She extends her arms, not like greeting an old friend but more formal, like one politician about to embrace another onstage. It's fake but she's so magnetic.

"He's not gotten much sleep. He's rambling. It doesn't happen often but when it does it can turn the world's smartest man into . . ."

"Sit," he says to her.

She looks at him, unaccustomed to this tone, then turns to me, plaintive, she shuffles to the love seat.

"I hired Alan Parsons," he says to me. "I asked him to contact you, discreetly, and"—he mulls over the word—"seduce you into looking into the Juggler."

"By shoving me into a train?"

He shakes his head and shrugs.

"I don't get into the details. I just knew you were the right guy."

"Why me?"

"You're like him," his wife says.

"Not in any way I can imagine." Not rich, famous, world changing, married to a beautiful, devoted wife.

He holds up his hand, asking his wife to refrain. "You are very talented. But your talent is outweighed by your curiosity. You overextend yourself."

Andrew says that he discovered my work when his team went looking for a journalist to award with his annual magazine prize. As he looked into my work, he became convinced that I had done a good job questioning Silicon Valley's implicit assumption about the inherent good of all technological progress.

"Okay, but why now? The Juggler's been on target for months, years. You've known about it."

He points out the window.

"Don't do this to yourself," his wife says.

I look where he's pointing. To our right, over the rolling hills in the direction of a concentration of residential lights.

"Los Altos High School. Another alumni of our after-school program killed himself."

The kid who jumped in front of a train. Just a few months ago. Anthony Gearson.

"But that doesn't have to do with your work." His wife stands.

"Wrong! Don't let me lie to myself. I love you. But don't let me lie anymore."

She's frozen again, her eyes half closed; she can't watch anymore.

He turns to me. "It's true that I didn't resurrect the Juggler technology." He explains that, in fact, he thought it was long buried. But he realized that his old partner, Gils, had revived it and sold it to a manufacturer with the backing of the Chinese government. Gils, he tells me, never knew about the negative neurological implications. On the other hand, Leviathan says, he had admonished Gils more than a decade ago that the technology didn't work and that it should not be sold under any circumstances. To sell it, Leviathan told Gils, would be unethical.

His wife interjects. "But you have to understand. Gils always lived in my husband's shadow. It's the same old story—Jobs and Wozniak at Apple, Gates and Paul Allen, to a lesser extent, at Microsoft—two co-founders at these companies, one is known as the genius and the other guy counts beans."

There's a moment of silence. She adds: "This was Gils's chance to put his stamp on the Next Big Thing, absent my genius husband."

He explains that Gils worked out deals to have the technology tested in a handful of day care and learning centers, after-school programs, and juvenile detention centers.

"It's up to industry! We have to police ourselves," he exclaims. He sees that neither I nor his wife understand his outburst. He explains that the old government social safety nets and regulations can't possibly keep up with technology and the deleterious impacts on the margins of technology. It would take the equivalent of the Food and Drug Administration, he says, to create policies around the potential downsides of mass consumption of technology.

"Technology is like food. We need it to survive.

But some technology is like brussels sprouts and some is like Twinkies. Some is arsenic." He bows his head. "We've swallowed technology whole."

"The industry is to blame?"

"Society is broke. We privatize our schools and our prisons. We've abdicated to industry. The corporation, writ large, is the future. It's got to take responsibility—to act responsibly. But how can we ask it to be other than what it is—to ask ourselves to be other than what we are?"

"Industry?"

He shakes his head, defeated. "There are no bad actors here. No malice. Just the usual human failings."

"Such as?"

"Greed, self-deception, envy." His wife again.

"What about Alan Parsons? He tried to bribe you. That's not malice?"

He nods a concession. "And he got his comeuppance through a heart attack. Fortune turned against him."

"Pure accident? Natural causes?"

He nods, yep. "But it brought me down too."

"How so?"

"My plan, weak as it might have been, was to get you looking into the Juggler technology without tying it back to my original failings. Gils didn't know about it. Sandy Vello, a mid-level manager, certainly didn't know. The Chinese didn't know. Only I knew, and Alan Parsons. He was smart and started putting things together."

"So why not just blackmail you and that would be the end of it? Why bother contacting me?"

"I guess he wanted to show me he was playing along and doing my bidding. He never actually had gotten around to directly blackmailing me, just dancing around it. And it might be that he wanted to use you to get more information."

I noodle it. "So the Juggler is not a plot to destroy young people's brains?"

"There's no malice with the Juggler, like I said. Unless you consider profit making to be malicious."

We fall silent.

"Why not just come forward, Andrew? Why not just tell the world about the dangers?"

"I'd be a rich, old, doddering fool."

"That's not why. I begged him not to." It's his wife.

He looks at her and says: "Don't you have anyone you love so much that it causes you to stuff down and deny the most obvious truths?"

I feel a terrible weight, Polly and Isaac, my inability to adapt to their absence, and the absence of the life I'd romanticized, a crushing truth in my life.

His wife chokes back a sob, the slipping away of her desperate hold on dignity. Is there little uglier than the most beautiful among us coming apart at the seams?

It dawns on me. He's not going to shoot me. He's going to shoot himself.

She falls to her knees.

"He has given so much to the world, not just the technology, but the charity." She looks at him. "You can't believe everything you've built has been without value. It's driven an economy, productivity, let grandchildren and their grandmothers talk over the

Internet. You've built an engine for twenty-first-century communications."

He takes it in. She senses she's gotten momentum.

"The Juggler is only one iteration of dozens of devices with dual edges—video-game consoles, phones, all the fast-twitch gadgets. You can't blame yourself." She turns to me. "Don't write about him. Write about the dangers of the technology, in general, to children. Don't ruin a man who has done so much. Don't make him the"—she chews on the phrase—"poster child for creating technology that bakes the brains of our babies."

He dangles the gun in his hand. I have this strange sense that the more she protests the more convinced he becomes of his own failings. I know what he's thinking: he can't believe his legacy, and the legacy of a region he helped build, will be a Brave New World. I don't know if he's right. I certainly agree with her that the Juggler isn't the only device. But it is the story.

"Andrew." She's pleading.

He shakes his head, and I realize they are having a silent communication more powerful and instant than email, more intense than anything a high-definition Juggler could deliver.

His arms fall to his sides. She looks at him, kneeling. As far as they are concerned, I am no longer in the room.

59

I make out the silhouette of the buzzard, willowy arms crossed over his chest, head cocked in attentiveness, at the ready to swoop, standing against a tree. But he makes no move to stop me as I drag myself to my car.

His inaction prompts my brain to reverberate with Leviathan's words "no malice." The phrase practically glowers at me with its beady eyes, challenging me to justify my rabid assumptions over the last few days about the emergence of a grand conspiracy.

Have I been subjected to terrific malice or just unfair play?

My movements have been tracked, and I've been followed. A man with a crooked smile clocked me in Chinatown but not in defense of a nefarious neurological plot. He was worried I'd expose his intellectual property and marketing plans. Love for her nephew motivated Faith.

On my part, I plunged into a reportorial frenzy because of the wounds to my head and the ones to my heart.

I climb into my car, Polly's car, the Audi that belonged to my dead ex-girlfriend and for which I now owe substantial taxes. Is this why, I wonder, I shouldn't own nice things, or date amazing women, or fall in love with them? You ultimately pay too high of a price.

As I drive Highway 280, I chew questions. Do I believe Leviathan? And do I expose him, or just the technology he helped create?

Forty minutes later, I arrive at my inherited flat. I walk into the living room and stare at the unused baby bouncer. I'm exhausted. I'm wired. I sit. I stare at the bouncer until my eyes glaze over. I pull out my laptop.

I start writing.

Three hours later, I have many pages. I've told the tale of the Juggler, its origin, the specific damage it may do to a generation of Chinese children and, the generally dual-edged nature of our technology.

I expose Andrew Leviathan, the white knight of Silicon Valley—itself the white knight of industries—is spawning a new generation of devices that retard development of our brains. I conclude that these ultra-modern devices have taken us backward neurologically. Bits destroy brain cells. The more we use supercomputers to juggle, the more primitive we become.

I put my head back, laptop still on my knees, and I begin to fall into sleep. I picture Leviathan and his wife, two truly connected people, undone by the image of him in shackles, accused of experimenting on children, causing the death of a little girl. Shame and incarceration, Leviathan's life having come full circle from his near-death experience in a cold war jail. Outside the cell I build for him, his doting wife stands, eyes streaked with tears.

I am not alone when I wake up. I am in an embrace, with my laptop. I've somehow started to cuddle it in the night. Convenient. I feel groggy but rested. It's 7:45.

My story is right where I left it. I read. It is not merely lucid, but gripping. In the push of a plastic button, I can send this to one of a handful of major publications—*Wired* or the *New York Times Magazine*. Maybe at last leap to the *New Yorker* or *Atlantic*.

I write a short pitch I can send to editors. I choose the *New Yorker*. The pinnacle. I fashion an email to an editor I know there in passing. I paste the pitch into the email. In the summary line, I write "No malice."

I put my finger on the send button. I start to push. I stop.

I picture Leviathan's wife, on her knees, pleading with me, connected to him.

I look at the baby bouncer. Protective foam packaging remains attached around the metal bar that encircles the bouncer.

I wipe my eyes. I stand. I walk up the majestic stairs to the bedroom, pausing halfway on the landing to take in a breathtaking view of San Francisco, and a giant neon glare of a Google ad appended to the side of a building.

It's nearly 8. There might still be time.

I quickly change my clothes, wash my face, and I hustle down to the car.

60

Just like I remember, she walks with the allure of a model but utterly without pretense. Like an apologetic model, wearing a baggy jacket, hands stuffed in the pockets.

She sees my car parked in front of the school. I roll down the passenger-side window. She hesitates, then walks over.

"I just dropped off Timothy." She clears her throat. "It's nice to see you."

"I know a place where we can get a doughnut."

She blinks. Faith must be wondering whether I am referring to the joint where she used to meet Alan Parsons.

"Not that place. The one I've got in mind is seedier. It got a C from the health inspector. Which keeps away the crowds, so it's usually empty. It's a nice place for small talk."

She leans forward and takes the door handle. She looks somewhere distant. "I'm not her." She looks at me. "I'm not anyone. Not anyone else."

I swallow. Some kind of acceptance, an effort to swallow my past, parts of it.

My fortune be damned.

Faith climbs into my car.

Keep reading for a bonus short story

FLOODGATE

Available for the first time in print

Introduction

In 1972, political operatives were caught bugging Democratic party headquarters at the Watergate complex. It was the nation's greatest political scandal.

Child's play. In 2012, the political scandal has gone viral.

1

August 21, 2012
8:07 P.M.

I toss back the shot glass and feel fire in my throat, just at the moment that the bar ripples with displeasure. It's a murmur gaining enough steam to rise above the thump-thumping of the Clash from the jukebox. Someone yells, "Sack the barkeep."

In my periphery, I sense that the cause of collective concern has something to do with what's on the TV. Without fully taking my eyes from the glass, I half gaze to my right into an upper corner of the bar, home to the gargantuan flat-panel television.

It's ordinarily tuned to sports. But someone must've hit the remote control. Now the TV shows a news channel, broadcasting a presidential campaign event. One of those town-hall meetings, where everyday Americans ask questions that sound way too polite to express how the polls indicate they're really feeling about the two candidates, the country, their lives.

I turn back to my empty glass. I let my eyes glaze. I consider what I'd ask if called upon at the town hall:

Hello, my name is Zach Coles. I used to work at the San Francisco Chronicle *newspaper, where I got paid to expose hypocrites like you and your corporate cronies. Then the economy imploded, I got laid off, and I do administrative office work that barely pays the bills. My question: Which of you has a plan that would get me my job back?*

I can't muster a smile at my own lies. Much of the time, my erstwhile newspaper job involved writing corporate earnings stories and doughy profiles for the business section, though I did have my share of kill shots. More than most. And I really lost the job not because of the economy, or not entirely because of it, but also thanks to the possibly heavy-handed way I once dealt with a spineless editor who shied away from tough stories and precise language. If you consider threatening an editor with physical violence to be too heavy-handed.

The bar returns to its sense of order, the channel evidently having been returned to its rightful place on ESPN.

I feel a guy sidle up next to me on one of the torn red vinyl seats that line the decrepit wooden bar. He settles in.

"Vodka?"

It takes me a second to realize he's talking to me. "Gin."

"Brave man."

I pick him up in the corner of my eye. He's as big as I am, which I wouldn't mention but it doesn't much happen. Rather, we're the same volume, different shape. I'm Laurel, he's Hardy. More like hearty. Bouncer shoulders, wrestler chest.

I sense that he's sizing me up too. Happens a lot when people see a wiry six-foot-six dude with a thick head of wooly hair and a beard that looks like seventies shag carpeting.

"Combination of burned-out taste buds and self-loathing—the gin thing."

Hearty nods to the bartender.

"Ketel One and another liver buster for my friend."

Bartender cups an ear. Can't hear over the music. My big bar mate points to the clear bottle of vodka he wants and then at my glass.

"To what do I owe the pleasure of your generosity?" I ask, still locked on my glass.

"Tough economy."

"Amen."

I'm not remotely in the mood for conversation. Just might say something like: don't think your drink is buying conversation. I'm doing a sudoku puzzle in my head.

The guy inhales his vodka. But he puts the glass down gently with chunky, ruddy hands.

"Want to add fifteen hundred dollars to your bank account?"

I sip my gin, feel the sleazy sizzle in my throat like I'm getting tattooed along my larynx, and realize just how much self-loathing. I don't look at him.

He says: "It'll take less than five minutes and everyone keeps their pants on."

Now I turn and briefly take him in. Late thirties, with droopy, confident eyes. A gummy face, jowls, like his cheeks got liposuctioned. Short hair-cut. Stretched taut over his square shape, he wears a sport coat made of thin fabric, which for some reason makes me think it must be tan. It's hard to tell in the dark, and the ear-splitting jukebox seems to diminish my ability not just to hear clearly but to see as well.

I don't have a regular bar. This one, the Pastime, is semi-regular, recommended by a journalist acquaintance who frequents here and swears by its antisocial atmosphere.

"No thanks," I say. "I don't do shakedown work."

I'm just assuming that's his aim. People see a big guy with a devil-may-care drinking problem and insufficient funds for a haircut and shave and assume anything goes.

"It's got to be ignominious," he says.

"The vodka drinkers always use the big words."

His vocab has almost perked me up but I'm unusually grouchy, which is saying something. I don't feel like giving him the satisfaction of asking him what he's talking about.

"Making coffee, filing manila folders, collating. Do you do collating as an administrative assistant?" he says.

Just like that, it's a whole new conversation—one where the stranger buying the cheap swill knows that I recently took a bottom-rung job as an administrative assistant because the first ten career options weren't hiring and because paying rent beats living in my trunk.

"Headline: Loob Award-winning journalist whose righteous indignation leads to newsroom violence is now forced to pay rent by collating," he says.

"Loeb." Not Loob.

The Gerald Loeb Award is the highest honor for business journalism. I won it five years ago, for the second time, at the *Chronicle*—before the economy imploded, cratering—among other things—newspapers, and causing layoffs of even award winners, especially the ones that once punched an editor for excising from a profile of a corrupt corporate executive a much-loved adjective.

Hearty leans in. I can smell the fish taco he ate sometime in the last hour. "There's a computer thumb drive in a safe in your boss's office. Probably in a folder. I'll give you fifteen hundred dollars to bring it to me."

He pulls out his wallet and spreads the bills, showing me hundreds of dollars.

"This computer drive has special meaning for me. It's an easy job. You have the key to his office or can get it, then find your way into the safe."

He doesn't seem sure what to make of my slight grin. Am I bemused? Bored?

"Three grand. Final offer."

"Absolutely, positively, no fucking way on Earth."

He tilts his head to the side, then brings his thumb to his mouth and chews on a nail. I glance long enough to see the bent and bumpy cartilage of a nose that's learned from experience.

"Figured you'd say that."

He reaches into his wallet and pulls out a photo. He holds it beneath the edge of the bar. I can make out a school photo of a boy, probably six years old.

"This young man would appreciate if you brought me the thumb drive."

"If the kid wants the thing, he can ask me himself."

He half laughs. "I will kill Ezekiel if you don't bring it to me."

I squeeze the gin glass and wonder: if this guy knows me as well as he thinks he does, then he knows that I've got anger management problems that manifest as physical violence, including twice in a newsroom. Once over an editor changing an adjective.

I set down the glass.

"I'm not humoring you anymore."

I stand up. I turn around to go.

"Meredith Canter," he blares.

I freeze.

Before I turn around, he walks up behind me.

"You broke up six years ago. She broke up with you, actually."

I turn to face him. "Guess what?" I say. He looks up at me—from six inches below.

"What?"

"I'm a tinderbox."

"She broke up with you six years ago. In a café in Santa Cruz. Love of your life."

"Righto. And I haven't seen her since. I've talked to her voice mail twice—on her birthday. I don't care who you are or what you want, but I won't get it for you or be intimidated by the fact that you know how to use the Internet or talked to some people who know me. Don't be fooled by my beard. Underneath here is someone who fights with enormous precision."

He holds up the picture of the boy. The bar is thumping with an old Scorpions song that I once loved to hate, and I'm feeling the effects of four shots of gin.

"Roughly eight months after Meredith split up with you, Ezekiel was born."

I take a deep breath. I'm doing the sudoku puzzle in my head.

"Bring me the computer thumb drive in twenty-four hours."

Hearty nods, turns, and slithers toward the door.

2

I turn back to the bar and finish my gin, and then his vodka. I reach for a half-drained Heineken that looks to have been abandoned. The bartender shakes his head, smiles cordially, points to the door.

I rub the side of my face and feel pretzel remains in the craggily brown nest adorning my chin. I brush them off. Life has grown, what's the word Hearty used—ignominious. Or tedious, pathetic, whatever is the right word when you drink other people's swill and scratch out a living filing other people's manila folders.

I look down the bar and catch the eye of my journalist acquaintance, Nat Idle. Nat's a bit sentimental for my tastes but he's a world-class journalist, picks up things, like the clear fact that I'd crossed words with some paunchy dude. Nat's looking at me with a head tilt, wondering: everything okay? I nod. I'm not in the mood for a partner. Besides, Nat's got a pregnant girlfriend, and doesn't need to get involved with this kind of jerk. I wonder if I once had a pregnant girlfriend, namely Meredith, before she dropped me.

I go after Hearty.

I've never liked running because it makes me look like a punch-drunk ostrich. So I walk/run/lope to the door, parting gawking revelers, seducers and their prey and push through the red door with the circular window.

I don't see Hearty.

I look at my grandfather's Rolex, the first thing I'd take with me in a fire and last thing I'd pawn when it comes to that.

It's 8:50.

I see Hearty. He's poked his head and arm out of the driver's-side window of a sedan that is parallel parked half a block away between an SUV and a Bug. He removes a flyer tucked under his windshield wiper. He tosses shredded flyer parts onto the pavement and rolls up the window.

I drunken-ostrich-lope toward the car.

He starts inching the car back and forth to extricate it from the parking spot.

With help from a streetlamp, I see his eyes widen as I jump onto the sedan. In the air, I twist my body so that I land on my butt. I can feel the hood dent under 260 pounds of thin fat man.

I slide off the sedan.

Hearty is out the door.

He's reaching into his internal jacket pocket. Gun? Knife? iPhone?

I lurch for the door and smash it into him, sandwiching his thick corpus against the car frame.

He smirks, unhurt. Standoff. Does either of us want to take the next step toward rolling around on the cement and trading broken noses?

"Zeke," I say.

"You see, I speak the truth."

"Gutter name. My grandfather was Ezekiel. Zeke. He killed my great-grandfather, a violent pedophile bastard and the mouth of the filthy river that became our gene pool."

"But you hate the name Ezekiel."

"Which also was the name of my great-grandfather, the pedophile. Of course that bitch would name her son Zeke. So, no, I don't think you're lying."

He says: "Meredith does seem like a bitch."

This is the part where I have no control. I lean my hairy bowling-ball cranium back and snap it forward right into Hearty's nose.

Satisfying crack of forehead against cartilage followed immediately by a momentary trip to the planetarium inside my eyelids. When my vision rights, I see Hearty buckle and regain his balance, smile slightly, practiced at taking a blow, nonplussed by the blood bubble that grows and pops and sends a trickle underneath his nose.

I know then I'm being set up, even before I feel the physical presence behind me.

I don't have time to turn around before some mallet or bat or baton wallops the back of my leg, just above the knee.

Hairy Neanderthal down.

I cross my arms over my head to stave off the next shot but it never comes. I dive for the feet of the soon-to-be savagely attacked bat wielder.

Then I hear the click.

Gunplay.

"Stop," Hearty says.

I stop. Beyond the threat of having my brain bisected by shrapnel, I appreciate the mature tone in his voice. It says: we're all adults here.

I look up. Hearty points a pistol in my general direction.

"I understand that what I'm about to say is something you will take great offense with," he says.

"*With which* I will take great offense."

"You're predictable. You did exactly what we thought you would. Exactly."

He wipes his nose on his soaking sleeve.

"You wanted me to know that you can take a thumping to the head."

"That we're smart and extremely tough. Take that into account when doing the math on your son's life."

I start to stand.

"Stay down," he says.

"Ignominious—word of the day."

Without getting a good look at the bat wielder, I see him take off. The street is dark and empty.

"What's so special about the computer file?" I ask.

"To you: it's worth fifteen hundred. Minus my medical bill."

The offer for three thousand must be off the table. Either way, I'm probably in the red.

"And if I get you the file, you're going to spare the life of some boy who may or may not exist and who may or may not be named Ezekiel and who is absolutely, positively, almost certainly not my son."

"Absolutely, positively, almost certainly."

He lowers himself into the car. He starts the engine. He leans out the window.

"Bring it back to this bar. Same time tomorrow."

I have to move so he won't run me over.

3

My neck hurts a lot more than my bat-smacked leg. The neck pain is a chronic condition caused from squeezing my Sasquatch body into something called a smart car. I won it in a raffle and am required to drive it for a year or give it back. On the side of the car it says: VitaWater: Smart Water Gets You Places.

Inside of it, I look like one of those model ships in a bottle—in this case, an aircraft carrier stuffed into an airplane-sized bottle of whiskey.

I drive it because I can't afford a car but I could afford $1 for a raffle ticket at the Fillmore Street Fair. I thought it was a raffle for the woman in the VitaWater sash. She had reminded me of Meredith, not just the long brown hair and the long thin legs, but the sidelong glance, like I held some powerful allure but also seemed deeply out of place in this world. Meredith, the true love of my life, used to give me the same look, before, like the guy said, she sacked me over iced coffee.

Did Meredith bear my kid? Do I have a reproduction running around? Did the Zeke-name skip a generation?

I'd call information on my cell phone to get Meredith's number but I haven't paid up on the prepaid calling plan. I'll use the phone at the office of Sandoval Political Consulting, where I currently work, collating and filing. A visit to the office kills two birds: use the Internet and phone to track down Meredith; do a little discovery to find out what kind of computer thumb drive is worth killing for.

I contemplate whether I might call the cops. But not before I know a bit more about whether I'm putting Meredith, and our ex-love child, in harm's way. Hearty says I've got twenty-four hours; that buys me a little time to play with.

It takes me two minutes to squeeze into my car and get comfortable, 10 minutes to drive to the headquarters of Sandoval Political Consulting. It's a single-story open-plan office, some Syrah-drunk architect's idea of bringing Eichler into the 21st century by making everyone and everything transparent through glass walls that separate the offices. I'll take old-fashioned cubicles; I like to overhear stuff and couldn't give a damn if people overhear me. Offices are for guys with secrets and unmet ambitions, two things I hate.

The place is dark, which surprises me. Fred works late, especially now, the eve of a presidential-year national election. We're gathering and making sense of mountains of data on the electorate, what they want and like, what they will want and like. We're part of the emerging Big Data industry. It feeds off of, and tries to track and synthesize, bil-

lions of fresh data bits, filled with evidence of tʰ
human condition, that appear in social networks
fast-twitch media sites like Twitter, caches of anonymous Google searches. A ton of research ultimately
backed up with old-fashioned phone interviews. We
look to find truths and hope social and economic
policy follows them, as opposed to following ideol-
ogy.

Fred is one of those prodigal engineers with
business sense who made it big first in the eighties on hardware, then again in the dot-com boom
with an Internet start-up. He tried to run for San
Mateo County supervisor a few years back but got
disgusted by the insincerity of the political process.
So, for a third act, well into his sixties, he's turning his millions toward monetizing his passion for
politics. He's truly nonpartisan, and so is our firm,
almost cynically so, which is why I took this over a
job making hoagies. And, when Fred hired me, he
promised I wouldn't have to join him in the high-
tech culture of burning the midnight computer
monitor. Interview went like this:

Fred: You look like a snacker. The cheese fish are
    for the customers.
Me: Then why did you call me for an interview?
Fred: You come highly recommended. You're smart.
    You're fair and you're tough. You can work your
    way up.
Me: From what? What does the job entail? What
    are the hours? What's the pay?
Fred: You want a job or not?
Me: Job.

Fred: Do you plan to hit me if I edit your work?
Me: Not today.

As I disgorge myself from my car in the empty lot, I'm struck that I'm almost more curious about what's going on than I am furious about being attacked. A part of me is glad to be back in the game, a game with evident stakes. Besides, I've moved well past the anger and into the opportunity phase. I'm going to talk to Fred, find out what's up with this computer thumb drive, track down the guys who did this to me, return serve, then reconcile with Meredith and my as-of-yet-unmet son, and drive off into the sunset in the smart car.

I do have my doubts that I've got a son. I figure Meredith would tell me. I don't doubt that there's a computer thumb drive with potent information on it. Politics is, obviously, big business. Billions at stake. Who gets elected dictates who gets what dough down the line. So if Fred's stumbled onto some powerful research, I could guess that someone might want it.

I slip inside the door. I pause. I listen. I'm betting the place hasn't been this quiet since the day after the midterms. It's quieter than a Mondale victory party. I look through the maze of glass walls, taking in a prism of shadows. We're usually a nine-person shop but we've stocked up to twelve in the months leading up to the election.

Despite my lowly status, Fred graciously gave me one of the glass-enclosed offices, the smallest. It was more for him than me. He'd come by and sit and we'd chat; or, he'd chat, I'd listen. And he'd

sneak a slug of the Dewar's he kept locked in m
bottom right drawer, and I'd tell him it was lucky
that he didn't make the desks made of glass too or
everyone would know his secret.

My office is in the back corner. Fred's is up at the
front, right behind the receptionist's counter. I'm
anxious to call Meredith but Fred's door is cracked
open and so I go with life's arrow theory, namely,
follow the arrows. I knuckle rap the door, causing it
to squeak and open a bit farther.

"Fred?"

No response.

I push open the door. I'm not sure what I see
first: Fred's safe on the wall behind his desk, open,
or Fred, lying at the foot of his desk, crumpled. The
grayish moonlight coming through the windows
over his bookshelves provides sufficient cover to
make out the knife in his chest and the blood seeping across the hardwood. It's a murder in sepia.

I make a quick start over to him and lean over
one of the few nice guys. I don't need a GED in
CSI to suspect the guy is long gone. And then he
twitches. A gurgling noise. A hiss.

"Fred."

Before he reacts further, or I can, I hear the noise
behind me. I turn. Behind Fred's door stands a
looming figure. Almost certainly the guy who put
the stick into Fred. Not the guy from the Pastime
Bar, or his aide-de-camp. Another knockout artist.
Some new danger. He and I both stand, four feet
apart, then half crouch, assessing, veritable sumo
positions.

When it comes to brawling, he's doubtless got a

better resume. The latest notch on his CV is prone behind me, in a death gurgle. But this jerk doesn't have anything on me when it comes to pent-up fury. I was pissed off even before I got threatened and found my boss lying near dead. And this assassin already used up his sharp object on that attack.

"You want your knife back or do this the old-fashioned way?"

He cocks his head, a foreboding moonlit silhouette. He's got a long face, horse-like. He takes a step forward. I see something in his hand. Another weapon?

A phone.

He holds up the screen, showing me the light, something I can't see.

"Your friends aren't able to answer," I say. "They're picking themselves off the pavement outside the bar."

At the mention of friends, he looks a bit surprised. "Scum got their comeuppance." Another punk with silky vocabulary. His low voice carries an undercurrent of chuckle.

We hear the siren, and I get it, instantly. He hasn't called the other thugs. He's dialed 911. Of course. It worked out perfectly for him. He got into Fred's safe, killed the poor fellow, and then I showed up, the gift of a fall guy. Nice night at the office.

He pockets the phone. He takes another step forward. I just growl, something way deep, the bad Ezekiel-gene in my heritage waiting a lifetime for this chance to put someone in a justifiable sleeper hold. I can see his plan; he's going to escape and he's willing to fight his way out to do it. I'm about to lunge when I hear Fred moan. I start to turn my head, just start, but it's enough for the guy to make his slip around the door. I've got no choice. Obvious priorities.

"Fred."

I hear the killer escape. I kneel next to Fred. I can hear sirens. They've got to be less than a mile away.

"Cavalry's on the way."

He shakes his head. His breathing is shallow and fast, like a dog hit by a car. He's still got that glint in his eye, the one I trusted, but it's fading into infinity. Then he smiles. Almost toothy. With obvious effort and excruciating pain, he lifts his arm from across his chest and he drops it to the floor. His hand opens. A tiny key skitters from his palm onto the bloody hardwood.

I catch his eye and he seems to acknowledge and implore me, a look including something, weirdly, like victory. "Hang on, Fred." He doesn't. He makes a gurgling noise and his eyes roll back. Gone.

I scoop up the key. I know just what it belongs to. The sirens get closer. I'm going to have to work fast.

4

I pause before leaving my deceased friend. I turn back to him, pat the right pocket of his stylish jeans. I feel what I'm looking for: Fred's cell phone. Might have his most recent calls. And goddamn if I'm not out of my own prepaid minutes.

I do a quick sprint by the open safe behind Fred's desk to assure myself that, as I suspected, it's empty. Fred's smarter than that. Or was.

Seconds later, sirens nearing, I'm awkward-ostrich-sprinting down the hall. I fling open my office door, working against seconds, skid to my desk. I lean down to the lower left-hand drawer. I fumble with the key. I always wondered why old man Sandoval locked up his Dewar's. Just figured he was cautious, like anyone in the reputation business.

I fumble around inside the drawer, pushing aside the fine liquor. I see nothing. No thumb drive, no computer file, no folder, or papers. Just the Dewar's. I lift the bottle, and I see it: a little drive, taped underneath. It's even smaller than a thumb, at least my fat digit. I palm it, stuff it into my pants with the phone, and jam out the side door, around the side the building and into my car.

I squirt away in the moonlight, my driver's door not fully closed 'cause I can't fold my body inside quickly enough. A block away, I pass a police cruiser, fast approaching, about to discover a dead body and evidence pointing to me as a killer. I'd better find an alternate theory.

Ten minutes later, I'm parking a block away from the Pastime Bar, just where this madness started. I'm flashing a bunch of obvious thoughts: Fred gathered some research that has so much significance to the pending election that someone's willing to kill him for it, and to threaten the life of a six-year-old boy named Zeke.

More than one someone.

There were the two guys who accosted me earlier, and the guy who accosted Fred to completion. That guy must've done some pretty violent cajoling to get Fred to open his safe, only to discover the mysterious computer file was not there. The key to finding the file was somewhere on Fred, and Fred managed to palm it and pass it off to me.

I flash on a memory of Fred once proudly showing me a picture on his desk, a photo of him with six toddler grandkids, three of the kids crying. Fred told me that you've got a better shot at getting 50 percent of the electorate to agree with you than you've got at getting 50 percent of the toddlers in any given photo to simultaneously smile.

I push the image of dead Fred from my memory and replace it with another recollection, that breakup conversation with Meredith, my ex. I'm stung by

mething that's shaken loose from the recesses of
ny brain: among the handful of reasons she gave me
for splitting was that she said that she thought I'd be a
great father, but *only if I wanted to be.* Those were her
words, I remember. I had just assumed she heard her
biological clock ticking and was baiting me to find
out if I'd commit to the next step of our relationship.

But maybe there was one already in the oven.
And she didn't like my shrug response when she
asked me about fatherhood. If I had known, would I
have shrugged?

I've walked into the alley behind the Pastime,
and I'm sharing standing space with two fetid
metal trash bins and two equally fragrant smokers.
They're inhaling in silence. Springsteen's "Rosal-
ita" pumps through the back door. I ask one of the
smokers, a tall, slump-shouldered lean-to with unkempt curly hair I can respect, if he could ask Nat
to come chat with a friend. Everyone here knows
Nat, my journalist acquaintance.

While I'm waiting for him to come back, I pull
out Fred's phone. I paw it until I bring up the Internet browser and I search for Meredith Canter, Santa
Cruz. Before the search returns appear, Nat does.
He's a head shorter than me, but who's not, with
a confident walk, like a former athlete, a face that
would be a little too pretty if not for the slightly
pronounced ethnic nose.

"What the hell happened, Zach? I heard you had
a scuffle."

"Nothing Advil can't solve. Did you get a good
look at the guy who came in earlier? Have you seen
him before?"

Nat takes me in. He's doing his thing, whic. studying people, and often identifying them a. breaking them down by their medical condition. Like, for instance, someone new comes into the bar and he'll say: psoriasis, or torn left ACL, or pigeon-toed, or degenerative bone condition, or some non-sense like that. He went to medical school before he became a journalist and he just can't seem to get past all that trivia he ingested. It's helped make him one of the most authoritative journalists on how the high-tech lifestyle impacts people's physiology, and their neurology. But Nat's penchant for always seeing pathology is almost a pathology unto itself. And, while I generally find it amusing, I've got no time for it now.

"Funny you should ask," Nat says. "Guy had me stumped. For a second, I could've sworn he's got Pickwickian syndrome."

"Nat, I . . ."

He thinks I don't understand what he means. "Rare condition. Most people don't survive it. Charles Dickens actually coined the name. There was something about that guy—a puffiness. Fat pockets that had been emptied out, like he might've overcome something as a child. Pretty unlikely, though. More likely that he's got an autoimmune disorder and the treatment is bloating him, or he's cushingoid, y'know, the puffy water retention that comes with heavy use of steroids . . ." He pauses. He looks closely at me, realizing something serious is going on. I see he's focused on my pant leg. There's a sticky stain from Fred's blood. Nat says: "You're not cut. So that's not your blood."

ignore him. "So you haven't seen him before."

Nat shakes his head. I nod. No biggie, not un-expected, and that's not really what I need his help with.

"Do you have your laptop?" I ask.

I've got to be among the tiny percentage of San Franciscans who don't carry a laptop or even own one. I've got a desktop, which does the job fine, but no way I'm going back to my Tenderloin flat to find out who is waiting for me with a bat or a knife or a gun or the trifecta. Nat's in the other 99.9 percent; he's always packing electronics, having given in to modern journalism in a way that I just haven't been able to stomach. Or maybe I'm just not cut out for it.

"In my backpack. You want to come in and use it?"

"Would it be okay if I use it out here?"

"Suit yourself."

He disappears again. I pull up the phone. Google has returned my results. The third one is a Face-book page from Meredith Canter. But I can't tell anything about her, or see her picture. Apparently, I've got to "friend" her first. *Hey, Facebook, she's not just my friend, she was the love of my life, and she may be the motherfucking mother of my child. I still gotta friend her to find out?*

Nat returns and pulls his laptop out of a ratty black backpack. I ask if I might sit in my car and use it for ten minutes. He tells me to pop back in and grab him when I'm done.

I squeeze myself into the car, in a darkened parking spot on a residential street, where I can't fathom anyone could think to find me. I insert the thumb drive.

5

Up pops some kind of multimedia file, maybe it's a Word document or a PowerPoint, I can't keep track of all the formats. It's got a heading:

Google Mayes County, OK, Data Center, server
#194657298.
Encryption code: A278444fSandoval93210

Then there is an image of a map of the United States. Each state is denoted simply by its shorthand initials, CA for California, OH for Ohio, and so forth. It looks meaningless, surely, on its face, nothing someone would kill for.

I run my cursor over the map, and, when I reach the first state, which is Maine, something happens: a little dialogue box pops up. Inside it reads: US SEN.: Andreeson (D) v. Sonol (R). Below that line, another heading in smaller font: HOUSE SEATS, and then a handful of more sets of names, like Johnson (D) V. Kyle (R), and Fern (D) V. Everson (R).

I'm looking at an electoral map of some kind.

I hear a noise outside the car and see a woman across the street with a barking dog on a leash. She's glancing my direction, and it takes me a second to realize why. I'm stuffed into this car like a Boa constrictor in a snail shell, and with a laptop perched on my steering wheel. She looks away and keeps walking. In San Francisco, it probably dawns on her, there's no length someone won't go to check their laptop, no matter how uncomfortable the physical position required.

I return to the electoral map. I notice that each name in each of the elections is underlined, a hyperlink. I click on the first name, Andreeson, vaguely recalling that he's the Democrat in a tight senate race in Maine.

A new window pops open on the right half of the screen. It takes a second for the format to come into focus. I'm looking at a document with four columns across the top. Left to right, the columns read: DATE, IP ADDRESS, SEARCH TERM DETAILS, HYPOCRISY POTENTIAL.

I increase this window so that it takes up the entire screen.

I look at the first few lines in the document:

DATE	IP ADDRESS	SEARCH TERM	HYPOCRISY POTENTIAL
2/27/11	174.16.258.1	How to bake chicken	Unlikely
2/27/11	174.16.258.1	Tiffany's bracelet	Low
2/27/11	172.16.254.1	Bifocals	Low/Modest
3/01/11	172.16.254.1	Portland, ME weather	Unlikely
3/02/11	172.16.254.1	Portland, ME weather	Unlikely

The list goes on and on, pages upon pages. [H]undreds of entries like this that cause my eyes to g[laze] over. I'm trying to make sense of it, looking f[or] some handrail, when several entries catch my eye.

DATE	IP ADDRESS	SEARCH TERM	HYPOCRISY POTENTIAL
6/30/11	174.16.258.1	Avoid Alt Min Tax	POSSIBLE/ CHECK
6/30/11	174.16.258.1	Alt Min Tax Loophole	POSSIBLE/ CHECK

I'm drawn to these entries both because of the "hypocrisy potential"—the only ones I've seen so far that read "possible"—and because "POSSIBLE" is in all caps. This, evidently, is important.

I've covered business long enough to strongly suspect what the "Alt Min Tax" stands for: Alternative Minimum Tax. It's a pain-in-the-rear tax that can really nail people in the upper-middle bracket.

I think what I'm looking at is that someone has done an Internet search about how to avoid paying this tax. Not just someone, but Dan Andreeson, the Democrat running for senate in Maine, or maybe someone using his computer.

I close this file. I go back to the map. I run my cursor over other states and wind up on South Dakota. Again, I get a dialogue box, with the senate race at the top and a handful of house races beneath.

In the senate race, the Democrat is Fisher, the Republican is Swan. I click on Swan. Up pops another huge laundry list. It starts.

E	IP ADDRESS	SEARCH TERM	HYPOCRISY POTENTIAL
4/19/11	162.94.116.2	Cheap airfares	Unlikely
4/27/11	162.94.116.2	Nike, size 10	Unlikely
4/27/11	162.94.116.2	RealClear Politics	Unlikely
5/06/11	162.94.116.2	Insomnia	Low/Modest
5/06/11	162.94.116.2	Signs child is gay	LIKELY

I read on, through hundreds and hundreds of entries, then see:

DATE	IP ADDRESS	SEARCH TERM	HYPOCRISY POTENTIAL
7/04/11	162.94.116.2	How long pot stays in system	HIGH
7/04/11	162.94.116.2	Getting THC out of system	HIGH
7/04/11	162.94.116.2	How to get THC out of body	HIGHEST
7/05/11	162.94.116.2	Duping urine test	HIGHEST

I pause to let myself put a fine point on what I'm seeing. It's a list of Internet searches. "IP address"—Internet protocol, if memory serves—refers to a specific Internet connection associated with the search. In more lay terms, it is the address of a computer, a number that, in effect, signifies a specific computer. In this case, evidently, the computer belonging to a Republican candidate for the senate, or a computer in his or her household.

The search term must refer to a specific Internet search on a specific date, something that someone

sought on Google or Yahoo or, what's the na
Microsoft's version, Bing?

That's explosive stuff, and private. Fred's so...
how tapped into these private searches. I pass ov...
that mind-boggling concept and consider the specific search terms.

The would-be Republican senator has looked for
how long marijuana stays in the system, and how
to get it out of the body, how to dupe a urine test.
Previously—I glance up the search list—the candidate has searched on how to tell if a child is gay,
and has made sporadic searches about ordering
OxyContin without a prescription from an overseas
pharmacy. Hypocrisy potential: high.

I close the document and I click on the file for
Steve Fisher, the Democrat in the South Dakota
race. I skim through the mostly innocuous entries.
Then I find a bunch of dates with entries like:

DATE	IP ADDRESS	SEARCH TERM	HYPOCRISY POTENTIAL
4/04/11	162.96.561.1	Threesome video	HIGH

And:

DATE	IP ADDRESS	SEARCH TERM	HYPOCRISY POTENTIAL
4/12/11	162.96.561.1	Bondage w/blood	HIGH

And:

DATE	IP ADDRESS	SEARCH TERM	HYPOCRISY POTENTIAL
4/17/11	162.96.561.1	Violent sex	HIGH

ok up from the file. I glance outside, seeing
iness and quiet on the residential street but
ing self-conscious nonetheless. I feel like I'm
olding something smoldering. It's starting to make
sense, particularly in light of the things I'd over-
heard Fred say about politics. He hated hypocrisy
and insincerity. He said that the reason that poli-
ticians can't solve real problems is that they can't
move beyond platitude. He wanted to use technology to bring truth to politics.

I think, sitting here squeezed into this car looking at this incredible document, that maybe he's figured out a way to do so in the most extraordinary,
and maybe most insidious, way in history.

What I'm looking at are the Internet search
terms of all the people running for higher office
in the United States. Somehow, Fred has managed
to tap into their computers, and record hundreds,
maybe thousands, of their individual searches, looking for behaviors and habits that might make them
unelectable. No, that's not right, I realize; it wasn't
that he was finding search terms that prove what
makes them unelectable, but rather what makes
them human.

Fred was going to expose the widespread com-
monality of people who cloak themselves as icons of
moral purity.

Maybe.

There are some reasons to doubt the veracity and
power of this document, both what it represents and
whether it's accurate. After all, even if he managed to
pull up this level of surveillance, how could he prove
that these aspirants of higher office were the people

sitting at their computers doing the Internet se.
Could it have been their spouses, family friends,
ness associates? And, even if it was them sitting at
computer, couldn't they claim otherwise?

But there is one major-league bit of evidence sug
gesting that this document is the real deal: someone
is willing to kill for it. More than one someone.

I return to the map and do quick searches across
the country, at house and senate races in California, Montana, Colorado, Georgia and Texas. Even a
cursory glance shows me that, with rare exception,
the documents have search terms that either are in-
cendiary on their face or, in the hands of the right
opponent or sensational media outlet, could bring
shame.

I look at the clock. It's 10:45. I've got to get the
laptop back to Nat. I make a copy of the file and I
save it to his laptop. I'm not super tech-savvy but I
manage to bury the document in some file library
where Nat's unlikely to look, unless he was expressly
searching there. And, without knowing what he was
looking at, he'd be hard-pressed to understand it.

I'm about to close down the machine, when I realize there's something I cannot resist. I return to
the map. I run the cursor over Washington, D.C.
Up pops a dialogue box with the two presidential
candidates.

I click on the incumbent. As the search-term
list materializes, I realize that I can't believe that
Fred would have been able to record the president's
searches. First of all, the president probably doesn't
do his own searches. And, secondly, even if the
president does search the Internet, there's got to be

sive firewall in the White House that would
ent such snooping.

The file opens. I nearly chuckle. Fred's a genius.
he search terms listed are from four years earlier,
from before he was elected president. And there are
a couple of striking ones, not eye-popping, but eye-
catching. Searches about marital discord, mild por-
nographic searches, a few medical conditions I'm
certain he wouldn't want the world to know he was
concerned about and that would make the year of a
late-night talk-show comedian. *Male yeast infection?
Erectile dysfunction related to stress?*

I turn to the challenger. I make it past the first
page when I come to a scattering of entries that
almost make me blush. One refers to a sex act that
some might perceive as unorthodox or even per-
verse. And there are a bunch of searches about how
to avoid paying taxes by parking assets overseas. I
can't believe this guy. What a hypocrite.

And I'm not sure I even want to know this about
him, or for that matter, about anyone else. It's like
this document is letting me look into his soul, his
digital soul.

I'm about to close the challenger's file and shut
the machine when something catches my eye. Atop
the challenger's file is an icon that looks like his
face. Beneath it is a file name with the extension
".mov". Now that I think about it, I realize I've seen
similar links inside the files of the other candidates,
but with their own faces as icons.

.mov—isn't that a movie file?

I click on it, feeling a sense of dread. Am I going

to see images from the sex sites the ca
thought he was surreptitiously surfing?

The file opens. The grainy movie starts to
It's an image of the candidate himself, from n.
breast up. His hair looks tousled, the slick loc
distinctly absent; he's got stubble, wears a white V-
necked shirt. He's facing the camera but seemingly
not aware of it. He's looking a few inches below at
something that has him rapt. He doesn't blink. He
swallows hard.

On the right of the movie screen, there's an information box. It shows a time stamp, indicating this
home movie was shot about five months ago, just
before 2 A.M. And there's a web site: Barebackbabes.

No, I realize, not a home movie. The candidate
didn't realize he was being observed.

"No way," I mutter.

I scroll back through a couple of other candidates
from across the country. Most have similar movie
attachments, 95 percent at least. "No fucking way,
Fred," I repeat. "How?"

I look at the laptop, near the top, the innocuous little opening that houses a camera, standard in
most computers these days, used for Skype or video
conferencing or whatever. "Jesus, Fred."

But better to confirm what I'm looking at than
do a wild conclusion leap.

Less than two minutes later, I'm back at the alley
behind Pastime. I poke my head in and ask one of
the regulars playing pool in the back if she might
tell Nat I've got his laptop. Not long after, Nat appears. I give him his laptop.

..wick is back," he says.

..arty?"

..Vho?"

The big guy from before."

He nods. I think over why he might be at the bar, even though we're not supposed to meet for another twenty hours.

"Is this guy a source?" Nat asks.

"Not yet."

"Is he following you?"

I don't answer but shrug in a way that suggests affirmation.

"You have a cell phone, Z?"

"I nod." Not mine. Fred's.

"You might want to turn it off," Nat says. "It's an easy way for someone to track you. They triangulate the signal, et cetera, et cetera."

"I miss being subject to a good old-fashioned physical stakeout."

He laughs. "Cell-phone surveillance is standard operating procedure for the 21st-century bad guy or cop. They can track you to a general area, within about three hundred feet, but not to a precise location . . ." He pauses. "This sounds serious."

I think about it. Maybe Hearty figured I'd be back here at some point and he wants to keep the pressure up. Or maybe this tough guy and his henchman tracked Fred's phone. So they know I'm in the area. I feel Fred's phone in my pocket. It's got a sticky smudge along the bottom. Blood.

"Tell Pickwick you just saw me out back and I'm reachable on Fred's phone."

"Fred?"

I look away and exhale, lightly shaking m
Not talking about it.

"You want me to call the cops?"

"I got this."

He cocks his head, takes it in. "You want som
one to ride shotgun?"

"You've got a pregnant gal. How's she holding
up?"

"Pauline. Polly. She's showing. She's tired as hell
but I can't wipe the grin off my face."

"You looking forward to having a kid?"

"You've got no idea, Z."

I love the look in his eye. I wonder if I'd have ever
felt like that if I knew I was going to be a dad.

"You need a head start—before I give a heads-up
to that thug?"

I shake my head.

Nat says: "I'm not sure what his medical condition is, but he's got one. It's going to cost him agil-
ity, leave him short of breath. Aim for the kidneys."

It seems like he's mostly joking. But I'm taking
the counsel to heart. I head back to my car. I feel
the sordid thumb drive in my pocket. I'm a tinderbox.

6

No sooner have I climbed into the smart car and revved the engine than the sedan with the dented hood—the one I pounced on hours earlier—comes around the corner. Hearty and his muscle. Just like I'd hoped.

They follow a half block behind me, keeping a respectful distance. I can imagine what they're thinking: I'm not likely to do something too rash as long as there's a possibility that they might kill some kid named Ezekiel who may belong to my bloodline.

I wonder if they know about Fred. Dead Fred.

I lead them down the peaks of Potrero Hill into the Mission flatlands. I'm waiting for something, an idea, a strategy. And then a wrinkle appears, wrapped in an industrial-strength pickup truck. I see it on the corner of Van Ness as I pass through on Sixteenth. I can't believe my eyes. It's being driven by the guy who killed Fred.

I recognize the long features, a mullet, upturned jacket collar and absence of any worldly conscience. In the streetlight glow, I see him catch my gaze,

and then his dull black eyes widen. He's not
sedan behind me, and its driver and passeng
clearly didn't expect to see them in the picture.

Interesting.

So maybe these guys aren't pals after all. If no
what's their relationship?

The pickup tries to turn behind me, but the
sedan speeds ahead and cuts it off. No, definitely
not pals. So it's me, Hearty and his muscle, and
then the pickup.

I pass a taqueria and a late-night Mexican bakery
and hear my stomach growl. I glance in the rearview mirror. I see the passenger in the sedan craning his neck back to eye the killer in the pickup. He
turns back to the driver, looking wary. This slow-
speed chase is looking more and more like a three-
way standoff, not two against one.

But how did the guy in the pickup know to find
me, or us, if the group isn't in cahoots? Could he
also be tracking Fred's phone?

I look at the clock. It's 11:25. I glance again in
the rearview mirror. I see the thug in the passenger
seat glance behind him, then put something on the
dashboard. A gun.

Near the freeway underpass, I slow down at a red
light. Wondering just how much trouble I've gotten
myself in by working under the assumption that I
simply must be smarter than these meatheads. But
these meatheads have guns and some killer motiva-
tion. Fred's phone rings.

I look down. Private caller. The light turns
green. I open the phone to answer the call and hit
the button to put it on the speaker setting.

"...ck's ticking." It's Hearty.

"...fty plan," I say.

"...What's that?"

"Call me while I'm driving so that I get distracted ...d crash into a truck."

"Don't worry. I won't allow you to die until I get the thumb drive. It's nonnegotiable. The information on it is irrelevant to you but is important to very important, and powerful, people. The technology can't fall into the wrong hands."

Technology. Interesting word choice.

"Whose hands would that be?" I ask.

In the second I wait for him to respond, the phone beeps. Another incoming call. Private number.

"Hold on."

"What?"

On the phone, I click to take the other call.

"You took Mr. Sandoval's phone." It takes me a second to recognize the voice of Fred's killer. But I'm not surprised to hear from him.

"Do you always refer to the people you kill with such formality?"

He grunts.

"I could use it to dial the cops right now," I say.

"But you haven't. You should. I'm sure they'd like to know the whereabouts of the guy who took that poor dead guy's phone, same guy whose fingerprints are all over his office."

I want to kill him.

Behind me, someone honks. Then another honk. I look up. I'm cruising too slowly as I pass the Opera House. But I'm lost in a thought, an idea, the out-

lines of one, fueled by my intensifying hatr
these guys, and what I saw on that thumb dr

I say: "Fred's phone isn't the only thing I
in his office."

"Meaning what?"

I punch the accelerator, the car pushing forwar
like my thoughts. The guys following me don't
seem much like they like each other. Maybe they're
competing for this thumb drive. Willing to do anything to get it. I need to up the stakes.

I take a flyer, vaguely remembering something I
read on the thumb drive, a couple of the searches.

"Colorado Springs."

"What about it?"

"A guy in a tight house race. He seems to have
a thing for watching the rough stuff. The kind of
videos where women really do not seem to be enjoy-
ing themselves. At least, that's what I infer he's into
from his Internet searches."

"You're bullshitting." It's not clear if this terrifies
or thrills him.

"Maybe he doesn't hurt anyone himself. Just
watches the videos. No biggie, right? Everyone's
got their deal. The thing is, it's not just him."

"What?"

"Another guy out of Denver. Similar tastes.
Probably just a coincidence. Though they do come
from the same party."

No response. Heavy breathing. I've got him,
even if I'm not sure how.

"It could throw the whole election," the horse-
faced killer finally blurts.

I've got it, or I'm pretending to. "Craters
rty in Colorado." Which party, I don't know.
iffing. "At least with the female voters. And it's
the beginning. It could cost an entire party the
ouse, the senate, who knows? Everything."

"Who knows about this?"

"Fred, me . . ." I pause, just for an instant. "That
guy in the sedan behind me."

"You gave it to *him*?!"

"You killed Fred."

"He was threatening me, this country. It was
self-defense. This is bigger than you, bigger than
me. It's about the country."

"Save it for Oprah when you get out of prison.
Hold on."

"What?"

I click back to Hearty, my brain racing.

He says: "You have the drive. What are you proposing?"

"Slow down. Two words for you: Colorado
Springs."

On my right, I'm passing the Tenderloin, my
apartment a few blocks to the right, then a mat-
tress store that has been offering the same grand-
opening prices for a decade.

"What about Colorado?"

I give Hearty the same spiel I gave the other guy,
but with a twist. I tell Hearty the other guy already
knows the story, all the info. I lay it on thick. "And
Colorado is just the beginning," I explain. "One
state after the next, one race after the next. Could
change everything."

"You're bullshitting," he says. I nearly laugh.

These guys sound like parrots. Parro[t]
frothing at the mouth, carrying heat. He[]
tests: "How could you give it to that guy[?]
killer."

"Not of kids. Gotta run. Battery's low."

I hang up, just as I reach Bay Street, a fork [.]
the road. To the right, downtown. To the left, the
marina, the Golden Gate Bridge. I see the light in
front of me start to turn yellow. I slow down to let
it turn red. I squirm around in the tiny cockpit so
I can open my window and pull the thumb drive
from my pocket.

I hold the drive out the window, extending it
high with my long ostrich wing. Showing it to my
trackers. Look, guys, the most dangerous secrets in
America. Come and get it.

I peel through the red light and turn left.

My dutiful trackers follow: continuing our cartoonish caravan; the putt-putt smart car valiantly
peaking at 45 miles an hour, the dented sedan, the
ominous pickup. I am trying to leave the impression
that I'm trying to get away. But I'm not really. I'm
just getting the last of the choreography together in
my head. Pick the right location. Somewhere dark,
shrouded, free of innocent bystanders.

I take a right toward the water, heading to the
marina, reminding me of Santa Cruz, those idyllic
days by the water with Meredith. I put her out of
my mind with a glance in the rearview mirror, see
the attentive thugs.

Looming above me, the Golden Gate Bridge.
Its bottom half gleams in the moonlight, the upper
spans splotched with fog. I've seen a million pic-

…n of moments just like these, aiming to
…ne swirling beauty of man's attempt to tri-
…ver nature, a gorgeous engineering feat, but
…nature, in the way of the fog, getting the last
…d.

That's it. Just what I'm looking for. Not the
bridge, the view. It's given me an idea of a place
where I can get a tactical advantage, if there is even
one to be had.

I'm pushing the accelerator as I putt-putt my
tin can up and through the Presidio. I'm trying to
get some distance between me and the thugs, but
manage just fifty yards or so. Within a few minutes,
I've powered through the ritzy Sea Cliff neighborhood and found myself in the quiet, tree-shrouded
edge of the public golf course that hovers along the
cliffs overlooking the Pacific Ocean.

Without warning, I pull my car over in a spot
along the seventeenth hole. I unfurl myself, climb
out, and start ostrich-loping.

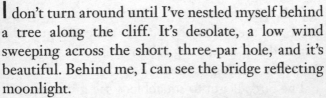

7

I don't turn around until I've nestled myself behind a tree along the cliff. It's desolate, a low wind sweeping across the short, three-par hole, and it's beautiful. Behind me, I can see the bridge reflecting moonlight.

I'm being followed by the parade of killers and would-be killers, the puffy guy from the bar and his pal in the lead, the horse-faced guy bringing up the rear, all huffing, just like me. But there's a difference: all three have their guns drawn. This is going to be tricky.

They've stopped, and spread out a bit, Hearty to the far right, his henchman just to his left, Fred's killer farther over still. They're all crouched. Battle positions.

I yell: "Promise you won't kill Zeke."

The three pause. They can't tell my precise location. I'm north of them, behind the tree, bushes surrounding, a good place to lose a golf ball, an impossible place for me to get shot, at least at this angle.

e my word." It's the puffy guy from the

: a dark purring of low-level laughter. It be-
to Fred's killer. "Your word?!" he exclaims.
rse wind gusts across the fairway. "You'll say
ything to get what you want. Don't listen to him.
Give me the computer drive and I'll make things
right."

Now it's Hearty's turn to guffaw. "*I'll* say anything?! Look in the mirror. You're in this for yourself, period. You want one thing: power. You'll do
and say anything to get it."

"Oh, shut the fuck up!" That voice belongs to the
third guy, the one closer to the middle, the guy who
whacked me in the leg. "You two are ridiculous.
Birds of a fucking feather."

The birds begin to squabble. I see guns pointed.
I've got them plenty heated up. This just might
work.

"I'll give it up, the thumb drive," I shout. "First I
want answers."

They're paused. They look in my direction. I hear
a foghorn in the distance. I work up some energy to
spout out my theory. I say: "Fred figured out how
to tap into the computers of all the candidates for
higher office. He's got their Internet searches. He
can expose their digital secrets, their secret desires
and queries."

I pause.

"It's private," one of the thugs says. "It's stolen.
Besides, it doesn't necessarily say anything about
their core values."

I ignore him. "He stored it all on some Google

server somewhere, in one of those n̶
warehouses. Someplace you couldn't pos̶
And he made a copy for himself, the on̶
pocket. You guys pieced it together. How? .̶
start threatening to go public?"

Another silence. Then: "You hear about the .̶
publican in Macon who pulled out of the twelft̶
district race?" It's the third guy, Hearty's henchman.

"Enlighten me."

"The local paper got tipped off to the fact she'd
been shopping around to find a discreet place to get
her daughter an abortion. She was ardently pro-
life."

"Fred gave it to them."

"It was his test case. We figured it out. Realized
he'd put together a dossier."

"We?"

They start squabbling.

"And the movies," I shout over them.

I prompt a silence, the low wind coursing through
it.

"He managed to get video of the candidates, in
real time, as they did their searches." I'm musing,
guessing. I'm picturing the image of the presidential challenger, hair tousled, sitting at his desk
doing some lurid search. Most of the search logs on
the computer drive had attendant movie files. This
part I can't quite figure.

"He used the cameras built into their own laptops, in a few cases, on their phones." It's Hearty's
pal again, the muscle, sensing my uncertainty, filling in blanks. "Everyone has a camera these days,
for videoconferencing or whatever. He just pro-

he devices to record every time there
nternet search. It's basic stuff. Think of
Internet searches you've done. You really
those are private. You think Google or Yahoo
n't know. It's their business to know. Fred fig-
ed out a wrinkle, pairing the searches with video;
m sure lots of bad dudes have been working on developing the same technology, or have it. More than
these two turkeys want the disk, they want Fred's
IP."

"Not true," Hearty protests.

"I'd absolutely deny it," exclaims Fred's killer.

"You really think your data is *that* secure. Jesus,
the Pentagon can't keep people out of its servers."
The third guy inserts himself over them. "What
makes you think you can keep people out of your
MacBook Air?"

"I've got a desktop."

No response. Maybe we've hit an impasse, or this
Luddite revelation is truly a conversation-deadening
admission. In the void, I have a realization.

"Which one of you guys is the Republican?"

No answer.

"One of you guys is a Republican, and one is a
Democrat. You're party honchos. You were working together to try to track down Fred and his computer drive. But then you turned on each other."

"Guy's a hypocrite," shouts one. "Oh that's rich,"
shouts the other. "You're destroying this country
with your lies."

"Hey! Enough!" My voice cuts through the
squabbling. I look up and see the rogue's moon; full,
shadowed by high clouds, just the way the old-time

pirates liked it so they could sneak up
leons.

"Come and get it."

I toss the thumb drive out into the middl
fairway, almost equidistant from the killers.
see it bounce in a patch of moonlight and se
somewhere in the darkness.

There's a moment of silence.

A gunshot rings out.

I peer into the darkness. A muzzle flash, then another. A blaze of gunfire. I see the puffy guy fall,
then Fred's killer. I tuck myself against the tree. The
flurry of firing slows. I peer out again. The henchman still stands, wobbly but walking. The guys on
the ground are moaning, bullet-riddled, moribund.

The guy walks over to the area of the thumb
drive.

"Help," he mutters.

"Who are you?" I shout.

"This is not my problem. These guys are crazed
hypocrites. I'm independent."

"Who?"

"Swing vote." He reaches down to pick up the
thumb drive.

Two shots ring out, from the fallen, writhing
killers. The guy in the middle goes down in a heap.

I hear sirens, distant, approaching. I crouch, listening. The thugs' moaning has stopped, the writhing ceased. I scramble back across the fairway. I pause
to look at the bodies. The puffy guy, the one who
threatened me, totally dead, looks to have dented the
grass with his heavy body. I'll have to ask Nat, but I
wonder if he could be suffering elephantiasis.

the other guy, the one who killed Fred. ...eceased. With his mane of a mullet and ...e. I make a note to figure out what medi- ...idition makes you look like a dead donkey. I ...oughly wipe down Fred's phone and slip it, fin- ...print free, into the dead guy's shirt pocket. The ...ops can make the connection.

I pick up the thumb drive.

I hustle to my car and jam myself inside. I drive back out through the Presidio. When I reach an overlook, I stop. I yank myself out of the car. I throw the drive into the ocean.

8

Back at my house, the next morning, I sign up for Facebook. I glance at Meredith's thumbnail picture. She's smiling with her eyes, not her mouth, and it makes me ache with nostalgia. I consider "friending" her. Too backdoor. Too snoopy.

Using my landline, I call information in Santa Cruz. There's a listing for Meredith Canter. I know it's her because the street address where she lives is in the neighborhood she always dreamed about. I don't think about it too much. I dial.

After two rings, the phone is picked up. "Hello." I lose my breath at the sound of her beautiful voice. Before I can answer, she says: "Hold on a second, please."

Then I hear scuffling in the background. I hear her say: "Hold on, Zekey, my love. Mamma's got to take a call."

I feel my heart break. If Zeke is my offspring, Meredith has a reason for keeping the secret. Maybe she suspects I'd be a rotten father, like my

ιe whole stinking bloodline. Or maybe it's
ιe and she doesn't want to hurt me.
ιg up.
ιotice the video camera perched on the com-
ιr. It came with the damn thing, supposed to be
r Skype. I stare into its black eye.

I think about all the searches I've done, looking for a job, passing late nights, buzzed on cheap gin, grazing on the Internet, indulging whatever whim, following links. Believing my behavior to be between me and my browser. Under the gaze of this electronic eye, unblinking.

Big Brother isn't looking over my shoulder, as the cliché goes. He's staring me right in the face.

I look at Meredith's thumbnail image on Facebook. I want to call her back, just to tell her: toss the gadgets, raise Zeke on paper and pencil.

I close the browser.

Some secrets were meant to remain buried.